Praise for the Legends of the Red Sun series

'...wton combines strange and vivid creations with very real
...d pressing concerns with estimable commitment and passion'
China Miéville

'...re labels just don't apply here. With *Nights of Villjamur*
...Mark has managed to incorporate so many wonderfully varied
ideas and themes' Peter F. Hamilton

'...*Book of Transformations* is a dark and original vision'
Guardian

'...eft melding of murder mystery, gang warfare, corrupt
...tics and full-blown war ... a rewarding experience' *SFX*

'...wton handles his multilayered world and diverse cast of
...racters with the assurance of an experienced author ...
...dly descriptive, compelling prose' *Publishers Weekly*

'...erb world-building ... the pages turn by themselves'
FantasyBookCritic blog

'This is such a pleasure to read . . . in years to come we will be talking about new authors and asking, "Are they the new Mark Charan Newton?"' *FantasyBookReview.com*

'The story is top notch, as we can expect . . . each book in the *Legends of the Red Sun* series has improved in every way, and *The Broken Isles* is no exception, with great writing, an exciting story, and engaging characters' *CivilianReader* blog

THE BROKEN ISLES

Mark Charan Newton was born in 1981, and holds a degree in Environmental Science. After working in bookselling, he moved into editorial positions at imprints covering film and media tie-in fiction, and later, science fiction and fantasy. He currently lives and works in Nottingham.

For more information and updates, visit his website
www.markcnewton.com

BY MARK CHARAN NEWTON

THE BROKEN ISLES

Legends of the Red Sun
Book Four

MARK CHARAN NEWTON

TOR

First published 2012 by Tor

This edition published 2013 by Tor
an imprint of Pan Macmillan, a division of Macmillan Publishers Limited
Pan Macmillan, 20 New Wharf Road, London N1 9RR
Basingstoke and Oxford
Associated companies throughout the world
www.panmacmillan.com

ISBN 978-0-330-52168-0

Illustration on page xi by China Miéville

1 3 5 7 9 8 6 4 2

A CIP catalogue record for this book is available from the British Library.

Typeset by SetSystems Ltd, Saffron Walden, Essex
Printed and bound by CPI Group (UK) Ltd, Croydon, CR0 4YY

Visit **www.panmacmillan.com** to read more about all our books
and to buy them. You will also find features, author interviews and
news of any author events, and you can sign up for e-newsletters
so that you're always first to hear about our new releases.

In memory of Frank Newton

ACKNOWLEDGEMENTS

Every book in this series comes with a huge amount of help from my editor, Julie Crisp, my agent, John Jarrold, as well as the fantastic team at Tor UK, who all do sterling work behind the scenes enabling me to continue writing.

For this novel in particular, I'd like to thank China Miéville for his palaeomantic role in creating the aesthetics of the Mourning Wasp. This was part of a challenge: he would draw a monster, I would have to write it into a novel. I think it worked out pretty well, but you'll have to decide for yourself.

In addition to this, I'd like to thank Den Patrick for naming the Mourning Wasp, as well as providing a source from Sebastian Venghaus, Scholar Vespidae. Thanks to Eric Edwards, too, for his neat historical references on *Vespa imperator khloros*.

The Mourning Wasp

By China Miéville

PROLOGUE

Jeza left the city alone and headed along the coast on horseback.

It was early, and her head pounded from a hangover. She was still a little dazed from all the cheap alcohol, furious with herself for having left her dagger somewhere under a table, and still contemplating whether or not her partner, Diggsy, was actually playing around behind her back. She should not have gone out, not with a dawn start ahead of her, but it seemed a good way of forgetting about those gestures, those second glances and the sudden in-jokes she didn't understand.

Jeza was an hour out of the city, far away from the comforting stone walls of her home, Factory 54, which she shared with a group of friends. She had left them there, too, deciding that this lead was one she should explore on her own.

The road south, along the coastline, was quiet. To her left, the chalk cliffs rose up from the sea; down below the surf ground upon the rocks. There were few clouds, and the sun cast its long blood-orange rays across the skies. Jeza pulled her green woollen shawl around her shoulders more tightly. Her breeches were thick, as were her boots – a present from Diggsy for her recent seventeenth birthday – so at least she was prepared for the rawest of conditions. As it happened, just a gentle breeze was all that challenged Jeza and her mare that morning.

One day, she thought, *I'll be able to live far away from the city. I'll be able to be out here, with my relics and my theories, and not have to scrape a living in Villiren – what's left of it anyway.*

The city was recovering, though – she had to give it that. Last night Jeza had been to one of the underground taverns, in a zone untouched by the recent battle, but one that had once again become dominated by gang types. The place had a post-war energy: those who had survived were too jaded by the heavy loss of life, or too euphoric from the victory, to care any more. Whatever a person's background, they were offered cheap drink and decent music, and that was just the kind of night she had needed. Even so, if she wanted to forget about things then coming out here would have done just as well. The view was remarkable. To her right she could see the fields that fed the city with cultist-treated crops; there were farmhouses, little smallholdings, and forests opening out into tundra. Beyond, the hills faded into the blue morning mists. Everything here was untouched from the recent battle, which had focused solely on the city itself.

Jeza rode for another hour at least. The sun banked. She scrutinized the horizon for any signs of the obelisk marked on her map, but it took a while longer before she could see a bleak structure puncturing the skyline.

As she approached the obelisk, which must have been fifty feet high, she noticed a figure sitting at its base, and a horse munching grass nearby. Her heart beat a little quicker. She didn't make a habit of visiting strange men outside the city, but she had a knife in her boot and a relic up her sleeve should he try anything.

Stop it, she told herself. *He's just a tribesman – they're as gentle as can be, despite what people say in the city.*

When she arrived and dismounted, she was surprised to see that they were both the same height, a little over five feet. His broad features and narrow eyes had a warmth to them; his skin was darker, presumably from spending a life out-doors. Long, black hair reached the shoulders of his dark waxed coat, and his breeches appeared to be of the same material.

'You are Jeza?' he asked sternly.

'Were you expecting anyone else out here?' she replied.

His smile widened massively. 'Good! You have some spirit. That will mean my trip won't be completely dull.'

'You speak Jamur very well,' Jeza replied.

'Do you think we nomads all talk in smoke signals?' He whistled and his horse came trotting to his side. It was a beautiful brown mare, with no saddle or any decoration. 'You have the coin?'

'Sure.' Jeza turned to her horse, and opened one of the saddlebags. She pulled out a heavy purse and tossed it across to him.

He caught it in his left hand, assessed its weight, looked inside, then placed it in a pocket. 'How does this young woman get money like this, eh? You mind my asking?'

'I have a job. My group struggles along. We do a little work outside normal circles, try to sell our wares. Deal in relics to cultists who should know better.'

He stared at her for a little while before nodding.

'I don't know your name yet,' Jeza observed. 'They never told me.'

'It is better this way. I do not want word getting back that I have defiled a sacred site.'

'So you work outside of your normal circles, too?' Jeza observed.

'I'm one of the few nomads who dare to do business with folk from Villiren. That is as wild as our people can possibly be.'

'Aren't you worried they'll trace this back to you anyway?'

'That depends,' he replied. 'I do not yet know what you intend to do at the site.'

'We'll do no harm, if that's what you mean. We respect your people's beliefs.'

'Well, that is more than I can say for myself,' he smiled, and with remarkable grace he leapt up onto the back of the mare. 'Come.'

*

Their horses trotted at a steady pace away from the sea and into the hills inland. The sun was high now, the shadows short, the temperature climbing above freezing. They appeared to be heading to the peaks in the distance, but after his initial conversation the tribesman became taciturn.

This time in silence, away from the distractions of the city, allowed Jeza to think of Lim, who was no longer with the group. His absence grew more profound each day. However, the group still felt near him, by reading his notebooks as if he was guiding them from another realm. He had been one of the most talented people back at the factory.

Stop it, she told herself. *You're getting worse. You had your chance, but he's dead. Besides, you have Diggsy now. Unless you haven't . . .*

They passed through evergreen forests and thickets of spindly bushes, back into tundra and then up a gentle stone path towards the grey cliffs. Birds scattered from the treetops, arcing up out of sight. Snakes unfurled in the damp under-growth, and she wondered how they could survive such cold conditions. There were wolves there, too, peering furtively from behind tree trunks.

Knowing little of her guide, Jeza half expected to end up the victim of an aggressive, Villiren-hating attack, but none came. They headed up a slope and deep into this ragged cliff region. The tops of the hills were crowned with snow, but little of it had fallen here.

And, as the horses navigated a path no wider than the width of a man's shoulders, with a hundred-foot drop to her left, she was grateful for the lack of ice. Jeza clung on to the animal, her heart racing every time she caught a glimpse of the steep drop.

4

'Have we much further to go?' she asked nervously.

'Don't be such a coward,' the tribesman laughed. 'They don't breed you city folk to be hard, do they? Anyway, it is not far now. Did you bring your source of light, as requested?'

'A light relic? Yeah, I brought a couple.'

'Good. Because we will need it soon.'

Wind buffeting them, they reached the mouth of a cave, a gaping hole some twenty feet high. Looking back, a beautiful vista presented itself. She could even see the obelisk now on the lip of the coast, the rolling farmland either side. In front of her, in the cave, there was only darkness.

'We leave the horses here,' he grunted.

After she dismounted, Jeza reached into the saddlebags for her relic. It was a crystal object the size of her fist, which she had attached to an ornate brass pole. She bashed the crystal on a rock and suddenly it began to glow. Not being an authentic cultist, she did not know the name. It didn't matter really – she simply referred to it as a torch, since it performed the same role as a flame.

'I stand impressed,' the tribesman said. 'Bring it this way.'

They entered the darkness of the cave. The torch picked out a pale, smooth stone, with a few markings that seemed to be writing.

The rock became coarser and darker, with scars of minerals, or coloured by dripping water. As they headed downwards, the dark and damp became more acute. Then the narrow pathway they were on suddenly opened up in front of them as if they had entered a cavern.

'What is this place?' Jeza asked.

'A burial ground, of sorts. Can you make your torch brighter like the sun?'

'Well, that's not particularly bright, but I can do that.' She struck the crystal twice more against the nearest rock and pointed it in front of them.

The cavern lit up.

5

First, the tribesman paused to read something on one of the walls. He muttered something vaguely affirmative to himself, before pointing out some of the drawings to Jeza. 'These are cave paintings,' he said, 'not dissimilar to the ones my own people once made.'

She was shown diagrams of bizarre creatures, unlikely things spliced together – lions or tigers combined with fish.

Jeza's nerves grew agonizingly tense. 'Will we be OK? We're not under any threat of attack, are we?'

'We will be fine!' the man laughed. His voice echoed for several seconds. 'People once lived in the caves, though no longer. They were only defending what was theirs – or protecting something that wasn't.'

'How do you know they're not here any more?'

For a moment he paused to contemplate her question. 'I hide in these caves sometimes,' he replied. 'I am not always a welcome person in my own community, because of my dealings with your people.'

'Because you make money from both of us?'

'A man must make a living somehow,' he replied, glaring at her.

*

The next room seemed even colder than the last. It was certainly smaller. Weirdly, there were tiny trinkets strewn along one side. Jeza brought the torch much closer, and could see offerings, prayer beads, strange feathered items, metallic cups, and weird scrolls that had crumbled to dust. There were markings on the wall, too, vast paintings now, with a variety of styles.

'These don't seem that old,' Jeza said, crouching by the offerings.

'They are not. When I first used this place as a shelter, I came across two women from a minor tribe, bringing items of honour to leave here. They were not the only ones.'

'Why?'

'Because they fear their gods, that is why.'

Gods? Jeza could ask questions all day long. Nothing here seemed to make much sense.

'Come and see this,' the tribesman said, 'and bring your light.'

On the wall was an enormous painting. It was rendered with a thick black ink that had stood the test of time. There was what appeared to be a bulbous abdomen and thorax.

'These lines here are wings,' he explained, pointing to one aspect of the picture, between the thorax and abdomen.

'Is this its head?'

'No, there is no head on this painting.'

Jeza stared at it, waiting for him to explain further, but he said no more. His tendency to give her limited information was frustrating. *Did he need more money?* she wondered. *Did he need more time?*

'We are very close now,' he said. 'Over here.'

She stepped to follow him and could then see he was now crouching beside a dark pit. 'It's in here,' he said.

She peered over with her torch. What lay in the pit astounded her.

Several feet long from tip to skull, it shimmered in the half-light; the bulbous abdomen was still there, as was the thorax – but there was most definitely a head. Rather, there had *been* a head at one point – now a huge skull lay at an awkward angle in its place. Mentally she began comparing it to other creatures she had seen, remains that had been sketched by her own hand and others, in a vague attempt to speculate on family trees, at how these things had come to be in existence. What family was it from? What was its lineage? Were there any remnants of this creature today; did it live on in other things?

But she drew a blank. Its presence stunned her.

Jeza shook her head in disbelief, and gave an incredulous laugh. 'Go on then,' she said. 'Tell me more. What is it?'

After a pause, he said, 'People from my tribe call it the Mourning Wasp.'

She breathed the name to herself, as if to confirm something so outrageous. 'Morning as in the morning, or mourning as in grieving?'

'The latter.'

'It's not a fake, is it?'

'I may have an interesting reputation, but I do not deceive. What you see here is real.'

'Tell me more.'

'What would you like to know?'

'How it came to be here.'

He eyed her for a moment, and he was impossible to read. His eyes reflected the light of the torch, almost startling her. 'There are folk tales, dating back to the Age of Science, a period where great beasts walked the earth, and monsters were constructed purely to see how far people could push their cultist-like powers. The wasps began a normal existence, but they were made massive by science, yet still they bred true. After the experiments there were thousands of them, and they all fled – on their own. It was said with the skull they became more intelligent. Their sentience, their solitary existence, their prolonged life and their awareness of dying out led them to be very miserable. Morose. Depressed. They lost much of their energy. It seemed they had no purpose. They mourned for their independence from their form, and in their final days they grieved.' He gestured to the remains of the Mourning Wasp. 'This is the second specimen known, but the best preserved.'

She regarded the remains of the wasp once again. Stubs remained where she assumed the wings would have met the creature's thorax. The specimen was in incredible condition, though the arts of palaeomancy were not exactly predictable.

'You think you can do something with this?' he asked.

Jeza scratched her chin. 'I'll need to bring the others here to help me take it back to the city. But I think I can, yes.'

ONE

Wind stirred the leafless treetops. Other than that, Commander Brynd Lathraea could hear nothing to cause concern, nothing out of the ordinary. Snow was settling deep in the Wych Forest.

Still, at least this is better than being in Villiren.

Just a few miles to the north, most of that city was now little more than a war-shattered pile of rubble. Each day since the fighting, soldiers had been discovering dozens and dozens of dead bodies, which were to be burned on pyres. His orders had been strict: this necessary evil was to continue until every citizen's soul had been freed. It was a messy business, but then the war had left a lot of mess behind. Entering through gates into this world, the Okun had made their way across the water aiming straight for Villiren, focused on the city's destruction. Brynd organized Villiren's defence and, though he could declare the operation a success, it didn't much feel like a victory when so many thousands of Empire civilians had been torn apart.

After that Brynd often preferred to be out here, to talk to the crows and run his hand along damp bark, rather than having to apologize to families for carrying their dead kin through the streets.

But he was not here to relax; he was here for business. A figure could be discerned nearby, beside her waxed canvas tent, lifting a flask to her mouth.

'Drinking on the job, sergeant?' he called out.

Sergeant Beale, one of the few surviving Third Dragoons, Wolf Brigade, dropped the flask. She peered around while grasping frantically for her sword. When her eyes settled on him, she didn't relax at all – in fact, she seemed even more agitated. This was no surprise: Brynd was used to people's reaction. He was an albino and his eyes were the colour of the sun. He was lean, with day-old stubble and a few inches of silvery white hair. His coal-black uniform, without armour, was immaculately clean and a sabre hung by his side. 'I'm sorry, commander,' Beale spluttered. 'I swear I didn't hear a thing. In fact, I haven't for days. And I don't drink on the job – honestly. Well, just enough to keep warm, sir, since I'm not getting much exercise.'

Brynd reached down, sniffed the flask, then screwed the cap back on before tossing it back to Beale. 'A waste of good vodka.' He looked around the forest, before staring intently at her. 'So you say you've seen nothing at all, sergeant?'

'No, sir.' Beale looked scruffy after five days in the mud and snow with little access to clean water. 'A garuda whizzed by during yesterday afternoon, and I've circuited this part of the forest every hour, but all I've located is some ruins, sir.'

Brynd strode casually over to her shelter and tapped the rope holding it between the trees. 'That's good work, putting this together. It's held up well enough considering there's little canopy cover.'

Beale said nothing, simply nodded.

Brynd continued to assess his surroundings, each individual trunk, clearings, the skeletal tree line, as if hoping to discern something. 'Five days and absolutely nothing, you say?'

'No, sir.'

'Good,' he replied mysteriously.

She frowned. 'Does this mean that I am to be relieved, sir?'

'No,' he replied. 'Not yet. A small unit of soldiers will be arriving within the hour with ... someone who might cause alarm upon first sight.'

'I've heard of a giant in the ranks,' Beale offered.

'She's not that big, if that's what you're thinking, but yes, it's her. What you may or may not see is to remain strictly within this forest, do you understand?'

Beale gave a quick nod, and that was that.

'How is the rebuilding of Villiren?' she enquired.

Brynd once again scrutinized their surroundings, like a paranoid man. 'It has begun, but you're better off out here.' He indicated the wilderness. 'This is where the real world is to be found, with trees and earth, not searching the veiled comments of businessmen for a kernel of truth.'

Brynd reached into his pocket, then unfolded a map, his breath clouding in the late afternoon chill. The sun was sliding over the horizon; the sky turning to the colour of dried blood.

'Do you, uh, have any duties you require of me, commander?' Beale asked, impatient and nervous in his presence.

'Do you mean,' he replied light-heartedly, 'what am I, the commander of your army, still doing here so late in the day?'

'I wouldn't presume—'

'It would be a fair question,' Brynd said. 'This is an issue of utmost secrecy and I can trust few people these days. However, a better question would have been why *you* were sent here in the first place.'

Beale remained silently annoyed with herself.

'It's all right – you just take orders and get on with it, I know. There's a lot to be said for soldiers like you, and that spirit will get you far in the army.'

Beale nodded.

'In an hour's time, about fifty soldiers will descend on this woodland. They'll take the main track through to those ruins you mentioned.'

'Sir.'

'You'll say nothing about what you may witness, nothing about what occurs here.'

'Indeed, sir. Though ... what will be occurring, so I know not to look?'

'You can look,' he said, 'though I'm not entirely sure what to expect myself.'

'Bleak times,' Beale said.

'You don't know the half of it. Were you there in Villiren from the start?'

'I'm afraid to say I was.'

'You're a brave woman.'

'Lucky, I'd say,' Beale added.

'Lucky?' Brynd gave a short laugh that emitted a cloud of his breath. Beale visibly shivered: the temperatures were plummeting as night approached. 'Luck would have had you elsewhere in the first place. But, by Bohr, a lot of good men and women were just hacked apart like nothing I've ever seen.'

'What was the death toll in the end?' Beale asked.

'The official estimate now stands at a little over one hundred and twenty-five thousand who died in or just after combat . . .'

'Shit . . .' Beale shook her head in disbelief. 'Pardon my language, sir.'

He waved her apology away. 'Though some of those deaths might be due to the cold weather and lack of food in the aftermath.'

'You'll see the place made good again, won't you, commander?'

The albino gave a shrug. 'We can but try. However, I'm not entirely sure that those events – that huge loss of life – weren't the beginning of something bigger. There are millions scattered across the Jamur Empire—'

'Don't you mean Urtican?'

'No,' he said and looked at her with intensity. 'The Jamur

lineage has been reinstated for the foreseeable future. Empress Rika is safe and placed in senior command once again.'

'But . . . I don't understand.'

'That's the least of your worries tonight, sergeant,' he said, and walked away. 'As you were – and remember to forget what happens later.'

Brynd wondered again what the former Emperor Urtica must have thought upon receiving his letter in Villjamur via garuda all that time ago, effectively annexing the city of Villiren from the Empire and taking what was left of the armed forces to support Jamur Rika. Brynd had received nothing in return, no indication that their declaration had even been read.

*

Later on in the night a torch flickered, moving between the branches; one, two, three of them now, all leading a small band of figures through the forest. Among the gathered silhouettes came Artemisia, a figure who towered over the others by at least a foot, and she moved with a fluid gait. At the front of the group walked Brynd, and he peered back to assess their progress.

He was surrounded by members of his Night Guard, the elite regiment that he led. More soldiers shuffled into line at the back, about two dozen archers with their bows poking up over their shoulders.

The group headed towards Sergeant Beale's post. She stepped out onto the path with her hand on her sword, and saluted Brynd.

'At ease, sergeant,' he called, his voice absorbed by the black, dead forest. 'You can fall in line with us at the rear now. We've scouts skimming around the edge of the forest.'

'Am I relieved of duty?'

Brynd considered this for a moment before he called out, 'Are you any good with a bow?'

'As good as any,' she replied.

'Good.' Brynd turned behind and gave some sharp orders. A bow was brought forward, along with a quiver full of arrows; he slung them towards Beale, and ordered her to fall in with the archers at the back of their unit.

They reached a clearing, the location of one of the ruins that littered the Wych Forest. Crumbling masonry of once-immense structures sprawled across each other, which was nothing new in the Boreal Archipelago, but here there was a key difference: none of these ruins was covered by moss or lichen like the adjacent deadwood – the smooth, pale stone remained blemish-free. This particular ruin seemed to have once been a kind of cathedral, with huge arches facing directly north. Little of the walls remained, but at the other end – opposite the slightly curved remains of the apse – lay a fully intact arch. It must have stood twenty feet high and, on closer inspection, its surface was remarkably smooth, like new – as if time had not touched it.

Artemisia moved past Brynd and marched right up to the archway as he gave instructions for the archers to line up in two rows extending from the archway, facing each other. Once assembled, they stood silently, in the cold.

The commander was not all that convinced. Of all the possible outcomes, the most likely would be that nothing happened, that this was all some ridiculous fantasy, and there would, in fact, be no extra military support coming his way.

'How much longer must we wait?' Eir asked out loud. She momentarily looked over to her sister, the Empress Rika, who remained impassive. 'We may freeze out here – it's so very cold.' The man behind her, Randur Estevu, placed his arms around her protectively and whispered something into her ear, which seemed to warm her up.

Brynd found their affection mildly nauseating. 'I haven't noticed.'

'Your enhancements,' she said, 'escape your attention. You

can't feel a thing, I'd wager. Meanwhile our bones will turn to ice.'

'We'll take as long as it takes, Lady Eir,' he declared. 'Besides, it's ultimately up to Artemisia as to how long we remain out here.'

The blue giant lumbered into view, bearing down on them. Brynd remained astonished by this alien woman who had burst into their world seemingly from nowhere, bringing the two Jamur sisters, and offering them her aid. She was wearing typical clothing for these islands: breeches and undershirt, but she wore an overcoat cut for combat, with a body-sculpted, brown breastplate that was adorned with a thousand minute symbols, none of which Brynd had ever seen in all his travels. Her hair was tied back out of her way, exposing over her shoulder the handles of her swords. She eyed them curiously, as if she was about to say something patronizing.

Then Artemisia beckoned forth three cultists, two men and a woman dressed in black robes, who were carrying a trunk of relics. She gestured for it to be taken towards the large archway, and the cultists trudged off hastily, their cloaks fluttering in the breeze.

'I will know soon enough,' Artemisia announced, 'how long it is we must remain out here.' Whenever she spoke, it seemed all those around her listened. She commanded respect. Brynd wondered what her position was in her own world.

'Have you all that you need?' Brynd asked her.

'For now,' she replied.

'If it carves a path in the wrong direction?'

'You have your archers.'

'And if it fails completely?' he asked.

'It will not.'

'But if it does?' Brynd pressed.

'Then, commander, it will be because your cultists have tampered with the technology. The theory, as I have stated, is sound.'

Her skills in the Jamur language had improved rapidly, even if her attitude had not.

For the better part of thirty days, she been working with the city's cultists; each night she returned to the Citadel in the centre of Villiren, where Brynd, Empress Rika, her sister Eir and the Night Guard were garrisoned, and she brought them relics. For millennia, cultists had monopolized these remnants from the technological glories of the past, even though they often only barely understood them; and now, for the first time, there were explanations as to their uses. Explanations both logical and full of absurdities. If only he could understand more of what she said. He wasn't interested in the theory, but their application – she was promising she could aid his army, and that was all he was bothered about.

So they had gathered in their numbers, here in the Wych Forest to the south of Villiren, to watch her apply this knowledge. What happened here would give Brynd some indication of Artemisia's true value to the people of the Boreal Archipelago.

The archway seemed to entrance her and Artemisia approached it with almost a religious fervour. As she retrieved a device from one of her pockets, Brynd stepped alongside her, under the gaze of the archers on either side.

'This is the archway then,' Brynd grunted. 'It looks a fine piece of architecture, but really – you honestly think this is the place?'

'Your scepticism does not favour you,' she replied.

'You mean *does me* no favours?'

'That is what I said. I would have thought that, by now, given all you have seen, you of all humans would be more inclined to possess an open mind.'

'It's my scepticism that's kept people alive!' he responded. 'You'd do well to remember that.'

It wasn't a confrontation, but she didn't acknowledge his

remark. The cultists lowered the trunk to the ground, and stepped aside as Artemisia loomed over it. Torches were brought closer as she lifted back the lid to reveal what to Brynd appeared to be the contents of a junkyard in Villiren – bits of piping, metal sheets, all items that could be melted down into something more practical like a sword. But there were stranger things there, too, wires and intricate compass-like gadgets, and materials he hadn't seen before.

He muttered disapproval of cultist trickery, and left it at that. Now was not the time to criticize: she was, after all, going to help him, help Jamur Rika, and help what was left of the Empire. Artemisia rummaged in the trunk.

'I will commence the build,' Artemisia announced, standing tall with two metal objects in her fists. She strode towards the archway and Brynd watched her work: at first she piled the relics at each side of the arch, and further away she began placing small metallic domes at regular intervals, stretching back through the ruins. She began connecting each of them up with a long cable, and then tied those around the arch. The process took the better part of an hour, and Brynd could sense anticipation and anxiousness from the archers.

Eventually, when Artemisia had rigged up an intricate latticework of wires, girders, poles and dials, it looked as if half the cathedral had almost been rebuilt out of this skeletal frame.

She turned to Brynd. 'I am now ready for the first attempt.'

Brynd nodded and marched along each row of archers, giving sharp orders, seething at their lack of discipline as they listened lazily to him.

This wouldn't happen with good honest army-bred soldiers, he thought. *Still, it's hired thugs or nothing.*

Once the archers nocked their arrows, Brynd ordered them to regard the space in front of the archway and to wait on his word before firing. Then Brynd returned to his position alongside Jamur Rika, who remained strangely stern-faced and emotionless. She was not the young woman he remembered from Villjamur, and these violent times had affected her deeply.

The wind groaned in the clearing. Dead trees rattled behind them.

Artemisia stood in the centre of the scene now. She unsheathed her immense blades and took both swords into one fist. Then crouched down to the floor, where she began tinkering with some small device exactly as a cultist might. She called one of the cultists over, and the woman rushed forward, remarkably servile, then the two of them conversed in whispers. A moment later the cultist ran back to make some minor adjustments.

Oh come the fuck on, Brynd thought. *This is taking forever*.

The sound of static was faint at first, but increasing in volume. The fabric of the air surrounding Artemisia became charged: a fine web of white light could be discerned, like a ghostly net; it became clearer still, hanging there – not a net, but some three-dimensional grid. Brynd peered around and could see this grid extended to the area they were now in, reconstructing the cathedral ruins in light. He held up his hand and it passed unaffected through one of the glowing lines.

The lines of archers held tight, impassive at the spectral architecture. For several minutes they all stood there, waiting as if nothing had happened. The lines began to fade, the form of a cathedral vanished into the icy night, and Brynd kicked his boot against a crumbling piece of masonry before marching up to Artemisia.

'Nothing, then,' he declared, but Artemisia stood staring at the archway.

He followed her gaze, and then he noticed that the darkness within the arch was different from that outside. Inside was an utter blackness, totally devoid of light, whereas outside he could see the edges of branches and tree trunks picked out by torchlight.

'An absolute nothing,' Artemisia confirmed smugly. 'This is, I believe, progress.'

'Where's this assistance then?'

'I never said it would come naturally. I may have to enter through here in order to retrieve it. No one on the other side would have known of my summons. This is merely a gateway.'

'The descriptions of the other Realm Gates were different,' Brynd said. 'They suggested a purple mesh of light – this has nothing.'

'There are different methods of construction – also, the light may be on the other side. This might only go one way. I would have to turn it around.'

'You mean, go in? How can we be certain you're not wasting our time – that you'll go back to your world and that's that?'

'Dimension,' she corrected. 'It is the same world. Why would I waste my time coming here in the first place? If it works, then I will be back immediately. Time works differently, I assure you.'

'Go on, then,' Brynd commanded. 'We might as well get on with it if our situation is as bad as we think it is.'

'Very well, I will return immediately,' Artemisia replied, and simply marched towards the archway – and then into a void.

Gasps came from the archers, and Brynd had to admit his own surprise at her nonchalance at the act. Then again, if she had breached worlds before, it might be second nature to her.

People began murmuring, and Brynd could hear the question arise of how long they would stay out here in the cold. Bitter disappointment was apparent on everyone's face; hopes began fading as the minutes passed.

But no sooner had the gathered soldiers begun to murmur when the archway began to emit light. A grid began to form, one similar to those that Brynd had heard about out across the ice, where it was thought that other races had infiltrated this world and gathered the invasion force that attacked Villiren. The purple lines of light bulged in hypnotic ways, as if a force were trying to push from the other side. The lines of light peeled outwards.

Brynd immediately called for order, stopping the panic from spreading and dragging the archers back to attention and telling them to focus their arrow-tips at the archway, because something was certainly trying to enter the clearing.

A moment later, a blue head pushed through – followed by its body.

It was Artemisia.

She appeared to be different, wore strange new clothing – dark armour with a red sun emblazoned on her chest.

'Prepare,' she muttered, and stumbled forwards.

Behind her, the gateway bulged again: this time in several places. Something pressed against it, then burst through – human hands, attached to ... yes – human warriors. Brynd had expected something stranger, given the nature of the recent invasion. He was almost relaxed at the familiar sight.

Then it struck him: *humans exist in this other dimension?*

Clad in body armour and carrying circular shields and short, thick swords, warriors tumbled forward out of the gate, flooding into the clearing. They all bore the same emblem on their chest and on the forehead of their regal-looking helmets: a hollow red sun.

Brynd turned to face his own military lines, ordering them to stand down: 'Take ten paces back for space, keep your aim squarely ahead. Do *not* fire.'

His men shuffled back into the darkness as these other-world soldiers continued flowing through the gates into the ruins of the cathedral, maintaining impressively precise ranks. There must have been two hundred of them. Here was a mix of dark-skinned and light-skinned men, some bordering on albino, and they were all broad and muscular.

Artemisia approached him. 'These are the elite of our warriors.' The pride was clear in her voice.

'Fine-looking soldiers,' Brynd admitted. 'Though I had hoped for more.'

'There are many more where they came from,' Artemisia replied. 'Tens of thousands, though of a more inferior quality. I located the ones that could be spared immediately. More will be brought soon enough. You should know I was gone from here for over five days in my nation. I also bring some news.'

Brynd nodded for her to continue.

'Frater Mercury, our creator, has already, it seems, made it into this world.'

'How? This is your ruler, right?'

'No – creator not ruler. Our society is democratic – there is no one ruler, but a working, interchangeable council of elders. Frater Mercury's work was in enabling us to exist and to breed more, but he has only ever advised.'

'What's he doing in our world?'

Artemisia seemed for the very first time to show concern on her face. 'I am not entirely sure. He had not . . . alerted any elders of intentions. It is a surprise to all of us. He has since left only a handful of messages.'

'I'm guessing you'll need to locate him,' Brynd said.

'A possibility, yes.'

'We're going to have to combine tactics – your nation, and ours – if we're not only to fight together, but also to live together peacefully. If you would head back to your world,' Brynd indicated the gate, 'I would like to meet with your elders. They should speak with Jamur Rika. We should begin diplomatic discussions immediately.'

Artemisia nodded. 'It could take a while to assemble them, but I will.'

TWO

To Brynd the obsidian chamber situated high up in the Citadel was becoming the nearest thing he knew to a home. As a soldier he could spend months away from the normal elements of life: family or friends or the comforting familiarity of daily routine. The Night Guard had long replaced his family and friends; as for a home . . . well, being shipped from mission to mission for more than half his life had long relieved him of any attachment. In that sense he shared more with the nomadic tribes of the Archipelago than with the people of this city.

The obsidian chamber had been the main war room for mounting the defence of Villiren. Blood-red volcanic glass lined the walls, upon which cressets were burning, mirrored in the glossy surface, and in the centre of the wide room was a vast oak table. A fire crackled in a grate. Thin, arched windows on one side revealed the harbour of Villiren, or what was left of it, and the sea beyond. The weather was unusually fine today: a few clouds scudded over the horizon, but other than that the choppy sea was a deep blue, the sky above slightly paler.

Brynd had spent many hours in here. Though he had seen more than his fair share of combat, much of his expertise had been concerned with logistics: food supplies, civilian evacuation procedures, military tactics, enlistment, all the time negotiating with the city officials – whenever they felt like engaging professionally, that was. Brynd hadn't seen the city's portreeve for many weeks now, the man presumably having long since fled. Now the city had fallen under military rule, and this suited Brynd just fine – it made Villiren all the easier to annex from the Empire.

He cleared the maps and draft budgets from the table and heaped them on his desk to look at later. Then poured himself a glass of decent wine that had been 'rescued' from the crippled cellars of a bistro by the citizen militia and took a sip.

There was a knock at the door and he called for them to enter. A muscular and the most thuggish-looking of the Night Guard soldiers, Brug, poked his shaven head around the door. Brynd could make out the tattoos on his thick neck as he stretched into the room. 'Commander, Jamur Rika says she's ready to see you now.'

'Does she, then?' Brynd muttered. 'You'd better bring her in.'

'Aye. She's a bit forward about it, if you ask me. Demanding, more than asking, to be brought here. Not the girl I remember.'

'She's Lady Rika now, Brug. Not a girl.'

'Not much of a lady, if you ask me. That the South Tineag'l vintage?' Brug said and indicated the bottles on the table.

Brynd nodded.

'Waste of a good wine, if you ask me.' Brug turned and exited.

Brynd lit some incense and then waited in silence, contentedly watching the flames of the fire. He closed his eyes; he could hear the footsteps of several people in the distance, possibly in the corridor beneath the chamber. Somewhere else was the crackle of cultist magic: hopefully they were working on *Brenna*-based munitions, very useful high explosives. Further away, possibly outside, was the smell of freshly baked sourdough bread.

Footsteps in the doorway: he opened his eyes to see Jamur Rika walking briskly towards him, accompanied by Brug. He rose to meet her, and bowed his head slightly.

'Jamur Rika,' he announced, 'welcome to the obsidian chamber.'

'So this is where Commander Lathraea spends his days?'

She looked around the room dismissively. He had never seen her looking so warrior-like. Had her snug grey uniform been black she could have passed for one of his own Night Guard. A gold, jewel-studded ceremonial dagger was fitted to her left hip, and her black hair had been cut shorter than he remembered, shorter even than Eir's. All the soft lines of her face, the creases around her eyes, the gentle mannerisms he recalled when he first saw her on Southfjords just months before, had taken on a harsher definition. Her transformation was sudden and disarming.

'And most evenings too, it seems,' Brynd said, effortlessly moving to his feet. 'My Empress . . .'

'Please don't call me that yet,' she replied.

'My apologies.'

She smiled wryly. 'I don't feel comfortable with what isn't yet certain. We are annexed – does this mean we are part of a republic? A freetown? I can hardly be Empress of just a *city*, can I?'

Brynd frowned and shared a glance with Brug. The big man simply shrugged and smiled to himself.

'Perhaps we can clarify some of those matters today,' he said. He started to move towards the table when the door to his office opened again and into the room walked Jamur Eir, Rika's sister, and Eir's companion – bodyguard and lover – Randur Estevu. Eir smiled serenely and greeted Brynd like an old friend, as she always had done. Randur, on the other hand, simply bowed with a ridiculous flourish; Brynd couldn't be certain if he was being respectful, sarcastic or a fool – or possibly all three. While Eir wore a simple brown tunic,

Randur was dressed in some fancy new shirt, frilled cuffs, a ridiculous collar, and his glossy cape. There were even a few braids in his hair.

'Is that a new sword, Randur?' Brynd indicated the rapier sheathed by his side.

'What a keen sense of sight, commander,' Randur replied, then – with a *zing* – he whipped the rapier out. Light shimmered off its surface. 'Fancy giving it a test later? I could do with the practice. Bored out my arse a lot of the time.'

'I'll see if I can spare a moment,' Brynd replied.

'I understand if you don't want to lose to me.'

'I will see,' Brynd said, cutting him short. 'Meanwhile, I would appreciate it if you adhered to martial policies: weapons are not to be carried about the Citadel, only upon exit to the city's streets. If we can't have discipline inside these walls, how the hell can we expect to export it outside?'

Randur sheathed his sword while glaring at Brynd, then grunted. He strode to the table, whereupon he began pouring himself some wine. Eir took a seat beside him, while Rika claimed her place at the head of the table. Brynd moved to her side.

Together they all waited patiently while administrators began to file into the room: lawyers, moneylenders, construction managers, cultists and then some more members of the Night Guard, who lined the room with their arms folded as a reminder of just who was currently enforcing the law in Villiren.

Brynd was expecting thirty-three individuals, but it felt like three times that when they were confined in this space, despite them maintaining a respectful volume, speaking only in hushed whispers to the people beside them while they waited.

Brynd rose from his seat and waited for them to fall into silence.

'Citizens, welcome,' he began, 'I have summoned you here

with difficult aims: to forge a new civilization, a new culture, a new Empire, to make provisions for the defence of the whole island and against the potential return of the Okun. And we need to do this together.'

He let his words sink in, and scrutinized the faces around him – some were passive, some wide-eyed.

'Any previous affiliations with the Urtican Empire are now terminated, and Villiren is a free, independent city currently under military rule, serving Jamur Rika, who is here seated beside me.'

All eyes turned to Rika, who sat with serenity amidst the whispers that now spread around the room. She waved her hand for Brynd to continue.

'At this time we are continuing to use the legal framework of the Empire. Villiren is a city without politicians, and many of you would probably think the place better because of it.' He got the laughs he intended, and smiled as he palmed the air. 'But I confess, these are serious times, and we face two problems that define our legacy. The first is this: the reconstruction of the city and the unification of a broken people. That is where you, the builders and bankers and lawyers and agriculturalists must talk openly. We must create employment for a people who have nothing, and we must feed them well. They must feel that they can participate in their own future, too. But the second problem may well prohibit any of this from happening.'

'What d'you mean?' someone called, a slender man with a thin moustache, who was called Derrouge.

'I'll show you,' Brynd replied. He called her name, and a minute later Artemisia stooped under the doorway at the back of the room. Everyone's gaze followed Brynd's own, and soon people at the back began clamouring to get out of her way.

'It is quite all right!' Brynd shouted. 'Please, remain calm – this is our ally, our comrade!'

In full war regalia, Artemisia marched through the parting, gasping crowd towards Brynd, and there she stood, towering over the room.

'What is it?' Derrouge asked.

'*She* is Artemisia,' Brynd replied, waiting for the room to settle. 'A friend.'

'Greetings to you all,' Artemisia announced, and Brynd thought he could see a smile on her face.

'You may recall that our recent battle here in Villiren was fought against a hitherto unknown race. Well, it transpires that in the world where this race originated, another war was being fought – against Artemisia's own people. She, too, was fighting the same enemy that we were.'

Brynd related the information he felt comfortable sharing about the breaches of the Realm Gates and the appearance of the Okun. With the gathered throng remaining in silence, he explained to them their situation: that their economy had been wrecked, that Villiren risked hyperinflation unless the moneylenders stopped giving money away and throwing people into debt; that the city had been annexed from the Empire, that Urtica had been notified, that they did not know where they stood in legal terms, and that these issues were the least of their concerns.

He refrained from telling them about the potentially false histories that all of these people had grown up with: the Church, it seemed, had offered a different explanation to the one Artemisia had brought with her, but that was another matter for another day. The split of humanity into a different dimension was perhaps too much to discuss at the moment. However, he clearly gave a context to her presence, and to that of the Okun, which had invaded Villiren so recently, and which were still being discovered in rubble-strewn pockets of the city, mostly dead, occasionally alive.

'The forces from other worlds,' he said, 'are going to continue flowing into ours. This cannot be stopped. They will bring with them – no, they've already brought with them – their long war. One side,' he gestured to Artemisia, 'is looking to settle alongside us. Their long-term opponents are . . . well, you have all met *their* ambassadors, the Okun. Their opponents would see all our cultures destroyed, humanity effectively cleansed, to make way for their repopulation of the Boreal Archipelago. You would have no farms, no banks, no buildings. No life.'

The noise in the room began to increase. Brynd waved to calm the hubbub, yet it had little effect. He caught the eye of his soldiers, who looked to him for guidance, but he shook his head. These weren't people who needed threatening – they had to work *with* him. Artemisia, it seemed, wasn't one for patience. She lurched forward, withdrew her twin blades from over her shoulder, and rested them on the table.

Everyone fell into silence, staring at the massive weapons, and then at her. No one dared say a thing.

'Thank you,' Brynd muttered.

Artemisia stepped back, satisfied.

'As I was saying,' Brynd continued, 'we can assume the Empire as we know it – our culture as we know it – is not as it used to be.'

One of the moneylenders, a man with a narrow face and blond beard, leaned forward and interrupted. 'How can we believe . . . what she says? What's to say we're not being used?'

A chorus of voices flowed and ebbed around the room.

Randur Estevu, surprisingly, stood up to answer. 'This *foreigner*,' he said, 'saved the fucking lives of Empress Rika here and Eir.' He gestured to them both. 'As well as saving my arse. I was bringing these women all the way across to Villiren, due to . . . events in Villjamur. Artemisia saved us from Urtica's men, cut down anyone who tried to capture us, and brought us all the way to Villiren. Not only that, but while you lot were probably pissed out of your faces, she killed a fair few of the Okun in the city on the way to see the commander here. Shitting hell, I'd personally vouch that we can trust her. For what it's worth.'

'Thank you, Randur,' Brynd said, 'for your colourful contributions.'

Randur slumped back in his seat and folded his arms. Eir placed a hand on his shoulder.

Brynd looked around the room trying to gauge the mood. It was hard to tell: these were people who made careers out of furthering their own interests. To suddenly think about the rest of society did not come naturally to them. 'I can understand the trust issue, but as Randur has pointed out, we shouldn't be so quick to dismiss Artemisia's people.'

'So who are these people? We know nothing.'

'They're coming soon enough,' Brynd said. 'Many of them are already here, south of the city.'

'What d'you mean?'

'We find ourselves in the middle of a conflict that we can barely comprehend, and from both a military and ethical point of view the only possible way we can continue is to side with Artemisia's people.'

'Tell us simply, commander. Is there going to be another war?'

'Indeed,' Brynd replied. 'And it might be one on a scale that we've never seen before, or are ever likely to again.'

'Good,' said one of the moneylenders, laughing. 'Wars are good for industry. I've investments in arms manufacturers and I can tell you business has never been better. The mines are thronging, commander, and the ore is flowing like a river. As is the money. We'll get some good employment out of this. You want jobs, we can get jobs. You want industry, we can create it.'

'A river of cash,' someone muttered, possibly the wealthy merchant Coumby, and a smattering of laughter moved around the room.

'I want to make an offer to all of you,' Brynd announced. 'For your participation in our plans, I will see that you each hold valuable positions in the new society we are seeking to forge. I'll need weapons made, a food supply chain established – you can use cultist technology freely for rapid yields if need be – and I'll need the money to build this army. We'll need our biggest ever enlistment programme, rolling it out across this and neighbouring islands.'

'You're asking us to bankroll some kind of revolution!' someone shouted.

'That is not *untrue*,' Brynd replied. 'It's been the way of things in Villjamur. Given that a new landscape is the inevitable outcome from war, I am seeking your backing. As I said, each of you will find the returns from your investments and your participations to be attractive and we can have a look about forming our own regulation for you – a different kind from former Imperial policy.'

'What form will our returns take?'

'New estates,' Brynd replied. 'New markets to control, new constructions to build across the Empire, and new statutes that need to be written. This will be a long-term plan, but in the first instance I will see land taken from the Empire, and handed over.'

'I imagine these new statutes will be complex, eh?' someone asked.

Probably a lawyer.

'Because we'll be sharing our world with aliens,' a merchant blurted out. 'Ain't that so, commander? There'll be foreigners here, sharing our towns. There'll be monsters walking up and down our roads and people'll be expected to just get on with it. Ghettos will form, mark my word. Things won't be the same.'

'It's the people who leave who create the ghettos,' Brynd said. In another time, in another setting, Brynd would have had that man roughed up for his tone. Instead he simply continued, 'Though much of what you describe may well be an inevitable consequence of them helping us, but don't forget they will be bringing with them their own industries, their own wealth . . .'

'They should be segregated – given their own land well away from the rest of us.'

'Aye,' another said. 'I ain't living with things like that walking the streets.'

'Please,' Brynd said, 'if we're lucky enough to be alive in the future, and to have a society, then we can discuss such matters; though I ask you to concentrate on what's happening right now, in the immediate future.'

Once they had accepted that statement, the questions followed from those around the table for another hour at least. Each of them demanded to know some fine detail relevant to only them, creating a disparate set of conversations. There were questions concerning payments, land divisions, how much ore would be needed and by when, and whether common land would be privatized – a firm no from Brynd. What surprised him the most was that few of the questions concerned Artemisia or indeed the inevitable war and races that would be crossing into their own world.

'I'm in,' said a balding, fat man in the corner smoking arum weed, wearing purple robes that almost matched the colour of his cheeks. It was Coumby, someone who once owned many of the buildings in Villiren, before they were destroyed. 'I got dealings in ores, and smiths, and the fishing industry.' He paused to take another drag. 'I've heard enough talk to last the day. I think I could be of use to you, commander.'

'Good,' Brynd replied loudly, optimistically. 'Thank you, sir. So who else can we add to the list?'

'Fuck else is there to do in this city?' the thin-faced lawyer chimed in eventually. 'I'm intrigued at the prospects of designing laws from scratch.'

'One thing,' Coumby muttered, then inhaled again. His

face was becoming obscured by smoke. 'This young lady here,' he nodded his head towards Rika. 'She's in charge, you say? You're the one doing an awful lot of talkin', is all I can see . . . What's her role?'

Brynd looked towards her. Rika had been impassive for much of the last hour. She had let him do the talking and the work, but now she stood up, and he stepped aside to wait for her to speak.

'He is,' Rika began, 'working on my behalf, because of my family's lineage, and because of the underhand methods that Emperor Urtica used to dethrone me. I have some connection with the populace. My father's reign was relatively popular – we expanded the Empire and provided stability. I seek nothing more than continuing stability.'

'Indeed,' Brynd said, 'something as stable as a Jamur ruler would be preferable. It would make any transition much easier to withstand. It would help morale, give people something to cling on to.'

'What's that to us?' Coumby asked, and there were gasps then. 'What'd you do if we all sat here, lass, as we are, and did nothing to help you?'

Even Brynd raised an eyebrow, anxious to see how she would take such talk.

Rika smirked, then laughed. 'You would probably all die, and I would do nothing to stop that from happening.'

'Tough talk for just a pretty thing,' another merchant said. Coumby laughed into his own smoke.

'What is your name?' Rika asked.

'Broun, Hant Broun,' the red-bearded rake of a man replied.

Rika looked to Artemisia and all she did was nod: the massive warrior stepped towards the merchant, hauled him spluttering from his seat and thrust him against the wall. He skidded smoothly up the obsidian surface as Brug leaned casually out of the way. With one arm thrust against his throat, Artemisia reached over her shoulder with her free hand and drew a sword out with a slick zing, and held the point to Broun's throat. Not one person tried to rescue Broun, whose legs kicked back against the wall to support his weight.

'Um, Lady Rika . . .' Brynd hissed. 'Call her off – we *need* these people on our side.'

'We need no one,' she whispered bitterly. 'They should *fear* us.'

'These men would rebuild our world for us!' Brynd snapped.

Rika said nothing but stared angrily at the table. Brynd called for Artemisia to release her grip, and the warrior woman simply removed her hand and let Broun crumble to the floor before she walked back to Rika's side under the gaze of everyone in the room.

Great, just great, Brynd thought.

'This,' Rika said, 'this is an example of what will happen to us all. See the might we are dealing with? This is someone who is *on our side*, who wishes to make a peaceful union with our nations. You can either work on your own, as you have always done, or for once you can put aside your own little empires and join together.'

'You mean,' Coumby said, 'unite to protect yours.'

Rika turned and glared at him, before nodding. 'If that is what you wish to call it,' she said, 'but what other option have you to hand? None, I can tell you that much. Either you unite for just a short period, with great rewards at the end of it for those of you who do, or all you've ever worked for will be destroyed anyway. We will have creatures much stranger-looking than Artemisia here coming into our world and destroying everything you have ever achieved, not to mention your friends and your family.' As the room fell silent, Rika moved towards her chair and sat down. 'Everything will be wiped out. Now, we need supplies, we need a building

33

programme, we need jobs and most of all an army kitted out to defend our shores. Put simply, we need your money.'

Brynd watched these impassive faces show sudden concern. At one end of the room, Broun was now on his feet, dusting himself down before he snuck out quietly, without his dignity. Someone nearby chuckled.

'I'm in,' Coumby declared, 'should the offer suit me. We can help each other. To our mutual benefit.'

Following Coumby's lead, a few other merchants threw in their hand, obviously wanting a slice of whatever was on offer.

'See, commander?' Rika whispered. 'A stern word and a little force is sometimes required. They need fear in them.'

'Of course,' Brynd replied. 'Well put, Lady Rika.'

THREE

A river of refugees, forty thousand long, stretched across the bleak landscape of Jokull, while in the distance in the direction of the ruins of Villjamur, a sky-city hovered, a black smear against the sleet-filled sky. There was a strange ambience to the scene, one of a people resigned to their fate, yet possessing an urgency to move nonetheless. It was as if they had accepted they would die, but didn't want to – not just yet.

Fulcrom, one-time investigator of the Villjamur Inquisition, now resigned but somehow with more authority than he'd ever wanted, turned his horse around to face the other horizon – in the direction of their travel. There were a few hills with patches of forest to navigate through, but other than that there was merely the endless tundra stretching into the distance. In front of him, a flock of geese arced a slow circle then – for a brief, dreadful moment he thought they were something else coming down to the ground.

In the periphery of his vision, a black-clad girl with a dark fringe bounded towards him.

'You miss me?' Lan asked.

Fulcrom broke into a reluctant smile. 'Did it all go OK?'

'Sure, not as much trouble this morning as last night. There are no serious threats at all.' Her slender face was caked in mud, her hair dishevelled. Lan's black outfit, once the hallmark of a Knight of Villjamur, was now a meaningless costume, though her deeds were still the same: pulling people out of harm's way. There was still plenty of work for her.

'Hmm,' Fulcrom muttered.

'What?'

'I don't like it when there are no threats. That usually means something's about to happen.'

'Ever the optimist, aren't you?'

'I'm merely being rational. It's not right when there are no signs of life up there,' Fulcrom said, indicating the sky-city. 'Whenever there's been a calm before, a blistering attack follows. Why should *now* be any different?'

'Well, in quiet periods we can get people moving quicker than before,' Lan suggested. 'We can get further along. That's something, surely?'

'I know,' Fulcrom sighed. 'I just wish we had more of these vehicles. We just seem to be bringing more communities on board every hour. I didn't even realize Jokull was this populated until now. Anyway, where's Tane?'

'I've no idea,' she said. 'He was with me when I ran from the confrontation last night, but I'm much quicker than him over any distance. I just assumed he'd make it back OK.'

Fulcrom nodded and regarded the scene. As if becoming sucked into a moving tide, people were being dragged into the ongoing mass of humans and rumels. A few thousand had become tens of thousands – twenty, then nearer thirty, as the villages and hamlets emptied themselves of people desperate to avoid the devastation heading their way.

At first Fulcrom was in shocked awe of the tide of new refugees. Then he realized that their presence here was, ultimately, a good thing. It meant that their civilization might survive a little longer.

'What's next?' Lan asked, jumping effortlessly up onto Fulcrom's horse behind him. She moved one arm around his chest and squeezed him closer. It made him feel normal again – albeit for a brief moment – though Lan hadn't quite been normal since they'd left the remains of Villjamur. She'd been thriving out here; her confidence had reached new heights, the people had seemingly forgotten or ignored the recent revelations about her past.

'Just keep going, I guess,' he replied.

'We're nearly at the coast though. Then what? Will the sky-city follow us? Do we go across the water?'

Fulcrom held up his hands. 'I'm hoping Frater Mercury will sort something out.'

'That's a bit like praying for divine intervention,' Lan commented. 'I didn't have you down as a particularly religious man.'

'That was before we had someone who's practically a god by our side,' he replied.

'Speaking of which, what's he been up to?' Lan asked.

'Oh who the hell knows? I tell him what I need, he delivers it if he feels inclined, though sometimes I'm not sure he even hears me. So, essentially, that's why I have some hope that we'll be fine when we hit the water.'

'So you *can* be an optimist,' she joked and kissed the back of his neck.

*

There were twenty-two earth carriages now, twenty-two behemoths constructed by Frater Mercury from the very fabric of the land. They had risen up from the ground with mud dripping off like water, and wheels had been created from debris and somehow bound to these enormous clumps of land.

These rolling banks of earth were enough to carry hundreds of people, and many of them sat clinging near the edges nervously. Each was pulled by a horse taller than a church spire.

*

Fulcrom, with Lan behind him, rode forwards alongside the lead vehicle. It was cold, it was *always* cold, but they had to keep moving. The sound of the vast rotating wheels was monotonous.

'He seems to have settled into our world quite nicely,' Lan observed. She indicated Frater Mercury, who stood on top of one of the towering horses.

Frater Mercury: a being summoned through to this world by a priest who was no longer in it. He was a head taller than Fulcrom, and his face was split down the centre: one side was bone, the other metal, and where they met seemed to be a perfectly natural design. His two human eyes, set amidst that alien facial architecture, were disarming for their familiarity. He wore a deep-blue cloak that seemed to hold other hues within it, and beneath that was a body-tight dark outfit, one befitting a soldier, and one which Fulcrom half suspected was Frater Mercury's body itself.

'For a god, he certainly doesn't act like one. If indeed he is a god.'

'I'm not actually sure what he's meant to be,' Lan said. 'I'm glad he's here though.'

Fulcrom was also grateful to have the enigmatic Frater Mercury travelling with them. Not only had he created these rolling earth vehicles, but when there had been assaults from the sky-city, Frater Mercury had turned to engage in combat – something remarkably impressive for such a frail-looking old man.

*

Stopping was a slow and laborious affair and, even though they had been on the run for several days now, the process had become an art.

Fulcrom took out a red rag that he had wrapped around a stick to form a banner. After indicating to the soldiers accompanying the lead land-vehicle to halt, Fulcrom turned his horse and rode backwards along the line, at speed. With the wind ruffling his wax cape, and Lan holding on tightly behind him, Fulcrom steered past the streams of muddied, cold and confused citizens of the Empire. He waved the red banner and called out to the soldiers, who he had requested to station themselves along the line on horseback, to act as guides and moral support.

As Fulcrom passed the crowds, he could see people collectively grabbing the reins of the gargantuan horse that towed their land-vehicle. Eventually, the thunderous strides ceased and the vehicles rolled to a stop. Everyone on board them looked dazed, as if they had just woken from slumber.

Fulcrom continued to ride for several minutes down the line and past each of the absurdly large horses, waving his banner at each one, giving the signal, watching to make sure they stopped – before continuing on to the next. When all of the vehicles had stopped, he rode back up the line with his hand in the air and his fingers and thumb extended: five hours, this signalled. They would stop for five hours.

They did not pause their journey often – because of the hassle and the threat of the invaders. With the slowly advancing city now a distant glow in the evening sky, Fulcrom gave the order for people to rest and set up camp alongside the vehicles. Each night he would keep his gaze fixed on the horizon, to check the sky-city wasn't an immediate danger.

Fires were lit. Crude tents were erected. Food rations were cooked and issued. Any health problems were dealt with and, now that a team with some medical knowledge had been found, Fulcrom could prioritize between the most needy and those who could wait a little longer.

Fulcrom had been heartened to see some of the tribespeople of Jokull, who had spent most of their existence living in fear of the Empire and its people, come forward to offer their help. They brought hundreds of animal skins for warmth and carcasses for food. It was a gesture that humbled him; he had nothing to offer in return, but it did not seem to matter. The

nomads simply handed over the gifts and disappeared back
into the twilight.

*

People milled around under the darkening skies and each face
that caught the fire looked set in a glum expression.

Still, at least the shock has gone. Initially many people had
been shivering and wailing manically or simply refused to
talk. But that stage had now, mostly, subsided into the grim
realization of what was going on. This was now life. They
had to get used to it or die.

In the brief respite from the monotony of travelling,
Fulcrom chatted with the few soldiers who had made it from
Villjamur, as well as some of the more active political types
who had put aside differences to help out.

In a way, Fulcrom thought dryly, *the anarchists had actually
got what they wanted.*

Villjamur was no more. The Emperor was dead. The
Council was not so much dissolved as destroyed. This entire
convoy, in fact, was comprised of self-organized cells, with
power distributed evenly. Indeed, this was what the anarchists
had wanted, but not the level of destruction. Perhaps because
of this, or perhaps the sheer acknowledgement that everyone
had to stick together, there were few of the same problems
of inequality and exploitation that there had been in
Villjamur.

And Fulcrom's memories of the city were tainted. He could
not forget his own grim experiences towards the end of its
existence: being thrown in a cell, his tail being cut off, all
because of the Emperor's wrath.

Eventually he settled with some senior officers around a
campfire, along with Lan and, finally, Tane. The catman liked
to keep aloof in these moments of rest – mainly because he
was wary of his appearance, uncertain of what others would
think of him. Tane and Lan no longer had the benefit of their
clifftop retreat, no longer had the sanctuary of anonymity.

They had to be here, with people, and that meant they had to confront people's fear of those who were different.

'Tane,' Fulcrom called out. 'Where were you today?'

'At the rear, for the most part,' he replied coolly.

'Was there a skirmish?' Fulcrom asked.

'No,' Tane said, flexing his arm muscle as if it ached. 'Nothing I couldn't handle, that is. But people are rather unprotected at the back of this convoy.' Tane's voice became louder, less feminine. 'All the soldiers are hiding at the front, as far away from the sky-city as possible.'

Two soldiers turned, big guys with a few days of stubble and wearing the colour of the City Guard. 'What the hell is he saying?' one of them muttered.

'I said,' Tane continued, 'that you're too fucking scared to stay at the back protecting the vulnerable people – that's where people are being picked off – not in big group attacks, but by curious hunting pairs.'

'It's not as simple as that,' Fulcrom said. Then, to the soldiers, 'I'm sorry. Please, just ignore him.'

'Ignore me?' Tane spluttered. 'These bloody idiots don't know the meaning of a day's work.'

The two soldiers lumbered past Fulcrom, almost knocking him to the floor, and trudged through the mud towards Tane.

Fulcrom staggered upright to see Tane's claws now extended. He was standing now with his legs wide, his arms open, taunting them. 'Come on then, chaps. Come *the fuck* on . . .'

Suddenly something blurred by and Tane was dragged away. Lan had pulled him back into the darkness with a flurry of movement, while Fulcrom ran back to stop the soldiers.

He caught up with them and palmed the air. 'Please, gentlemen, we shouldn't be fighting each other. Tane is raw – he's recently lost a friend, a close colleague. These are difficult times for all of us.'

'We've all lost friends,' one soldier grunted. 'We've lost

friends, family, houses, everything we've ever bloody well worked for. You think we don't feel any pain about this?'

Tane took deep breaths and bowed his head. Lan soothed what, to Fulcrom, seemed an unlikely outburst from Tane. If any of the former heroes of Villjamur were known to have troubles with their temper, it was Vuldon. Vuldon who had been killed trying to save lives as the city crumbled.

Whether or not Tane felt guilt for *not* being there, Fulcrom couldn't work out. What was clear was that, for better or worse, Tane was quieter now. There were few opportunities for his jokes, fewer venues in which to present himself as the evening's entertainment, the centre of attention, no more parties. Everyone's lives had been irreversibly changed.

'Guys, why not head back to the campfire,' Fulcrom said. 'There's a little warmth there, a little meat that the tribes have brought us.'

'Aye,' they both said wearily, and turned to head towards the flames. People were staring at them, waiting to see what might happen next, but eventually they, too, moved on.

Fulcrom stepped across to Tane and Lan.

'Tane,' he said, 'I know I'm not in command of you, but for whatever Bohr-forsaken reason, I seem to be influencing a lot of what goes on around here. There are people much, much weaker than you, who need some inspiration, something to look up to, and something to comfort them, to assure them that they're safe, that they might live if they carry on this journey. Whenever you slip up like that, it makes everyone's lives a fraction harder. It makes all our work more difficult. Do you understand that?'

Tane lifted his head with as much pride as he could muster. There were retorts in his expression, Fulcrom could see that; witty one-liners or just a dismissive remark; nothing came from his lips, no apology, but that silence was all Fulcrom really needed.

Fulcrom placed a hand on Tane's arm and looked him right

in the eye. The feline pupils were wide, his furred face rippled ever so slightly in the breeze. Tane's hair had grown a lot since Fulcrom first saw his transition under the cultist treatments, but there still remained an air of dignity and respect. Even now, after his performance with the soldiers.

'What's wrong?' Fulcrom said softly.

'It just seems all rather futile, don't you think?' Tane replied, his voice returning to that familiar, refined tone. 'Just a few days ago there were some plans and probabilities to help shape our day. A degree of comfort could be found in that. What now, eh?'

'We press on,' Fulcrom said. 'We get our rest, we gather more people, we protect them against any attacks, and we move forward. We don't look back. We don't think about the worst, though we plan for it.'

The wind picked up, groaning in the distance. The sky was now indigo, the flames of campfires littered the foreground, and the smell of cooking meat lingered in the air. He could see families nearby had daggers or short swords out on top of blankets, just in case something bad was to happen.

Fulcrom, even with his tough, rumel skin, began to shiver. Lan put her arm around his waist, resting her head on his chest, and Fulcrom wondered just how well he would be coping if she was not there to soothe his worries.

*

Screams woke him.

He bolted upright, the blankets sliding off him. Lan was already awake, rolling the sheet back, letting in the noise from the clearing: to one side, the land-vehicles were lined up behind each other; to the other, people were beginning to surge forwards.

Fulcrom stumbled up, brushing his clothes. He wrapped up the blankets and bundled them into a small bag, which he slung across his back, then picked up his crossbow, bolts, and a blade.

43

'What's going on?' he called out, though no soldiers were nearby.

Lan and Fulcrom watched in confusion – it was still dark, and campfires had become smouldering ash piles. One of the moons was overhead, its faint glow cast down upon the scene. There must have been a hundred people moving to scramble to the other side of the land-vehicles. A few soldiers on horseback rode back the other way with their weapons at the ready.

'Can you see Tane?' Lan asked.

'No,' Fulcrom replied. 'Are they coming for us? I can't see anything.'

Lan craned her neck to look up. 'Not from the air at least. I'm going to see what's going on.' With that, she bounded up towards one of the land-vehicles, used one of its wheels for leverage and took huge arcs through the air and out of sight.

If only I had such powers, Fulcrom thought, as he trudged over the ice-cold mud. His pulse racing, he headed towards a family pulling their small handcart hastily through the clearing.

'What's going on?' Fulcrom asked.

The father, a slender, bearded man in a baggy jumper, stopped and urged his family to go on. 'I'll catch up.' Then, to Fulcrom, 'There's word of things coming out of the far end of the forest, sir.'

'Things?' Fulcrom asked. 'What *things*?'

The man shrugged. His eyes looked tired. 'I've only heard word, like. I don't know really. We're just getting the hell out of here before the sun rises.'

'Can you give me any description?' Fulcrom asked, wanting to shake the man. 'I need something to go on, anything.'

'Word . . . word is that ghosts have started attacking, that's all, sir, I swear.' The man looked this way and that, then back to his family.

'Thank you,' Fulcrom sighed, gesturing for him to return.

44

People swarmed past now, and Fulcrom began hassling others at random to ask them what they had seen. Again, only the suggestion of ghosts. Spectres. Glowing things. Only hearsay, nothing definite, which frustrated him.

Fulcrom jogged towards the head of the convoy, away from the noises, where dozens of soldiers had now stationed themselves, but had not yet moved into action – instead they were slouching by one of the fires. Further up, standing alongside the front leg of the furthest horse, Frater Mercury stared out into the darkness.

The soldiers stood to regard Fulcrom.

What the fuck are they doing just lying around? he thought to himself. 'Evening,' Fulcrom announced, 'we've reports of events at the western end of the convoy. People are looking for help.'

'We don't know what to do,' one of the younger men said. 'We're waiting for orders.'

'You pick up your swords and bows and you help them,' Fulcrom urged.

Two looked at each other, another one – older – seemed to get the idea. 'Gather all those wearing Empire colours like before.'

Fulcrom nodded. 'Good, and hurry. I've heard odd reports of spectres – which sounds different from what we've dealt with before.'

The soldiers split up – some went to locate their horses, others moved on foot. Ahead of the convoy lay the limits of the woodland and, beyond, the vast expanse of grassland and tundra, much of it buried underneath snow. There were no lights of towns or villages, only darkness.

Fulcrom headed up towards Frater Mercury, moving around the legs of the gargantuan horse, which seemed to remain so still it was statue-like.

When Frater Mercury spoke it was directly into Fulcrom's head. *What do you want now?*

'The rear of our convoy is under attack, I believe. People are saying that there are ghost-like killers – spectral forms.'

Frater Mercury contemplated his words without expression.

'Did you hear my words?' Fulcrom asked.

Of course. It takes me time to remember the language.

'Are they from the Policharos?' Fulcrom asked, using Frater Mercury's original term for the sky-city.

Yes, he replied. *I know what they are.*

'Are they a threat?'

Yes they are.

'Then would you be able to help?'

It seemed to take the greatest effort for this man – this god, perhaps – to oblige Fulcrom's request. Why was there no sense of urgency?

I will follow you, if I must.

*

They located two black mares and rode off to the western end of the convoy. Fulcrom was impressed by Frater Mercury's finesse at riding, the ease with which he moved in the saddle and directed the animal. People seemed to be moving more quickly, the further west they rode, and there were more panicked expressions upon people's faces.

Fulcrom tried to peer further ahead but the forest was too thick to make anything out. His frustration grew. Fulcrom began to worry that leading the refugees through a vast clearing in the forest had been a mistake. He had hoped it would provide cover from two sides, wood for campfires and potential food. He forced his guilt from his mind: he could not possibly know what he was dealing with.

Panicked faces became more distressed; there were piercing screams in the distance, then – through the darkness – Fulcrom could discern glowing forms.

'Oh fuck, no . . .' he breathed. 'What now?'

They had reached the fringe of the convoy. Jamur soldiers,

perhaps a hundred in all, as well as citizen militia who had picked up arms, had formed a line of defence stretching perhaps a hundred feet from one side of the clearing to the other. Along the fringes of the trees, archers were firing into the open.

As Fulcrom approached, he could see beyond them stood blue-white glowing forms, exactly like ghosts, and they were brandishing swords. They did not wear military armour: in fact, they seemed to be sinewy muscle and tendon, as if stripped of skin. Their faces, too, were featureless. Only their swords seemed real: huge curved blades that shimmered in their own light.

Two Jamur soldiers were suddenly carried back through the lines, their arms bloodied and blistered. One man was unconscious, the other screamed, his face creased in agony. He shouted, 'It's fucking burning me, it burns, get it off!' before being taken to one side where his screams became whimpers.

Fulcrom scanned the crowd of soldiers and civilians for Lan: there she was, on the far left, much to Fulcrom's relief, hauling two people out of the combat zone to safety. It was then that Fulcrom noticed the dead bodies – civilian casualties – that lay around.

So many of them ... this time we're surely finished.

A burst of soldiers moved forward, shields locking behind to protect the next row. From his horse, Fulcrom watched the men move to engage the spectres in combat. The ghost-warriors seemed undisciplined; they fought like feral savages, though for the most part the soldiers were holding them off. Yet more of the ghosts came from behind, twenty, forty, maybe more flooding into view. Fulcrom could not see the sky-city, could not see where these things were coming from.

'Frater Mercury,' Fulcrom called across. 'Please, help us. What do you suggest we should do? Do you know how to stop this?'

The god-like figure remained inert, merely observing the scene. He gave no sign of having heard Fulcrom's questions, but instead he nudged his horse in a tight arc and behind the thin line of Jamur soldiers.

The soldiers moved back and locked their shields again and, from their flanks, archers released another wave of arrows. None of them connected with their targets; the arrows merely passed straight through and struck into the earth beyond.

Frater Mercury emerged onto the field of combat and rode out into the centre. Fulcrom heard commands for the Jamur soldiers to hold their position and for the archers to cease firing. After Frater Mercury pulled his horse to a stop, the scene fell eerily silent. The ghost-warriors ceased their movements across the clearing then began to confer with each other, their movements oddly fluid. More of them came in from behind, brightening the night with their glow. They seemed to swarm, ooze and drift rather than make coherent progress, but soon they began moving towards Frater Mercury, slower than before and more cautious.

Frater Mercury stared at the approaching figures and began wailing in a bass tone, almost melodic at first, then something far harsher.

The spirit figures paused on the spot and their glow faded to something duller. When Frater Mercury ceased his noise they became more obviously animalistic and less supernatural. The god-like man held up a hand and Fulcrom watched in awe as a sword whipped from the grasp of one of the Jamur soldiers and travelled – through the air – towards his outstretched hand. He snatched it firmly, dismounted from his horse and advanced on foot towards the former ghosts, who were now cowering like frightened children at his approach. He held up his other hand and another blade emerged through the air and landed in his palm with little effort.

Fulcrom now struggled to understand the action, but he

saw Frater Mercury lurch forward and bury one blade into the chest of an enemy. As the sword connected, the creature began to redden at the point of impact, and burst into flame. Screaming horrifically, it lurched back and forth, burning from within, before retreating off into the distance. Several others of its kind began to follow and, with their backs turned, Frater Mercury threw another blade like a spear: it connected with one of them, creating yet more flames and high-pitched screams. Again, he held his hands aloft, like a prophet, and – again – he seemed to haul more swords from the clutches of a nearby soldier. One by one, Frater Mercury warded off the remainder of the ghosts until the last of them scrambled, alight, along the periphery of the forest.

Satisfied his work was done, he slowly walked back to his horse, without acknowledgement of the events or his actions, mounted the mare and nudged her in a slow arc around the row of shocked soldiers and back towards the east.

*

It was the dignified thing to do, Fulcrom thought, to light a pyre for the fallen.

Fifty-three people in total had been found dead, the vast majority of them with burns or weird abrasions from physical contact with the ghost-warriors. Those who had survived were in agony and many remained unconscious long afterwards.

As Fulcrom was on his way back towards the chain of refugees, he thought he caught sight of Lan crouching by a body at the edge of the forest. When he came closer he noticed she was shivering and in tears. The body resting on the damp earth beside her was one he knew all too well.

Tane . . .

He took a deep breath and bent down beside them.

'Is he unconscious or is he . . . ?' Fulcrom asked, gesturing to Tane's body.

Because of the late hour and Tane's dark uniform, Fulcrom

49

struggled to make out how much blood the werecat had lost, but the open wound below his right ribcage was enough to tell Fulcrom what he needed to know. He placed a hand on her shoulder.

'Yes, he's dead,' was all Lan could manage.

They rose together.

'We hadn't always got on,' she breathed, 'but I had very few people I could rely on in this world. It shouldn't have happened to him . . .'

Fulcrom didn't say anything. He had found Tane frustrating to work with, but very effective – if a little too brutal – at helping to reduce crime in Villjamur. But he felt a fatherly attachment to him, and was deeply saddened.

'Did you see what happened to him?'

'He had pulled a dozen or so individuals from the path of those white things,' Lan said, her arms still around Fulcrom. 'He'd managed to find a blade and was trying to attack them when one of them must have caught him. I was the other side of the clearing when I heard his scream, but couldn't reach him quickly enough because of the combat and all the soldiers. It was only when the fighting moved on that I could find his body. So I brought it to the side and let him pass away quietly. He was so silent at the end – he just couldn't say a word. It seemed so unnatural.'

*

The pyre was a hasty affair. What wood could be gathered from the damp forest floor was piled haphazardly and all the bodies wrapped in any rags that people could spare. Smoke plumes drifted back in the direction of Villjamur, downwind, carrying with them the rancid smell of the burning dead. Fulcrom had tried to approach Frater Mercury about doing something perhaps to bring Tane back to life, but his requests were stubbornly ignored and the god-man simply walked away. Instead, Tane's body would join the others.

Hundreds of people tentatively came to pay their respects,

many of them wary about remaining too long in one place – Fulcrom included. People raised the question of whether or not it was reckless to light beacons that would reveal their whereabouts; perhaps this was true, Fulcrom told them, but it was clear, given the recent events, that whatever was after them knew perfectly well where they could be found.

He would light these pyres. Respect would be paid.

Frater Mercury attended the funeral burning, but despite Fulcrom persistently quizzing him about what had happened, the god-thing gave no explanation as to what the creatures who attacked them were, or indeed how he had dealt with them; they seemed a minor inconvenience to him. The figure merely regarded the flames, which were reflected in the metallic half of his face.

Fulcrom and Lan moved closer, Lan with her head on his shoulder, him with a blanket wrapped around her shoulders.

'Will we make it to the coast after this?' she whispered.

'So long as we have him by our side,' Fulcrom said, indicating Frater Mercury, 'I would think our chances are decent. The only question is, is he actually here to help us? Given the sacrifices to bring him into this world, we still have little idea of who Frater Mercury is, or even what he wants, let alone whether he can get us to the coast.'

Four

She waited for him from within the shelter of an old doorway in the heart of the Ancient Quarter of Villiren. Diggsy had promised to take Jeza out tonight and he was true to his word. They were headed to her new favourite bistro, which had replaced the one on the seafront with the constantly steamed-up windows and the delicious crab cakes – that had been destroyed in the fighting. She had been devastated by its loss at first, until she realized it was silly to mourn a bistro when so many people had died in the war. Still, it was the little things like that which hurt just as much – the little pleasures she had previously taken for granted, which had been rendered important once they had been lost to her forever.

A lot of things took on a new context after the war. Once-important issues, such as what clothes she was wearing or what they might eat that night, didn't seem to matter as much, not when the bodies of tens of thousands of people were being swept from the streets. Arguments with others seemed futile. She realized how close death could be, and that seemed to fill her with a sense of urgency – to do things, something, anything, though she didn't quite know what.

Diggsy sauntered down the street towards her. He had made an effort with his hair, and wore customized breeches. He was also sporting a hooded jumper she had asked to be made for him with money she earned selling a bunch of dodgy relics. The sight of him warmed her insides. She smiled widely.

When he arrived, they kissed. He smelled good tonight and his tongue tasted of peppermint. He walked with his arm around her, and she liked that it was so casual. The stars were starting to show.

Everything felt right.

*

'What d'you think our next creation should be?' Diggsy asked, before tucking into a mouthful of young, boiled sea trilobite. She laughed when he had difficulty prising open their shells, but she fared no better. She half wished she could bring some of the tools from their workbench, but that might not have gone down too well with the owners of the bistro.

The Mourning Wasps . . . she thought. *The shells were tough. Like armour.*

'I think we should really get to grips with the Mourning Wasps,' she said. 'I want us to work with the military – with that albino – and if we really work hard on the Mourning Wasps instead of procrastinating, we will get work with them.'

The waitress, a middle-aged lady with a limp, came over to ask them for their drinks order. Jeza wanted the wine while Diggsy, as always, stuck to water. He gave her that smug look of his: the one that questioned why she was drinking yet again.

'It's all right,' she replied.

'Don't you think you drink too much these days?' He meant it innocently. He laughed and smiled at her, making light of the issue.

'I like the taste,' she replied. 'Plus it's nice to unwind – my mind needs some way of relaxing after thinking about flesh matrices all day long.'

'I know, I just worry about you, that's all.'

As the waitress clanked the bottle and glasses on the bar,

Jeza looked around. It wasn't quite the same as the harbour – there wasn't the same smell, and the windows were generally clean – but the place had a little charm about it, with polished tables, stone tiles on the floor, high wooden beams with bottles balanced on them for decoration, some with candles in.

'I think you're right,' he said.

'What?'

'About what we should create next – on commission. I think you're right. All of us at Factory 54 do.' He leaned forward and held her hand. 'Look, there's something I want to ask.'

'Ask away,' she replied coolly. Secretly her heart was thumping away with expectation.

'You know, I've been speaking to the others,' he began, 'and we've all been thinking that we should have some kind of representative. Like a boss. We've never had to deal with anyone other than ourselves, and now that we're in a position where we'll have to deal with stuff outside our usual world, we're going to need someone to lead us. To have those conversations. We're not kids any more, and have to start taking things seriously. We felt you should be in charge of all those kinds of things. To look after all of the gang at Factory 54.'

'Wow,' she replied. 'I mean ... yeah. I'd love to. It's not what I thought you'd say ...'

'What were you expecting?' he asked playfully.

For you to say you loved me. 'Nothing,' she lied. 'But this – I mean, everyone wanted me to be in charge?'

'Yeah, everyone. Even Coren.' Diggsy laughed at that. 'I guess it's probably what Lim would have wanted, too.'

She looked down at her plate for a moment. Then she met Diggsy's gaze. 'What kind of things will you want me to do exactly?'

'You're the real brains, we all know that. You see the bigger picture while we lose ourselves in the detail of animation. Coren's too full of himself to care about such things. Me, I'm too laid back and just want to enjoy things as they are.'

'And Pilli?'

Diggsy shrugged. 'You're the smart one, Jeza. You should be the one to deal with the guy in charge of the army. You're much better than any of us at that sort of thing.'

'Really?'

'Really, and maybe it's why I don't want you drinking all the time.'

'It's not *all* the time,' Jeza replied with a frown, but still, she couldn't contain her excitement. She leaned over the table and kissed him, and sat back happy and determined. But first, she resumed her dinner and everything tasted just that little bit better than a moment ago.

*

They finished their meal and headed home, to their room at the top of Factory 54.

It wasn't much, but it was nice to have everything all in one place, and certainly better than most other cultists lived, surviving in a windowless room with little but a few technical manuals to play with. As it was, most of their existence was actually spent in or around the factory. Every flesh-being, every mechanical device, every crude relic was manufactured by the team. Most of the meals she ate, most of the boys she'd slept with, were all under the one roof.

The hour was late, nearly thirteen, and a little tipsy from the drink Jeza shambled up the rusting metal stairs. Suddenly she realized what a noise she was making and then tried to act stealthily to make up for it. Diggsy chuckled as he pushed her towards their bedroom.

They opened the door, and she pulled Diggsy to the bed,

one soft beam of moonlight hitting the wall behind them. Haphazardly, she pulled off his clothes, then her own, before dragging him clumsily under the bedclothes.

He was tender, too tender and too slow at times, when she wanted that little bit *more*. He did this thing with his tongue, which she appreciated, but he was more hesitant than she really liked.

Enough . . .

Jeza pushed him over on his back, climbed on top of him and, once he was hard and inside her, she began to fuck him aggressively.

A little later and they both collapsed in a state of sweaty breathlessness. She'd needed that, even though he barely lasted five minutes. What was it with good-looking guys? Did they just not try that hard to hold it? Still, it had only been their fourth time. Maybe things would improve as they grew used to each other.

The room seemed hazy, she could taste the drying alcohol in her mouth and, just about satiated, she passed out.

*

Jeza woke up in the night, paranoid. Diggsy lay asleep beside her, his arm sticking out of the bed; she pulled the sheet over him to keep him warm, climbed out of bed and walked to the window that overlooked the streets behind Factory 54.

Hidden somewhere behind the clouds or over the horizon, none of the moons was present, and the place was in darkness. She stood there, naked and cold, suddenly afraid of what she was getting herself into.

She remembered the screams from the war. These streets were, not too long ago, littered with carts that carried dead bodies from the centre of the city. She remembered people crying and the carts becoming more frequent. Some of the bodies had limbs missing, and even though she spent her time working with the animation of flesh, her experiences had not desensitized her – she knew that they had been real people.

At the time they had all felt survivor guilt. They felt they should be doing something to help – but, as she said at the time, their contribution would come through what they were good at, not lining up to die with so many others. *Now* was their time. She knew that, and liked that the commander spoke to them like real people and didn't dismiss them like other cultists.

She was only eighteen. Part of her wanted to spend time studying and drinking and sleeping with Diggsy. If she was to represent those who worked at Factory 54, would she be some kind of commander herself? When money began to flow in and out, would she be in charge of its distribution? Would she be assuring the commander that they would hit deadlines?

What seemed a wonderful idea in the bistro began to cause her concern and she realized, then, that she would not be able to sleep well.

Instead she reached into the drawer beside the bed and pulled out a small sketchbook and pencil, and immediately began to plan out what their next monster might look like and how it would function in a war like the one that had just passed.

'What're you still up for?' Diggsy asked groggily.

'I'm . . .' She paused. 'I'm just thinking about projects, that's all.'

'You're crazy,' he said, smiling. 'Knew you'd be excited about being in charge. Let's worry about that in the morning, yeah?'

'Yeah,' she said. Sighing, she tossed her sketchbook to one side and climbed back into bed, allowing Diggsy's warm body to consume her.

*

In the morning Jeza headed down the metal staircase with the sketchbook under her arm. Seeing the mess, she put it on the table and began clearing up the plates and beakers, the crusty bread and the warm cheese, from the night before. No one else was up yet; she was often the first down each day and liked the silence of the morning routine. It gave her time to think before things became hectic and Coren began wittering his usual nonsense at anyone within earshot.

The factory was cold so she began lighting the firegrain stove they'd hooked up to a larger system, which in turn channelled the heat around the entire building in one fairly efficient system. It coughed and spluttered like someone taking their first few drags, as the rich grain sparked and fired up.

That was usually the alarm call and, true to habit, moments later some of the others began stirring, banging drawers or doors upstairs.

'Fucksake, Jeza. Don't you ever sleep?' It was Coren, lumbering down the metal stairwell, his heavy steps clanging as he came down.

Shortly after, Pilli strolled gracefully downstairs, wearing some fashionable jumper and boots with her laces undone. She sauntered into the kitchen area, said good morning, turned on the firegrain stove and placed the kettle on it.

The three of them sat down at the crude, stained table while the sun reached a point above the rooftops that shone a beam of light across them. The kettle began to boil; in the distance the firegrain system coughed.

'Whose turn is it to make breakfast?' Coren asked, his gaze flickering between the two girls. He yawned.

'Yours,' Jeza replied, glaring at him.

Pilli smiled, pulled back her hair to tie it. 'Are you going to let him near the stove after last time? He tried to cook with a relic!'

'Hey, those fish were edible,' Coren protested. 'They tasted fine.'

'Sure – once Diggsy scraped them off the ceiling for you,' Jeza said, standing. 'OK, I'll cook some oats. Happy now?'

*

After breakfast, Jeza gathered them all around the table, Pilli, Diggsy, Coren and Gorri, so that they could get on with business. At first she wanted to make some formal announcement, something to clear the way forward. She had rehearsed a few lines in her head but they all sounded ridiculous. In the end, she opted not to acknowledge her new position at all – it seemed to be largely a label she wore outside this room.

'So,' she said, 'getting on board with the military—'

'I'm excited,' Gorri burst out. The young lad with red hair smiled at her. 'We're going to make a fortune.'

'It's only money,' Pilli said. 'I just love the fact that we're finally going to be *acknowledged*, you know?'

'You wouldn't care about the money, rich girl,' Coren said, leaning back on his chair and gripping the rim of the table, 'but for us dregs, this'll sort us out for *years*.'

'Hey, guys,' Jeza interrupted, 'we've not got any money or prestige yet. Don't you want to see what the plan is before you start spending the money you don't have?'

'Go for it,' Coren said.

'OK,' Jeza said. 'If our plan works – and even if it doesn't we can still sell these on – I suspect they're going to want some beasts for use in warfare, something more akin to a weapon. For that I think we can mass-produce the Mourning Wasps. But for a start, how about selling the soldiers something that's not too distant from what they already have, something we can maybe clone and produce quite a few of?'

'Mass-produced specimens?' Diggsy suggested. 'Some kind of monster?'

'Not even monsters in this case. I'm thinking we give them a soldier that's bigger, stronger – purely weaponry enhancements at first. Something that doesn't even require anything but themselves.'

'Hmm,' Coren stared. 'Sure, sounds OK, but it's a little dull.'

'It's an investment,' she replied. 'It's something they'll feel comfortable with at first. They might not feel good fighting alongside something as weird as we can create, so it's best to break them in easily to what we can provide.'

'We don't exactly churn things out at 54,' Diggsy pointed out. 'It could take weeks just to get a few enhancements. How long have we got?'

'Working on Lim's time theory, I think that we can produce what I've got in mind pretty quickly.'

'Time theory . . .' Coren repeated, nodding his head. 'Like it.'

'So with that in mind . . .' She placed her large sketchbook in the centre of the table and began to describe what she'd drawn. 'Look, I like the idea of Knights – they're pretty noble things throughout history. They're also warriors that will kick the shit out of things. This is how a knight used to look, but with *biological* armour. From that specimen of the Okun we took, just after the invasion, we can replicate its shell structure to form armour, as you can see here. Other than that, it's pretty much a standard soldier, but much more resilient.'

'How can you ensure this will be able to fight normally?' Pilli asked. 'This will, presumably, need to have some finesse on the battlefield?'

'You're missing the point here. We're not making anything sentient at first. If we make just the armour, we can just sell that straight to the military. Using time theory in the replication process, we really can churn these out. They're big enough to fit a human and, because it's the shell material, as light as cloth. Afterwards we can start thinking about filling in the armour with something cloned and fleshy.'

There was a moment's silence as everyone contemplated her drawings.

'What's it called?' Coren asked.

'I'm not sure. Black Knight Armour?' Jeza suggested. 'That's something the army would fall for.'

Coren nodded again. 'Is it easy to replicate and mould the shell?'

Jeza looked to Diggsy. 'What do you think?'

Diggsy leaned back in his chair, lifting the front two legs up as he gripped the edge of the table. He seemed to contemplate the sketches a little longer before he said, 'Yeah, we've done it before, haven't we, Pilli?'

Jeza suddenly felt her heart beat a little quicker, but forced away her concerns. *Not the time or the place* . . .

'Absolutely,' Pilli said. 'Jeza, this is marvellous.'

Coren said, 'Looks like it was the right choice putting you in charge of us lot.'

'Seconded,' Pilli said.

'Thirded,' Gorri said.

Coren stood up, grinning. 'Doesn't stop you from making post-meeting drinks though. Put the kettle on. Mine's a tea.'

*

They had found the Okun during the fighting in Villiren, when they had been investigating reports of new relics recently discovered in the Scarhouse district. The five of them had wanted to get there before other cultists or the gangs got the relics for themselves, to put them on the black market.

It was Lim who had pointed out the corpse. The creature must have strayed away from its own lines and then died from severe wounds to its torso and neck, but the rest of the body remained intact. No longer interested in relics, Lim dragged it out of sight into a side street until he could fetch the others, whereupon they decided to keep it.

They brought it back to Factory 54. They wanted to study it and hopefully provide useful information to the military. Jeza had thought to herself that it seemed to appease their guilt for not being involved in the fighting. The boys seemed to feel it most – the guilt, the pressure that they should be doing something. Herself and Pilli had pledged that they would enlist if they did too, all together, the lot of them. But they did not sign up; they remained in the factory, listening to the sounds of war in the distance, occasionally retreating to the secure basement workshop in case the defensive lines were breached. Of course, they never were.

She had never known how Lim was killed. They simply found his body after a skirmish a few days after finding the Okun. He had bled to death from a cut to one of his major arteries. It could have been related to the war, or simply a casual murder, such was the way of things in Villiren at that time.

There had been daily reports of the ferocity of the attacks by the Okun – how they had cleared the island to the north of human and rumel life, how they had swarmed out of metallic vessels into Villiren harbour, how they had eradicated people effortlessly. That the commander had managed to prevent them taking the city was beyond any of their reasoning; but he had, and these things were – for the moment – not a threat.

She had to admit the Okun were frightening life forms, more sinister than anything they could ever create. Lim had commented at the time that nature was occasionally a sick beast herself, and could create weirder things than they could imagine themselves.

A blend between a hominid and a crustacean, the Okun were huge, bipedal creatures. Though alien-looking, they never seemed *too* alien – they possessed eyes, arms, legs – all in pairs, which seemed to suggest they were more a result of a perverted branch of evolution, rather than something monstrous from another realm. That was the military line, anyway, that they were flooding in from another world entirely, though everyone had their doubts about such claims.

With the Okun corpse back at the factory, the group immediately began a kind of post-mortem. Lim needed to know everything about its inner workings, about its structure, the way muscles functioned. He rolled up his sleeves, got all the tools organized, and together they got to work.

They bled its black, acidic fluids, which sat unused in containers. They tried for a while to cut through the shell, but in the end resorted to cutting through the joints and cutting flesh underneath the shell plates so that they could lift the segments whole. There were around three hundred different shell armour segments, the largest being a chest plate, the smallest being tiny forms of protection around their claws. Underneath, once the flesh had been cut away, they were amazed to see how similar it was to human or rumel anatomy, though augmented, transformed through alien means to be something genuinely awe-inspiring. There were two, slightly larger hearts, and four equivalents to the lungs. There were more tubes akin to veins and arteries, and strange, copper-coloured wires that led through the neck to the head.

The most difficult thing to prise open was the head. The gang tried all sorts of tools, but eventually used relics to burn open one side. When they managed to get it open, they stood back in disbelief: there was hair-thin copper wiring and dozens of small, metallic square plates with grid-like patterns etched into and raised up from the surface. There were objects that looked like gemstones, which they could not identify, and which were imbedded in a jelly-like substance that burned through their clothing yet not their skin. It was both organic and mechanical, with no clearly defined facial structure whatsoever.

The Okun, the most hideous and wonderful thing they had ever seen, was now reduced to hundreds of fragments. For days at a time, each of the group set about trying to establish whether or not anything could be gleaned from these pieces. They took detailed sketches of the way things slotted together, listed potential materials that these might have been made from, and how certain parts reacted to substances from their own world. But they were ultimately dumbfounded by the intricacies of its body. It was, quite simply, too much for them to understand.

All except the shell.

The shell was not all that distant from the chitinous exoskeletons found throughout the Archipelago, but this seemed more tactile, flexible and impenetrable. They decided they wanted to re-create it and Lim, after Jeza aided him, began to use a particularly large relic they had discovered to cast crude moulds to regenerate certain sections.

Reflecting on the process, Jeza now realized she'd loved working with Lim. He was so passionate and cared deeply about what she thought, what she felt. He encouraged her line of thought as much as his own and he trusted her opinions and did not dismiss one of her suggestions, no matter how wild it was. He was sensitive and she was intoxicated by his Varltung accent, and his broad face. Perhaps, looking back as she did now, she realized she had possessed deep feelings for him. He was special in a way no man had ever been. Such feelings weren't comparable to those she had for Diggsy, of course – that was based on raw passion. Lim never seemed interested in any of that kind of stuff, never mentioned girls or sex. Lim's energy was funnelled entirely into his research. He loved discovery. She loved him for being ever elusive. Despite her scientific ways, she could never quite work Lim out.

Why did I never say anything at the time?

*

In the afternoon sunlight, which spilled through a large circular window on the top floor of Factory 54, the group took the Okun's dark, glossy exoskeleton out of storage and laid it out across the workbench.

First they separated it into several large sections, sifted through the pieces, deciding which section to concentrate on, before settling upon one of the breastplates.

'It has to be this,' Jeza said. 'It'll sit over people's most vital areas . . .'

'Speak for yourself,' Coren smirked, grabbing his crotch as if to hammer the point home.

'Idiot,' Jeza sighed. Then, to the others, 'It'll sit over the major organs: the heart, the lungs, the parts that can't be repaired on the battlefield.'

Jeza lit several lanterns while Coren and Diggsy began to assemble the relics and tools. She fetched the notebooks from Lim's unused room and, for the next hour, they began to work through pages and pages of his detailed instructions, most of them simply on how to operate the relics.

'You OK?' Diggsy asked. 'You look pretty upset.'

'I'm just concentrating,' she replied. Had Lim's death really affected her this much? It was a strange process, following his words; it was like having him there and alive once again, but he was dead – she *had* to keep reminding herself. *I have to let him go.*

Two relics the size of industrial equipment were dragged to sit either side of the breastplate specimen. The relics were called *Haldorors*, 'true of word' devices – they translated materials and re-translated them – or, in some cases, replicated them, in whatever shape or form was desired by the person setting the relics. The units, almost as tall as Jeza, were crafted from copper and silver, and possessed intricate ancient lettering that none of them had ever seen in a book, let alone understood.

Jeza made tweaks to the devices according to Lim's notes on other creatures, moving the second of them about two armspans further down the workbench, so they were no longer opposite each other. She altered the frequencies and the measurements on the sixteen extra dials they had built into it, mainly by trial and error.

The relic was activated by placing a brass cylinder the size of her arm into the slot at the back, a process that was not immune to Coren's crude innuendo. Diggsy switched on the second device and they all watched as a web of purple light spread out across the exoskeleton and hovered in the air above. The little crackles of energy never ceased to impress her; they signified ancient knowledge being reused, a line that spanned tens of thousands of years. No one spoke during the process, they were too focused.

Exactly as Lim's theory described, a second replica of the breastplate began to fade into existence alongside. It finally materialized whole, in its own separate web of purple light, and when they were quite sure the process had finished, Jeza shut off one device, Diggsy the other, and soon all that was left was a dull hum, the faint smell of charred leather and a little smoke as if someone had blown out a match.

Jeza and Coren moved over to the cloned piece and inspected it, waiting for the thin, pale-blue smoke to dissipate. Coren prodded it, first with a metal rod to see if it was genuine, if it was physically there and not some illusion; then when he was more confident, he jabbed it with his finger. 'Still warm,' he said, and waited a moment longer while Diggsy and Pilli dragged the two *Haldorors* out of the way and against the wall.

Eventually, Coren picked up the original breastplate in one hand and the newly 'translated' one in his other. The others watched him, waiting. He moved them this way and that and wafted them around in the air, smiling. 'Same light weight, same feel.'

'Guess Lim's tricks never fail to work,' Diggsy said.

'Is this what we want to show the military?' Coren asked. He placed the breastplates back down while everyone turned to Jeza. They waited for her to speak, a new phenomenon for her, and she had to admit not entirely unpleasant.

'We need to move our *perceived* roles on from spurious cultists – and in fact a bit of a motley crew to boot – to something more professional and businesslike. To most laymen, we might as well be casting runes or muttering dark spells.'

'Go on . . .' Diggsy urged.

'Now we know we can do this,' she continued, 'we should try to take things further, to show them what we think a more complete piece of soldier's armour might look like. I think we should try our best to show the finished item. First we write to that albino commander. Get him here, see if he's interested in the concept. Now's the time. Later when we have refined this and he sees what we can sell him, he'll have no trouble opening the Empire's coffers.'

'Now you're talking,' Coren said, and slapped her on the back.

Diggsy gave her a warm smile and placed his arm around her in that casual, cool way of his, and she couldn't help but notice Pilli turning away now to fiddle with something on the workbench.

FIVE

She was back in Villjamur, back with Rika.

The warm sunlight falling through her opulent curtains was enough to tell her that this wasn't quite real, though she didn't know why. Bright coloured wall hangings and bed sheets, all the books she could wish for, trinkets and toys littered the floor. Everything seemed so pristine. Too pristine. As ever, there was frantic activity outside their bedroom door, which she took to be something to do with her father or his entourage.

Sometimes, when she heard such noises, she would close her eyes and hope that he'd come in – if just for a moment – to see how she and her sister were getting on, what they were up to, how they were feeling. It rarely happened, though. And yet . . . now she thought of it, Rika wasn't actually there. Her bed was a mess, so she had obviously been around recently, but she couldn't see her anywhere. Eir called out; no reply came. She was utterly alone.

Sighing, Eir stretched fully, pushed herself up, out of bed, and walked to the windows, her legs feeling heavy. The whole movement seemed such an effort. This was the second time she realized something wasn't right: her black hair was much shorter than before.

Pulling back the curtains, light flooded the room, and she squinted to see the rooftops of Villjamur. Always mesmerizing, always awe-inspiring, she could look down on that city a thousand times and never become complacent with its complex, labyrinthine layout. Each time she looked over the many levels of the city, over the winding rows and dreamlike spires sometimes lost in the mist, her imagination would flare happily.

A garuda flew by, drifting in an arc over the city – no, it had turned and was heading towards her. The bird-soldier glided in, his vast wings extended, his bronze armour glimmering in the morning sunlight. It swooped to her window and, with a thud, gripped the window frame to one side.

He had a panicked look on his face. He tried to sign something to her with his one free hand but she couldn't understand him.

'What's wrong?' she asked, trying to climb up to open the window.

But it wasn't any good.

'What's wrong?' she asked again. 'What's wrong?'

*

A jab to her ribs lifted her from the dream. She opened her eyes in a cold, dim chamber, with the wind rattling something outside and a man to her right.

To be fair, she didn't mind the man at all. Randur looked back at her with a soft gaze, his dark hair falling in front of his face. He was propped up on one elbow, wearing only a thin cream tunic which was a size too large for his lithe frame.

'You were dreaming,' he told her.

Slowly she realized she was now awake, and curled in towards him. 'I . . . It felt like that, even though I was asleep,' she said. 'It felt like I *knew*.'

'You're a lucky thing,' he said. 'If you know you're dreaming, I'd have made myself imagine I was lying somewhere a great deal warmer than this ice palace.'

'You could always put more clothes on,' she replied, rubbing her eyes.

'Nah, I don't like it.' He waved a hand. 'I'm from the islands. We sleep with little on – preferably nothing. It's much more comfortable that way.'

'You were always bed-hopping on the islands.'

'True, but I'm a one-woman man now.' He laid back down and moved in to kiss her shoulder. When he held his lips there, his warm breath was delightfully sensual on her skin. It seemed a world away from her dream. 'You should know that.'

His routine never grew old to her, even though they had been together for quite some time. The playful words always drew her out of her reflective moods. These days his charm was one of the few things that brought a smile to her lips, and she knew all too well how rare it was to be happy in this city.

'What were you dreaming about?' he asked.

She gave him a summary, dwelling on the garuda at the end. 'The garuda was trying to tell me something, yet couldn't. It appeared urgent, as if he had a message for me.'

'Perhaps he was telling you to put more logs on the fire,' Randur replied, and wafted a hand in the general direction of the smouldering ashes in the grate.

She slapped his chest. 'I'm serious. It felt . . . wrong somehow. It was very disturbing.'

She looked across to him; he was now lying face down, his head in the pillow. With two fingers she brushed his hair from his face. 'What will you do today?'

'Same as usual. Lounge around, wait for a decision to be made. Maybe head out into the city, see what's happening there. Might see if I can get some decent clothes.'

It was frustrating for them both, she had to admit, not to have much direction now. For all the adventures they'd had on the way to Villiren, and for all it had changed both her and her sister, their arrival in the city had not been what she expected. Instead of every day being a matter of survival, now their time was spent on politics and bureaucracy, and Randur was chafing at all the conversation and lack of action.

And then there was the issue of his mother, the very reason he had gone to Villjamur in the first place. He spoke little of her these days, given all that had happened; Eir knew he thought of her often though. She could tell from his unusual silences.

Randur lifted his head to look at her. 'You don't have to feel sorry for me. I like doing nothing. We get fed, and I can bask in the glory of escorting two of the most important ladies in the Empire around the city. The soldiers in the Night Guard seem to have welcomed me on board after I told them of our travels.'

'What *exactly* did you tell them . . . ?'

'Well, I might have embellished the story a little. You have to with those types – they're as competitive as you get. Besides, they expect it.'

'Do they, indeed. Well, I might have a word with the commander and see if he can make use of you.'

'Oh, for Bohr's sake,' he said cheerily. 'I'm all right – and you're not my mother.'

The final word hung in the air just a little too long for her liking.

'Well I'd certainly like to see more of the city. The commander has shown me just a little, and there are people out there who could do with our help.'

'But . . . you're one of the Jamur sisters,' Randur said. 'You should be in here, arranging the affairs of state or something.'

'After all the lectures you gave me on snobbery, Randur Estevu, you're the last person I'd expect to say such things.'

*

Brynd entered the room with a plan in mind. Lady Eir was seated in one of the few regal-looking rooms that once belonged to the portreeve. Amidst the smoke of incense, she sat on a cushioned chair with her knees drawn up to her chest. When Brynd approached she barely turned away from the oval window that overlooked the harbour. A brazier burned to one side, offering just a little warmth, and he stood by it to enjoy the glow.

'There isn't much to look at, I'm afraid,' Brynd said.

Eir looked up at him. She was wearing another plain outfit, not one usually associated with such a powerful family, with a blanket pulled over her shoulders. Though still young, she no longer looked as innocent as he remembered in Villjamur. When people grew older sometimes there was a look about them: they could seem more resigned to their fate, or simply tired of life, no matter what their age. Right now Eir seemed to be a little of both.

'Your sister,' he continued, 'was unusually determined yesterday. I've never known her to be so . . .'

'Merciless?' Eir asked. 'She's barely my sister any more. We hardly recognize what each other says.'

'Yet still you stand by her,' Brynd said. 'An admirable quality.'

'Foolish loyalty, perhaps,' Eir replied. 'Families, you know how they can be . . .'

'Don't do yourself a disservice.'

'What else can I do then?' she asked. There was a hint of desperation in her voice. 'Tell me, you aided me when I was Stewardess in Villjamur for that short while.'

'You managed the affairs of the city very well, if I remember correctly.'

'What use can I have here? Rika is in command, and you control the city's infrastructure. I want to help, Brynd, I want to do *something*. Neither Rika nor myself have ventured far from this building. The days are long here, Brynd, and I feel utterly useless.'

He contemplated her words and crouched beside her. She had grown too thin on the road, but had since recovered: the colour had returned to her cheeks, there was more flesh on her bones, but her spirit was nowhere to be found. He had watched the girl grow up within the world of her father's madness and, in his periods of rest from missions or more formal attachments in Villjamur, he had spent many days in her company. Those were simpler, happier days, of course, but he had never seen her quite like this.

'I think you should see more of this city,' he offered and, breaching all the code of manners which had been installed in him by her father, extended his hand for her to grasp. 'You may find it inspiring,' he continued. 'You may find what you seek, right here. Come, I'll show you now.'

She placed her hand in his, and rose.

*

They ventured out on two grey horses from the Citadel, him in the resplendent uniform of the Night Guard, her borrowing some drab military gear so that she wouldn't stand out, and with a thick cloak around her. The horses plodded steadily down the long slope, their breath clouding in the air, and then on to the slush-strewn streets of Villiren.

The snow came and went, mixed with a little rain. Artemisia had suggested that it was the Realm Gates that affected the weather patterns in Villiren, though Brynd never queried this. There was too much to take in, but now he thought about it the weather never quite seemed to commit to the much-talked-about ice age.

As the two of them looked around the streets, Brynd noted that even though there were fewer people here than had been normal, there were still a surprising number of civilians milling about on the main road down towards the enormous Onyx Wings. So many buildings had been destroyed in the war that the three pairs of structures, each a couple of hundred feet high, now dominated the skyline of the city.

They rode in the direction of Althing, but Brynd's idea was

to arc around and back to the Old Harbour. If Eir wished to see the city, then he felt it important that she witness the worst-hit areas first.

The operation to repair the city was ceaseless. Brynd had ordered what was left of the army to more manual duties, which ranged from helping locals to board up broken windows, to organizing the clearance of rubble so that the streets were clear for transport. Carts would be loaded with materials, and any stones that could not be reused in construction were to be piled outside the city limits.

Corpses were often pulled out of collapsed houses. Now there weren't as many and the city had already shared in collective grief they were taken to the southern tip of Villiren where they were burned en masse. This operation was now carried out each morning so that the brightness of the funeral flames would not show at night and undermine morale.

Wherever it was suspected that enemy soldiers were hiding – be they red-skinned rumel or Okun – experienced units of Dragoons were ordered in to root them out. Brynd didn't want them killed unless they provided too much of a danger; instead he wanted them taken to underground holding cells where Artemisia could interrogate them. So far, only eight had been captured alive, with another seven killed as they attempted to flee. None of the captives had proven much use so far.

Brynd explained to Eir how the city was being rebuilt and organized as they moved along the edges of Althing, and she listened without interrupting. He enjoyed talking to her; it helped to clarify things in his head, and he began to feel encouraged by the amount of progress they had made.

Now and then, civilians in rags would approach, telling them that they had lost everything and begging for money. They were all ages, the youngest a girl barely out of childhood, the eldest over seventy. On the first two occasions,

Brynd let Eir hand over a few coins from her purse, but after that he cautioned her.

'Lady Eir, nearly everyone in this city has lost something – if not everything. If you keep opening your purse for everyone who asks for money, you'll have nothing left.'

'Oh. I didn't realize. I'm sorry, I'm probably making things worse.'

'You wouldn't be expected to know how many desperate people there are.'

Brynd gave a gentle kick so that their horses moved at a swifter pace through the approaching crowd, all holding their hands out for change.

*

Passing a greater volume of civilians, Brynd and Eir approached one of the few reopened irens, a vast and sprawling market situated in a relatively intact plaza.

Under the late afternoon sun, hundreds of people milled about between rows of trade stalls. While things had not quite returned to normal, there were ad-hoc stalls here: those dealing in metalware to melt down into weapons, or clothing cut from hessian sacks, which had been provided by the military – some of them still bore the seven-pointed Jamur star beneath gaudy dye. Scribes were offering writing skills, some women were leaning against perimeter walls, openly offering their bodies. On one side the fish markets had come to life again, bringing much-needed food to the people of the city.

'It might not look much at the moment,' Brynd said, 'but this is a vision compared with what it was like when you first arrived.'

'I remember it well.' Eir's expression was unreadable. She looked impassively across the scene for some time without speaking. Then, she said, 'When I left Villjamur, I had only positive memories of my father's once-glorious Empire in mind. This is not exactly how the family dream went, I'll admit.'

'I didn't realize you were so attached to those dreams,' Brynd said.

'Neither did I until recently,' Eir replied. 'Still, I think I need to face reality, don't you?'

'Having escaped your own – very public – execution, traipsing halfway across the Archipelago to get here, and brought our only hope of an ally – I'd say you've faced reality.'

'You're very kind to me, commander – you always have been. I always found it easier talking to you than any of the guards who were attached to myself and Rika. Your loyalty to the Jamur lineage has been unquestionable. And now, even now . . .' She gestured to the thronging iren. 'Even now you rebuild this in our name.'

'Come. Let's head down this road – there's a lot more to see.'

*

There were sectors of the city so badly damaged by the war that, after the clearance of rubble, there was nothing left but a skeleton neighbourhood. Stubs of stone were scattered irregularly throughout one region heading towards Port Nostalgia – or what was left of it. There was little to remind them that these streets were once inhabited.

'This place saw the worst of the fighting,' Brynd said. 'And remember I told you about the huge being that emerged from the city and trailed out towards the sea?'

'It came this way, then,' Eir realized. 'By Astrid, it must have been enormous.'

'I never saw it myself,' Brynd said, 'and the reports that came in were inconsistent. Those who witnessed it first-hand suggested it was some primitive sea monster made of crackling light, though that sounds like an exaggeration to me. Whatever it was, though it nearly killed the Night Guard

76

while we were saving people, it also took a chunk of the enemy forces occupying this sector of the city. It did us a favour, in the end. Somewhere we must have had some remarkable allies.'

'Both fortuitous and . . .' Eir paused as she took in the scale of devastation.

'Just fortuitous,' Brynd added. 'Everything that was here can be built again, more or less. They're only buildings. The alternative was much less appealing.'

A unit of Dragoons wearing bright-red sashes rode by quickly on horseback, five men in all, and another followed a few moments later, moving much more slowly due to pulling a cart. Each of the riders saluted Brynd as they passed and offered the Sele of Jamur, before moving on down the street.

'What's going on here?' Eir asked.

Brynd considered the question. 'We should follow them. I think you should see this as well.'

They turned in line behind the Dragoons, pursuing their cautious route through the debris. The group continued for several minutes, eventually approaching the fringe of a more built-up region, one that had not been totally decimated. The terraced houses were largely featureless, flat structures, with once-brightly painted wooden doors now covered in dust and flecks of blood. Many doors had been scrubbed clean again by returned owners, though one of them still had an arrow-head embedded in the wood. One road was relatively clear, with a small pile of rubble in one corner.

At the far end, where the Dragoons were now heading, a dust cloud floated above an end-terrace, which had recently collapsed. A few neighbours had clustered around to examine the damage without offering much help, but the Dragoons dismounted and began to clear them out of the way, before they set to work.

Brynd and Eir came closer to see that half the end house had just buckled over. It was an area of about fifteen feet wide now reduced to a mound of stone, with broken furniture jutting out of the gaps. It wasn't the first time this had happened since the war, and wouldn't be the last.

As the skies clouded over and the dust settled, the Dragoons set about climbing further into the debris. Four soldiers formed a chain along which they passed chunks of masonry. Brynd and Eir dismounted from their horses, approached the scene and offered their help.

'Nah, you're all right. We'll have this sorted soon, commander,' said a tall, bearded officer with a wry smile. 'It's our job, like.'

With a remarkable nonchalance they continued the chain of operation, the heavy men grunting as they moved some of the heavier stone back first. Two of the other soldiers had run further along the street to flag for civilian assistance and, after returning unsuccessfully, one of them was sent on his horse to fetch more troops.

Brynd turned to Eir. 'This has been the main operation since the war – clearances of property, of streets, seeing that structures are safe. We tried to keep a log of all the progress, though it probably isn't as efficient as I'd like.'

'These are people's homes, though. How do you log the emotional distress this causes?'

He knew what she meant. He led a life of numbers and logic, and in the clean-up he couldn't afford to take such things into account.

A middle-aged woman with straggly brown hair and dressed in heavy, drab robes, burst forward onto the scene. She dropped her bags, and began to wail into her hands. Brynd watched as she sank to her knees on one side of the collapsed building, crying, 'My boys, my boys.'

Eir rushed over to the woman and knelt by her side. Brynd watched the former Stewardess of the Empire hold her as the woman emitted great, heaving sobs into her shoulder.

Seeing Eir react to such raw human emotion, and so

quickly, made Brynd contemplate whether the sheer scale of these losses, or even the war itself, had began to numb his senses, and chisel away at his compassion. The Night Guard were enhanced in any number of physical ways, but the ability to offer a shoulder to cry on did not seem to be one of them.

The soldiers eventually uncovered the dead bodies of two teenage lads and loaded them gently onto the cart. Their mother, with Eir still gripping her hands tightly, leant on the cart, pressing her tearful face into one of the boy's dirtied, bloodied shirts.

While this continued, Brynd walked along the street to knock on the doors of several of the houses.

Two people answered, only one of whom knew the woman well enough to take her in. It was an elderly woman who seemed fit and healthy and sane, and Brynd told her what had happened, pressed a few coins into her hand, 10 Sota in all, and instructed her to buy food and look after the woman.

As he returned to guide the woman towards this temporary sanctuary, he thought to himself, *If I keep opening my purse like that, for every dead body, I'll have nothing left ...*

*

Brynd and Eir rode back in contemplative silence. Eir's mood was different now, though he couldn't tell how exactly.

'Are you glad you came out here, to see all this?' Brynd asked eventually.

'*Glad* is not perhaps the right word, but I am certainly grateful for what you've shown me. I'm happy you're going about things the way you are – seeing that these people have jobs, houses and food.'

'I'm not as alert to human and rumel needs as yourself, Lady Eir. You were very good earlier.'

'Well, such emotional things probably aren't necessary for a military man when you've so many other things to worry about; but you have compassion in your heart, and that is what these people so clearly need. Compassion.'

I'm glad someone thinks that, Brynd thought, as they neared the imposing Citadel.

'If what Artemisia tells us is true,' Eir continued, 'if another war is genuinely coming, what will happen here in Villiren?'

'I'm not sure I follow,' Brynd said.

'To these people, I mean. Will they be expected to fight again?'

'Some will be more willing than others.'

'And the rest of the island – the rest of the Empire's citizens?'

'I don't know yet, Lady Eir. Although Artemisia's people could provide significant support, we should plan for all eventualities, war or no war. Though I suspect that war is more likely.'

'On which front?'

'Your guess is as good as mine, Lady Eir. It may be that we have to mass an army to defend some other corner of the Empire, or it may happen in Villiren again.'

'One final thought,' she added.

Brynd indicated for her to continue, then steered his mare towards the cobbled road that led up directly to the Citadel. A unit of soldiers began to move forward but, on recognizing him, moved aside to let them through.

'Please, no more of this *Lady* Eir. It hardly seems fitting any more. Just Eir will be sufficient.'

'As you wish,' he replied with a smile.

'Commander,' one of the soldiers called.

Brynd looked away to see a sergeant running towards him. When he reached his side he held up a letter. 'This arrived when you were out, sir.'

Brynd took the letter, thanked the man and placed it in his pocket.

*

Night-time traditionally brought out the worst elements in Villiren, though the war had put a stop to most of that. When he had first arrived, Brynd had found underground drug dens, whorehouses importing kidnapped tribal girls, and a black market larger than the Imperial registered channel. Brynd could not concern himself with these matters; he had his mind set on the defence of the city. When the war came, this more *colourful* side of the city was forced to the fringes and beyond – out of sight, out of mind. But now the more insalubrious kinds of city life were finding their way back to the heart of things, where money and people met.

Brynd headed out on horseback along with two young archers from the Dragoons. They were riding towards a sector of the city right on the tip of where Deeping met what used to be the Wastelands, a former area of new growth that hadn't lost its old moniker. There were rumours of illicit goings-on here, but he had other matters on his mind after reading the letter.

Brynd dismounted and tied his horse securely to an iron bollard alongside some former industrial works, while the two archers remained on standby, their eyes fixed on the surrounding shadows. The streets were wide and largely featureless, the buildings no more than a storey high for the most part, until they reached one area that appeared to be a row of large disused warehouses. Along this stretch of road, homeless people were gathering around small fires, their hands out for warmth, their faces illuminated by the flames.

There was a warehouse at the end with a large double door, on which the number 54 was painted crudely in white. The building was vast and reminded Brynd of some of the industrial fishing units near Port Nostalgia – just like the one in which he and some of the Night Guard had nearly died. It had a gently sloped pyramid-style roof, with ornamentation at the top.

This must be the place, then, Brynd thought as he approached.

He banged three times with the ball of his hand and waited, peering around into the gloom. Then he waited a little longer, watching a dog trot from one side of the street to the other before it disappeared into the darkness.

Eventually, after a clang of bolts, Brynd found himself facing a slender young man in his late teens or early twenties, with short blond hair and a wide smile. He stood a little shorter than Brynd, and was wearing what looked like overalls. His face was smeared with grease.

I've come all the way out here for this youth?

'Hey, it's the Night Guard commander,' the lad beamed. 'Can tell by your eyes. Glad you could join us, man. You got our message, right?'

There was no salute, no signal of respect. 'Would I be here otherwise?'

'True, true. Hey, come in, it's freezing outside.' He backed away and let Brynd walk in. The door closed with a thud behind, and the young man bolted the door.

'What's your name?' Brynd asked, his voice echoing.

'Diggsy,' he replied.

'Funny-sounding name,' Brynd said.

'That's just what the lads call me. Real name's Thongar Diggrsen.'

'I can see why they call you Diggsy.'

'Hey, you've got a sense of humour. Was beginning to think you were all po-faced.'

You would be, if you'd seen what I'd seen, boy.

'Lead on, Diggsy,' Brynd gestured. 'I'm keen to see what all the fuss is about and hope that I haven't wasted my time traipsing across the city for no good reason.'

'Right you are.' Diggsy turned and walked down a dark corridor. Though Brynd could cope with the poor lighting, how Diggsy was finding his way in front of him was a mystery, but the lad seemed to move as if the passage was committed to his memory.

Something didn't make sense: why was someone so young occupying a factory? Was it his home? The building smelled like a blacksmith's workshop, of charred materials and molten metal. There was also the tang of cultists down here, too, that weird, unmistakable chemical odour from messing with things people shouldn't.

'How long have you been working here?' Brynd enquired.

'Now that's a question,' Diggsy replied. 'Way before the war, if that's what you mean. Pilli's father was one of those ore-owning types, and she knew this building of his – like quite a few others – wasn't being used at all. Anyhow, Pilli's good stock – not like her father – and so this has become our headquarters for the most part.'

'Headquarters? So are you part of an official order?'

'Ha, no. Hell no. We don't like to get involved with other cultists. They can be shitting well poncey if you ask me. All about structures and etiquette and whatever. That's not our kind of thing – we prefer to live by our own rules, in our gang.'

'How many are in your ... *gang*, then?' Brynd felt the situation was growing increasingly absurd. The way this Diggsy talked, his mannerisms and nonchalance, his references to his social circle, suggested this was all going to be a complete waste of time.

'Depends on when it is. We lost one in the war. Got the odd seasonal, but that dried up a year back. Oh, watch the corner here – it's a sharp one.'

'I see it. You didn't want to join in the war effort yourself?' Brynd asked. 'We had people far younger than you.' They turned to the left, along a narrow corridor, the sound of their feet occasionally scuffing along the smooth stone.

'We were too busy, to be honest. Sounds lame, doesn't it? But seriously, once you see what we've got, I think you'll understand.'

Diggsy's voice suddenly gave off a lot of reverb. They had entered a large chamber, lighter with a lot of energetic conversation and laughter at the far end. Brynd could smell arum weed mixed with cooking meat. There were four, maybe five people there, and they turned to face Diggsy when he hollered out to them.

Diggsy turned back to Brynd, gestured with wide arms, and smiled. 'Welcome to Factory 54. I think you'll like it.'

Brynd looked around to take in the scene. All around the walls and hanging from the rafters were bipedal structures, things made from junk that looked like immense hanged men. They were metallic and flesh and perhaps even something else, with leathery attire and what looked like massive trays on the floor. 'By Bohr . . .'

'Aw, this is nothing,' came a girl's voice, a young redhead with a slender frame and freckled face. 'This is the shit that doesn't work. We've been trying forever to get things to work, but life isn't that easy to manufacture. Isn't that right, Diggsy?'

Brynd eyed her and Diggsy. Judging by her look towards the lad, there was a history between them, that much was certain.

Brynd stepped closer to the large trays, which contained weird-looking brown fluids. 'Could someone bring me a flame over? I'd like to see this as clearly as possible.'

Some of the others laughed.

'I wouldn't do that if I were you, chief,' Diggsy said. 'Get a flame in that stuff and we'll all be eating breakfast in another world.'

Brynd soaked up the scene. This building was immense, which meant all these hanging creatures were larger than he originally thought. He stepped back to take in their expressionless faces, if they could be called *faces*. They were so creased, stitched and folded they seemed as if they were old sacks. Some of them wore open fissures, which had dried to black. They were bizarre specimens. The fact that they were a parody of a human or rumel kept him from believing that this was in any way unethical.

'Where did you get these from?' Brynd asked.

'We *made* them, of course,' the red-haired girl said, wandering over. 'Or resurrected them in many instances.'

Brynd asked for her name.

'Jeza,' she replied nonchalantly.

'Your name was on the letter,' he said.

She nodded coyly.

'Presumably you all know me – Commander Brynd Lathraea, leader of the Night Guard? Leader of the military that has applied martial law across the city.'

'Yeah, we got you,' someone replied.

He hoped to lend a little gravitas to his presence, but they showed little sign of acknowledging that. 'Let me get this right in my head: you're similar to cultists, then? You use the old science in new ways?'

'More or less, in layman's terms, though we don't really like cultists,' Jeza said. 'We deal with them, but they're *way* too cliquey, and they speak in all these prophetic riddles, it's ridiculous.'

'So you use their technology,' Brynd observed. 'That is to say, I'm guessing here, this was all done with the assistance of relics.'

'It was and it wasn't,' Jeza said. 'There's a whole mix of things – relics mainly, but we use some tribal refinements too, not to mention with palaeomancy you're dealing with the creations of the natural world itself.'

'I don't think the commander needs to know all the details,' Diggsy interrupted.

'Sure he does,' Jeza snapped. 'Think about it.'

85

'What's wrong with you tonight, Jeza?' Diggsy said softly.

'We need him to trust us,' she replied, then turned to Brynd. He noticed that her face revealed underlying conflicts within her. 'Isn't that right, commander?'

'That depends what you need my trust for.'

Jeza took his arm in an informal manner and directed him along the lines of constructs, through the semi-darkness. Shadows seemed to exaggerate the sinister appeal of these things, but Brynd couldn't help but wonder what they'd look like on the battlefield.

'None of these function, right?' Brynd asked.

'If you mean move around like a living thing, then only some of them do. We've actually got a couple in an adjoining chamber, which are a little more polished, but just take in all of this for a moment. You can see the potential here, can't you?'

'Of course,' he replied. 'But what were you saying about the technology behind them . . . ?'

'Yes, we work with a mixture of tribal knowledge and cultist science. Cultists haven't really touched on this stuff – to our knowledge at least. They concentrate on the bits of science and the discipline of technological lore being handed down through the generations. They're too full of shit to look further afield – you know, the tribes have some pretty power-ful stuff, but no one gives them the time of day. They just dismiss it as magic.'

'You have me intrigued,' Brynd said.

'I guess we were all lucky to have Lim.'

'And who,' Brynd asked, 'is Lim?'

Jeza sighed. 'He died during the fighting. But he was really, really good at this stuff. He came from one of the tribes on Varltung, which is how we got to work in this way.'

'Off Empire? How did he make it out here?'

'He ran away, came across on his own, learned the languages, did it all the hard way. They've got cultists on Varltung, too – did you know that?'

'I didn't,' Brynd admitted.

'Well, they have. Anyway, so Lim knew stuff that we didn't. Spoke Jamur well enough to explain his findings to us.'

Brynd's interest was most definitely piqued. He would indulge these youths a little longer. 'You all just meet then. He comes to Villiren—'

'Because anyone can make a go of things in a place where no one cares,' Jeza said. 'No one bothers us. No one pays us attention.'

Brynd nodded for her to go on. 'You have my attention.'

She looked around at the others who were approaching to hear the conversation.

'We all found each other, more or less. We're the kind of people who fell through the gaps – either dead parents or kicked out of home or runaways. Those kind of things make you grow up fast.'

'You've done all right for yourselves by the look of it,' Brynd said. 'But I don't understand how a bunch of street kids could have come across cultist technology.'

Diggsy laughed. One of the others was shaking their head. Jeza said, 'You don't know much about cultists, commander.'

'Excuse me?' Brynd replied.

'I mean, you might think they're all high-powered and respect them and stuff, but ... what you might not know is that some orders take in kids.'

'Of course, I've heard of such things.'

'Have you heard of abuse rings? Have you heard of cultists taking in dozens of young children promising to show them all the riches they can imagine, only to lock them in window-less rooms? Bringing them out just to test technology on them, or sexually abuse them.'

A silence fell in which Brynd considered the way Jeza spoke. She seemed totally unmoved by her past.

'My apologies,' he said eventually. *Tough kids, these ones . . .*

'Ah, think nothing of it, commander,' Diggsy said. 'We

were the lucky ones. We managed to scrape some knowledge together and get the hell out of there – others are still trapped, being beaten or worse. We got out, we stuck together and used the only thing we had – our knowledge of relics.'

'Not to mention stealing a load of relics when we ran away,' Jeza pointed out.

'True,' Diggsy smiled faintly, sadly.

There was a charm about these youths that Brynd admired. They'd done things the hard way – there was a lot to be said for that.

'So tell me the details of what you've achieved here,' Brynd suggested. 'I want to know what makes your work so special.'

Jeza told him, in approximate terms. Cultists were vague and spoke in heavy jargon, but she explained things in a very simple way. Lim could conduct rituals with relics – remnants of old technology as well as gemstones and tribal accoutrements he had brought with him from Varltung. There were tribes who worshipped such things in distant, remote valleys of that island. And sources of energy were provided to reinvigorate dead 'cells' – or make body parts quite literally spark into life. Jeza called it palaeomancy. The others chimed in with colour and examples to clarify this life science. Brynd concluded he would never fully understand the ways of a cultist.

'Tell me in plain terms: what can you offer the army?' Brynd asked.

'As I indicated in my letter we're developing things you might be able to use on the battlefield – though these are currently still in development.'

'I still need to *see* something.'

Jeza nodded and sauntered off into a dark corner of the room, where she rummaged around on a shelving unit. She returned a moment later clutching a small black item, and handed it over to Brynd, who examined it.

It was the size of a plate, half an inch thick, smooth on one side, and slightly curved. He attempted to bend it, but couldn't, then tried a little harder – but still did not move it out of shape. 'What am I looking at here?' he asked.

'This is the material we've made. It's strong and durable, and a fraction of the weight of metal, but not at all finished. We can make armour from this material. And we're nearly there.'

*

A couple of them headed outside to get some more cheap wine they'd been storing in the ice. The rest of the group sat around with Brynd on upturned crates, sipping wine from wooden cups. They offered him one of their many hammocks, but he politely declined.

'You weren't involved in the war,' Brynd said, 'so what made you contact the authorities now?'

'Word was that you were looking for new forces,' Diggsy said. 'We saw them posters you put up all over the place. I reckon we're in a position to supply you with some of those *forces*, depending on what you need.'

'Yes, of—'

'It'll cost you though,' Jeza replied coolly. 'We've also heard that bankers are looking to give a lot of cash to the army. If we can get a little contribution for working with you, we'll be happy enough. That could change all our futures. There's nothing wrong with that, is there?'

They were young, but definitely not stupid. Brynd took a sip of the wine and winced. One of the girls – Pilli? – chuckled and said something about no one liking their drinks.

'Of course if you'd rather we sold this stuff elsewhere . . .' Jeza started.

'No,' Brynd replied, 'that won't be necessary. We can arrange a contract, I'm sure. But I'll need to see what you've actually got first, and I'll need guarantees – you see, you're a lot younger than people I normally deal with.'

'Just because we're young doesn't mean we're unreliable,' Diggsy said.

'I mean, just look at what we've achieved so far,' Jeza said. Then, to Diggsy, 'I knew no one would take us seriously.'

'I didn't say that,' Brynd said. 'What we're dealing with here is something quite unnatural and untested, and – to be honest – I have no idea if what you've got can be deployed in military use yet. For example, can I make requests?'

'We can look at that, sure,' Jeza confirmed. 'But before we go on, we just want to know you're interested.'

'There are many details I wish to mull over,' Brynd continued, 'but you should know that yes, I *am* interested – and I can assure you that money's not a problem.'

Brynd placed his cup on the floor and stood up. 'Hopefully then you'll be able to buy better wine for your guests.'

He offered a smile and extended a hand to Jeza. She looked up at him with amazement, as if she had not expected him to take them seriously at all.

'Write to me again, but next time I want to see something finished and ready to test.'

She shook his hand. 'Sure, we'll have something in a day or so. You won't regret it.'

As Brynd left with the Dragoon archers, he realized that this was one of the few times in his life when he'd met a group of people who did not appear startled by his skin colour.

SIX

A day later, Brynd rode south on his mare, with Randur Estevu alongside him on a skittish grey colt, which he did not seem able to keep under control.

Late afternoon sunshine was sliding from the sky, leaving an oily residue across the clouds.

The road out of the city was lined with wiry horses and oxen. Bored-looking beasts trudged along the mud-tracks hauling felled trees to the lumber yards or huge chunks of stone for the masons. At this hour, there were dozens of them making their way to the city before the sun set.

'These are encouraging signs, young Randur,' Brynd called out, gesturing at the line of traffic. 'These are the building blocks of the new age. The city will be rebuilt. Life will be restored to what it was. This gives me hope.'

'Well, not to be annoying about it,' Randur replied, 'but anything's better than the pile of shite that Villiren was a while ago, let's be honest.'

'Your mood is still sour, I see.' Brynd pulled his horse to slow down to a more casual pace, so that he could sip some water and contemplate the gentle flow of people. 'Any chance it will improve, since we've a way to go yet? I would have thought this country air would've done a rural fellow like you some good.'

'Bugger has it done me any good. It's cold out here, and I'm hungry, if you must know.'

Brynd chuckled and said nothing.

'What're you laughing at?' Randur asked. 'Do I amuse you somehow? Look, chap, not all of us have had our senses slapped into some new state where we can't feel anything any more.'

'A little. You remind me of an old comrade,' Brynd said. 'He was a good friend, actually, and he was just as pessimistic as you.'

'I wasn't always this bad, you know. Doesn't seem that long ago that I was chipper and looking around for little but a decent plate of meat or a lady's sigh. So, what happened to him, your comrade?'

'He died.'

'Oh,' Randur replied. 'Sorry to hear that. Was he killed in Villiren?'

'No, he died just before as it happens – we were on our way here, to Villiren,' Brynd replied. 'It was our first encounter with the Okun, just an outrider group – a couple of hundred of the Empire's finest. Got himself fatally injured but that didn't stop him in his dying moments dragging a pile of relics to collapse the ice long enough for us to get out. He saved the Night Guard and a good few soldiers, and allowed us all to get back to the city so that the defence could be maintained. If it wasn't for him, I suspect, Villiren would have fallen. He was a good one, ultimately. Bitter and jaded, just like you, and would have gone to great lengths to avoid doing any work. Just like you.'

'Hey, I've done my fair share,' Randur grunted. 'I've saved Eir from execution, as well as your *charming* Empress Rika. Took them from right under Urtica's eye, and I brought them all the way out here. I think I've earned a rest, don't you? Especially from that woman Rika. You can deal with her sourness now.'

'Tell me,' Brynd began, 'did anything happen to Rika before you brought her to Villiren? She seems rather different these days. You went through quite a journey, so it seems. That's enough to change someone's outlook . . .'

'You're ferreting out why she's such a miserable sow all of a sudden, aren't you? Truth be told, I don't know. She was always boring, right from when I met her, but at least there was something gentle to her then. Now, she's . . . Well, there's a glint in her eye that wasn't there before. You could call it a darkness in her heart – she's no longer a docile girl, no longer some meek former priestess. She wasn't the same after she met Artemisia. I take it you were told about us being on her ship?'

'Yeah, Rika and Eir told me about that. A ship in the sky – quite remarkable.'

'Ridiculous if you ask me, though the flying monkey things were fun. Anyway, things changed then, on that ship. I wouldn't like to say that it was Artemisia's doing, but Rika felt like that warrior woman was her god. She was in awe of her right from the off, and didn't seem to want to question her like we did, me and Eir. Then – and here's the really weird part – they took the same chambers at night. Heard groaning, but didn't know if they were, you know . . .' He raised his eyebrows at Brynd. 'Getting their end away.'

'I understood you from your expression, thank you,' Brynd said. 'You don't know for certain? This could change things.'

'The old pervert in me likes to think they were – just to loosen Rika up a bit, you know? But truth be told, I'm not sure. The groans could have been from pleasure or pain.'

'What happened after that?'

'Well, next thing you know, Rika suddenly toughened up a little. At the time I was just grateful she stopped being so useless and passive – things would happen with a little more certainty.' Randur let out a sigh. 'I've no doubt we're all doing the right thing by Artemisia, having witnessed what I have, and having been protected by her blades. But Rika's a different person by a long way. And I just hope . . .'

Brynd remained silent, hoping Randur might continue. The wind stirred, sliding across this bleak landscape.

Randur pushed back a lock of his long black hair, and flashed him a grin. 'I bet after saving the city you didn't anticipate handing over the reins of the Empire to such a bitch.'

Brynd grunted. 'You should have more respect for the woman who leads so many people into this new era.'

'Thing is,' Randur replied, 'how much respect does the woman have for her people?'

*

They rode on for the better part of an hour until the road petered out, becoming nothing more than a muddy trail. The lights of the city faded from view, and the darkness and silence of the countryside became something more complete. Stars were brighter and the temperature plummeted. It wasn't long before all they could hear were the sounds of the horses' hooves and the animals' breathing.

They navigated east around the edge of the Wych Forest, and up a long, gentle slope that seemed to go on forever. Even at this hour, one of the moons cast enough light to suggest that nothing had been moving around here for days, not even any animals. The horses walked slower wherever the snow deepened; Brynd was careful not to injure them on this terrain. The further inland they travelled, clouds suddenly began to mass, obscuring the stars, and Brynd could smell the smoke from campfires some way off.

They're here at least . . .

Brynd halted his mare, dismounted, and tied her to a broken tree stump.

Randur followed suit, and then stepped alongside him. 'Is this it?' he asked. 'Where are they meant to be? There's nothing but snow and the odd dead tree.'

'We're not quite at the top of the hill,' Brynd replied. 'I

want to walk there cautiously because I can hear them over the other side.'

'I can't hear a thing,' Randur moaned.

Brynd ignored him and marched a little further up the slope. The ground was frozen solid. It began to rain, gently at first, then came heavier drops – again, he noticed, not snow, but *rain*.

'For fucksake,' Randur said, drawing up his hood, 'I don't know why we couldn't just ride to the top.'

'Though this is a friendly visit, we need to see what they're made of,' Brynd replied, pulling up his own hood. 'We need to see what they've got, what their capabilities are. And, most of all, we need to *shut the hell up*.'

Brynd moved cautiously up the slope for a few minutes. He kept looking around for any signs of scouts, but he could see none. It annoyed him that they had no one guarding the perimeter.

Randur followed, rather reluctantly, and whispered, 'Hey, I think I can hear something now. What can you see?'

As Brynd crested the hill, the scene down below presented itself slowly.

Row upon row of yurts and tents stretched in precise rows as far as he could see. Fires, set within immense cauldrons, were burning at regular intervals, at intersections in the lanes. Meanwhile, strange shapes lumbered in the half-light, occasionally illuminated by the flames.

Immense and ragged banners rippled in the evening breeze, each bearing exotic insignias, with strange shapes and curves to the designs. Meat was being cooked in aromatic spices that he couldn't recognize, but which reached him even at this distance. And, all around this vast site, humans and rumels – with other, similar-looking life forms – were sitting in enclaves or standing to attention as they were addressed by some more senior official. Brynd estimated that there were twenty or thirty thousand warriors down there, and Bohr only knows how many beyond. Some wore bright armour, some were covered in dark cloaks, but what struck him was how *similar* they looked to people from his own world. Their attire was not more exotic than could be found among the cultures of the Boreal Archipelago – a fact that was both comforting and unnerving. It was as if there were some shared characteristics, some common essence between the two worlds. That seemed to confirm the new histories that Artemisia had provided. They were cultural cousins.

Randur came up alongside him and, with his jaw open wide, managed to say, 'Well bugger me. Would you look at that.'

'Impressive, isn't it?' Brynd replied.

'Well you wanted an army, chief,' Randur said. 'It looks like you've got one.'

'Not quite. We've still got to persuade them to fight with us.'

The two of them remained stationary as they examined the expanse beyond, contemplating just what this could mean, until something barked in a language Brynd did not recognize.

He knew what that meant.

Cursing to himself for letting his guard down and his senses slip, he held up his hands, leaving his sabre by his side, and suggested to Randur that he do the same. Then Brynd searched his surroundings in order to locate the source of the voice.

'What's going on?' Randur asked.

'It's all right – they've scouts, and in a way that's what I wanted to find out,' Brynd muttered. He addressed the approaching warriors who he heard somewhere in the darkness. 'I am Commander Lathraea of the Night Guard, senior officer of the military in this world. I have liaised with Artemisia in seeing that you were brought here.' On noting no reply, he ventured, 'Welcome to the island of Y'iren . . .'

'Albino,' came the strained reply, followed by whispers in a foreign tongue.

'Can you see them with your fancy vision?' Randur asked.

Brynd scrutinized his immediate surroundings: the hilltop was dark, and he could only discern spindly bushes or the contours of the landscape. The voice, still giving orders in some strange tongue, was definitely coming from down the slope, but there he could only see crooked trees or lumps of rock or frozen mud. It alarmed him that he could not see them with his enhancements.

A twig snapped nearby, his attention shifted. Now he could see something: the rain was clinging to four opaque forms that were marching towards them. It was the water that defined their presence, the edges of their bodies, rather than the bodies being physically there.

'I still can't see anything,' Randur said.

'I see them.' Brynd pointed towards the four water-covered shapes. 'You might struggle in this light, but they're very definitely there. Four of them.'

'Fuck, I can see their footprints in the snow.' Randur shuddered and moved to draw his sword.

Brynd held back his arm. 'It's all right. Remember, they're on our side.'

'Don't see why they have to creep up like this.'

'It's good,' Brynd replied. 'They mean business, and we need armies that mean business, instead of littering battle-fields with their inefficient corpses.'

Brynd held up his arms again and declared some basic greetings.

The figures became quite still, before fading into existence. The hominids possessed dark skins that reminded him of his obsidian chamber for their faint sheen. With no discernible hair, and a strange headband bearing tribal symbols, they stood a good foot shorter than himself, and each one was clutching a dagger. They were lean and, unbelievably for the weather, clothed only in light bronze armour and baggy breeches. They must have been freezing, but they showed no signs of suffering. As they came nearer he counted five of them, all in all; their movements were fluid, and their muscles looked tough and wiry.

'I am Commander Brynd Lathraea from the city of Villiren, representing Jamur Rika, an ally of Artemisia.' He repeated himself a couple of times but could only hear the wind in the distance.

Then he got a response: 'You . . . both of you, come . . . Come with us.'

Brynd couldn't tell which of them was speaking, though their voices seemed warped and distressed. It might have been all of them speaking simultaneously, for all he knew. 'At least we can communicate,' he whispered to Randur, who looked petrified. Brynd addressed his otherworldly comrades once again. 'Yes,' he said, nodding and smiling to make sure they understood. 'We bring you no harm.'

*

'I thought they were meant to be on our side?' Randur moaned.

Marching through the rain at knifepoint, they headed down the slope towards the encampment. Even though they traversed the hill in a wide zigzag to make the descent easier, they still managed to slip occasionally on the mud. Each time they did, their captors showed no signs of concern. They merely waited impatiently for Brynd or Randur to stand up again, brush themselves down, and continue towards the camp.

It seemed an eternity, that walk. Brynd realized that what he was about to witness was very special, and also that he was an ambassador for his entire people. Perhaps he should have brought Artemisia, but he had not anticipated an actual meeting – he only wanted to see them from afar.

As they entered the fringes of the encampment, past the yurts made with thick fabric and enormous brass cauldrons, Brynd was overwhelmed by the noise and smells of this suddenly present civilization: the odours of unfamiliar food, and the harsh clamour of a new language. Here was a new city, of sorts, that existed on no maps.

Brynd didn't know where to look first. So many oddities presented themselves to him: beings of perplexing shapes, uniforms of subtle shades, markings etched across metal, insignias on flags. In addition to the creatures who had located Brynd and Randur, there were others wandering past them. They were some degree taller than the humans, green-skinned, long-limbed and remarkably slender, with a smooth elongated face and two black eyes. They wore tight leather tunics and their light steps barely marked the mud and snow as they moved gracefully past.

He did not know their customs, but, out of habit from dealing with tribespeople throughout the Archipelago, Brynd made sure not to lock eye contact with anyone, and asked Randur to do the same, so neither would accidentally cause a confrontation. It seemed to be an instinct not to offend anyone, but it was difficult as Brynd could not help but feel how these creatures were pausing to look and stare straight back *at them*. Here, *they* were the oddities – they were the exotic specimens on parade.

They passed an area where enormous bronze chariots were lined in neat rows, some covered by mesh-like cloth to protect them from the rain. Brynd caught the briefest glimpse of one: an opulent carriage with spiked wooden wheels and polished metal glimmering in the nearby torchlight. Further along, black muscled horses – finer and more aggressive than any he'd seen before – were being led into larger and more impressive tents to shelter. Somewhere in the distance came singing, which moved along a harmonic scale, and then he heard drumming. Nearby huge sides of animals were being turned on spits as they roasted over fires. It took two of the tall, green-skinned creatures to turn each spit.

Then, within a vast clearing, he witnessed perhaps the most resplendent sight he had ever seen.

It was their wings he first noticed: immense, jagged and jutting into the air; and when caught in the cauldron fire they stood out clearly against the night sky. They reminded him of the Onyx Wings in Villiren, and were just as imposing – in fact, he realized he never knew the history of those statues. Could they have been related in some distant way to these creatures?

Then, when Randur and Brynd came nearer, the creatures' bodies could be discerned moving slowly, their pale under-bellies revealed, with darker skin on top. Their heads were disproportionately smaller, relatively flat and squat with narrowed eyes, and within their wide maws were numerous, minute yet dangerously sharp-looking teeth. Each whole being was held in place by immense chains tied to posts the size of ancient trees.

Dragons, he thought. *The very stuff of mythology.*

There were five of them, at least in this clearing: beyond, chained to further posts, more could been seen drifting about, their wings extending and folding, possibly agitated they were not soaring in the air. Soldiers seemed to be moving around between them in a training regime.

Brynd glanced across to Randur and said, 'You're unusually silent.'

Randur stood agape, apparently not knowing what to make of all this.

That would make two of us . . . he thought to himself.

*

Brynd and Randur marched for some time through the centre of the encampment and Brynd still could not take it all in. He required more time than a mere walk-through, more hours to sit and observe and perhaps engage in some kind of conversation with these people. And it was not just for the fact that this was an event in the history of his world; no, he needed to understand how they would function, how many of them there were – and, more importantly, what their strengths and weaknesses would be on the battlefield.

He would find out soon enough, no doubt.

Eventually they reached a wide, hessian-coloured tent, which bore insignias made from gold leaf, or something very similar. The very top of the tent contained a look-out platform: two or three soldiers stood up there, bipedal, hoofed, with human chests and huge, angular heels, and what looked from Brynd's position to be bulls' heads. Each was carrying a spear.

'They must have gone to some lengths to cart all this stuff here,' Randur suggested.

'They were ready for war,' Brynd said. 'War should be all they know, judging by what Artemisia has told us, having fought against their enemy for millennia. These are people on the run.'

They were led to a vast tent where dozens of warriors were seated in a large circle, on rugs made from animal furs. It was dark in here, with a glowing brazier in the centre burning spices, and standing around the perimeter were more of the bull-like soldiers with their spears gripped firmly in their hands. Whatever language was being spoken faded to silence on their entrance as everyone turned their way.

The two of them were prodded forward, through a parting gap in the crowd. Brynd felt the thrill of excitement of new races, of new sentient species. He was concerned that he might say something stupid and betray his entire race. *I hope they might be more forgiving of me.*

In the centre of the gathered warriors, several considerably older humans, rumels, and members from the other species were seated on cushions. Brynd couldn't quite make out their faces in this light, but they were grey-haired and frail-looking men and women. Even one that possessed the head of a bull seemed aged and tired, a little frayed at the edges.

Through hand gestures, Brynd and Randur were instructed to sit alongside them.

There was another bustle of activity nearby and a young soldier was beckoned forward. He was a fine-looking man, lean and broad-chinned. Brynd felt an attraction that leapt across the cultural divide. His armour glimmered in the light of the brazier. He took off his helm and knelt before the elders. Words were exchanged. There was an announcement of sorts and Brynd suspected that they were being introduced to the other warriors.

There were signs, in the faces of these old men, that this was an important moment, that they were just as nervous as Brynd. The kneeling soldier leant in to hear a whisper from one elder, then the man shuffled towards Brynd and, in a broken Jamur accent, one nowhere near as refined as Artemisia's, said, 'You were . . . *tress-pass*. On our camp.'

'I meant no trouble. I came to see what was here – if you were *established*, if you had settled in your temporary home.'

The soldier translated to the elder, before returning. 'There should be official channels . . . We would make you a guest.'

A relief. The discussion would not continue to be about their incursion.

'Next time,' Brynd replied, 'we will remember.'

As the soldier translated, Brynd turned to Randur. 'What do you make of this?'

'Honestly,' Randur whispered, as if furtively, 'they're not all that . . . weird, or anything. I mean from Artemisia's appearance, I had expected more. Even in her seeing-contraptions, the images of the cultures she showed us seemed darker. But I guess, up close, they're nothing wilder than some tribes you get out in the sticks, or some of the strange folk you get rambling around the city.'

'Indeed,' Brynd replied. He felt both comforted and disappointed in the fact that this alien people were not utterly alien. As Randur suggested, many of their characteristics – respect for a group of elders, hierarchies, customs of welcome – all of this could be found in many tribes scattered throughout the Archipelago. Brynd had expected more, but he was glad of their vaguely familiar customs. It would make negotiations less intimidating.

The translations continued back and forth. Brynd explained his minor mission: he came because he was curious, because he wanted to see for himself how many of them had come to the Boreal Archipelago. They, in turn, quizzed him on the geography of the island, of the people who lived here, of more abstract points like the quality of the air and the direction of the ocean currents. They asked him about food and where they could store what he imagined to be their livestock. They wanted to know in which direction the sun rose and how frequent the tides were. There were questions on hours of daylight, what herbs or crops grew locally, what stone 'grew' nearby, and how many people lived on the island. They asked how many gods lived here, and questioned them about deities that Brynd did not know about.

Some of the warriors, later, came closer, many of them decorated in skulls he did not recognize, and wearing layers under their armour made from rough animal hide. They asked about his weapons – indicating the sabre by his side. They queried the material, on how it was held, and he showed them. He made sure to communicate around the translator through his smiles – it seemed important for them to know he was happy they'd come – and some of them smiled back. He would, after all, ask them to spill blood for the preservation of his people, too.

My people . . . get that thought out of your head. You're not the bloody Emperor.

Brynd plucked up the nerve to ask if these elders were the

rulers of the incoming races, a question that could potentially cause insult, but they did not seem bothered.

'We are . . . approximately third, fourth, seventh, and tenth in command,' the warrior explained.

Brynd nodded, glad he was not wasting his time, impressed at the seniority dispatched to the island. Brynd complimented them on their camp, on the impressive races and animals that stood outside, at the discipline and organization. He enquired about the animals that looked like dragons, expressing his admiration for them and wondered about their purpose.

The elders smiled and seemed to like that. They used the word *spakov*, which he committed to memory. 'Do you fly them?' Brynd asked. 'How do you use them?'

They are used in battle, came the reply, much to Brynd's delight. They also help to transport warriors to inaccessible places.

The soldier translated, 'You would be happy, yes, to fly with the transport?'

Brynd eagerly nodded his answer. 'I would indeed.'

The evening went on, with Randur remaining silent, observant, and Brynd wanting to learn more about these newcomers. If these people would be integrated with their own culture, then he would not make them feel unwelcome.

After a couple of hours of exchanges, Brynd and Randur were escorted back through the camp, past all the exotic races and back to the hilltop where they were discovered. There, they picked up their horses, and rode slowly back to the city.

SEVEN

It was the morning of his rest day, something that tended to be little more than a token gesture rather than a genuine opportunity to put his feet up. However, today he had somehow found himself with a couple of free hours. He had left two of the other Night Guard soldiers in charge and their only orders were not to bother him.

He sat alone by the fire reading a book of social philosophy he'd taken from the Citadel's library. Sunlight streamed in through the window of his personal chamber. This was a simple place with a large bed in which he could stretch out fully, a few nicely designed pieces of dark-wood furniture, a stone floor, and a fire. The window, too, was an improvement, as it overlooked Port Nostalgia and the sea beyond. Outside it was a calm day, with enough sunlight to suggest it might melt some of the snow.

It was good to get the time to think alone. It energized him. As soon as he stepped outside his door, the incessant questions and demands would begin. This side of the door he had a book and a fire and that was all he needed.

Overall, things seemed to be shaping up well. He might have a decent army. A ruler was in place. There was a chance the city could be rebuilt if the money flowed well enough. From these embers, something resembling an empire could be rebuilt. There had still been no word from Villjamur though. Had Emperor Urtica even received his message, and what would be the consequences of his decision?

There were so many unknown variables that he felt he should just close his eyes and wait for the trouble to find him. The best he could do was make sure they were prepared for every eventuality.

*

It couldn't have been more than two hours before there was hushed activity outside his door. Brynd put his book down, stoked the fire, and sat back in his chair, waiting for the knock that came just a moment later.

'It's unlocked,' Brynd called out.

Brug poked his war-scarred and shaven head into the room, 'Uh, commander – sorry to bother you while you're off duty, but . . .'

'It's all right, Brug, you can enter.'

The thuggish-looking Night Guard soldier was speaking just outside the door and now stepped inside, his tribal-inspired neck tattoos more noticeable in the light of day.

'Were you talking to yourself?' Brynd enquired. 'Has madness claimed you?'

'No, not yet,' he smiled. 'There's a garuda outside who says she'll only speak to you.'

'Send her in immediately.' Brynd stood up quickly, anxious for a report.

Brug disappeared, gave some orders in the corridor and a garuda marched into the room. She was a brown-feathered soldier, with white plumage around her face and downy feathers over a tightly muscled torso. She wore black breeches, held with a belt that carried two daggers on her hips, and she held her gold helm beneath one arm. Two massive wings were folded neatly behind her back.

'Sele of Jamur,' Brynd said, and the garuda returned the greeting in hand-language. 'Name and rank?'

Wing commander Elish.

'Have you brought news?' Brynd demanded.

She seemed a little tired as she signed, *I have indeed, commander*. Her hand movements were intricate, her fingers graceful as they traced the forms of the military code.

'You were sent to survey Jokull if I remember correctly,' Brynd said, partially to remind himself because he had dispatched so many garudas recently.

That is correct.

'What did you see there?' he asked.

I have seen that Villjamur has collapsed.

'Excuse me? Is this a translation error, wing commander? How do you mean "collapsed" exactly?'

Precisely that, commander. Villjamur is now a ruin. The many levels of the vast city have been destroyed. Buildings lay ruined. Bridges have been reduced to rubble. The city has collapsed – there is no one there left alive. I perched on a ruin in the morning sunlight looking over this new topography, and I saw nothing move at all. The only people who were there were dead, buried under stone or their bodies dismembered.

Brynd absorbed the report, breathing deeply to maintain a sense of calm. It seemed unthinkable that the jewel in the Empire's crown was no more. 'What happened there – and what of the populace?'

Something came from the skies, I believe. That thing is still there and it chases what remains of the populace across the island. It hunts our people. It hunts them still.

'What did this thing do, and what is it?'

I am not sure entirely. I could not get too near as it is well protected. There are beings that fly around it to maintain safety. But it is a city like no other. It maintains its presence at altitude through ways I cannot fathom. From it, individuals of complex races are delivered to the ground. There, they create havoc in the towns and villages. To my knowledge they have moved across Jokull in what is a systematic act of genocide.

The people from Villjamur – those who survived what must

have been a dramatic assault – are travelling at pace. It should be said that there is some hope – a plan of sorts appears to be in operation. Whoever is in charge has constructed strange land-crafts on which many of the refugees flee, though the rest continue on foot or on horseback. They are moving ahead of the slow-moving menace in the sky.

Well, this was at least a silver lining. 'How many refugees are there?' Brynd asked.

So far, estimates range from forty to sixty thousand.

Brynd looked at the garuda in disbelief. 'As many as that? What condition are they in?'

Healthy, for what it is worth. They are stretched out over a vast area. It is difficult to make a precise calculation. More seem to be joining their mass each day and there are outriders and those sourcing and distributing food. I was impressed with the organiza-tion. They have cultists with them, and a handful of Imperial soldiers.

'Are there any signs of Emperor Urtica?' Brynd enquired.

There are no traces of him or any form of government. I have seen no councillors and, as I signed, there were simply a few soldiers remaining with the refugees – they were the only symbols of authority. When I flew over where Balmacara should have been located, much of the Imperial residence was not to be found. It was, presumably, in the crumbled remnants of the city. I cannot see that Urtica would have survived.

'That would explain the silence regarding my message to him,' Brynd said, and wondered, *Did he ever read it before the city fell?* 'The refugees, where are they headed?'

They are travelling in a direct line to the east coast. I would guess that their main aim is to stay ahead of their attackers. They are doing little more than trying to get away and survive.

'And when they get to the coast . . .' Brynd said. 'What do you think will happen?'

The wing commander made no movement of her hands, and remained impassive, awaiting instruction or question.

'I'm asking your opinion now,' Brynd said. 'How urgent is their situation? How do you rate their chances of survival? Are there enough vessels that will help them leave the island?'

I would say, commander, that unless they receive immediate military support and food aid, when they reach the coast their progress will be halted. When the presence in the sky catches up with them, it will be unlikely that so many people will survive the onslaught. There will be more of Jokull's people with them by this point. It would be a massacre.

Brynd nodded. 'Thank you, wing commander. I would like you to make some sketches later – I'd like to get an impression of what this apparent city in the sky actually looks like. But for now, take a night's rest. Tell Brug that I've said you are to be provided with a chamber – you've earned it. And good work, Elish.'

Thank you, commander. The garuda gave a tip of her head and headed out the door.

Brynd closed it behind her, and rested his head against the wood for a moment. Then, taking slow, deep breaths he picked up a pad of paper and a pencil, then sat back down in his chair, once again in the warm glow of the fire.

There, he began planning how he would organize the rescue of this train of lost souls.

Eight

Over the next twenty-six hours they continued the process of refinement on the exoskeletal armour. Day became night, and still they continued to work on their plans. While the others were working on the material, little Gorri did what he did best, concentrating on developing Jeza's designs into something they could work with. He had come up with some variants on the armour design. In a flurry of words he enthusiastically suggested his changes to her.

'Though I'd actually like to speak to a soldier, once we get this sold – and get the cash! – just to get a fully formed idea of the mechanics of how they'd use this, you get me? The kind of ways they wanna use a sword and generally kick the shit out of the enemy, so I can get a better idea of how it'd work in action and, anyway, there's no point me shaping this for people only for them to hobble about in something they can barely move in because you might as well have them wearing an iron box!'

'These sketches are more than fine,' Jeza replied. 'Really. They'll be perfect for a prototype.'

While he continued talking at her, she took his drawings over to the *Haldorors*, and programmed in their various measurements, quotients and angles. They set up the relics to translate the original into this more calculated form.

And it worked. First time. *Just like that.*

They had managed to modify the original breastplate into

one that would fit over a human or a rumel. In a jubilant move, Coren donned the resulting piece of armour, which slotted crudely over his head. It was a little bland – they would have to embellish it for future designs – but it did the job, and covered his entire torso successfully.

'It's bloody light, I'll tell you that much,' Coren announced. 'Hey, who's got a sword?'

Diggsy strolled forward. 'Just so happened to have one on standby.' He lifted something from a side-bench and unsheathed a dirty rapier-style blade.

Coren smiled. 'Come on then, *Throngar*. Let's see what you've got.'

'Just be careful,' Jeza said, hiding her head in her hands. After two sharp clangs and a burst of whooping laughter from Coren, she looked up.

Coren lurched back and forward as Diggsy struck him with the sword. Each time it glanced off harmlessly. Coren stood still with his arms out wide and Diggsy grunted as he thrust the tip of the blade right at him. The sword made a dull thud on impact; Coren simply beamed.

'We get our designs finalized, get the commander's buy-in,' Diggsy said, tossing the sword away. 'I reckon we can make more of these than we think. We'd have to test whether or not the later ones we produced were weaker than the original – one of the side effects is the redundancy of the original translated material.'

'We'll make another few examples then,' Jeza said. 'This didn't take us all that long – let's make some more. I want to see more than one sample to show the commander. Meanwhile, let's get a letter to him about this – tell him that we think he'll want to see what we've got.'

The others got to work again, and Jeza looked at this recent organization and efficiency with a great deal of pride. *We're really going to mean something to the city now.*

*

III

Brynd sat opposite the group of youngsters, not quite know-ing what to make of them. He had received their message and come all the way out to the factory as soon as he could make it, this time leaving just the one archer outside the door for security. The message this time was curiously rather bold, suggesting there were big developments, and he came armed with huge amounts of healthy scepticism.

If there was one thing these young cultists were likely to create, it was trouble, but he gave them the benefit of the doubt. Sitting down at a table in their workshop he felt utterly out of place and wary that although not exactly an old man, he was certainly not a young one any longer. He also felt that he had spent so much time in such formal surround-ings, in Balmacara or the Citadel, that this kitchen-workshop hybrid, rammed with cheap plates and scraps of food, was mildly unsettling. He realized he was becoming a bit of a snob.

You need to get out on the road again, he told himself. *That'll be humbling enough.*

The girl, Jeza, started to hold court again. She began with a little presentation full of sketches which he found endearing, but mildly annoying.

'Please,' he said eventually, 'I've some urgent planning to get back to. May we get to the essentials? Your original letter promised nothing short of a revolution.'

'Indeed,' Jeza replied, and nodded to two of the lads, Diggsy and Coren, who snuck off quietly. Jeza spoke briefly of the Okun, a race with which Brynd was uncomfortably familiar, and the lads returned. One of them was wearing plain-looking body armour, the other, Diggsy, carrying a sword, which he handed over to Brynd with pride.

Brynd waved his hand, stood up and said, 'I've got my own, thanks,' and unsheathed his sabre. It glimmered briefly with cultist sorcery and the lad simply stared at it in awe.

'Now we want you to strike Coren as hard as you can manage.'

'Are you sure?' Brynd asked. 'I didn't get to the top of the military without being fairly useful with a blade.'

'Go on,' Jeza said, 'it's quite all right. This is the whole point. Just use your blade the way you would do normally – on the battlefield or in a duel or whatever.'

'But only on the armour,' Coren laughed awkwardly, slapping his protection. His face turned sour. 'No, really.'

Coren took a wide stance and held his arms out away from his body. At first Brynd made a quick, effortless stab towards him. His blade pinged off, and Coren did not move.

He beamed. 'Go on.'

'All right,' Brynd said. First of all he walked around to see where the body armour was fitted, so that he wouldn't injure him, and then he commenced with some more vigorous moves, striking the body armour in various zones, harder and harder, until he began to break sweat.

Coren stood there, his eyes closed, as Brynd continued this mock-assault. Brynd tuned in to his enhanced strength and began using the same force as on the battlefield. Coren hardly moved and the body armour did not even show signs of scarring.

Brynd ceased his attack, just a little breathless, and sheathed his sword. Once he regained his composure, he asked, 'What material is this?' and tapped the breastplate. 'It's not even dented.'

'There's more,' Coren said. 'See how light this is.' He lifted the body armour off his torso with remarkable ease – for the same size piece of equipment made from metal, it would have required another to help with its removal.

Brynd asked, 'Where did you get this from?'

'We made it,' Jeza said. Then she slowly explained the process behind its construction.

'It's made from Okun shell?' Brynd asked. He ran his hand through his hair. 'The concept . . . it's abhorrent.'

'No, no,' Jeza continued. She walked around calmly and waved to test pieces. 'One is the Okun shell, the other is a replica of its . . . *fabric*. We've used, um, what you might call cultist energy to re-create it. It's *not* the same thing – you wouldn't actually be wearing an Okun shell, far from it, and you wouldn't even know it until you told someone.'

'I fought against these things, you see. Relentless and brutal – like nothing I've *ever* witnessed before. They possessed such power and killed so many of us.' His mind flashed to the combat within the narrow lanes of the city: blood spurting against high stone walls, soldiers being savaged, their remains being stomped into cobbles; then the smell of burning flesh on the funeral pyres night after night as innumerable souls were set free.

'And just think,' Jeza said, 'if you were able to use such a negative in acting for good. This substance is tougher and lighter than anything the military currently uses, right?'

'Right,' Brynd admitted.

'We could make this armour for you,' she said. 'We can't promise in what quantity just yet, but enough to mean something.'

Brynd asked to hold the specimen and studied it in immense detail, tilting it this way and that, attempting to bend it with his strength. 'If I gave specifications,' he said, 'if I provided samples of our own armour, the design and so on, would you be able to meet those requirements?'

'Sure.' Jeza looked across to the others, who remained silent during this discussion. 'We're even working on designs for other parts of the body, too – legs, arms, head.'

How could such young minds produce this quality of technology?

Brynd's mind began fizzing with potentials. He imagined row upon row of soldiers equipped with this war gear; fast-moving ground troops who would be well-protected and more mobile than ever before. There would be less fatigue, fewer casualties.

Brynd extended his hand to Jeza. She looked at it for a moment, uncertain of what to do.

'We've not yet talked money,' Jeza said, and moved her hands to her hips. 'But I'd be happy to do that as well.'

Brynd raised an eyebrow. *Smart. Businesslike. Took guts for her to say that.* 'We'll talk money soon enough. I need to speak to the accountants before I can make any offers. Be assured you have me on board. I'd like to visit again, very soon, and see what more you can offer. How soon can you make two more? A day, two, three?'

'Now we know we can do that in a day easily. We've done all the hard work.'

'Good, because this . . .' he held up the armour again, 'this could change things.'

NINE

'Artemisia . . .' Brynd called to her where she was stood on one of the balconies of the Citadel. The blue warrior-woman was staring out across the sea. It was a grey day, with sleet-filled skies and a rough surf. Whereas at street level the repairs to the façades of buildings suggested some sort of progress, from this vantage point much of the wreckage of Villiren could still be seen. Ruined building after ruined building rolled down to the shattered harbour front; many were devoid of interiors, others were propped up by scaffolding. It was in this region where Brynd had witnessed the ferocity of the other world meeting his own; it was hard to shake those horrors from his mind.

'Commander,' Artemisia replied. She continued to regard the cityscape. A gust of wind buffeted her, sending her hair spiralling around her shoulders. Those two large blades never left her back, in clear contradiction to the regulations he was trying to establish. 'How does it go with the money men?' she asked.

'As positive as can be expected from dealing with their sort,' he replied, now standing alongside her. 'They do not have an altruistic bone in their body. They exist solely to make themselves richer and, if society just so happens to be reconstructed at the same time, then that is simply a happy coincidence.'

'I am surprised,' Artemisia continued, 'that this is the state of affairs here. Where I come from, we do not allow so much wealth to sit in the hands of so few – that way leads to great power imbalances, and it is very difficult to get things done. Our elders are experienced, yes, but they rotate their roles with newcomers each cycle.'

Brynd sighed with a smile. 'Here it gets even more complex. The money men, as you put it, need laws to protect their wealth, which is why I've brought in legal assistance to form a set of laws – a universal treaty – once all this mess is over. I've made it clear that construction of society is the highest priority.'

'You are a man of great vision,' Artemisia said. 'Yet for one who is so optimistic, it seems you are perpetually unhappy.'

'I don't get paid to be happy,' Brynd said.

'You do not, it seems, get paid at all at the moment,' Artemisia pointed out.

'I see your Jamur is improving vastly,' Brynd said bitterly. Then, 'I've had trouble finding you for a while – what have you been up to?'

'I have been here and there through the gates, many times. You have come across the assembled forces, I understand?'

'Indeed, and it's a most impressive array of forces. I was speechless when I saw them – a most successful effort.'

Brynd thought he saw pride in her appearance then: a subtle changing in her posture and expression.

'However,' she continued, 'it does not at times seem to be enough, for so many have died in our world. We want to evacuate many more of our civilians here as well as the military – because on your islands there is sanctuary. We need to settle here. We are losing everything of our home.'

'Your resources will be a hugely significant help to us here,' Brynd said. 'This is a different world. I know the geography of it better than an emperor cooped up in a high tower. My men have shed blood over most of it. Trust me, the landscape here is different, the people are stubborn – but we'll need to work *together*. Once we have victory behind us, we can settle any differences, but we must remain a united force, no one-upmanship.'

'You have our promise on that, commander.'

'Good. Because I need more than your promise right now – we need your help. I've received a report that up to around sixty thousand civilians are currently fleeing across the island of Jokull. Villjamur has collapsed completely, and nothing remains there.' He described in detail the presence of the sky-city, of genocide, and of the strange land-vehicles.

Artemisia questioned him, but he could give little detail. And for the first time today she actually faced him. 'Two matters here. The first is that, as I suspected, our . . . enemy has done what they always threatened to do. That is a matter that must be dealt with. But secondly, and of equal import-ance to our culture: as I told you before, our creator has broken through to your world of his own accord. These land-vehicles – he has made such things commonplace in our world. If these vehicles are as you say, then it suggests to me his location may well have been found.'

'Then you'll want to investigate this also?' Brynd suggested.

'This is of interest to us and I understand, also, your concerns for civilian life. What needs do you have of us?'

'I have some suggestions for a military operation,' Brynd said. 'It will require you to liaise with your people gathered to the south of the city and, if possible, to have a reply by sunrise. By which time I will have gathered enough of our own military forces, which have been regrouping and rebuild-ing ever since the defence of Villiren.'

'What is your *plan*, commander?' Artemisia asked.

'That depends,' Brynd said, 'on which of the many races I saw in your encampment are able to join us.'

*

Early evening, and hail pummelled the outside of the Citadel, creating an ambient noise that soothed Brynd's agitated mind. He couldn't hear all the activities of the corridors, all the hubbub from the floors below – a moment of peace after an afternoon engaged in the business of arguing with lawyers. Spending just half an hour with a lawyer confirmed to Brynd that a military life had certainly been the right path.

It occurred to him, on the way back to his room, that if the remains of Jamur society were to blend with another, alien culture and customs of both must be respected, then existing laws and dictats – ones based upon ancient and religious decrees – would have to be adjusted.

There was a pounding on his door – he assumed from the heavy thumping that it was Artemisia. He leapt up from his chair and called her in.

'You bring news?' he asked.

'I bring news.' As ever, it was difficult to tell much from Artemisia's appearance. 'Tomorrow morning, at sunrise, you will be able to utilize the better part of a thousand soldiers.'

He considered the value they would add. 'And the transport?'

'The elders agreed – more units are being brought through the gates ready to be dispatched when the sun is at its highest. You will need to inform your soldiers of this and tell them to get what sleep they can before the mission.'

'I'd like to be briefed on the differing capabilities of your people,' Brynd said. 'I witnessed a great range among the races.'

'I will have this written down for you for the morning.'

'With regards to the transport . . .' Brynd started.

'You will,' Artemisia finished, 'be briefed on how to handle the journey. There are specially fitted . . . I think the best word is "cargo" holds for many people to be carried at once. For now, get rest, commander, and make sure that your meals tomorrow morning are consumed more than an hour in advance of the flight.'

*

Before Brynd could brief the members of the Night Guard, and to suggest they use cultist enhancements on their weapons when they woke, he called in on Rika and Eir. They were in another chamber in the Citadel, a vast space that had been hastily decorated and cleaned out of respect for them, so that they could have somewhere to be at peace. Richly decorated with highly polished wooden furniture, lavish tapestries and an immense, ornate fireplace, it was once used as the former portreeve's bedchamber. Incense burned in one corner, making the room feel calming. Eir was standing by a small washbasin, and turned to regard him, though Rika remained seated.

He greeted them and informed them of his intentions.

'You should,' Rika said, 'remember to inform me of such things first, before making such bold decisions in my name.'

Like hell I should . . . 'Indeed, and for that I can only apologize. You see, we had to act urgently. I've hardly had time to breathe.' Brynd gave a short bow of apology, not his most sincere, he had to admit, before glancing to Eir. He noticed then that there were stains on her arms. 'Is that blood on your skin?'

She glanced down self-consciously. 'Oh, no . . . well, technically yes, this is blood, but it isn't mine. I've been helping out in the city and I didn't clean myself up properly before I left. That's why I'm at the basin.'

'What were you doing?' Brynd asked.

'There is a small hospital near Port Nostalgia, which needed some assistance, and I offered my help. I'm not exactly doing a lot around here. I wanted to do my bit, so I've found a small role helping to nurse some of the injured from the war. Suffice to say it is rather different from the role I am used to . . .'

'It isn't fitting,' Rika hissed, 'for a girl of your position. Our blood must ensure it stays out of such affairs.' There was something vaguely animalistic about the way she tilted her head.

'Did you not do similar things as a priestess?' Brynd enquired. 'Surely Jorsalir clerics assisted in such matters?'

'They did,' Rika replied. 'That was then . . . But times have changed.'

'I'm certain the people of the city would appreciate the gesture,' Brynd continued, and Eir smiled proudly back.

Rika, on the other hand, looked as grim-faced as ever. Her expression lacked any of the serenity of her youth.

'When you have finished your next mission,' Rika said, 'I have commenced establishing laws and legislation so that we are set for rebuilding my father's Empire.'

'Now might not be the best time to mention this,' Brynd began. 'I'd hoped you would have wondered why there are so many of the Empire's people on the road. I thought you had been briefed.'

'No. No one has told me anything. Speak.'

Brynd told them about Villjamur. That it was no longer there. That citizens urgently needed to be evacuated, which is where he was going first thing in the morning.

Clearly distraught, Eir sat down with her head in her hands. 'All those people, dead . . .'

Rika declared, 'Which means we must rebuild as quickly as possible. We must harness the power of citizens to fight and to fund our efforts.'

Brynd wasn't sure if he agreed with her or if it confirmed in his mind how she was developing into a deeply inappropriate leader. There were none of the qualities he hoped for. Perhaps she had inherited her father's madness.

'I'm sorry to bring such news, but I'll do everything within my power to see our people are brought to safety. I've seen to it that enough resources – both in terms of personnel and rations – are being diverted accordingly. Ships have already set sail with cultist-enhanced grain, to cope with what may follow. I've dispatched messengers to settlements with major ports to release all seaworthy vessels to our cause. I don't quite know what to expect when we arrive, but hopefully all of this will catch up with us, and be enough to guarantee survival.'

'Shouldn't you be there already?' Rika demanded.

Brynd held his sigh from being too audible. Would the woman not give up? 'I'm investigating swifter methods of transport, Lady Rika.'

'Very good.' Rika gave no further indication of her mood.

'Look after yourself, commander,' Eir offered, with a look of concern in her eyes. 'You've done nothing short of help prop up the remnants of ... of this culture. Stay safe. We'd struggle without you.'

'I haven't scheduled any immediate plans to die just yet,' he replied with a wide grin. 'But thank you and, please, excuse me.'

He began to back out of the room.

When he reached the door, he heard Rika call out, 'See that you do get them back and spend as little as you can. We will need what money we have to allow full integration with Artemisia's people.'

'You're keen to see integration is smooth?' Brynd stepped back in the room slightly.

'We shall see that we keep our promise – I feel our people, too, must pay their fair share of their own future.'

You, in your new guise, will make not only a poor leader, but also a dangerous one, Brynd thought as he left the two sisters in peace. He continued along the dusty stone corridor, fuming. *With such reckless ideas, she'll be usurped within days. I can't allow that to happen . . .*

*

Tonight he could finally dispatch three soldiers on horseback to Factory 54 with the deposit of money to pay for the new Night Guard armour. What the group would do with such cash was anyone's guess, but by now he had realized these were not normal youngsters. They had acquired a knowledge beyond even some cultists. Perhaps because they were not like ordinary cultists, he actually started to believe what they said.

Brynd paced back and forth behind windows at the front of the Citadel, quietly fuming at what had become of the Empire. His entire life had been spent building it up – to see it trashed so quickly was frightening, he had to admit. The sound outside the window indicated his soldiers had returned. He looked down out of the window as they drew up at the front of the Citadel with a cart. Dozens of vast crates were stacked on top; the soldiers began unloading them and hauling them into the Citadel. He went to see the delivered product and a few other Night Guard soldiers sauntered in, curious as to what the commotion was about.

'What's in the boxes?' Brug asked.

'An experiment.' Brynd opened one of the crates. Inside was the soft glimmer of their new black armour, each piece – be it a helmet or a breastplate – bore a white, fist-sized seven-pointed star of the Empire. It was a nice touch.

Our very own shell . . . A shudder went through his body at the thought of it: that the things which contributed towards so many deaths would now become their new form of protection.

It was an impressive development from the previous version he'd seen; they had worked quickly, too. He lifted one of the lightweight pieces of armour and placed it over his own head and body. He adjusted the straps around his ribs. It fitted the contours of his body naturally and felt as if he was wearing nothing heavier than a waxed raincape.

'Looks impressive. What's it made from?' Brug asked, rapping the armour.

'Just a new alloy,' Brynd replied. 'Cultist enhanced – I've been doing a little digging into new suppliers. Here.' He handed one over to Brug who seemed braced for something heavier, and made an expression of surprise at its light weight. He marvelled at the texture, at the craftsmanship, and began testing it for rigidity. A few others filed in behind him, curious.

'Incredible,' Brug said. 'You can't even see any joins. This thing robust?'

'Why not try for yourself?' Brynd drew his sabre and offered it to Brug. Rubbing the back of his shaven head with one hand, he took the weapon, then stepped back to take a more formal combat stance. Brynd readied himself and tensed: just like Coren had done at the factory, Brug gave a tentative prod at first, poking the blade into the armour, then commenced with firmer strokes. Having placed his faith in the technology, Brynd merely smiled. Some of the others began laughing – even Brug, who eventually stopped his assault.

'What about more rigid tests?' Brug enquired.

'Give it a shot.'

Brynd lifted off his armour and placed it on a workbench. Several of them set about finding whatever blunt objects they could find in the vicinity and, with a breathtaking lack of logic, began to hammer down blows on the armour hoping it would bend or dent.

Nothing.

Hardly any scratches, not even a minor indentation. Despite the muscular enhancements of the Night Guard soldiers, despite their cultist-treated weapons, it seemed very little could make an impact.

Brynd used the moment of their quiet awe to inform them that they would be trialling it for tomorrow's mission. 'I would consider the conflict tomorrow to not be anywhere near as intense as the defence of Villiren.'

'Thank fuck for that,' someone muttered dryly. A few awkward chuckles spread about the room.

Brynd smiled. 'Though nothing's ever easy, as you all should realize by now. Now, this new material replaces our current body armour – it's made to similar specifications as the previous design, so there should be no problem there. I know normally we give things a go in training sessions, but I think the potential of this could be vast. The only difference you should find is that this is significantly lighter. You'll not tire as quickly and you'll have more mobility. You'll be able to take just as many blows, if not more.'

'Sounds like a no-brainer to me, commander,' said Tiendi, the only female member of the Night Guard. Her shoulder-length blonde hair seemed a stark contrast to the more aggressive-looking men around her, but she had been every bit their equal on the battlefield.

'Indeed,' he replied. 'I'm glad you think so too.'

'Only,' she continued, 'are these only kitted out for men? Some of us, you know, are crafted a little differently . . .'

A few chuckles. 'You'll be relieved to know there's one made with adequate room for your form. Now, are there any further questions about this or about the mission tomorrow?'

There were a few predictable queries regarding the briefing he had given them earlier. Further questions about tactics and formations. Brynd encouraged them to think of such things, to take a part in strategic planning and offer suggestions.

Managing soldiers was more than barking orders on the battlefield. These were the elite, the best fighters in the Boreal Archipelago, treated, trained and enhanced to be without peer, and they needed to be prepared.

'Right,' Brynd concluded, 'you should all get some sleep. We wake before sunrise. Supplies are all sorted – you don't need to worry about that. I don't anticipate us being on the ground for long – perhaps a week at the most if things go wrong – but I've already dispatched several units of Dragoons by longship. It will take them much longer to get there, but when they do they can relieve us and permit us to fall back. The mission is not territorial – I want to stress that. It is a rescue mission.'

Brynd watched them file out of the room, a mixture of expressionless faces and determination. No one at this level really looked forward to engaging in combat these days: at least, no one who had survived and remembered the battle for Villiren.

TEN

Fulcrom didn't think he could maintain optimism and reassure everyone for much longer. While the refugees and soldiers around him seemed calmed by his attitude, he believed in his own words and gestures less and less as the hours went by. People considered him a leader – many still called him 'investigator', others recognized him from Villjamur, though he wore no garb or symbols of the Inquisition and had left his medallion somewhere in the rubble of the city.

Even if he still wore it around his neck, it would represent nothing. Any previous structures seemed irrelevant now. Existence fell into two categories: those who could muck in and look after the others, and those who needed guidance. Some were using terms of leadership whenever they addressed him: boss, chief, sir. He waved them down and asked to be called simply Fulcrom, but they didn't stop doing it, and soon their expectations seemed to weigh down on his shoulders.

Their hopes became his burden.

He found joy in small things: children finding the time to play the odd game amidst these ruined lives. Or a puppy looking up from a basket being carried by an old man. A few entertainers engaged in spontaneous juggling acts, lifting the mood of the crowd. Storytellers pulled people in around campfires in order to forget about the evils that tormented them. There were rumels, like himself, and of all colour skins

– brown, black, grey – helping their human companions, and vice versa, without a single hint of racial tension. There were people from immensely wealthy backgrounds – lords and ladies, retired military officials, landowners – all reduced to poverty; the poor, trained by years in the caves, helped them out with advice on ways of looking after themselves. It was, Fulcrom had to admit, immensely touching.

Occasionally something might fly overhead, too quickly for him to discern, but it was enough to cause panic on the ground. Enormous gouts of people would surge towards the woodlands or throw themselves in soft snow, and all that happened was that more people would suffer from frostbite or pneumonia. And each day, a few more people would die.

*

Eventually, after many days trudging across the wilderness, two outriders returned to the convoy and brought their horses in alongside Fulcrom. A man and his daughter, both well-built individuals, were protected by wax raincapes and woollen hats.

'The coast, investigator, it's the coast,' the woman said. 'It's within reach. We'll make it before sunrise if we continue straight on through the night.'

'If we take rest it will be well into the next day,' Fulcrom called. 'That means we'll be exposed to attack for longer. We've been OK the last two nights, but I don't want to risk anything – we should expect an assault.'

'People are tired, investigator,' the man grunted. 'Should let 'em get some rest.'

Fulcrom shook his head. 'Many have been on transport, and of course they'll be fine through the night. But the others will have to manage. I don't want to risk the sky-city catching up with us. We've gone two nights without an attack, without any sightings. I'm not a paranoid man, outrider, but I think it pays to be cautious. Could you live with the guilt otherwise?'

'No, no,' the man said. 'My apologies.'

He watched the two outriders turn and ride into the distance before disappearing into a dark forest. Soon it began to snow – yet again. Within the walls of the city it never seemed so bad; out here, each fat flake seemed to press against his face with greater intensity.

*

The next hour was slow going. The dirt road crossed increasingly boggy terrain before leading them uphill. Fulcrom remained mightily unimpressed with this route.

'This hill goes on forever,' Lan mumbled from behind, squeezing her arms tighter as if to prompt him into speaking.

'Sorry,' Fulcrom replied glumly. 'It's the only route we can take. It's the most direct way to the coast. It's all we can do.'

'I wasn't complaining about your navigational skills, I was just saying,' Lan replied. 'What's wrong?'

'I just wish we could hurry, but we can't force people to go any faster. I want to get to the top of that hill as much as you do.'

'Will we see the coast when we're up there?' Lan wondered.

'I very much hope so,' Fulcrom replied. 'We should be able to see in every direction from the top, and maybe see how far behind they are, and if any more are on the ground.'

They went on horseback alongside the lead land-vehicle's front wheels, and far enough away so that the horse's immense hooves would not crush them.

That would not be a dignified end, after all I've been through, Fulcrom thought.

The convoy then moved through a landscape littered with spindly bushes and the occasional deep pool, which people stumbled into by accident. He pitied those that did, and pitied himself that he could not help everyone. There were thousands of people behind him; how could he choose to divert medical attention to everyone who stumbled or caught frostbite?

These must be the decisions of a god, something he did not feel comfortable with. Besides, one god-like figure among them seemed enough. Frater Mercury, the being who had been brought through to this world, seemed more like a statue than a god, as he perched on the lead horse. The figure simply stood regarding the vista: it must have been quite a view up there.

Upwards, slowly upwards.

Low clouds vanished leaving white wisps that trailed into the distance. Sunlight materialized, bright red and disarmingly warm at times. The crest of the hill was nearby, and Fulcrom decided to break free from his position and gallop towards it. Wind lashed his face, but he desperately wanted to get there. It seemed more important than anything.

The horizon lurched into view suddenly, the sky seemed brighter . . .

'We made it,' Lan said. 'We did it.'

Eventually, the hill flattened out to a plateau; the wind picked up even more, but this time it came with a heavy coastal tang of seaweed or salty air. Down below, perhaps a good mile away from where they were standing, the sea met the rocky shore. The surf was lively; great white waves licked their way towards land. For some distance there was nothing to see except for an old military fortification or two, which might provide some shelter for those who needed it the most, and several vast, still rock pools. Birds were hovering on wind currents above the sea, in the deep distance. On the downward slope there was more grass poking up beneath the melting snow, perhaps brought by warmer currents, but it was enough to make him hope the supposedly decades-long freeze might come to a premature end.

'What next?' Lan asked.

Fulcrom took another deep breath of the coastal air, clearing his mind. 'Well, I say we head down to the shore, then see about whether or not the land-vehicles can become sea-vehicles. As for the rest – we can either hope for more help from Frater Mercury, or we can scour the coastline for old sailing vessels. None of the outriders has found anything for us yet, but I've not given up hope. We really must set sail as soon as possible. We must.'

Turning his horse, Fulcrom examined the scene behind.

The closest it had been yet, the sky-city was a dark blot on the western horizon. It must have been just two or three miles from them at the most now, and from this new viewpoint its hideous glory was exposed to its fullest.

Twice the size of before, the thing seemed born from a baroque nightmare: loosely adhering to the shape of a sphere, it was as if a moon had made itself present just above the ground. Vast spiked pillars stuck out into the air around it and around them tiny black dots flew in slow circles – Fulcrom dreaded to think what they might be. Other structures appeared to be ribbed, or ribs themselves partially absorbed into the surface. There were glossy, bulbous things, and the shadows of grid-like rows, perhaps resembling some strange roads or streets. There were irregular flashes of light coming from within these hollows, containing explosions that defied logical thought. The sky itself appeared to veer away from its presence; instead of blue sky perfectly meeting its edges, there was a darker colour, smears and stains that were perhaps emissions from the city itself.

This thing – this monstrous city – had pursued them across an island, depositing bizarre life forms to attempt to murder those it had not slaughtered already. Fulcrom was not in awe of it any longer – he was furious at what it had done.

Beneath it, the tide of refugees flowed towards him, up the slope. The immense horses that pulled the land-vehicles came first, and he could see the vast grooves the wooden wheels had left across the distant landscape. Even if their progress had been swifter, they weren't exactly difficult to follow.

'We've made it this far,' he said, 'we've come so close.'

'It's not over yet though,' Lan said. That fierce determination had set in her eyes once again, filling him with positivity.

'I'm scared, Lan. I seem to have become the centre of this.' He gestured towards the refugees. 'This isn't what I'm used to.'

'It's not what any of us are used to.'

'You're right,' he replied. 'It's just ... what if we don't make it? If we get away from here, then what if we perish on the seas?'

'Then we perish knowing we damn well tried. The only other option is staying and certainly dying here, on land. We've come too far to do that. I refuse to, in fact. Now come on, let's—' Lan jerked her gaze away at the sound.

There was a tremendous ripping noise from the west and, up in the sky, possibly directly above the rearmost of the refugees, part of the sky-city began to detach itself.

Even though it was a good distance away, Fulcrom could see one of the vast, spiked pillars separate from the main structure and lower itself to the ground slower than if it was falling naturally. There was a strange, ambient silence now, like being in the centre of a storm. Eventually, it connected with the earth, landing like an arrowhead in what Fulcrom thought was marshy terrain. He waited for the sound to follow, some bass shudder to denote its presence on the ground, but nothing came. Again, a lingering silence. The wind now began to change direction. Sounds began to travel further, voices being carried on the breeze.

'What do you suppose *that* is?' Lan asked.

'Nothing that comes down from that thing,' Fulcrom said, 'has so far been beneficial to us. I have no idea what could be next.'

The descended structure lowered its other end, so that it

eventually lay flat, stark and black against the snow. Barbed and smouldering as if hot, something seemed to flip down on its right-hand side. Out of it spilled a dark tide.

'Warriors...' Fulcrom muttered. 'More of them. Dear *Bohr*, please, let there be no more.'

'Is this it then?' Lan asked. 'Is this where the trail ends? Do we just send out the order for everyone to flee wherever they can?'

'I don't know,' Fulcrom replied. 'We've faced attacks before. We've done all right. If people just disperse, they'll die.'

'We've never faced that many – just look at those numbers. They're filling up the whole landscape already.'

Lan wasn't wrong. Swarms of these dark things seemed to occupy the terrain quickly; some began to take the form of orderly rows and regiments, tightly packed and intimidating.

'It's hard to see, but this looks like a concentrated attack,' Fulcrom agreed. 'There's only one guy who can do anything about this.'

Fulcrom shouted and waved to get the attention of Frater Mercury, whose towering horse had now caught up with their own standard-sized animal. Eventually the god-thing stepped off the horse's back, drifted down and connected with the ground effortlessly, using one hand to stabilize himself. Frater Mercury's half-metal face shimmered in the afternoon sun; his cloak stirred in the onshore breeze. Fulcrom and Lan both dismounted, and then Fulcrom approached him.

I have been summoned, the voice said in Fulcrom's head. *Why?*

'Can't you see?' Fulcrom replied hesitantly, then jumped down from his horse, where he gestured to the sky-city's latest manoeuvre. 'They're coming for us. This is it for us. We'll die right here if you can't help.'

Frater Mercury turned his head for a moment then returned his gaze to Fulcrom. Whatever he was – if indeed he was a *he*, Fulcrom only had a priest's word for it – Fulcrom hoped he would be able to provide some assistance. 'What can you do to help us?'

What would you have me do for you?

'I'd like to see our people survive whatever is going to happen.'

We all die eventually, Frater Mercury said. *It is a freedom, of sorts.*

'I don't care for philosophy right now!' Fulcrom said with irritation. 'We've got tens of thousands of people coming up this slope and I want to see all of them live a little longer. Now, do you have any idea what is going to happen?'

Yes, Frater Mercury said.

'What?' Fulcrom demanded.

Slaughter is what will happen. But one gets used to it. I have seen enough for dozens of generations. I am indifferent to it.

'I refuse to *get fucking used* to it,' Fulcrom said despairingly. He felt Lan's presence now, as she held his hand – a gentle, soothing touch. 'I don't know what your plans are exactly, but it is *my* responsibility to get these people to safety,' he continued, ignoring the fact that he had previously thought otherwise. 'Can you provide anything – anything at all – to help me do this? You've done it before, but this threat seems huge. Whatever you need from this world we can help you – I'll do my best, for what it's worth, but please . . .'

Silence. If Frater Mercury understood Fulcrom's words, he showed no sign of it.

'Don't forget, I did help to see you brought into this world. Why did you come anyway if it wasn't to help us?'

To die, Frater Mercury said mysteriously. *For freedom. You have seen my tricks, as you call them, and you wish for many more. Think, dear rumel, what it is like to have millions of people demand such miracles again. It starts off very simple. The task of seeing that a child does not die of an illness.*

The requests become larger after this: governments offer their allegiance if I can provide tools to create their worlds. I oblige and find myself locked in endless, endless councils and must sit through infinite pleas for assistance. Over the millennia, war comes – on a scale which sees my creations rise up against each other – my own children fighting against each other. The side I choose, the side of peace, is outnumbered vastly. Ultimately my children die. And then the world begins to end – slowly, dully, predictably, when time finally runs out. What use is any of it? Who can tell.

I have become imprisoned by the neediness of my creations. Yes, I seek freedom, too, but I first wish to see the landscapes I helped to populate. I would like to know how my … my work has flourished in this realm before I see to it that things are ended.

'Your work,' Fulcrom interrupted, 'as you put it, is about to be fucking wiped from existence soon. Is that how you wanted to see it? If you did indeed create these things, is this what you hoped would happen? You have the choice now to not let many of your so-called children die in a genocide. This is not dignified.'

Dying rarely is.

'Please,' Fulcrom said.

After a lengthy silence, Frater Mercury added, *There is an endearing persistence in your mind, rumel, though it is a story I have heard many times before.*

'Look, all I ask is that our people get the chance to move east across the seas,' Fulcrom pleaded. 'There we can seek our own military personnel or somehow organize ourselves naturally. It at least gives us the time for a fighting chance. We didn't ask for this,' Fulcrom waved to the airborne threat, 'this is something that has been brought out of nowhere. I would not have so many people die at once. If you don't like making decisions any more, let me make this for you.'

Frater Mercury seemed to consider these words – or that's what Fulcrom hoped. He looked again to the swarms of the enemy that had extended so quickly and so far across the landscape.

What would your wishes be? Frater Mercury asked. *You who have designated yourself leader of these people. I know you feel the* burden – *it is a burden, is it not? – so please, tell me, what do you first require?*

Fulcrom's heart skipped a beat. He had to think quickly. What was the most urgent thing, protection at the rear or seeing that they could leave the island? *Think, man*, he told himself.

'The land-vehicles,' Fulcrom said. 'I want them to travel through water, first, but I want more of them. I want to get all our people over this hill, down to the shore and simply to carry on eastwards. Is there any way you can do this before it's too late? Can we get more vehicles to do this? We need to be quick, because we both saw the power of this thing. All we're asking for is a little more time.'

It is possible, Frater Mercury replied. He spun then walked down the slope.

'Now what?' Lan asked. She was now on foot, her arms folded in the chill of the coastal wind.

A noise in the distance, like a horn: the swarms began to move forwards at the rear of the convoy. Fulcrom could see in the clarity of the late afternoon sun how the refugees from Villjamur and Jokull were being attacked.

'*Now what?*' Lan repeated. 'What's he going to do?'

'I don't know,' Fulcrom said.

'We should try to fight,' Lan said. 'Defend the people we can. See if some can escape in time – or until this Frater Mercury decides to help.'

'You're right,' Fulcrom said. 'I'll give the order.'

They began to move towards their mare, watching the crowds begin to move past them and over the slope.

'We'll probably get killed before nightfall,' Lan said nonchalantly. 'I'm fine with that, but before that happens, I just wanted . . . I never got a chance to say thank you – for giving me something I've never had before.'

Fulcrom placed a finger on her lips. 'It isn't a charity I'm running. I'm in love with you, Lan, or had you not noticed? Now then.' Fulcrom placed his foot in the stirrup and levered himself up. He offered to take Lan's hand, even though she didn't need it. She just tuned in to her internal powers and leapt up effortlessly.

*

After giving instructions for those at the head of the convoy to continue downhill towards Frater Mercury, Fulcrom and Lan galloped down the line, passing the miserable and concerned faces until they met up with clusters of soldiers. Fulcrom had been careful in planning their route to navigate close to the few military installations, outposts and training camps that were scattered throughout the wilderness. The further they travelled, the more soldiers they accumulated. Granted it had not been much, perhaps a couple of hundred troops here and there, but that was better than nothing. Just as importantly, Fulcrom had located a few cultists who had lost most of their relics, but still clutched a few items that might come in useful – and now was just such a time to try.

As Fulcrom and Lan dashed down the vast line, he gave the orders for any soldiers, cultists and anyone who could bear arms to follow. Those on horseback came immediately and the rest progressed quickly on foot, brave and determined.

Even from this distance, Fulcrom could already see the horrors that lay ahead.

The swarms that had spilled from the alien structure were individual warriors all right, but they looked like nothing he had ever seen before, not even what came down into Villjamur. Their armour looked more like black shells . . .

These are no ordinary creatures.

His small group of defenders eventually arrived at the rear of the convoy, where the black things were lining up to face them. The sun was sliding from the sky, over the distant hills and behind the enemy. The sunlight was right in Fulcrom's eyes. *Yet another disadvantage.*

He estimated that perhaps four or five thousand of the black creatures had now assembled.

'It's horrific,' Lan breathed. 'Look at them all.'

'I'd rather not,' Fulcrom replied, dismounting from his horse.

'I'll see to the people's safety again,' Lan said from the saddle. 'Do you want me to stay and fight? Wherever you want me, I'll go.'

'No, do what you do best, help people, and be careful,' Fulcrom replied, holding her fingertips for a little longer. 'Make sure everyone gets their chance to get up that hill and out to sea.'

Lan smiled softly and nodded, before riding towards the last few hundred people.

No kiss goodbye. No longing embrace. To do so would have seemed to tempt fate.

'I hope that's not the last I'll see of you,' he whispered.

Remnants of the City Guard, Dragoons and Regiments of Foot began to adopt their pre-planned formations, which was essentially two standard lines of defence.

They stood now near the base of the hill, which flattened out to a vast stretch of abandoned farmland hardened by the snow and ice. There were two largely dead forests either side of these fields, up on slightly higher ground. Aside from that, the terrain was even, just a barren, featureless stretch of land. It would make the fighting straightforward, though Fulcrom didn't know whether or not that was a good thing. He marched over to a band of cultists, seven of them who had remained loyal to the cause of the convoy, united by their homelessness. Some had brought crude catapults, and such weapons were very welcome right now. The cultists began assembling their makeshift war gear on the spot. One had a sack of relics which she brought down from a nearby cart;

another began dragging their catapults – three in all – into a neat row.

They were like none Fulcrom had seen before – like enormous wooden crossbows, the height of a human or rumel, and each sitting on a two-limbed stand. They didn't look as if they should stay upright, but they did.

Fulcrom moved around behind the cultists offering a simple suggestion. 'I want you to use these catapults as heavily as is possible. Show no mercy. Don't hold up. Give everything you've got.'

'Ballistas, mate,' one of them said. 'They're ballistas, not catapults. And we'll do our best. We've got a few hundred munitions, mate. All depends on the torsion springs mind – these are pretty old. Still, should do the trick, eh?'

'Yes,' Fulcrom replied, having no idea.

He watched them load up with munitions and aim them towards the enemy lines. In order to get a better view of the scene, Fulcrom climbed up onto the nearby cart. The few hundred Empire soldiers had formed a row now, protecting the rear of the convoy – it might not be much, Fulcrom thought, but it was at least a layer between them and the refugees.

Behind, the cultists had lined up the three ballistas and were now making minor adjustments to the mechanisms, before aiming them at the enemy.

It looked futile, Fulcrom had to admit. 'What's the furthest you've ever shot one of those things?'

''Bout half a mile at best,' one replied. 'Why, how far away are the fuckers?'

'I'd say nearly half a mile,' Fulcrom said.

'Right you are, chief. Want us to fire?'

'Might as well,' Fulcrom said.

'Uh, investigator?' one of the cultists was pulling at his legs. Fulcrom looked down and then up to where the man was pointing. In the sky, on the other side this time, there were yet *more* forms – drifting down towards the other side of the convoy about a mile or so away.

Fulcrom held his hands over his head. 'Shit!' he shouted despairingly. 'What now? Are we not hunted enough already?'

'Fucked if you do, fucked if you don't, eh?' the cultist said.

'Well, I don't know about you,' Fulcrom said, 'but I'm not going down without taking down some of that lot. You with me?'

'That's the spirit, chief,' the cultist laughed and returned to the others. 'Ready, lads?'

'Release your munitions,' Fulcrom ordered.

The cultists each pulled a lever at the back of the ballista and Fulcrom barely had time to notice the munitions launch off with a *thwack* into the distance. They rocketed in huge arcs and, for a moment, Fulcrom thought they were going to fall short, but they carried on going and eventually connected with the ground. Something flashed: a moment later came the sound of explosion. A disproportionately large purple fireball began spreading and smoke bubbled and billowed upwards into the sky.

Fulcrom felt his spirits soar. Soldiers in the front two rows were visibly excited.

'Not bad, chief, eh?' one of the cultists said, slapping another on the back. 'Right, next one.'

Another set of munitions were released and sent arcing through the sky. They closed the distance gracefully, before once again causing fireballs. This time Fulcrom saw enemy numbers caught up in the upward-billowing inferno and he felt the cart shake beneath him.

Those things are horrific, he thought; for a moment he felt deep sympathy for whoever was on the opposing side. But then something hardened inside of him. These repugnant things deserved everything that could be thrown at them.

Another munition, another fireball; four, six, ten, and still they kept coming – the cultists showed little mercy, but the black-armoured enemy continued to march, through the smoke, towards their Jamur lines.

It's the waiting that's the worst part of all this, Fulcrom thought as he drew his sword.

Despite the munitions that thundered into them, back over their first rows, and thinning them out randomly, there was no stopping the sheer flow of . . . creatures. Fulcrom felt a lump in his throat. The creatures were running now, not marching, great swarms of them approaching the base of the long and gentle slope. Soldiers in front of him readied themselves.

It was not difficult to predict the bloodbath that would occur, but this was the right thing to do – to die here. If they could hold out long enough for as many of the refugees to make it out to sea, if Frater Mercury had managed to develop some way of crossing the water, then thousands of lives would be saved.

Yes, that's not a bad way to go, Fulcrom concluded.

A flicker of movement overhead caught his eye. 'What the hell is that?'

Two, six, ten and more, enormous reptilian creatures – with a wingspan of dozens of feet – swooped down and lowered themselves onto the field of battle, directly between the Jamur soldiers and their enemy. The gargantuan beasts bore giant wooden crates on their backs and, as soon as they had landed and stooped lower, the crate doors burst back: soldiers were revealed inside, gripping on to ropes; they filed out and jumped down onto the ground and drew their swords . . .

'They're wearing Empire colours!' one of the cultists screamed.

There must have been over forty of these enormous reptiles now on the field of battle, each of them deploying Imperial reinforcements, and more were landing by the minute, more swooping down from the sky.

Where had they come from?

'It's the Night Guard!' the convoy's defenders shouted. 'The fucking Night Guard are here!'

The reptiles, having released their cargo, one by one extended their wings and launched themselves back into the air; strong downdraughts of wind whipped across the soldiers on the ground.

Fulcrom could barely believe the scene: thousands of the Empire's soldiers were now standing between the convoy and the enemy. Spearheading this new assault were the Empire's finest warriors, the Night Guard and, at the very front, stood the famous albino commander.

In the distance, the enemy had paused, as if to assess their new situation. The Empire soldiers began beating on their shields like tribal warriors – it was like nothing Fulcrom had ever witnessed. The air was now filled with a new confidence, a relief, a knowledge that this was not yet over.

A shaven-headed man wearing the black uniform of the Night Guard ran over to the convoy troops in front of Fulcrom to announce what was going on and what would shortly happen, and what would be required should the lines fall. His voice was bass and authoritative. A few people turned and pointed towards Fulcrom, and the soldier nodded his acknowledgement.

'The enemy we face are called Okun,' the Night Guard soldier announced. 'They are brutal, but we have defeated their kind once already.'

'Thank you for coming!' another soldier shouted.

'Aye, they were about to charge and kill us, no doubt.'

'Well, we're here now,' the Night Guard soldier replied, grinning. 'Yeah, that's right – we stand together with you.' He gestured with his glimmering sword to the distance and shouted, 'And we've come to fuck them up! Now are you with us? Are you prepared to die to save your people?'

A cheer went up and, seemingly satisfied with the noise, the man returned to the elite regiment.

The albino commander was now giving some orders, though Fulcrom couldn't discern what. There were movements of the Empire troops, a discreet reorganization. Units began to file off in different directions, giving further breadth to the defence. The ground thundered. Rows and lines became staggered, formations took more complexity. Archers fell in behind the Night Guard and Dragoons, and stood now just before the original convoy defence, two vast rows of them with longbows. The speed with which they had organized themselves was impressive.

Then it became clear that there weren't just the Imperial soldiers here: there were humans wearing uniforms that Fulcrom didn't think were part of the Empire, clothing that was more primitive yet far more ornate, and they looked as if they meant business.

And, remarkably, there were beings of another species entirely.

There were creatures, bipedal, bull-headed, and very tall – hundreds of them, armed with spears and round shields. They took their positions at the very front of the Empire's defence, ahead of the Night Guard. There were green, lizard-like things armed to the teeth with a variety of weapons, and they began stalking their way along the flanks.

The commander shouted more orders and Fulcrom's gaze was then drawn once again to the archers, who nocked arrows, each with a fat flame at the tip; and there was a deeply unnatural chemical smell that drifted towards him on the breeze. He had no idea what was making that fire, but these weren't any standard arrows, that much was certain.

In the distance, the enemy commenced their charge.

Everyone waited.

The commander held up his sabre.

Half a mile's distance eventually became just a few hundred yards and the commander lowered his arm: hundreds of flaming arrows were suddenly loosed and slipped through the air . . .

They plummeted down on the enemy, clattering against their shields or armour and setting off hundreds of small explosions. The thickness of the enemy's charge diminished noticeably, and another wave of arrows was lined up then without hesitation loosed into the air.

Again they hailed down on the enemy; again they thinned out the ranks. Black forms were sent collapsing to the ground. There was enough time for one final wave of arrows and explosions before the archers hauled their bows over one shoulder and marched out quickly to the flanks of the formation.

Closer still, the advance of the Okun was creating a thunder that vibrated through the earth.

Now the bull-men readied themselves to charge into the enemy, tipping their spear-tips forward; they galloped onto the battlefield, closing the gap towards the thinned and broken lines, their speed phenomenal, then they ploughed into the advancing Okun with a sickeningly loud noise, smashing the black forms down, stomping on their bodies, slamming spears into faces.

While they rammed themselves forward, a few of the Okun managed to find gaps in the line and filtered through.

The commander was marching up and down the neat line of the Night Guard who now had their weapons drawn. A large humanoid suddenly lumbered alongside them, blue-skinned and holding two wide blades that seemed so large a normal human would have struggled to lift them. This figure posed nonchalantly next to the commander, who showed an acknowledgement of her presence with his sword-tip.

The Night Guard lifted their shields to their chests, and the Dragoons followed suit. They took a fighting stance.

Fulcrom hoped they would hold the line but, surprisingly, the Night Guard began to edge forward while the Dragoons held the tight row behind. Spearsmen stepped in and prodded the tips of their weapons through, and the Dragoons locked their shields to form a vast, spiked wall.

The blue figure strolled forward into the arena of battle, showing no knowledge of Imperial decorum. As the Okun approached, the blades began to whirl in its hands and with remarkable grace it cleaved into the enemy as if it was a sport.

At the same time the Night Guard broke away from their formation and engaged with the enemy in small clusters with swift, life-stopping moves; their blades sliced through the air at a ferocious velocity, finding postures and styles that Fulcrom had never thought possible. The speed and grace was breathtaking; they made warfare look like an art form. Some of the soldiers fought individually, each one surrounded by two or three Okun, yet still the enemy creatures seemed outmanoeuvred.

It was only when they were this close, some just a hundred yards away from Fulcrom, that he could see the Okun for what they were: grotesque creations, something between a hominid and crustacean. He shivered at the thought of having to fight one, yet here the Night Guard were making it look effortless.

Still some of the Okun broke through and proceeded towards the Dragoon shield-wall. The soldiers held their line firm as the Okun clattered into their armour. Fulcrom couldn't see what happened – his attention was drawn to the air yet again. Arrows started to sail over their heads from different angles as the archers on the flanks fired randomly. The explosions thinned out the enemy's next assault wave, stopping any chance that they could create much of an impact.

Having slaughtered the first wave of the Okun, the Night Guard regrouped. The very front line of Dragoons peeled off from the main combat zone, filtering back through the rows; a fresh line stepped forward. Fulcrom smiled at the efficiency of it all – those soldiers who had stepped from the front had their wounds tended to by military medics or cultists.

As the sun slipped lower, fading from the day, the Okun came again in dribs and drabs and small, vulnerable bands. The initial threat of their sheer mass had been nullified. It seemed a half-hearted effort at best and they were dispatched with the same efficiency as before. Row after row of Dragoons piled forward, seizing on islands of Okun, whilst the Night Guard themselves continued to fight like beings from another world.

The albino commander led from the very front, his presence on the battlefield unmistakable. Pale face caked in blood, and shifting back and forth with the agility of a dancer, he hacked and slashed his sabre into the gaps in the Okun shell, striking more vulnerable flesh. He exuded a confidence that Fulcrom admired and envied. All of Fulcrom's fear had gone.

The adrenalin rush had dissipated as the minutes rolled by. He couldn't tell precisely when it happened, that the threat was pushed back to the point where it was no longer a threat. Darkness came rather suddenly. Fulcrom looked up and noticed the sky-city had drifted slightly northwards, perhaps having hoped there would be nothing left here to see. A moment or so later a cheer started, somewhere at the far end of the defensive line, which progressed towards him.

Euphoria . . .

ELEVEN

'They tell me you're in charge around here,' said Commander Brynd Lathraea. He wiped his face with a small rag, leaving a few smears of blood across his cheeks, but it was better than before. He was a handsome man, remarkably pale-skinned, with eyes so dazzling they unsettled Fulcrom at first. There were other soldiers in the distance, milling around, and signs of order were returning to the refugee convoy.

'I doubt you can call it *being in charge*,' Fulcrom replied with a dry chuckle. 'Most of this has seemed so completely beyond my control.'

'It often feels like that, doesn't it? But I can assure you that's quite natural. The skill comes from eventually discerning the planned chaos from actual chaos. I've heard remarkably good things about you. It seems that without your leadership we may not have had any people left to defend this evening.'

Fulcrom didn't know what to say. Had he succeeded? It didn't feel like much of a success.

'Do you think the Okun will return?' he asked.

'Not at night, I'd say,' the commander replied. 'We found from the defence of Villiren that their military activities took place during the day. I can't work out their response to daylight – perhaps it has something to do with their biology – but such things ultimately work in our favour. Though I cannot vouch for any of their kin.'

Fulcrom nodded.

'Walk with me,' the commander requested. They turned and began trudging back up the slope, military personnel surrounding them. There were quite a few stretchers being carried to the hastily set-up medical tents with several dozen injured soldiers, some of them clearly not human.

'Now tell me, Investigator Fulcrom – what the hell happened to Villjamur?'

'When were you last there?' Fulcrom asked. 'A lot changed, even before we were forced to flee.'

'I left before the Empress and her sister were set up for a crime they did not commit and were due to be executed on the city wall. They escaped. Urtica became Emperor.'

'Is that the official story now?' Fulcrom asked. 'That they were in the clear?'

Brynd nodded. 'As much as these things still matter, yes. We're annexed from the Empire now,' he continued, looking around, 'but that is a situation which seems out of date considering there seems little from which to be annexed.'

'That's putting it mildly.'

Fulcrom gave as accurate an account as possible, starting with Urtica's crackdown on law and order. 'In the Inquisition, we thought it would be good – that we'd have powers to do our job thoroughly. The crackdown went rather far, though. The military upped their patrols on the streets and started harassing those from Caveside. Crime, ironically, started to rise.'

'Soldiers shouldn't be on the streets like that,' the commander observed. 'They're not trained to deal with civilians in that way.'

'I agree with you on that. Well, given the tensions in the city, things were bound to escalate. A woman called Shalev arrived in the city and organized the Cavesiders. She came from the cultist isle and she was remarkably efficient in targeting structures of power. The rebels became so efficient, in fact, that the Emperor panicked. He was beginning his programme of repairing the city and didn't want a revolution on his streets – and so he created the Villjamur Knights.'

'And they would be . . . ?'

'Cultist-designed heroes. I was in charge of them, as it happens. There were only three of them and they were each given special powers to help fight crime. A little like the Night Guard but more specialized. Only one survives now, and her name is Lan. At the same time the underground movement had swelled to a point where tensions were simply too much. I've heard talk that there was an attempt on the Emperor's life and that he was assassinated, but that all became overshadowed by the presence of the sky-city.'

'Indeed . . .' the commander said. 'Do you know where it came from?'

'I don't know,' Fulcrom continued. 'One moment there was nothing but the usual grey skies, the next it was just there – dropping creatures into the city and massacring people.'

'You seem to have handled it well,' the commander observed. 'Getting everyone out here like this, getting them all moving – that kind of thing isn't simple.'

Fulcrom grimaced. 'It just . . . happened, really. No one knew what to do. I've not even mentioned Frater Mercury yet.'

'Frater who?'

*

The man who invented the rules – you'll see.

That's what the rumel investigator had said – the man who invented the rules, and the man who could probably save them – if he chose to do so. This, then, would be the person Artemisia mentioned back at the Citadel, the one so important to their world.

Brynd walked with the affable investigator up the slope, a little exhausted now despite the fact that the battle had been relatively simple compared with Villiren. His mind was thoroughly engaged in processing the mess that the Jamur Empire had become. Although a staggering number of people had died, more deaths had been avoided, and he couldn't help but feel satisfied that the battle had proven successful. The Okun had been comprehensively defeated, thanks to combining forces with Artemisia's people – an important gesture. Also, his new armour was everything he had hoped for.

When they crested the hill, Brynd stared in awe at the scene below. Enormous, strange vessels were drifting out to sea, the crude, flat outlines more akin to floating islands than ships, and how they were moving without sails was anyone's guess.

'That is what Frater Mercury does,' Fulcrom said enthusiastically next to him. The relief was clear on the rumel's face. 'He changes all the rules.'

'What are they?' Brynd asked.

'They *were* land-vehicles,' Fulcrom said.

'We had reports of such things, but *what* are they?'

'So far as I can tell, exactly that – they're moving vehicles crafted from the fabric of the earth itself – quite literally. Frater Mercury – the man, being, *thing* I mentioned – possesses some qualities that we can't fathom.'

Fulcrom then explained the emergence of this being as the result of a priest coming to Villjamur, brought through worlds by means of some arcane ritual.

'What happened to the priest?'

Fulcrom shrugged. 'Gone. Presumably killed during the events in Villjamur.' Fulcrom hesitated before continuing. 'The priest said some strange things, about our history not being as we believe it to be.'

'Yes, I know,' Brynd replied, looking around cautiously. 'We have figures from the other realm who can confirm this was the case.'

'These figures,' Fulcrom said, 'will they be looking for Frater Mercury?'

'Yes, I'd say that's very likely. That will need to happen before the next phase.'

'What's that going to be?' Fulcrom asked. 'The next phase.'

Brynd turned back to face the sky-city, which was defined only by the absence of starlight. 'We'll need to take that thing down and wipe out anything it's brought to ground and that does not wish to exist peacefully. There are no gentle solutions, and very little room for negotiations. At the same time, we have to accept that we are going to have to share our world with other species. There is plenty of land, many islands that are sparsely populated, but I can't imagine it's going to be a smooth journey.'

'How do you plan to take down the sky-city?' Fulcrom asked. 'It's already obliterated Villjamur.'

'First, we're going to complete the evacuation, get ourselves to safety and, once we have time to build up enough of an opposition, then we can begin to consider our real options.'

'In the meantime,' Fulcrom said, 'we lose the island of Jokull?'

'The Empire may have collapsed, but we still have the people,' Brynd said diplomatically. As he looked to the future, he had already lost his emotional attachments to the concept of the old Empire. 'Life as we know it has changed and a new world will form – for better or worse. We need people to shape these events, however – people like you.'

Fulcrom turned to watch the ships again. 'I've never really contemplated what I'd do next. Getting off the island was all I could think about for every waking hour. How could I help?'

'There will need to be a force similar to the Inquisition – even for a transitional period. Not just in Villiren, where we're currently based, but the new plans would need defining for further afield. And I tend not to trust many people from Villiren.'

'I've heard it's a pretty fast and loose city.'

Brynd laughed. 'Yes, you could say that. And that was *before* the war, so imagine how problematic things are now. No, now I'll need good investigators, and a different form of street policing. We're carving our own future at the moment – but you should be a part of that, given your achievements and leadership skills.'

A figure bounded towards them, descending from above; Brynd tensed and moved for his sabre.

'It's all right,' Fulcrom said. 'It's Lan, one of the Villjamur Knights – the group I told you about. She's the last remaining one.'

Brynd examined the newcomer: she was lithe and athletic, with a strong, overgrown dark fringe and an outfit as black as night. There was a strange symbol on the front, now muddied: a white cross set within a circle. 'A Villjamur Knight,' Brynd muttered, and nodded. 'Fulcrom here has been telling me about what happened in Villjamur. So you fought crime on behalf of Urtica?'

'Something like that,' she said with a half smile, and he knew by her sarcasm that she wasn't some pre-programmed Urtican puppet. Lan gave them a report on what was happening with the civilian movements. 'There are now twenty craft transporting roughly two or three thousand people.'

'How are they travelling?' Fulcrom asked. 'What's taken the place of the horses?'

'Nothing,' Lan said and then laughed gently. 'The horses are walking on the surface of the sea – it was incredible to witness. They seemed tentative at first but whatever Frater Mercury did to them – or the sea, or both – they're now happily treading on the surface as if it was sand. We've had to space the vehicles wide enough apart so that the waves created don't soak the people. There're enough freezing to death already.'

Brynd nodded and gestured to the horizon. 'I've seen to it that every seaworthy vessel is sailing to this island to help with the evacuation,' he replied. 'Garudas are helping with their navigation – we didn't quite know where the exit point would be – but we should have a few thousand fishing boats, longships, trade ships, whatever we can get our hands on, all landing ashore over the next day or two.'

'Will that be quick enough?' Fulcrom enquired.

Brynd frowned. 'I just don't know. The dragons are transporting another few thousand soldiers so we'll have more troops ashore before sunrise. We can form several lines of defence, to ensure the safety of the civilian population. We're doing what we can.'

'I think the people will be more than grateful,' Lan said. 'Now, I should really get back – there were a few fights over who should be evacuated first. You would have thought people could stick together in times like this. Anyway, I have to make sure more conflicts don't break out.'

'Excellent suggestion,' Brynd said.

Lan touched Fulcrom's arm, and he smiled back at her. She turned and jogged into the distance. Brynd noted those final tender gestures Fulcrom had made towards her, and questioned their status.

'We are partners,' Fulcrom confessed, 'in more than one sense.'

Brynd nodded and thought no more of the comment. He was relieved simply to have met two decent individuals. The future would need people like them.

*

Hours later, sometime between midnight and dawn, the sea-vehicles returned to the shore. Someone clattered a crude copper bell and started shouting in an attempt to rouse people from their slumber, and for the next wave of evacuees to assemble. There weren't enough craft for the job – people just had to wait.

Brynd didn't think it was possible to sleep out here anyway, what with this breeze moaning loudly as it drifted along the coast. A salt tang lingered in the air, and smoke from wood fires was still pungent. He watched in disbelief as the immense horses approached the shore. On the back of one of them stood a much smaller figure, which he assumed was Frater Mercury.

Presently, civilians began surging towards the shore. The tide was out, and many began slipping on the seaweed-caked pebbles. Brynd walked over to a unit of senior soldiers nearby, where he gave orders for a few hundred of the Dragoons to try to organize the most vulnerable – the elderly, the very young, mothers – to evacuate first. Anyone who could last another night was ordered to stay.

There were impromptu farewells between families, and Brynd found the sudden, touching scenes actually moved him – which was surprising, given his recent lack of emotional engagement. Perhaps it was because he was back on Jokull, or perhaps because he had seen just how vulnerable a population could be.

Fulcrom joined him to confirm that all was going well with the next phase of the evacuation, and that any signs of trouble were beginning to fade.

'Quite a sight, isn't it?' Brynd asked.

'Yeah, it's certainly something,' Fulcrom said with a wry grin. 'Especially now it's less of a burden and the responsibility's yours I can finally enjoy the sight.'

'The burden becomes less of an issue after a few years of doing it. You learn to filter out those kinds of thoughts, for better or worse. Besides, whatever we do someone will end up being hurt or angry with us.'

'How do you know what the beneficial choices really are? Will there be democratic choices in this new society? We all know the Council elections were a joke.'

'What would you have in its place? Tell me – you're someone who has worked with the law for all your life.

Where does it *fail* people?' Brynd gestured with an out-stretched arm towards the evacuees.

'It's not really my place to say, commander.'

'I've spent a lot of my years listening to people who have *no idea* about how things work on the ground. You've been there, and seen a great deal of turmoil. You saw what happened in the last days of Villjamur. I'm only interested in an opinion, man – you won't hang for it.'

'This is a new regime then,' Fulcrom replied. The rumel appeared to think about the question for a moment, but Brynd didn't hurry him. Eventually, he said, 'Ideally you'd have representatives for the people. I would say that, without a shadow of a doubt, the serious events in Villjamur would not have happened if people had had some say in the matters that affected them. You could have neighbourhood represen-tatives, perhaps, especially if there are going to be communi-ties of different species. All the law books in Villjamur were geared up around protecting land or property in one form or another; presumably when you're drawing new lines on a map that won't be so easy. They'll need someone to champion their concerns. They'll want land of their own, too, to make a living from.'

Brynd absorbed the sage words of the rumel investigator. Brynd's time had been spent enforcing a type of law on people in far-off cities, and he had seen the difficulties and scepticism and failures first-hand; the investigator had experi-ence of what happened when a society looked inward, which was the direction Brynd was now having to contemplate.

'Forgive me for bringing this up, commander – our discus-sions are rather high level. I hadn't expected to be discussing the future of the Empire – or whatever's left of it. I always assumed the Night Guard's concerns were military strategy. I think what I'm asking is, who's leading us and who gets to decide how to run a new regime?'

'Empress Rika,' Brynd replied curtly.

Fulcrom nodded and appeared to contemplate her reclamation of the throne of the Empire. 'You don't seem too impressed with that.'

'Your powers of observation are acute, investigator,' Brynd said.

'It always seems odd that our history is populated with kings or emperors – or in this case, Empress.'

'She's not strictly an empress any more,' Brynd said, 'for as you can see, there's very little left of the Empire's main structures.'

Dawn broke, shadows flittered away as the first light of day rose up from behind, lighting the remarkable view before them.

TWELVE

Eir, former Stewardess of the Jamur Empire, sister of Empress Rika, found herself in unusual settings for a lady of her status. The rooms weren't exactly inviting – the structure had been built using large stones from a collapsed monastery, though apparently the architects had not thought about bringing many of the windows with them. Light came only from cressets, candles and fireplaces. Just a few decorations were littered about the place – a few religious trinkets and some donated rugs that gave off a bad smell, which was only disguised by the worse odours from dried blood or buckets of urine.

Using a cloth soaked in a water and oil mixture, she washed around a man's wounds; they hadn't become infected, thanks to the quick work of one of the nurses, so it probably looked far worse than it actually was.

The man smiled through the pain as she dabbed the longest wound that stretched up along his ribs. Water trickled down his torso and he shivered. One of the other nurses briefed Eir earlier: he had become injured in a fight when he intervened in a quayside skirmish. Two women had been assaulted by a gang of youths, and he had stepped in to scare them off. The youths overwhelmed him: two knife wounds under his ribcage had freed him of a lot of blood, but he had been incredibly fortunate to gain the attention of some people nearby, who knew about the hospital.

'You have good luck on your side, if you managed to find yourself here,' Eir said softly.

He looked at her, smiled, and then his gaze drifted to the wall behind her. 'Well, miss, some might argue that my luck was not so good that I was knifed in the first place.' He was one of the more polite patients here at the hospital – a pleasant-natured forty-year-old, who seemed honest and decent, and that was the most any nurse could hope for.

'I don't suppose it's too much to hope for a few more logs in the stove?' he asked.

'I'll see if one of the nurses can bring some more in,' Eir replied.

He glanced up at her again. 'I've not seen you around here much.'

'No,' Eir replied. 'I don't get the chance to volunteer that much.'

'It's nice that anyone can really,' he said, and laid back on the bed. 'You don't look much like a nurse.'

'And you don't look much like a hero,' she replied dryly.

He laughed. 'No, I guess you never quite know that you'll be the one to step up when you need to.'

Eir placed the pan of infused water to one side and began to rinse the cloth of blood. This was only her third time spent working here, and already it had not panned out quite as she thought it would. For some reason she had imagined rows and rows of beds, clean sheets, fresh water, and nurses tending thankful patients. The reality was starkly different: makeshift beds; reeking donated blankets; water that had to be boiled from melted snow; rats scurrying along the edges of the room before disappearing into shadows; and patients, when they were not being sick or coughing up blood, were either ungrateful, drunk, or the men leered at the nurses and tried to touch them up when they got a chance. Luckily Eir had not so far been affected; she kept a dagger in her boot and, thanks to Randur's teachings, knew how to use it.

Perhaps things would change. Before Brynd had left for deployment on Jokull, he had told Eir that, because of her request, he had secured a large loan from the banks to fund this hospital. What was more, they would be able to create hundreds of new jobs as well as serve the injured and sick. He said they might be able to build even bigger hospitals – because he would rather have a healthy working population that could help rebuild the city, than more bodies to heap on the pyres.

*

She headed out of the ward to find Randur, to see what he was up to. Today was the first time he had accompanied her to the hospital.

The corridors were surprisingly airy, a contrast to the dark and depressing wards themselves, and the tall windows facing towards the east brought in deceptively warm sunlight on the stone. She passed a few other nurses on her walk, and none of them could fully accept that Jamur Eir – of the royal lineage – wanted to help out. It had made socializing and blending in difficult. However, she had managed, so far, to keep news of her identity away from any of the injured or sick. It was only the guard, a soldier from the Regiment of Foot who had been sent here against her protests by Brynd, who gave any suggestion that Eir was someone different. Luckily for her, he kept himself mostly out of the way, and decided the best way to waste away the hours was to flirt with other nurses.

Presently she heard a clanking of swords echoing along the corridor, and she quickened her pace to see what was going on. As she entered a small antechamber, two nurses burst past her with expressions of disapproval on their faces.

There, in the antechamber, Randur was demonstrating various moves of *Vitassi* with his rapier to a group of four young children, each one clutching an old blade. They were mimicking him as he progressed through one of the basic series of moves.

'Randur!' she gasped.

'Ah,' he replied, and pressed his knuckles to his hips. 'I'm afraid, my little brothers and sisters, that we must reconvene at another time.'

'Oh damn,' one little girl said.

'Sorry, young maiden. Boss's orders,' he replied with a bow.

'Randur,' Eir snapped, 'where did you find these children?'

'They were hanging about the place waiting for their relatives to get better. They wouldn't stop bothering some of the nurses, so I thought I'd relieve the ladies, so to speak, and educate these young ruffians in the finer arts of *Vitassi*. They learn pretty quickly at this age. The moves stick easily.'

'That is not the point, Randur, it is hardly fitting for them to be running about with blades in a hospital, now is it?'

'You've got a small dagger in your boot.'

'That is not the point – they're children, Randur, and it's dangerous for them to be holding swords. What if they injure themselves?'

'Well, they're in the best place for it, eh?' Randur said. 'Anyway, these young things need to learn how to fight one day.' He turned to the kids. 'Come on, you lot, we can do this again tomorrow.'

Grumbling, the four children filed out, each one handing their rusted blade back to Randur, who then stood them in their rack in the corner of the room.

'They're no more than a few winters old,' Eir said, quieter now.

'What does winter mean in an ice age? They were grateful enough and they'd just be annoying the nurses otherwise. Besides, they will need to learn to protect themselves some day.'

'This should only go on if their mothers and fathers are made aware of it.'

'Sod their parents – what's better than being able to protect themselves in a tricky situation?'

Eir took a deep breath. 'What's wrong, Randur? There's no need to get angry about this.'

'I'm not angry.'

'Yes, you are. What's wrong?'

Randur sighed and made a flamboyant gesture with his arms. 'Nothing. It's all right for you. You've got something to focus on now, haven't you? You're helping out and I approve. This is quite a change from the spoiled little girl sat inside the pretty castle on the top of a hill.'

'You can contribute here if you want.'

'It's not really what I'm cut out for. I want to help with things, sure, but there's a lot hanging over me.'

'Your mother?'

'Yeah,' he sighed, 'for one. I'm scared of heading out there – she's probably died by now anyway. That poison, even though slow, would have got to her by now. And even if not, what do I do – turn up and say I've not got a cure, that I'm a failure?'

'She never expected you to cure her anyway. She packed you off to Villjamur thinking that was best in an ice age. And it was. You met me of course.'

Randur gave half a smile.

'You know, your sister should be down here too.'

'She has other things to think about.'

'Yeah,' Randur replied. 'I'm sure she has.'

'Meaning?'

'I saw her, the other night, walking around the corridors of the Citadel muttering to herself. Seems as though she's gone a bit crazy? It's all because of this thing with Artemisia – it's gone too far.'

'You shouldn't talk about her like that,' Eir whispered.

Randur moved a hand to her shoulder. 'You know as well

as I do that she's not the same woman any more. It's as if she's smitten by Artemisia and needs her presence, else she just can't handle herself.'

'Has Artemisia put her in some kind of trance, do you think?'

'Who knows?' Randur said. 'We'll never know what happened on Artemisia's ship, will we? Rika thought that she was a god – despite the fact that most of what Artemisia stands for contradicts the whole Jorsalir thing. It could be mental – or, yeah, maybe Artemisia did do something to her.'

'Why would she do such a thing?'

'To help the alliance between worlds? To make sure Artemisia got what she wanted? It could be anything.'

'I hope that isn't the case,' Eir replied. 'We need Rika to be on her best form if she's to take the helm of whatever Empire emerges from all of this.'

THIRTEEN

The western coast of Folke was a welcome sight. The sun was rising, illuminating the shoreline. A few birds skittered about the rocky shore before veering out to sea. A thin, flat layer of cloud drifted by above the land. The conditions were as calm as they could possibly be for a landing. Brynd put four of his Night Guard brethren on board, who had acted impressively in getting this hefty yacht cutting through the waters so efficiently. They were not natural sailors, but they had remembered their training manuals to the letter, and now the sails snagged tightly in the wind, and the boat lurched towards the east.

Brynd stood at the bow contemplating the island ahead, waiting to see signs of life.

The military had decided to stay until all civilians were on the sea-vehicles or some reclaimed vessel, and either were now at sea or on the island of Folke. The evacuation had been completed successfully and there had been no more attacks.

Brynd was grateful for that.

'Sele of the day, commander,' Investigator Fulcrom said. The rumel then yawned and stretched. 'Time at sea certainly helps thoughts germinate, doesn't it?'

'Indeed, investigator,' Brynd replied.

'You seem troubled, commander.'

Brynd gave a wry smile. 'I've been troubled for years; it doesn't bother me any more.'

Fulcrom smiled. 'Have you any more thoughts about what we'll do next?'

'I've done nothing *but* that. This much is clear to me: while the sky-city remains, I doubt we can form a peaceful future. We can't build a new multi-racial culture, we can't decide on how land is to be allocated. We can't do any of this when we know what it can do. One island was cleansed even without its help, and now Jokull makes two . . .'

'Frater Mercury can pull off a trick or two,' Fulcrom said optimistically. 'He could come in handy.'

'You're not wrong about him, investigator.' Brynd now looked towards Folke's coast. He could just about make out the forms of those enormous horses moving across the fields. They were now unattached to any vehicle and instead tromped about the landscape freely.

'I noticed you had some assistance from . . . well, they were people *not* of our world. They'll be useful again, surely?'

'I've no doubts about that,' Brynd muttered. 'They've not just come here to fight. They want to share our islands with us, too.'

Fulcrom seemed to stare at Brynd for a while, blinking in the morning light. 'You have doubts?'

'I have doubts.' *Their ambassador has corrupted our Empress: yes, I have my doubts*, Brynd thought. 'We should prepare to land. Gather your things and,' he added with a smile, 'you might want to wake your lady, too.'

He pointed out Lan who was asleep on the deck, under a pile of blankets, the gentle breeze stirring her hair.

'She's had a busy few weeks,' Fulcrom chuckled.

*

Their boat was forced to navigate through thousands of vessels now abandoned a little offshore and, once through, they sailed the final stretch. Brynd and a handful of his soldiers jumped ashore in the shallow waters and waded the final few feet to land, carrying their weapons and supplies.

Brynd was pleased to see that the military had followed his plans and had everything under control. There were small encampments where names and details were being recorded for any families or friends on other islands, and for official records. Food parcels were being handed out. Tents were being set up in the fields just to the north. Two dragons were flying into the distance, presumably having just dropped off supplies of food or blankets. There hadn't been much to come from Villiren in the first place – but it showed wonderful altruism that the suffering could find something to give the refugees.

To one side, Lan – the former Knight of Villjamur – landed gracefully. Brynd looked back at the boat where Fulcrom was tentatively disembarking.

'Did you actually leap from there?' Brynd called over.

Lan turned to face him. 'Sure. It's not that far. When you've spent a few weeks clearing the distance between the bridges of Villjamur, this is pretty simple stuff.'

'And you can fight well?'

'Well enough,' she said. 'Though I was trained more for one-on-one encounters.'

Brynd nodded. 'We'll certainly have use of you, miss.'

He turned to watch the shore, where he hoped to see some of Artemisia's people. Sure enough – and to plan – they were there, carrying supplies and distributing them among the evacuees. To his surprise even Artemisia was helping, lumbering up and down the beach with piles of blankets.

Brynd spotted a shaven head approaching him, fellow Night Guard Brug. 'Commander,' he called, 'everything is running to schedule. Aid is arriving regularly via dragon transport, people are now being treated for serious illnesses or wounds.'

'What about the plans for resettlement?'

'We've the three encampments here, with three more planned further inland. The Dragoons are heading there right now to set them up.'

'We shouldn't remain here for too long. I imagine this could become a front for another battle. The camps should be dispersed as soon as people are recovered enough to press on. Do we have any estimates of numbers?'

'Somewhere between fifty-five and sixty thousand, at the last survey, but it's hard to tell with so many small children.'

Brynd cringed.

'That's good, surely, commander?'

'Good that we saved so many; bad that so many must have been killed in Villjamur or are still somewhere on the island, destined to join the dead. There were a good few hundred thousand in Villjamur and the caves alone, plus the refugees outside – not to mention the rest of the island. How many of those died, we'll never know.'

'Aye, sir. It's saddening. We have a few large funeral pyres planned for those bodies that made it over with us. Out of respect, at least, we will get them out of the way tonight.'

'Do it while it's still light – you don't want the people seeing the pyres at night or families will be wailing non-stop. I'd also like riders sent to all the settlements on this side of Folke – they should know what is happening.'

'Aye, sir.'

'How are Artemisia's soldiers coping?'

'Reasonably well as it happens. Your idea for them to deliver and dispatch food aid was a good one – it seems the refugees have accepted their presence, even if they might fear them on first sight.'

'The way people react to their fear will ultimately define our future,' Brynd replied grimly. 'It's important that, at every given moment, someone from their world is seen to be standing alongside our military or is involved in medical or social assistance.'

'You're fully committed to the partnership then?'

'I'm fully committed to peace,' Brynd said. 'You've seen the other option available to us.'

'I wasn't doubting your orders, sir. We're all right behind the scheme.'

Brynd glanced at Brug. 'Do I *dictate* too much?'

'Pardon, commander?'

'I'm no longer just making military decisions,' Brynd replied. 'I'm interfering with the matters of an emperor or empress. It is one of the key tenets of the Night Guard not to assist in creating a military ruler. And here I am, acting like one . . .'

'You have the people's interests at heart, sir,' Brug said.

So do some tribal dictators, Brynd thought. *Even if I consult the Night Guard, that's a military ruling force making decisions.* If Brynd felt awkward making decisions, there was a reason for it – people should indeed be deciding matters for themselves. *Just not yet.*

'See to it that the Night Guard muck in with the aid until nightfall, and then we'll head back to Villiren in the morning. It will do the people's morale some good to mix with the regiment. And make sure you raise their spirits – just don't let things get out of hand.'

'With the poor wine brewed on this island, sir, I seriously doubt they will.'

*

Brynd made his way up towards the abandoned farmyard, which the military had commandeered as their local head-quarters. It was a large, nearly decrepit, whitewashed building, positioned at the edge of an enclosure surrounded by high, dry-stone walls. Old farming implements had been left scattered around the place, tools that looked more as if they were used for torture than agriculture. Troughs were upturned or on their sides; the door of the vast barn had been discarded and, judging by the charring, long set upon by local youths.

A light shower came and went, but brought no snow. Perhaps it was the coastal breeze but the weather seemed less and less like that of an ice age. There were much warmer spells of late and, though it was not necessarily anything more than a hunch, the signs of nature suggested it was more than that: buds were starting to show on dead-looking plants; new shoots had started to form. It made Brynd contemplate yet again whether the astrologers who made their predictions about the long ice age were simply wrong.

He continued along the muddied road that, thanks to the military, had already become well-trodden and slippery. Gloops of mud were thrown up at his black uniform, and he was forced to step up onto the grassier verge, clinging to the stone wall, so that he did not fall in the quagmire.

In the field opposite, cream and brown tents stretched as far as he could see, with little spires of smoke rising from inside them and out. Brynd paused to watch: it reminded him so much of the refugee camps outside Villjamur. There was so much activity here that it seemed some primitive city had been set up overnight. People milled about in between the rows. A priestess was holding her sermon against a small outbuilding. From the look of it, there were even a few people who had begun businesses – upturned crates and made temporary market stalls, and they were selling whatever bits and pieces they had managed to bring along with them.

Brynd continued on his way, until the muddied road went through a zone that had been sealed off, and was for military personnel only. To one side two young soldiers were slouched by a low, dry-stone wall, sitting on two barrels, muttering to each other. For a moment he tried to glean what they were saying about the refugees, and was soon disgusted at the subject.

'. . . One of them even offered to suck my cock for a few coins.' They both laughed. In a heartbeat, Brynd stormed up to the soldier who spoke, gripped him by his throat and pinned him back against the wall. 'And what was your reply to her then, *soldier*?' he snarled.

'Commander . . .' the man spluttered. His face was covered

in dirt, his eyes were wide. 'I ... Nothing happened, commander, I swear.'

'Sir,' the other man said, 'he's full of nonsense. Don't listen to his stories...'

Brynd released his grip, listened to their measly excuses and took their names.

'If you hear of anything like that going on, you come to me first,' Brynd said. 'These are our own fucking people – *we* serve *them*, or have you forgotten that?'

'No, sir,' they said in unison.

'I'll personally give a dozen lashes to anyone who abuses any of these refugees – in whatever fucking capacity that shows. I'll cut your cocks off myself if I have to. Have I made myself clear?'

'Yes, commander,' they said, both now terrified, and nodding.

'Good. Get back to your units,' Brynd ordered, and waved them aside. He watched them gather up their things and shamble into the distance. Of course, such abuse went on in the army – word spread quickly through the ranks – and there was little he could do to stop it, no matter how hard he had tried over the years. Those in power would always use it in inappropriate ways. He didn't mind at all if the men, or indeed women, visited whores – he had done it himself, of course – but to abuse the Empire's *own people* and take advantage of Villjamur's desperate refugees was a line he would not cross. It was essential that the people trusted the military. Brynd continued into the run-down farmhouse, which was the new hub of operations.

Although it obviously hadn't been lived in for years, a little military efficiency had helped: a pile of broken furniture had been stacked outside, while other smaller pieces were being burned in a huge firebox against the far wall. There were flagstones for flooring and a large wooden table, at which Artemisia was seated. Three Dragoons paused, as they strode through the room, to salute Brynd and he returned their gesture.

These were all signs of business as usual, that they were on top of everything.

'Welcome, commander,' Artemisia said. 'Were the people who lived here once all, how is it said ... dwarven? These buildings are not fit for children to stand in, let alone one of your human or rumel people.'

'You help fight in a battle and a low ceiling is what worries you the most?'

'It was a good skirmish, was it not?'

She continued to examine the maps and various lists that were strewn across it, and he could see that she had been making notes.

Brynd sat alongside her. Somewhere outside, he could hear someone busily chopping wood. The blue sky in the distance prompted his thoughts to the change in weather.

'Tell me, the gate through which your enemy gained access to this world. How many of them are there?'

'They are numerous, though many are located above the seas, so were of no practical use until the ice formed as a result of the cold being emitted.'

'So though the cold weather – all this ice – isn't natural here it's far worse in the north. Is that anything to do with the Realm Gates?'

Artemisia remained expressionless. 'Of course, commander, it brings you the ice from our own world and expels it into yours. You think your world is cold? My comrades can dress lightly here. It is a paradise compared with ours, which has now become an endless winter. This is what it is like at the end of the world. The land there is almost utterly dead: we would perish if we remained there for another of your years. Our people had heard stories about a sun; those who sired me told me about it, many generations ago, and we do have certain texts that depict its path through the sky. But it was never anything like I have experienced here – so bright and red. When I first came through – long before I brought my ship, on a purely investigative quest – I spent the better part of a day watching your sun moving through the sky from one side to the other. There were no clouds that day. Its movements did not tire me. I sat, and I watched, and I marvelled. Then I returned to the gloom from which I came, to face the war that had been fought for generations; I knew then my elders' plans were correct. We had to leave but, alas, it seemed our enemies were burrowing through time and space in their own way. Those Realm Gates indeed brought the ice from our world. So powerful is their effect it seems they altered your weather patterns, too.'

'You've closed one up – the one on Tineag'l, with your ship, after the war in Villiren – and it became warmer then. We're not in an ice age here, are we?'

'Your scholars were all fools,' Artemisia replied. 'They would do well instead to open their eyes and observe the world.'

Brynd had learned to look past her bluntness. *It's probably deserved and, if not, then it's a welcome challenge.* 'Presumably if you've shattered one gate, you can shatter some more?'

'It is possible, yes.'

'If you want to stop them coming into this world, then it seems like a good place to start,' Brynd added dryly.

'We can do that – though it would only make a difference to your climate.'

'How do you mean?'

'Our enemies have,' Artemisia said, 'all arrived anyway.'

'In the sky-city?' Brynd asked.

'A crude term for the Policharos, but it is accurate enough. They are here in vast numbers, in that vehicle. Whatever happens in the near future will settle matters, finally, and it will occur here, in the Boreal Archipelago.'

'Are you suggesting they've put everything in that thing? Their entire culture?'

'It sounds improbable, commander, does it not? Yet it is truth. They, too, know there is precious little time in our own world. The elements have removed the luxury of choice. Our sources informed us that they had been making arrangements for a large-scale exodus, and that they had sourced a way of transportation for the whole construct, both through space and time, to this world. That action itself removed their biggest threat, Villjamur.'

Brynd fought back his annoyance. He knew that the destruction of Villjamur was a trifling matter to Artemisia, and that she had probably seen more death than he had in his lifetime, but to him – to his people – it was a world-shattering event. 'I take it this sky-city should be the focus of our plans? That we should somehow disable it.'

'I can barely begin to describe its complexities.'

'Try me,' Brynd said.

'As you observe, it is a city. It is a vast, complex . . . urban structure, well-fortified and containing uncountable numbers of roads, not to mention the housing there, that covers the majority of the surface. There are even structures made from the blackened bones of humans. They have built this for the purpose of redeploying an entire civilization, here on this chain of islands. They are, it seems, a significant step ahead of us. What's more, they are now perfectly prepared to populate the island of Jokull.'

'You know this is their plan?'

'It's a strategy for survival, commander. It is what you or I would both do. Admit it. Now that it has been cleansed of life, the island is *theirs*. What may happen is that just a few of the sky-city's outer structures will commence to fall to ground, at first, whereupon they will form the basis of new cities – only to take the rest so that they can expand elsewhere.'

'They can't do that so quickly, can they?' Brynd asked. 'They can't just fucking *take* an island like that.'

'You have just witnessed them taking your island, have you not? Now, of course,' Artemisia continued, 'there is the matter of further invasions, the systematic eradication of your people. They will strike this island next. Then the next. They will not stop.'

The recent victory suddenly became quite hollow. Indeed, Brynd felt sickened and now stared glumly at the table. He had tried to view the situation as optimistically as possible, but all he was doing was dressing over a severe wound. 'What do you suggest then?' Brynd asked.

'We should have a series of plans commencing with the massing of a combined army and ending with a confrontation against them – and sooner would be better, because then they will not have spread themselves across the various islands. They will be much more difficult to remove, if that is the case.'

'How big would an army need to be to tackle them?'

'I can bring the better part of half a million soldiers.'

'Half a million?' Brynd exclaimed.

'It is not enough, I know,' Artemisia declared.

I was thinking the opposite . . . 'Just how many people will we really need?'

Artemisia raised her hands in a gesture Brynd took for a shrug, though she had not yet learned the subtleties of human interaction in this world. Perhaps it meant more in her own. 'Twice as many, at least, for that is how many they will have with them.'

'Is that the entire population you've brought with you?' Brynd asked.

'No. There are many people who are not born for war, just like in this world – more fragile races. What has arrived will make up the majority, but the others will be of little use just yet.'

Brynd's mind flitted across various problems. He began to think about where these creatures – no, these *people* – would reside, and then about how he might locate so many soldiers. There were, perhaps, a hundred thousand potential warriors he could find at the most – and most of them would be civilians. They would need training, armour and weaponry. The youths back in Villiren suddenly came to mind, and he felt a strong desire to see what they were able to provide.

'You seem distracted, commander,' Artemisia said. 'I hope you are still capable of assistance in these matters.'

Brynd's temper flared, but he wasn't going to let her see it. 'I'm simply contemplating the logistics of the operation, Artemisia. Now tell me, you're a military ambassador, as such, though you're a fine warrior also. Who will be responsible for planning this operation?'

'You will be the senior representative from your world, of course.'

'And from yours?'

'I will consult with the elders and see who they deem suitable. It may be that they deem it suitable for me to continue as the point of contact, for I am relatively senior. I understand the subtleties of your culture better than they do, and can translate messages to them easily.'

'You do that,' Brynd said, 'because—'

There was a knocking at the door. Brynd called out; a soldier opened it and poked his head in. 'Commander. Investigator Fulcrom is here, and he says he's got someone rather important . . .'

'Good, send him in,' Brynd ordered.

A moment later, Fulcrom strolled in and nodded to Brynd and there was a strange-looking individual in tow. Suddenly Artemisia was dropping to her hands and knees. Beside her chair she bowed deeply, her arms out straight, palms to the floor. He could not have imagined a more bizarre transformation of her character.

'Well,' Fulcrom said, frowning at Artemisia, 'being a fan of evidence, I suppose all this might confirm Frater Mercury's status as a god of sorts.'

Brynd moved across to examine Frater Mercury, and Artemisia made no signs of moving from her position. 'Frater Mercury,' Brynd began, 'welcome to the Boreal Archipelago. I must first thank you for saving many lives.'

There was no sign on the individual's face, faces, that his words had been registered. Brynd tried not to stare too much at the two perfect halves of his face. Alongside him, Artemisia finally clambered to her feet and stepped cautiously forwards. She began speaking to Frater Mercury in their native language. The noises were guttural and unnerving.

Brynd cleared his throat and addressed Artemisia. 'Perhaps we should get him back to the outskirts of Villiren. While we're there, we can bring your elders together with Rika, and we can discuss the immediate future.'

Artemisia paused but ignored him.

Fulcrom moved beside Brynd. 'I suspect they've a few issues,' he whispered.

Brynd took him to one side, out of Artemisia's earshot. 'How do you mean?'

'Well, I have a hunch, but it's no more than that. Who's the blue person?'

'A warrior from another world,' Brynd replied matter-of-factly. 'One of the ones on our side.'

'Right.' Fulcrom seemed bemused and shook his head.

'Out with it, investigator,' Brynd pressed. 'What's your hunch about the newcomer?'

'Frater Mercury – if he's a god to this woman here – which I'm certain he is in a manner of speaking, indeed to all of us – then, in their world, I believe he was something of an *imprisoned* god. Part of the reason he broke out is to see what's left of the world he abandoned before it was too late and his creations smashed it all up.'

'So you think she's persuading him back perhaps?'

'He can probably hear what we're saying, by the way,' Fulcrom whispered. 'He's choosing to ignore all of us. He is, in many ways, like a child who wants simple freedom, out of curiosity more than anything else. I can't understand much about him – considering he is meant to be connected to us – but I suspect he's suffering inside. He feels the pressure of it all. Coming here was a release from those burdens.'

'And yet,' Brynd ventured, 'you asking him for help in our world has already put more pressure upon him.'

'It's certainly possible.'

'What state is his mind in?'

'It's hard to say,' Fulcrom replied. 'I think stable, but I don't know him well enough, nor do I know what "normal" is for him. What I do know is that he's almost an omnipotent individual – his involvement could mean you manage to get the future you plan for. If not, it could mean a future that none of us is a part of.'

Brynd breathed deeply, weighing the investigator's words in his mind. 'I'll let Artemisia finish with him, then I may try to get a few words with him – that is, if Artemisia will let me.'

The blue-skinned woman's voice was pleading, her words tumbling out of her mouth in a torrent he couldn't understand. Eventually her sentences faded and Frater Mercury remained impassive to what she said. Artemisia sat back down at the table, and for the first time since he had met her she seemed quite disturbed.

'Is everything all right?' Brynd enquired.

She looked up at him. 'We need to get back to the encampment as soon as possible. I will see to it that the dragons are brought here before nightfall.'

'Are you taking Frater Mercury with you?' Brynd asked.

'Of course!' she said with irritation. She rose up from her chair petulantly. 'Unless you wish to return to Villiren via foot, Commander Lathraea, I would urge you to set straight your affairs here as soon as possible. Make what arrangements you will.' With that, she marched back over to Frater Mercury, muttered something in their own tongue, before they both left the building.

Brynd watched through the windows as they made their way along the edge of the wall and out of sight.

'They may be from a different world,' Fulcrom said, 'but they're certainly as temperamental as people from ours.'

Brynd laughed, and found the thought vaguely comforting.

Fourteen

Jeza was keen to explore the nature of the Mourning Wasp before she resuscitated it. She had paid to gain access to what was left of the city's private underground libraries. Knowledge was power, of course, and in Villiren you didn't get something like that without paying for it.

Information was barricaded within tiny rooms situated mostly in the Ancient Quarter, an area that had remained unaffected by the war, and they had been kept in good condition by either aged cultists or old scholars weighed down by nostalgia. She examined shelf after shelf for information on the Mourning Wasp, thick tomes coming apart at the bindings, all kinds of exotic books written in various languages, though she could only understand a couple of them. Some were in remarkably good condition – facsimile copies or translations made by scholars, and with useful annotations.

Jeza had disregarded unreliable authors, researched others, but slowly began to piece together the origins of the Mourning Wasp.

There were mentions of an enormous Pale Emperor Wasp, *Vespa imperator khloros*, by a scholar called Vendor Hast, which was the earliest mention of the creature. Hast's scribblings seemed a little inconsistent, so she did not set great store by his theories.

The most encouraging text was written by an Ysla-based academic called Venghaus, who had written on what he claimed was an encounter with something called the Mourning Wasp. He was more specific in his observations: saying that the creature's overactive saliva gland secreted a substance that corroded its flesh, thus leaving it with a mostly skull-like appearance. He had suggested the use of 'heavy clubs and cudgels' for dealing with the pest – the numbers of people on his expedition had been halved upon contact with the species. Venghaus was the only writer to have made a sketch of the creature, hovering in the air. It looked both macabre and mesmerizing. Of the ability for people to sit on top of the wasps, as depicted in the cave paintings, Venghaus did not mention anything.

*

Despite the effects of the war, Villiren was still a busy city. The streets had begun to settle back into their old ways: bawdy bars kicked out those who were a couple of drinks the wrong side of the night, only for them to then go and piss their expenditure up against the wall around the back. People in long waxed coats began offering her dubious substances from the shadows, illicit fluids or bark scrapings, which could either heighten your experience of the evening or do absolutely nothing, depending on the dealer you found. There were working girls here, too, though far fewer than before. They stood almost between the moonlight and the shadows, trying to catch the attention of passers-by. Behind them, their pimps loitered, knives tucked into their sleeves, waiting. Land trilobites had returned as well, their strange, shiny shells catching the light from windows as they scuttled into the alleys. Though these waist-high creatures had once found work carrying tools for the stevedores, ever since the presence of the Okun no one really trusted anything with an exoskeleton. Now trilobites could be found drinking from puddles or scouring mounds of rubbish for existence.

The dark economy flourished.

Any hopes Jeza had that the war might have purged such

goings-on from the streets of Villiren had vanished. Nothing would stop these discreet forces. Yet despite the dangers, in spite of the rancid smells and questionable people, Jeza did enjoy these evenings. The bitter coastal breeze brought her to her senses after a long day spent cooped up in the factory. It made her feel alive. And there was a definite buzz around the group ever since their first genuine commission from the commander. A downpayment had come through and they were now in possession of the one thing they had craved for years.

Respect.

The manufacture of Imperial armour had not stopped when Brynd left the city on his urgent business. He said he would return promptly once a small matter was seen to, and she took the decision then to industrialize their process further. They opened one of the many unused rooms in the factory, cleared out junk and rubbish, and employed some friends of friends to kit out the place as a vast storage facility so it would become a warehouse for armour. It wasn't long before they had the better part of a thousand of the new-style breastplates on the racks. The gang tested their work on other sections of body armour until they had enough examples to show Brynd. Then they started their first thorough explorations on the art of raising the Mourning Wasp.

They could do this without having to do shitty conversion jobs for cultists. They now had the luxury of having money. Some of the gang had resisted the urge to buy the first thousand things they saw. Even in a post-war Villiren, they could still get their hands on nice clothes, decent drinks, tasty food. The army paid well, it seemed, and the group couldn't quite work out what to do with all the money. Jeza decided she would save hers. She would perhaps see if she could get a passage to Ysla, where the cultists lived in some kind of utopia. The weather was warmer there.

Somehow news had got out concerning their manufacture

of military gear and there had been a request to meet her, one on one, in a tavern on the far side of the Ancient Quarter, in an area untouched by the war.

The note came from a man called Malum.

She thought to herself, what if the deal with the army collapses? What if the commander had to pull out of the contract? If she was going to be a legitimate businesswoman, she would need another plan, something to fall back on.

So she had decided to go on her own, yet for her own safety was secretly wearing one of her own pieces of armour designed to fit her small frame. *I don't want to get stabbed with all that money sitting there unspent in a bank vault*, she thought.

*

As she headed towards the agreed meeting point, by way of the enormous Citadel, she noticed something strange occurring down one of the side streets. There, amidst the rubbish sacks discarded by the nearest bistro, was a hunched figure rooting around in the darkness. For some reason, Jeza's curiosity got the better of her and she sauntered cautiously towards the person: it was a human, a woman and, surprisingly, her black clothes seemed to be well cut, though more fitted for combat than anything else. In fact, everything about the quality of the clothing and neatness of her hair suggested that she was from a good background.

Not a beggar then, Jeza thought. *Has she fallen on hard times?*

Jeza tentatively said, 'Hi,' and the woman snapped around to face her. Blood was drooling from her mouth and smeared all over her right cheek, but she didn't seem injured. In her hands were the remains of something fleshy. Jeza's gaze followed the trail of blood by her feet and back up the alley – this suggested that the rest of the fleshy thing at the woman's feet had been dragged here. It had not been found here, discarded by the bistro.

That realization made Jeza's skin crawl.

The woman looked at her – right through her, in fact, as if

she was in some kind of trance. Jeza remained utterly still. Somewhere in the distance she heard a pterodette screech.

'Who are you?' Jeza asked the woman. 'Do you need any help?'

The attempt at conversation seemed to draw the woman out of her state. Her gaze relaxed, and settled more naturally on Jeza. 'Are you all right?' Jeza held out her hand, though drew it back hesitantly when she remembered the bloody flesh.

'I ... I must be going,' the woman muttered, her voice incredibly refined, her accent from the west; and suddenly she dashed past Jeza and back out into the city. She had dropped something on her way and, after peering around cautiously, Jeza examined it—

She lurched back in horror. It was a child's arm, and very definitely mauled around the fleshy muscles of the forearm. Who was that? Had they *killed* a child? The woman seemed far too *normal* to have done such a thing.

A bell-tower struck in the distance, and Jeza realized she had to be moving on. Reluctantly, and now feeling a little sick, she stumbled out of the alley and back into the night.

*

The tavern was surprisingly clean and decent for Villiren. It had all its windows intact and the door had not been ripped off its hinges. There was no graffiti on any of the walls and no bad smells. Though it was crammed into a row of white-washed buildings, it seemed big enough to hold a regular flow of respectable clientele.

Inside was a large fireplace near the bar, and plenty of warmth. She ordered herself just a tea – she didn't want to drink when she had to be alert – and took a seat in a plush armchair by the fire. Brass accoutrements hung on the walls, with shoddy-looking paintings, and a fug of smoke had stained the ceiling. There weren't as many people inside as she thought there would be, but those who were there seemed solitary, quiet types, which suited her fine.

She sat for a while contemplating the place. Eventually a man with stubble, wearing a long wax coat and a tricorne hat, approached her. He was handsome, bore a scar or two on his face and moved towards her with an effortless cool.

'You got my message.' His voice was gravelly. For a moment she thought she saw two animalistic fangs in his mouth.

She nodded.

'Good,' he replied. 'Name's Malum.'

'Jeza.' She watched him slump into the chair with grace.

'So then, you're the girl who's got the underground talking.'

'I try not to listen to rumours,' she replied.

Malum laughed and she couldn't tell whether or not he was mocking her.

'Look, I'm interested in your military gear,' Malum continued. He smiled. He looked around sheepishly before he leaned in a little closer. 'You're doing business with that albino commander, am I right?'

Jeza nodded, intrigued as to how much he already knew about the dealings. She was, for now, thankful he was treating her like an adult and not speaking down to her.

'Does he pay well?' Malum asked.

Another nod; she didn't want to betray the commander.

'You're a closed book, young lady,' Malum said. 'I respect someone who's got secrets – but you can treat me like a business client. I'm interested in purchasing your wares, and I'm also interested in the range of wares that you deal in. Trust me as much as you want to, but I don't do business with people I don't believe in. I have faith in your operation. I like what I've heard.'

'What's your business exactly?' Jeza enquired.

'I'm a trader, of sorts,' he replied coolly. 'I tend to deal in whatever I can get my hands on, in just about every ware you can think of; but I also deal in private security, or settling scores for people. Sometimes a contract needs enforcing and, in the absence of any decent Inquisition around here, businesses need a little kick now and then. I'm increasingly in demand – things are changing in Villiren.'

'What things?'

'Tensions, mainly. You know of the aliens to the south of the city?'

'I've heard a little about them, but not much.'

'Big encampment – like a new city filled with all sorts of weird, deadly creatures. It's causing a lot of worries with many important folk in this city, business leaders, local representatives, bankers. They're worried that these things are just going to come and take over when the city needs stability. They don't belong here, you see. They'll upset the balance and do strange things. There's talk of creatures coming in to the southern fringes of the city and eating pets; even one report of a child being eaten by them.'

Jeza thought of the woman earlier, in the alleyway. 'It's a difficult situation that everyone in this city finds themselves in.'

'Those aren't your words, that's the commander speaking,' Malum grunted, but he didn't seem angry. 'It's all right for the likes of the powerful – they can get to make decisions and influence whatever they want. For the average man or woman on the street, this is really frightening.'

'Do you see yourself as a man of the people?' Jeza asked.

Malum eyed her. She couldn't tell a thing about his thoughts from his neutral expression.

'Not as such.' He smiled. 'But there's money to be made in representing their concerns.'

'At least you're honest,' Jeza chuckled dryly.

'That, young lady, I am.'

There was a pause in conversation while two men ordered drinks from the bar, and Malum and Jeza waited until they had moved on.

'So,' Malum continued, 'I find myself in an interesting situation. I might be looking for all sorts of solutions, to help appease concerns of the city folk, so I'd be intrigued as to the kinds of things you deal in. Tell me what you're all about.'

Jeza explained the operation at the factory, glossing over the new armour and finishing with her ambitions for synthetic creatures. She skirted over the intricacies of the operation, but let him know just enough – that they were good, that they could be trusted. Malum remained silent as she talked, letting her do all the work.

Once she had said her piece, Malum spoke again.

'Now, I can't tell you my specific business with representing the interests of the people of this city, but I can tell you this – I'm interested in all you have to say, particularly with these *creatures*. I've always been a fan of such beings – they can cause a lot of damage.'

'I don't want our creations causing harm!'

'They won't be – I wouldn't worry. All I'm interested in is *helping* people.'

'You're sure?'

'You make me out to be the monster here – you're the girl that makes them. I'm a businessman, plain and simple.'

'Good.'

'Now,' Malum said, standing. She could see a small blade sheathed at his hip, and for the first time she became nervous. 'I'll be in touch, Jeza. I needed to know what you had and I'm impressed.'

Jeza had a vague thought that if he was a criminal of sorts, he wouldn't be able to match the military. 'We do charge quite a lot, given what the commander has given . . .'

Malum gave a wry smile. 'I can afford twice whatever he's paying, don't you worry. I'm a professional. I'd also like to see some of these creatures for myself, when they're finally finished. How long, do you think, until they're ready?'

'They'll be ready when they're ready,' Jeza replied, 'but you should know that most of them never make it.'

Malum seemed satisfied with her answer, and slunk out into the night, leaving Jeza with an uneasy feeling. However, if she cancelled potential business purely because someone made her feel uneasy, they would never make a living.

*

When Jeza arrived back at the factory, the others were still up making their usual racket. They were eating fried fish, which she could smell from some distance. The place was a mess again. It seemed no matter how much money they had, no matter how much respect they were accumulating, they would forever be kicking around boxes of junk, food containers, or empty bottles.

'Guys,' Jeza announced profoundly. 'I think it's about time we hired a cleaner.'

'Place is fine as it is,' Coren called out. 'Besides, we've too much sensitive stuff here – cleaners could go messing with things they don't know about. Anyway, how'd it go tonight? Who was the mystery man?'

'It went pretty well actually,' she replied. 'His name was Malum and he seemed interested in the monsters. Said he could pay well, too.'

'That's the main thing,' Coren replied.

'Yes. The thought occurred to me that we'd need a back-up if the thing with the commander fell through. If we can get this guy on board we can build up a decent and secure set of projects. Diggsy, did you buy those new relics that were uncovered in Saltwater the other day?'

'Yup,' he replied. 'We've got two crates of them sitting in the next room. It was a good idea to spend some money investing – there might be some really useful things there. I've heard about a few underground markets after buying these – there are levels below ground that not even cultists know about. We're about to enter a much bigger scene. There's also a few pieces that might help with the development of the Mourning Wasp and speed that process up.'

'Jeza, what's on your mind?' Coren asked. 'You look as though not a word of that went in your ears.'

'I also saw something weird tonight. There was this woman – decent-looking, well-to-do type, and she was . . . well, she had a child's arm in her mouth. It was like she was in a trance.'

'Oh, you've seen the Cannibal Lady,' Coren said excitedly. He stuck his fork into a piece of fish before dropping it on the floor. 'Aw shit.'

'You know about her already?' Jeza asked. 'Is that her name then?'

Coren leaned back up and put the fallen fish in his mouth, much to everyone's disgust. 'They're calling her that, yeah,' he continued, while munching. 'And I don't know all that much, just that there's been talk in a few of the bars around the Ancient Quarter. She's been spotted quite a few times, and on each occasion she's been seen, it's been the same thing – her, somewhere secluded, munching on flesh. They say she's some kind of animal.'

'Do they say where she came from?' Jeza asked. 'Is she one of the creatures from the south of the city? Malum mentioned there had been sightings of things coming into Villiren and taking people.'

'Could be.' Coren nodded. 'Though they say this one didn't so much as come from the south, but was here already. People are whispering that the Cannibal Lady comes from the Citadel.'

FIFTEEN

Malum spotted the poster nailed to a decrepit noticeboard outside a Jorsalir church, deep in the Ancient Quarter.

It was late morning, the skies had just cleared after a quick shower, and the cobbles shone brightly in the sunlight. A flock of seagulls swooped by overhead. The day's traffic had calmed after the throng of the dawn markets, allowing him to contemplate the notice in peace.

But Malum read the information in disgust.

The notice was a piece of pro-alien propaganda from the military; it played on the fears of the populace and tried to appeal to their sense of self-preservation. It explained what was happening with the alien peoples camped to the south of the city and that without their aid against the Okun – or worse – Villiren, and the whole island, might be destroyed.

How many of these posters were around the city, he had no idea, but the military were obviously trying to get the people to accept the aliens.

'Imperial filth,' he muttered to himself, and ripped the poster down, chucking it into a puddle.

Cheap tricks, he thought. *I'm going to have to tear these down and raise my own game in the war to get people behind the gangs – and behind me.*

Malum buried his hands in his pockets, and headed to an agreed meeting point outside a tavern.

Four members of his gang were loitering outside, one of

them with a huge hessian sack at his feet. A black horse and a large, sturdy wooden cart pulled up a moment later, and the cloaked driver nodded to Malum. One by one, his comrades climbed up onto the back of it, the final one hauling the sack and carefully lowering it on board.

'We're good to go,' Malum called over to the driver, then hopped onto the back.

The cart turned in a large circle and rode south-west through the city.

*

An hour later, they found themselves in scrubland, just beyond the poverty-stricken district on the edge of Villiren. There was nothing here but snow, mud and a few copses of trees. It was much colder in these exposed conditions, and much quieter, but at least the skies were still clear.

'This'll do,' Malum shouted, and the cart drew to a halt. 'Right, let's get to it.'

The gang disembarked and began to set up the gear from the hessian sack. They unveiled a large harpoon catapult, one previously used for whaling, arranged it so that the tip pointed up into the sky at an angle of around sixty degrees.

Malum asked for the harpoon to be loaded to test it out.

'Let it go,' he said, and one of his men released a harpoon with a *thunk* – it rocketed into the sky, almost out of sight, almost touching the base of a passing cloud, before falling to the ground some distance away, beyond a copse.

'I'm impressed,' he said. 'Good work, lads.'

They mumbled their thanks before loading it up with something else entirely – a relic they'd bought from a new cultist contact, a woman who worked from a rented apartment in Saltwater. It was a thin silver tube, with a pointed end, and in many respects looked exactly like a harpoon. The only difference was that when this reached the highest point in the sky, it would detonate, stunning anything within fifty feet.

'How long till one comes, boss?' one of his younger crew asked, a swarthy, grubby-looking guy not long out of his teens.

'This is the route garudas take, and at least a couple come by after noon each day,' he said. 'We'll just wait it out and fire when we're ready. For now, just scan the skies and the first of you to spot one gets drinks all night on me.'

*

It was the better part of an hour and Malum continued pacing around the mud, contemplating his strategy.

'Hey, Malum! One's coming now.'

Malum stood by the catapult and gave the instruction to fire when it was within range. The avian drifted in an arc towards Villiren, a stark silhouette against the bright sky.

Thunk.

The relic was released and travelled right towards the bird – and, at its peak, the device gave a spark of purple light. The garuda immediately fell from its flight directly to the ground, and the gang began hollering their excitement.

'Nice work, now let's get over there,' Malum said. 'Tie it up, get a sack over its head, and load it onto the cart. We deal with the questions in the city.'

*

As the moon broke free of the clouds that night, while Malum pored over his crude accountancy, he was informed that the garuda was now fully conscious. They had dragged the brown-feathered creature underground, to one of their bolt-holes. There they stripped it of any Imperial armour, held back its arms, and his men laid into it, giving it several blows to the back of its wings, before striking it repeatedly in its stomach.

The thing gave off a hell of a noise, and Malum called away his men. Gripping a lantern, he stepped closer to the creature, which was slouched against the stone wall. He noted its impressive plumage and gently speckled face, its huge beak, muscular arms and torso.

'You don't talk, we get that,' he growled. 'But we know that you fuckers can write.'

He nodded for one of his men to bring a piece of paper and a pencil, and placed it on the floor in front of the garuda.

'We'll be back in an hour,' Malum said, 'and in that hour you will have written down all the movements of the alien races that are going on around the city. I want to know exactly what the threat is to Villiren, *where* this so-called threat is, but mostly I want to know if the Okun are anywhere near the city. And if you don't, we'll break off one of your wings.'

As he walked away, he whispered to one of the more senior of his gang, 'Make sure you dump the body out of the city when you're done. We can't have gossip of this getting back to the military.'

Sixteen

The flight to Villiren was rough. A harsh wind came from the north, rocking the transportation cage so hard that even Brynd thought they stood a good chance of falling to their deaths. Two rows of his regiment were facing each other in one part while, towards the back, men from the Dragoons sat hunched, holding on to ropes: they were above the wing muscles, and were getting the most vicious treatment. It had been fine coming south, flying with the wind in their favour and almost gliding the last stretch. Things weren't even this bad for an oarsman on one of the larger Imperial longships. At least three of the Night Guard soldiers threw up and only Tiendi, the woman, seemed to be at all easy, moving around and talking to people as if this was some cosy tavern.

A few holes in the roof of the vast wood-and-metal cage permitted enough light inside to indicate that they still had a little while left before nightfall.

'How long's left, sir?' Brug called across to Brynd.

'About another hour at least, given these winds,' he replied.

Everyone's face was glum. They just wanted the flight over. *Understandable*, Brynd thought, as another blast of wind rocked the cage.

'How are you holding up, investigator?' he called across to Fulcrom, who was sat a couple of places to his left next to Lan. 'Glad you accepted our offer of a ride now?'

The rumel tried to laugh. 'Well, it's quick at least. It beats sitting on a horse for days or being tossed about on the waves for just as long.'

'I'll say,' Brynd replied. 'Lan, are you coping all right?'

'I'm good,' she replied. 'I used to work as an entertainer – as far as I'm concerned, it's the only way to travel.'

'Are these otherworld people – are they OK with you using this method of transport?'

'It was their idea,' Brynd said.

'Seem like good people, these ones,' Fulcrom replied.

Another leading question, Brynd thought. *He'll do all right.* 'They're certainly very positive in working with us.'

'What happens when we get back?' Fulcrom asked.

'First we'll ride into the city, and send outriders ahead to announce our coming. We'll do the usual post-battle propaganda before briefing Jamur Rika on the latest events.'

'Would she not want briefing first?'

Brynd paused and contemplated a diplomatic response. 'In an ideal world, yes . . .'

*

Not even boredom itself is as dull as this, Randur thought.

He decided that he had found a new place *beyond* boredom, a part of the emotional spectrum that he would not wish on his worst enemies.

And what the hell has become of me?

As he so often did after dinner, he headed along the corridors to chat to some of the serving staff, to see if he could glean a little juicy gossip about the mechanics of the building; despite his new-found position near the top of the remnants of the Empire, he still preferred to mix with people who had a few stories to tell, who had a little spirit about them, but there was precious little gossip to be found. Apparently since the departure of the former portreeve of the city, everyone had been on their best behaviour.

He noticed tonight that Rika had eaten very little at dinner, but afterwards, when he was in conversation with one of the administrative staff, he saw Rika marching by with a strange pace about her. His curiosity was piqued and he moved around the corner to see where she was going. She strode confidently along the stone-paved corridors on the ground level of the building, heading towards one of the rear exits.

Now where's that lass off to?

He threw on a thick cloak, managed to find his sword that he had stashed away, and decided the most productive thing to do would be to follow her.

What else, he thought, *is there to do?*

The element of subterfuge had brought a sudden burst of excitement back into his life.

*

It wasn't as cold as he thought it would be tonight, and the sounds of Villiren were enticing once again. His blood was pumping properly. It felt good. He could hear the sea in the distance, grinding against the geological forms of the bay and harbour; he could hear people talking, glasses being smashed, dogs barking. Comforting sounds for someone if they were used to them.

Quickly, he trotted down some steps, and around the corner where Rika had gone; there, he scanned the immediate streets for any signs of her.

He caught a glimpse of her – in that same dark, military-style garb she had taken to wearing. Her black hair had been cut even shorter, her skin growing abnormally pale, so she wasn't hard to recognize in the light of some of the ornamental beacons flaring around this district.

The place was less of a mess than before. Rubble was gradually being cleared by community teams; a lot of travellers provided cheap labour to help out with odd jobs around the city. Taverns were doing a good business, too, which was a promising sign.

Citizens here seemed more of a threat than the average person in Villjamur. People there may have wanted a fight or two, but in Villiren the challengers looked as if they might actually win a fight with him.

Rika seemed to have no destination in mind, just taking a random route around the city. Though the streets were no longer constructed according to any available map, she wandered about the place as if she was drunk or overdosing on arum weed. She would head down one street, only to round a corner and head back along a parallel street. She took full circles and went down some only to come straight back up as if she'd met a dead end – except she was free to pass through.

And this woman is to lead the new Empire? Randur thought. *She can't even lead herself at the moment. It doesn't really bode all that well.*

Whenever she passed citizens, she would veer into their path and scrutinize them before lurching away again, leaving them startled and hurrying on.

Is she looking for someone? Over the course of a few minutes, Rika became increasingly animalistic, he noticed: her stance might become a crouch, her walk would transform into a scuttle.

Suddenly she disappeared from sight. *Shit!* He ran along the street down the entrances of every alley to see if he could spot her, but he found little but rotting food waste, cats, or old men urinating up against the wall. He continued for several minutes and, as time passed, his search seemed increasingly futile. Eventually, assuming he had lost her, he decided to head back the way he had come to the Citadel.

But then *there*, in one side street behind a destroyed theatre, where the old buildings of the Ancient Quarter met the debris of war, he spotted her hunched over in a corner. She was doing something, but in this light he couldn't quite see what. He walked to the end of the street and cautiously poked his head around the corner from a slightly different angle.

She had something in her mouth, and he thought for a

moment that she might have been eating litter, but it was something far worse.

Randur was agog.

You are shitting me...

Rika was eating through an arm – one that was still connected to a corpse. She nibbled into it like a fevered fox. It seemed for a moment as if the ambient sounds of the city had fallen away entirely, and Randur could hear the sounds of delight and little groans of pleasure that Rika was emitting as she dined upon the dead flesh.

And the victim was indeed dead – he had been a young male with blond hair, still in his teens by the look of it. The dead boy's head tilted backwards and both his mouth and eyes were open in an expression of sheer horror. His throat had been cut cleanly, marked by a line of blood, and a gore-covered blade lay beside his body on the ground. The sleeve of his coat had been ripped or sliced open to expose his arm, and a cap had fallen to one side.

Randur was vaguely aware that it might be a good idea to tell someone about this, and soon, but he couldn't help but stare at the gruesome display. He waited to watch enough of what was going on to be utterly sure, to be confident that he was indeed watching the former head of the Jamur Empire chewing on human flesh.

Once the initial shock had worn off, Randur became entranced by her actions and tried to work out what she might be actually thinking. She was no longer normal – they all knew this – but how could a girl of religious purity transform in such a way?

Rika continued for several minutes, hunched as she devoured the flesh. She had begun with the arm, then moved on to one of the boy's legs, which, Randur supposed, were logical, fleshy places if this was a wolf attacking, so was she genuinely hungry? He made the connection with her lack of appetite at dinner, though that was a bit vague.

She froze. She looked up.

Randur's heart seemed to stop, and he tried to turn back before she could see his face, then sprinted along the street, jumped up on a crate, grabbed a piece of guttering and slithered into a concealed position on a flat rooftop.

His heart was racing and he was out of breath. But at least Rika had not seen him. Well, *hopefully* she had not seen him – he couldn't be entirely sure.

Randur lay there for some time, for ten or twenty minutes, maybe even longer, every now and then peering over the side to see if she was still there.

Satisfied that he was safe, he slid back along the roof tiles and flipped himself down over the edge. He made his way back to the scene of the crime, curious. When he looked around the corner, Rika was no longer there. Randur approached the body and pushed it over with his boot: the neck wound was clear to see, as was the absence of flesh in certain areas. She had eaten her way through half an arm and just a little thigh.

This would need reporting.

*

He walked back to the main thoroughfare and eventually attracted the attention of a Dragoon out on city patrol. After a hurried explanation, he guided the slender, young soldier back towards the body, which was still there.

'You sure you didn't do this yourself, eh? Guilty conscience n'all that?' the soldier replied.

Randur explained who he was, the companion of Eir, and where he had come from. 'So I have better things to be doing with my time than chopping up strangers in dark alleys.'

'Right you are, sir, I'll get the lads to bring a stretcher and we'll record this. You sure you didn't see who did this?'

'No,' he lied. Randur waited for the logical question of *Then how did you come to find the body?* But it seemed this soldier was not the brightest of sorts.

'OK,' the soldier said, shaking his head. 'You would've thought after all the fighting people would've seen enough killing, wouldn't you?'

*

Randur walked hastily back towards the Citadel, constantly checking over his shoulder. The night was deepening, and he had been out for well over a couple of hours. He realized Eir would probably be worried and, no doubt, would berate him for not letting her know where he was going.

As he reached the streets within a few hundred yards of the approach to the Citadel, he could see there was something of a lively atmosphere growing. People were here in their hundreds, milling about the streets expectantly – and there were quite a few military types too. The noise grew. It seemed peculiar since a little while ago there was nobody about. Randur pushed his way forward, glancing to and fro to locate gaps in the crowd.

He turned to a middle-aged couple. 'What's going on here? Why's everyone out and about?'

'The Night Guard is back,' the man replied. 'There is news of their arrival tonight. They say they saved the lives of many *thousands* of people on Jokull.'

Randur thanked the couple and continued on to the Citadel.

The crowds were at their most dense immediately outside the front ramp, so he pushed his way around the side to one of the other entrances. He made his way inside, nodded to those guards he knew on the door, and quickly tried to process what he would do.

I'll tell Eir – I'll have to, he thought. *It won't be easy but there's no other choice.*

Up the stairs and along the corridors, he continually brushed past administrative staff busying themselves for the arrival of the Night Guard. Eir would, perhaps, be readying herself also. Breathlessly, and sweating from the adrenalin buzz, he went along the higher levels towards her quarters. The guards let him through swiftly, and he knocked on her door before entering.

Rika.

There she was, sitting opposite Eir at the table; Eir, now dressed in an ornate blue dress with heavy woollen shawl, stood up to greet him.

'Randur, where have you been?' she asked. 'Have you not heard that the Night Guard are approaching the city? They were victorious! Brynd did it.'

'Yeah, I heard talk of it and came back.' Randur couldn't take his eyes off Rika. He just kept staring at her, trying to gauge whether or not she knew he had been following her, and that he was aware of her vile secret. 'I, uh, I needed some air. I'm sorry. I should have told you.'

'It's nothing to apologize about – I simply wondered. Are you feeling OK? You look a bit distressed.'

'Nah, I'm fine,' he replied. 'So, was Rika out as well?'

'Yes,' Eir replied, 'both of you it seems have become creatures of the night.'

Creatures of the night ... That sounds about right. Monstrous witch.

'What did you get up to, Lady Rika?' Randur asked as innocently as he could manage. He sauntered around to her side of the table, trying to get a closer look at her face, to see if there were any signs of her nocturnal habits.

'I had a minor discussion with local business representatives. They were not trivial matters.'

'Is that so.' Randur eyed her a little longer, but there was nothing in her expression to suggest her terrible secret. For a brief moment, he began to doubt that he had seen her out at all, and that it had been his imagination playing tricks on him.

'Randur,' Eir said, 'you'd better get ready for the arrival of the Night Guard. An impromptu ceremony is being organized. You'll need to look your best.'

'An easy enough task,' Randur replied. He was wary about leaving Eir in Rika's company, but he decided that Eir would be able to look after herself. He moved in to kiss Eir on the cheek before heading to their quarters.

*

Randur wanted to find something smart enough to wear, but not so ostentatious that it would feel out of place. He was beginning to understand what being partnered to royalty was like – that he would only really be an important person when in close proximity to Eir. He was aware it was a vaguely effeminate sensation, but it wasn't the first time he had been accused of such things. And he was eating well, had a great lady on his arm, and he didn't mind an excuse to throw on a breathtakingly outrageous pair of trousers.

Just that psychopathic, flesh-eating sister to deal with, then. To be honest, Randur, you've probably had stranger ex-girlfriends.

These stone chambers were cold: he had spent a few moments getting a fire going, which he'd appreciate later once everyone had gone to bed and he returned to a warm room. He splashed some water on his face and hair, brushed the thick dark strands back, and began to take off his shirt in exchange for one more suitable for the occasion.

Standing before the open wardrobe, he thought, *Black, very definitely something black after a war. Sombre. Memory of the fallen brave heroes. Besides, everyone looks good in black. Just hurry along – you don't want to leave Eir that long alone with Rika...*

He was about to reach for something when he heard a scuffle against the brickwork, and paused to listen carefully. Certain it was not something in the fire or outside his room, he considered the chimney breast. He took cautious steps around the place. The noise would stop for a few seconds, only to start again, like a bird or a rat scurrying along the walls outside. There was no balcony to this room, so it was probably something trapped within the brickwork or a bird stuck in the chimney, or perhaps even rats down below somewhere. *No, very definitely coming from outside...*

He opened the window to see if he could fathom just what the noise was –

He jumped back, gripping his sword hilt.

It was *Rika*, her face pressed up against the glass, her eyes wild. She gripped the edges of the window frame and he had no idea why she had not already fallen below. Within a heartbeat she vanished to one side, leaving only a circle of steamed-up glass where she had breathed against it.

She knows, Randur thought. *Shit, she knows...*

He had to do something tonight. He had to tell the commander before Rika intercepted him.

The witch will not feast on my flesh.

*

From the alien camp south of the city, where the Night Guard had landed back on the safer soil of Y'iren, they waited for the remnants of their own army to congregate. There, those who could took to horseback and began the journey back to Villiren. The rest would have to continue on foot and join them later.

The Night Guard ploughed through the dark countryside and Brynd, not for the first time, was acutely appreciative of the benefits of his enhanced vision. The wilderness opened up in front of him, bleak and desolate, community after community struggling to make an existence in the harsh weather. The road north was relatively straight and flat. The hours passed slowly. Grass became farmland became villages until the urban sprawl that was the southern tip of the city, the Wastelands, appeared. There was little in way of celebration at their return to this sector of Villiren and, where people had gathered, they simply looked on in curiosity.

But the Night Guard rode into the older parts of the city as heroes. Their victory had travelled ahead of them, via garudas and outriders, who had done a good job of spreading the news far and wide. Hundreds of citizens turned out to welcome their heroes home, running alongside the obvious routes to the Citadel; then, as they neared their headquarters, people came in their thousands.

The gathered masses began to cheer and whistle, and trumpets sounded, in a rare display of Imperial pomp. There were dozens of beacons lighting the route, and some of the older army standards had been raised above the Citadel, flapping in the breeze above the crenellations.

'This is like the good old days,' Brug said. 'Remember when we'd ride into Villjamur and people actually gave a shit?'

Brynd returned a knowing smile. 'People care when they feel threatened; their lack of attention simply meant we were doing our job well enough.'

'You're more optimistic than me,' Brug told him.

Brynd had to admit this felt good: his pulse raced and the air felt suddenly sharper. They hadn't experienced this sort of appreciation in years – subduing tribal skirmishes was not particularly celebrated in Villjamur, they were merely the expected thing, despite the brutal efficiency of some of the tribes.

Six mounted Dragoons met them, before guiding the army on the last part of the journey to the Citadel – it was more a formal gesture than a necessity, but Brynd was impressed at how the military was remembering some of the old traditions in his absence. A raised platform had been erected, another unexpected event, but Brynd realized that someone would want him to address the crowds – and that fitted in nicely with his own plans.

The command to halt rippled back, and gradually the horses came to a standstill. Brynd dismounted, while the others remained in position, tightening into neat lines with military precision. Brynd walked forward and some of the administrative figures greeted him, then guided him towards Eir and Rika.

He spotted Randur lingering in the background with a strange sense of urgency on his face, desperately trying to get Brynd's attention. And amidst the cheering he just about made out Eir's relief at his safe return.

Rika merely asked, 'Is Artemisia with you? Are her people coming?'

'No, my lady,' Brynd replied. 'She's awaiting further communications. They've a few matters of their own to deal with.' *And I need to ensure the people know that they are our allies before we bring them into the city . . .*

He was ushered to the platform and he climbed the steps two at a time. Directly in front of him, the army was lined up beautifully, impassive amidst the hubbub of their welcoming. People were pooled on either side, their hands in the air, chanting a range of slogans that blended into a hum of noise. Torches moved through the crowds like slow fireflies. There must have been several thousand people piled into these wide streets to listen to what he had to report. Brynd soaked it up, thriving on their energy, before he held aloft his hand for silence. It took the better part of a minute for the noise to die down enough so that he could begin his impromptu speech.

'We return as victors,' Brynd began. The noise immediately built up and, once again, he held his hand up for silence. He waited. 'We return as victors, and with new allies – new friends of our own races who helped us save the lives . . .' he paused before his exaggeration . . . 'of over a hundred thousand refugees who were fleeing atrocities on Jokull and, in the short term, we issued a comprehensive defeat to our enemies, the Okun, the same ones who tried to take Villiren from us – we stopped them here, and we stopped them on Jokull.'

Another noise of approval echoed between the high stone walls.

'However,' he announced, 'I am afraid to report that there was an unimagined catastrophe on Jokull. The legendary city of Villjamur has fallen, and the man who falsely claimed the Imperial throne – the former Chancellor Urtica – is dead.' There was a murmur that moved through the crowds and Brynd could not tell whether or not they were angry or ambivalent. 'What is left of the Empire is in a fractured state and, given the damage, it may take many, many years to fully regain the glories of the past. Villiren's position – this great, healing city – was not certain until now. But I can tell you this: Villiren, this city which we are proud to stand in, is the new jewel within the Empire's ashes. It is the new centre-point. It is the hub of the new era. Villiren receives the glories it deserves.'

The crowd slowly built up another cheer.

'This will benefit us all,' he continued, 'because the city will expand, and it will be the focus of development plans. Where there is an opportunity, it will be taken. Where the city is broken, it will heal stronger. There will be jobs and commerce, and we will see greater democratic rights and social rights for the poor – with one condition.'

He left the statement hanging there, looking across the rows of now expectant faces. Then he waited just another moment more, because it was important they knew what awaited them.

'There is only one thing that stands between us and the paradise this city can become. The very people that assaulted Villiren have taken the island of Jokull for their own and they will move from island to island until they reach us. All I ask is that all healthy individuals offer their services to fight for this noble cause: you will be fighting for your future, for your families, and for your homes. Without such assistance, I dare not think of the consequences ... If you remain alive afterwards, this world will be a perilous place.

'However, if we are victorious, you have my word that

there will be access to hospitals for the poorest, initiatives to ensure all families are fed, and the new governing bodies will see an investment in new industries to see that there will be jobs for all those who return. We will see you are looked after. We even have the finances to pay decent wages for those who join up.'

There was a hubbub, but he couldn't tell what they were thinking.

'Of course, there is one other path available to us – a path I would not like us to choose, and that would be to do *nothing*. We simply carry on as we are and we do not fight. We will most likely see ourselves encircled in this city again – under siege once again. I believe you will agree with me in thinking that to be an unfavourable option.'

People had been stunned into silence. They had come here in their thousands to celebrate something – anything, per- haps, given what happened to Villiren – and while he had them there Brynd had moved them straight into the next stage of his planning. He knew he wouldn't have such an ideal opportunity again. He could feel the gaze of the Empress, and probably the bankers and the lawmakers around him, fuming that he had not consulted them on any of these matters.

'These islands will be united against the forces that have invaded from beyond our realms of knowledge,' he continued. 'But you should know we are not alone any more. This recent victory was only possible due to help from friends elsewhere. They are . . .' He searched for the word, knowing it would be crucial. 'Neighbouring races. They are, indeed, our neigh- bours, from a place off our known maps, but they are friendly and skilled. Some of them look just like you, just like me. Some of them look . . . a little different, but they are still our neighbours and our allies and they helped save the lives of our people. They offered many of their own as sacrifice. These neighbours are very different from our enemies – these alien races that seek to destroy us. We must welcome them if we are to defeat the aliens. They are our friends in our hour of need.'

The mood was different again: hesitant, confused.

'But tonight is a time for rejoicing.' His voice became noticeably more upbeat. 'With our allies, our military has – for the second time – defeated the alien terrors that seek to ruin our lands and our peoples. Let me tell you it was a spectacular display, one that served our people proud. The future is a much brighter place than it was several days ago. And all of us within those walls' – he gestured to the Citadel behind him – 'will dedicate our lives to ensuring Villiren's safety and prosperity.'

Brynd turned to walk from the platform and trumpets began to sound, the noise ricocheting around the streets. Only then did Brynd realize how much his heart was racing, how his palms were sweating. He stepped down to ground level, where he was guided like an emperor towards Rika and Eir. It felt strange, being sheltered like this: he was the one who should be protecting people.

An avenue opened up through the staff and military personnel for him to walk back to the Citadel.

Suddenly, Randur Estevu – of all people – lurched into view from his position alongside Eir. 'Commander,' he grunted, 'it's urgent I speak with you.'

'Can it wait?' Brynd replied. 'I've just returned from a mission, if you haven't noticed.'

'Appreciate that, sir, but this is absolutely fucking serious.' His voice was more discreet now, and he kept looking back towards the Jamur sisters, who were being marshalled up along the main track inside. 'It concerns your plans for the future,' he added. 'It concerns ... *her*.' He tilted his head towards Rika.

Brynd nodded. 'I'll quickly settle some affairs. Meet me in my quarters in one hour.'

'Right you are, commander,' Randur replied, and shuffled his way back towards Eir's side.

What a curious fellow, Brynd thought.

*

Brynd opened the door to his chamber and Randur practically collapsed into the room. He stood up straight and peered behind him out of the door.

'You seem quite the paranoid man,' Brynd said with amusement. 'Paranoid men don't handle secrets well.'

'I can handle a secret all right,' Randur replied. 'It's creepy, bat-shit-crazy women I can't handle.'

Brynd gestured to a chair by the fire, then closed the door behind Randur.

'Would you mind bolting it too?'

'As you wish,' Brynd sighed, and obliged.

Randur shuffled over nervously and took his place in a wonderfully ornate wooden chair. He frowned and struggled to ease himself into it. 'Not very comfortable, this chair of yours. I would've thought someone in your position would use something more comfortable to rest his arse.'

'It keeps me from falling asleep too much by the fire,' Brynd replied, taking the seat next to him. 'Now, would the loving partner of Jamur Eir be good enough to tell me why I can't get a moment's peace on my return? What is it that you find so urgent and secret?'

'Right you are, boss,' Randur said. He leaned forward in his chair, rested his elbows on his thighs and began his story.

He reminded Brynd of their exchange on Rika's change in personality and behaviour. What he then went on to describe caused a great deal of discomfort to Brynd.

'So there I am, in the middle of the city, and she's eating the kid's arm.' Randur leaned back and held up his own as if to prove his point. 'She's biting the flesh like some rabid – no, not rabid – a *starving* dog.' He gave a remarkable level of detail, location, time of day, lighting, who else was around, whom he reported it to – enough to convince Brynd that Randur believed what he saw.

'Don't think I'm mad, will you?'

'I did already.' Brynd tried to remain expressionless. 'And you're quite certain that it was Rika? It couldn't have been someone else?'

'I didn't see her kill anyone, I'll say that much, but I saw what I saw. I came back here when I lost her to find her back with Eir. She claimed she'd been out on business. What's more, when I was in my room earlier she was there at the window.'

'What happened?'

'She just vanished, like some spirit.'

'You're absolutely sure of this?' Brynd pressed. 'It seems more than a little fanciful that she was just hanging about outside.'

Randur shrugged. 'I'm just telling you what I've seen. I'm not asking anyone to believe me – but given that you're about to make this woman the centre of your new world, I thought you might like to know she's one wave short of a shipwreck. Might not go down well with the electorate once she starts eating them.'

'Colourfully put,' Brynd muttered and considered the matter for a while longer. Was there any reason not to believe Randur? They had both witnessed Rika's deterioration, and Randur had personally seen her safe passage across the Archipelago. He harboured no grudges that Brynd knew of, either, and now his demeanour seemed genuine. Brynd knew the look of panic in someone, and Randur was displaying it here genuinely. Despite his sceptical nature, Brynd was inclined to believe that there was something in what Randur said that was probably the truth.

Which was a deeply distressing realization.

'What do you think you'll do about her?' Randur asked.

'I'm not entirely sure, if I'm honest, but I believe you saw what you say you saw.'

'Huh, which means you could think I had the eyes of a madman.'

'It's a very thin line between a sane person and a mad one. Some suggest that the only difference between perceptions of sanity and madness is the status of the person in question.'

Randur grunted a laugh. 'I've seen some weird shit in my time, I can tell you, enough to last me a lifetime. I saw what I saw. This was an extraordinary sight.'

'I've no doubt you felt it was.'

'Do you think it's related to Artemisia?'

'In what way?'

'Well, Rika does seem rather keen on the woman – emotionally attached. It's a bit like love gone wrong, their relationship.'

Brynd regarded the flames of the fire as they began to die down. He reached forward to throw another log on, and gazed as the flames licked at the wood. 'She enquired about Artemisia earlier – it was the first and *only* thing she asked of me. Not how the battle went, not how many casualties there were, nothing about the refugees.'

'Look,' Randur said, 'I'm no politician, but is she really the kind of lass you want to be putting in front of folk? Do you really want people to put their support behind someone who's not all there?'

'She is the Jamur heir,' Brynd replied. 'It is as simple as that.'

'Madness took her father, didn't it?'

'It did. I was there when he fell to his death.'

'Oh,' Randur said.

'This isn't the same kind of madness. It was paranoia that affected her father, and was an affliction that accumulated slowly over the years.'

After a pause, Randur said, 'I only hope Eir keeps her wits.'

'She'll have to with you as her partner.' Brynd smiled.

Randur's own smile faded. 'Look, chief, to be perfectly frank, I'm a bit worried – she was outside my window. You know what I'm saying? She *knows* that I saw her. She *knows* that I'm a threat – and is no doubt worried I'll tell you about her secret.'

'Well, she'd be right,' Brynd pointed out.

'Oh very funny.' Randur stood up and pointed at Brynd. 'If I end up as some midnight feast, with all my youthful limbs bearing her teeth marks, I will personally come back as a spirit to haunt you. And I'll be twice as annoying when I'm dead.'

Brynd chuckled and waved him down. 'Don't worry, Randur. Firstly, you're with Eir each night, right? Rika would not bother her sister, I wouldn't have thought. She's had hundreds of opportunities to kill her – or indeed anyone at the Citadel. No, I'd say if she's hunting in the streets, she doesn't want to be seen – perhaps she's aware of her own urges, and is therefore trying to avoid being caught in the act.'

'I don't know – I think we can safely assume she's not right in the head,' Randur said, and began to saunter around the room. 'Anything could happen.'

Brynd turned in his chair to follow Randur's steps. 'OK, I'll have two soldiers stationed outside your door and we can make sure your window gets boarded up – we can claim it's broken.'

'I'd appreciate it.' Randur picked up one of Brynd's swords from the rack against the wall. 'Decent blade, this.' He began to work through some moves that seemed a little genteel at first, then Brynd could see some real flair there.

'We've not had the pleasure of sparring yet, have we?' Brynd asked. 'Perhaps we can see what you're made of soon.'

Randur finished a series of moves with a flourish. 'I'd like that,' he replied. 'I was without doubt the best swordsman on my island. I fought my way across the archipelago to keep the Jamur flame burning. I'd say I'd hold my own.'

'That is if you're not eaten in the night.'

'I don't especially like your jokes,' Randur said. 'They're not actually funny.'

'Who was making a joke?' Brynd replied coolly.

Randur grunted his reply. 'So, what will you do regarding Rika's position?'

'I need to sleep on it first,' Brynd replied. 'The mission has drained me somewhat, and I think it needs the clarity of a good night's rest before I actually engage with the situation.'

'Fair enough,' Randur replied, and moved towards the door. 'But it might be worth having her followed, in case you're not sure whether or not to really trust me.' He flipped back the bolts and opened the door cautiously to see if anyone was outside. He waited a good minute before he was confident and then he glanced back into the room. 'Thanks for taking the time to listen.'

Brynd gestured wearily. 'I appreciate you telling me – honestly, I do.'

As Randur closed the door, Brynd sighed and approached the window. He moved his hand to draw back the curtain – paused, bearing in mind what Randur had said about Rika – then with a swift flick of his arm he pulled them open.

There was nothing there, no creature scaling the walls, no mad former Empress. Only the cityscape of Villiren presented itself and Brynd stared down on the glistening beacons and lanterns around the harbour. He had only just arrived back from fighting and wondered if the situation could get any worse. If what Randur said was true, and rumours broke out across the city, Brynd knew just what that would do to his plans to get the remains of the Empire moving forward.

Will there be any end to this? How bad will things have to get?

SEVENTEEN

Jeza decided it was time to return to the location where the Mourning Wasp had been discovered. Though she had taken small samples to assess its potential, she alone could not have conducted the complex experiments to take it back to the factory.

She brought Coren and Diggsy with her this time, and they helped her with their sophisticated equipment. The boys cursed the rain that lashed against their faces on the journey there, and cursed the ascent on their skittish horses. But, eventually, in the sanctuary of the cave, they saw what Jeza had found and were astounded – as she had been herself.

As she stared at the remnants of the original Mourning Wasp once again she realized that the find managed to fulfil that need in her life, the thirst for knowledge.

It seemed to fill the void of answers in her own existence.

Like some of the others at the factory, Jeza had grown up without knowing her parents. She told herself she didn't care about this. She had been lucky, though, and had somehow managed to scrape a decent existence alongside cultists, who had taught her to read, had instilled in her a sense of curiosity.

Jeza felt a strange kinship with these forgotten creatures of the past; and she was determined not to be forgotten. So she wanted to make her mark.

And she would do that through palaeomancy.

Coren laughed a little, pushed a few strands of black hair

from his eyes. He walked around, folding his arms around his stocky midriff. 'I'll give you this. It's the best find you've made.'

She examined his comments for any traces of sarcasm and then beamed with pride and said, 'Thanks!'

They unpacked their relics and set to work. They built a frame over the pit using small silver rods, so that after an hour it seemed as if a metallic spider had been at work on some alarmingly brutal web. Once this was in place, she began to attach the necessary wires to a thaumaturge unit, which in reality was no more than a two-feet-square box, but she struggled to lift its weight on her own. Finally, she attached a large glass vial to collect what she liked to tell others was the distilled essence of Time. What was collected was essential to the re-creation phase back in the factory.

They switched on the equipment. Light shot along the wires and the silver metal mesh began to glow purple, illuminating their faces. They stared down on the work in progress. The exoskeleton on the Mourning Wasp began to stutter in and out of existence, then, soon after that, so did the skull.

After the better part of an hour, what remained was a translucent set of remains. This was the bit where she felt guilty, that these beautiful almost-fossilized remains would never be the same again. In the right light, it would seem as if a ghost lay there on the floor. She checked the vial and it had indeed filled up with a murky-looking fluid. She unscrewed it carefully, sealed it, and placed it in a bag – for the next few hours, it wouldn't leave her side.

After the operation the three of them crouched down by the side of the Mourning Wasp. It now lay there both in and out of existence, half of it removed, half of it to remain there indefinitely.

'We're done,' Diggsy sighed, placing his arm casually around Jeza's waist.

'Finally,' Coren muttered, 'we can head back to civilization.'

'I like it out here,' Jeza replied. 'It gives you space to think.'

'Think about what? There's nothing to think about out here. There's nothing but rain and rocks. No wonder this poor thing decided to end its days. If it lived in the city, at least there'd be something to think about.'

'Well, there's not a huge amount left in Villiren these days either.'

'True, I'll give you that,' Coren said.

'Anyway, let's head home,' Jeza said, 'I want to get started on bringing him back.' She gestured to the inconsistent form of the Mourning Wasp.

*

Later that night, back at Factory 54, phase two began. With the rest of the young group gathered around excitedly, Jeza and Diggsy reconstructed the metallic web around their large marble workbench, while Coren complained that his legs ached and sat glumly in the kitchen area watching them. Still, she liked that it was her and Diggsy doing this; it was something else for them to bond over, something else to share.

For the better part of an hour they arranged the rods and this time she had to make sure that they were all tilted according to the correct angles. More than once she had to consult her books, because she was always forgetting an equation here and there.

Pilli had lit a few coloured lanterns nearby, lighting the room with a warm glow. Jeza could smell food being cooked as she walked around making minute adjustments. There were sudden shouts and weapons clashing outside and for a moment they thought the war had restarted, though Gorri ran back in saying it was just a few of the gangs engaged in a turf fight.

'Great,' Jeza muttered. 'I guess soon even we'll have to start paying protection money.'

'Nah,' Diggsy replied. 'I've heard they're too busy trying to build up numbers from the war. It'll be a while yet.'

She turned back to her work, inserted the vial containing the essence of the Mourning Wasp and watched it drain into the rods. Then, she stood back as they began to glow.

Slowly but surely, as she expected, a form started to materialize before them on the workbench. It stuttered into existence, and then became cohesive.

Once the rods were removed, everyone in the group – even Coren, whose legs were mysteriously no longer aching – shuffled across to see the results.

It was the Mourning Wasp, and it maintained the same slightly curled pose that it had in the cave.

'It's strange,' Jeza said. 'The skull seems to have arrived complete, yet the rest of the body is still translucent.'

'Your bit of kit always worked better on bone. It was designed by cultists interested in the necromancy of humans and rumels, don't forget.'

'Yeah, I guess so. Dammit, this is going to mean another failure.'

'Don't be so harsh on yourself,' Diggsy said. His startling eyes disarmed her anger. 'It's too early yet. Besides, we could think of something.'

'How? We need a complete body – a full exoskeleton – if we're to do anything with this.'

Little Gorri pushed in to get a closer look. The kid needed to visit the barber, since his red hair almost covered his eyes. 'I know I spend most of my time with designs and stuff, but you could always use the Okun parts, eh?'

Jeza looked at Diggsy, and then at Coren, who made a face that said it was worth a go.

*

Jeza puzzled over the theory for a day or two. She lay on her bed, surrounded by fossils perched haphazardly upon shelves, which she'd hoarded in her childhood. She held one in her hands, a small spiralled shell now blended with rock, mystified as to its purpose in life. She examined her notebooks on shared characteristics of fauna, to see if there were any patterns that might be of use. She looked at massive charts, complex family trees spread about on vellum across the walls, which only she could really fathom – though much of that was down to her dire handwriting. She had spent much of her life wondering where certain creatures came from, but the Mourning Wasp was all the more difficult to assess given the fact that cultists had a penchant for tinkering with the fabric of life.

Diggsy entered the room only at night, and the two of them lay alongside each other in a passionless state. She still churned through speculative theories in her mind, all the time wondering what might happen.

If she could somehow ensure the Mourning Wasp's form was stable, by using something from the Okun material – and even its biological matter – then the creature would surely be able to survive. Then they could easily reproduce it.

When she was certain Diggsy was asleep, she leaned over to retrieve the small box containing Lim's notebooks. For a long time she was scared of opening them, scared of what she might feel, but as soon as she looked across his theories and formulae she put aside whatever emotions she had felt – still felt – for him and got lost in the magic of his silence.

Eighteen

The new criers of Villiren began their work early.

Like an invasion force, several of them penetrated the streets of Saltwater, Althing, Scarhouse, Deeping, the Ancient Quarter, what was left of Port Nostalgia and throughout dribs and drabs of the Wastelands, wherever there might be people who would listen.

In a bright-red doublet, black breeches and black tricorne hat, which Brynd had commissioned for their newly formed role as official information distributors, they marched forth bringing news. While last night those who were interested in the wider world had gathered to see the Night Guard's return, there were still tens of thousands of people who had not turned up, who were either too busy or uninterested in things beyond their streets. Brynd left the Citadel, to follow the criers' progress and gauge public reaction from the corner of road junctions. At the back of his mind, he wondered if he'd witness the Empress gorging herself on some poor unsuspecting soul . . .

It was a chilly, sharp morning, and a sea mist had drifted onshore, leaving its ghostly impression upon the streets. The criers' voices seemed to come from nowhere and gained greater significance in these conditions. They rang their bells, and issued forth the news that Brynd had scripted for them.

Villjamur had been destroyed. Tens of thousands of people had fled. The Imperial forces came to their rescue and were victorious. There was a roll call of some of the few senior military names who died. There was a reiteration of the victory, that the enemy had not just been defeated but comprehensively beaten. The first message was simple and repeated itself from street to street, verbatim. People seemed to acknowledge the words and perhaps mutter a comment or two to someone nearby, but otherwise citizens seemed utterly uninterested or unimpressed.

Good, Brynd thought, *they don't feel threatened or concerned. It's business as usual for them.*

A little later on in the morning came the second wave of messages: the man who called himself Emperor is dead. All Imperial powers have henceforth transferred to Villiren. The Jamur lineage is to be reinstated. Military law continues from the aftermath of the siege.

Then the third and final message of the day: good news. We have powerful new allies to the south of the city. They supported us in the war. They bring prosperity to our lands. Our friends will help us keep the vicious enemies, who have destroyed Villjamur, at bay. Only with our new friends can we succeed. Together we will create a new, wealthy, safer world for our children. It is important we welcome them. The Empress extends her hand of friendship.

It occurred to Brynd how people barely reacted to Rika's name, and he hoped – when the time was right – she could continue making public appearances. He felt it was important for people to buy into a stable leader.

He walked down one of the main thoroughfares to Scarhouse, and into an iren, as this last piece of news was absorbed into the city. Traders looked up, customers paused in their browsing. A weird silence fell here.

Together, prosperity, important, welcome, safer, wealthy, all words that Brynd had agonized over. Their tone was right, he felt, and it should plant a positive seed in people's minds. He could never predict just how people would react. People could not care about the most important matters, issues that directly affected their lives, and yet something exceptionally mundane could spark riots. The criers might not be enough, however. It occurred to him that, yet again, he would also need to get the Jorsalir Church on board, much as he loathed to do so. Their help had been crucial in mustering volunteers for the war effort; their help would also be a necessary evil in getting the message across that a transition to a new culture would be harmonious. How helpful would they be in the face of new cultures coming to these islands?

Brynd made a safe assumption that there would be plenty of trouble to come. What would be the consequences of integrating their two worlds? Humans and rumels did, generally, get along – though that took centuries to happen. Perhaps they should settle on different islands altogether, and build separate communities, in peace.

Nothing like this had ever been attempted, and his inexperience was showing. The only thing that was right in both his head and heart was for there to be acceptance of each other's culture.

And that required sound propaganda.

*

Whilst continuing with his morning patrols, and keen to see some of the city after his brief mission on Jokull, Brynd decided to pay a visit to the youths at the factory. He wanted to give them the good news regarding the success of their armour in battle, to tell them he would be ordering plenty more, and to see what else they could do.

The fog began to clear, and he could see the streets around the factory were quiet as always. Few people seemed to want to travel here, and why would they? There were few irens, few stores, few taverns. The place needed renovation; the streets should be thronging with activity. What happened to these factories and why had they mostly stopped working?

Since he had helped to organize a successful defence of the

city, Brynd wanted to improve Villiren vastly. He could see so much untapped potential in the city. Here was an area that needed injecting with money to get production going again, to get people moving in and spending money and creating jobs. So much could be done – there was no reason this area couldn't become an engine room of the future city, a trade hub.

*

He eventually reached the factory where the youths were. There, he banged on the door loudly and waited. Very distantly he thought he could hear something inside, like a grumbling.

Or a droning noise. Or was that growling?

Then there were loud footsteps running over a metal frame, and someone calling from one corner of the warehouse to another, before silence fell. Then, nothing.

He thumped on the door again, then regarded the street as a few flakes of snow fell to the ground before melting away. He waited a little longer.

Eventually someone came to let him in and the bolts slid free.

'Commander!' Jeza stood in the doorway, covered in muck and looking totally flustered. Her red hair was tied back, and strands of it flitted across her face in the morning breeze. 'Oh, we weren't expecting you back just yet.'

'Have I come at a bad time?' Brynd asked, curious as to what was going on.

'No, no, it's that, I ... Look, you'd better come in.' Jeza skipped aside from him to enter. He plunged into the semi-darkness behind her and waited for her to lead the way again.

'How was your business out of town?' she asked. 'Did you get everything sorted?'

'It was a battle.'

'Literally or figuratively?'

'Literally.'

'Oh my,' she replied. 'You should have said.'

'I didn't want anyone to know at the time,' Brynd replied. 'Though you could have guessed with my recent orders. So has the team been keeping well?'

'We've certainly been a bit busy,' she said, leading him through the dreary corridors. 'You said you were in battle then – so, does that mean you were *testing* the armour?'

'That's correct, yes.'

'And . . .'

Brynd laughed. 'It stood up exceptionally well, Jeza. None of us who were wearing it bore any injuries where we were protected by it. What's more everyone reported back on the weight and mobility improvements. We're going to want a *lot* more of it – as much as you can manufacture.'

'Oh that's great!' she replied. 'I'll show you how we've improved our production methods.'

'Very efficient of you,' Brynd said.

Jeza directed him towards their seating area, but before she did she paused and her expression changed to one of concern. 'Now, I know I said you didn't come at a bad time, but just to warn you, things are . . . OK, I'll not shit you – they're a little bit lively in there at the moment. Things have gone wrong.'

'Should I be worried?'

A sudden clamour erupted the other side of the door, and it sounded as if quite a few things had been knocked over with an enormous clatter. Jeza cringed. 'No, no,' she said, and shook her head vigorously. 'Not at all. It's just that . . . an experiment or two is underway, and I think maybe it's getting a little out of hand . . .'

'I understand,' Brynd said. 'Do you want me to stand to one side until you sort it out?'

'That . . . yeah, that might work. OK, you ready?'

He nodded and she opened the door.

Brynd stepped in behind her and immediately looked

upwards. Though he couldn't quite fathom its precise shape, something enormous, and with many legs, was drifting across the ceiling. It was covered in a slimy skin and making an unnatural, guttural noise without really opening its maw. Its head was lolling from side to side and it lumbered its way awkwardly across to a platform on one side, where it then cowered in a corner.

'What on earth is that?' Brynd enquired.

'Experiment number eighty-something . . . Eighty-three I think.'

'Could you expand on this, just for a curious soldier?'

'You know, we're in the business of creating all sorts here, and this is a bit of prep work to see if the regenerative technology will work on something else, which I think it might. We're in the trade of *horrors* and grotesques – which is precisely what this is. We make monsters.'

'It doesn't look especially horrific,' Brynd observed. 'The thing looks more frightened of you.'

'Stupid beast.' One of the other lads entered the room, the laid-back handsome blond, who placed his arm casually behind Jeza's back. 'Yeah, we're not great at refining their moods just yet.'

'But once we get the formula right . . . Don't forget, this is only to see if we can activate the life form. Regeneration and palaeomancy and the like. We've got something else in development, but there are a few essentials you need to get in place before you gamble. We've only got one of those specimens, so it's a bit like doing trials beforehand.'

The creature suddenly sprinted across the platform and into the shadows above, knocking over some crates and sending rusty relics spilling onto the floor with an enormous racket. Two others from their group ran after it across the platform, the first time Brynd had noticed them, and disappeared through a hatch and into another room. Howls came from the distance.

'Fuck,' Jeza said, and she and Diggsy ran forward to try to clear up the mess on the floor.

Brynd sauntered up to them and watched.

'Oh they're everywhere,' Jeza said. 'We'll have to clean up later.' She stood up in a huff, with her hands on her hips. 'Later, yes. First let me show you the warehouse, commander, since you've come all this way.'

'I'd appreciate that, thank you. Then we could perhaps have a chat about logistics and then I'll leave you in peace.'

There was another racket and a curse from the other room.

'I doubt there'll be much peace for a while,' Jeza muttered.

*

Jeza showed Brynd their new ad-hoc facilities, which entailed opening up more rooms of the surprisingly deep factory. She lit a few lanterns on stands in the centre of one particularly large room, which he did not need to help him see, but they did cast a warm glow across the rows and rows of shelves.

Sitting upon them were hundreds of pieces of glistening armour.

'We cleaned this area up,' Jeza announced, 'and dusted down these units, and they were great for storing more pieces of armour. We've been making all of this since you left and we probably have just over a thousand complete sets now. We would have made more, but I didn't want to over-commit – you know, in case you didn't want any more.'

'This is impressive. Over a thousand?'

'Yeah, and we can make more really quickly. It's simple, once the kit is set up. We should probably discuss how many you're going to need and by when, because I've a *few* private clients that have been discussing other forms of work and I'd really like to plan our workload. We've come a long way in a few weeks.'

'I'll say,' Brynd said. 'Is there any chance of exclusive contracts . . . ?'

'We do a lot of things here, commander. I wouldn't want

223

the guys to just make armour all day long. They'll soon go their own ways – they can be a fickle bunch, but I love them for it. To keep them sane, they'll want to work on other things.'

'I understand,' Brynd said. 'Tell me – these so-called private clients of yours. Why would they be after armour?'

'Strictly speaking it's not armour, sir, but other creatures.'

'This could be a matter of great importance to the Empire,' Brynd stressed.

Jeza shook her head. 'I'm sorry, commander, but as much as we generally loathe them, we want to operate like many of the other cultists in the city, and we adhere to a strict code of conduct. That way we ensure clients come back to us and not elsewhere.'

Brynd's curiosity was now piqued, but he did not want to assert himself too strongly. He needed Jeza's talents; he needed her industry. Upsetting her could impact upon the outcome of a battle. He looked once again over the rows and rows of armour, contemplating just what he'd need.

'I want to bring more samples of standard-issue Imperial armour to you,' Brynd said, 'body armour, shields, helmets, the works. My specifications would only be to improve upon it in the same way you have already.' He paused, knowing that if he discussed numbers, it would most likely cause concern. 'We're going to have to sign contracts that forbid you to discuss these matters with anyone – anyone at all – which, if breached, are punishable by fairly strict means.' She looked worried suddenly. 'It's fairly standard stuff,' he added. 'Just to protect Imperial assets. It's the same thing we use for people like ore merchants.'

'OK,' she agreed.

'Excellent. I'll have the contracts and the samples brought to you as soon as they're ready, along with quantities of what we'd need, roughly by when, and how we'll collect it. You can return with some estimated prices. Meanwhile, I'm interested in these other things you're creating – these so-called *aggressive* creatures. Do you think they can be used easily as a weapon on the battlefield?'

Jeza nodded. 'It's funny you should mention that because I'm working on something that might be really, really useful. I can't say too much right now, in case it crumbles, but it's looking good – and I think it might work because . . . well, you saw for yourself that we had a successful regeneration earlier.'

'I'm intrigued,' Brynd said. 'When you have something final, cost it up.'

*

Brynd headed quickly back to the Citadel, whereupon he immediately called for an emergency meeting of the Night Guard.

They filed one by one into the obsidian room, garbed in their crisp all-black uniforms, and took their places around the vast table that dominated the room. Once they were all settled, Brynd closed the door – and locked it, which raised a few eyebrows. He then stoked the fire so that it roared loudly before he took his place in the centre of the table, facing his regiment. As soon as he was seated, a respectful silence came. Afternoon sunshine fell across some of the gathered faces, revealing cool and attentive expressions.

'Before I start,' Brynd announced, 'I want to thank you for your roles in the defence of Jokull. That was an *outstanding* mission, one which you should all be proud of. I have rarely seen an enemy dispatched so efficiently, nor can I recall having seen us work with any other forces so well, and it does our army credit. Morale will be raised as a result. We can see that the enemy, the Okun, are vulnerable on the right occasion. This is an important message to spread.'

A murmur of appreciation spread across the table.

'Now we're back in Villiren,' Brynd continued, 'I want something done and it is of the utmost importance. I would like Jamur Rika to be shadowed at all times – in the most discreet manner available. Whoever follows her – and I recommend this is not a solo mission – should remain at a distance and unobserved. She should not know you are watching her. No one should know where you are going. I want you all to take shifts doing this, and it should be something that occurs all night and all day.'

'Why the cloak and dagger, commander?' Brug asked. 'I mean, what should we be watching for? Is she likely to be attacked?'

'As I mentioned, this is not a normal mission,' Brynd continued. 'But it is a particularly sensitive case. It is unlikely she will be attacked and, to be honest, this is not the focus of the mission. I've received a report from a respectable source that Jamur Rika has formed unnatural habits. Not a word of this leaves the room.'

He paused. The soldiers nodded.

Brynd cleared his throat. 'She has been witnessed eating the flesh of the dead.'

No one gasped – that wasn't the way of the Night Guard – but some of them raised their eyebrows. Brynd informed them in detail of what Randur had seen, gave his impressions on the matter, and tried to reassure them if they doubted the chain of command.

'I want her tracked, so we can really assess the situation. I have . . . planned accordingly, if this turns out to be true, but it is simply too early to tell. I'm interested in surveillance only for now. Any questions?'

No one responded.

'Finally, on to more fitting business,' Brynd said. 'It is time we prepared for war once again. Our next move – and ultimately, I hope our very final move – will be to remove the sky-city from the skies and rid the Archipelago of anything it leaves behind.'

'Do you think that is possible?' Brug said.

'After the defence of Villiren and the rescue from Jokull, I'd say anything's possible,' Brynd replied. A few of the others muttered their agreement on that sentiment. 'Now, the question is how we go about this and, if I'm honest, I do not yet know. I want to consult with Artemisia and her people. You will all help me in this matter, as I wish you to become ambassadors for our culture. It goes without saying my trust in you all is beyond question ... I'll want you to mix with their people and help glean information on their military. Though Artemisia is going to assist in such matters, I'd like to know troop capabilities, what weapons are at our disposal. What creatures, even. We might bring many of them into the city, to begin the process of integration.'

'Do we have to fly again?' Mikill joked. He was a slight man, and young, so the others had quickly ribbed him about not being able to handle the rough journey across to Jokull. A few chuckles broke out.

Smiling, Brynd said, 'Yes, it wasn't exactly what I'd call comfortable, was it, but look at how quickly we could respond to the crisis there. What other methods do these new people possess that we can use to our advantage?'

'A change in your tone there,' Syn pointed out. He had that quiet, dangerous look about him, the one most of the Night Guard muttered about when he wasn't around. 'You've gone from talking about friendship and harmony to exploitation for our own advantage.'

Brynd contemplated the statement, before nodding. 'You're quite right, Syn, on both counts. I don't think they're mutually exclusive points. We do need to live harmoniously with them, but they also possess many powerful creatures for us to use.'

'We could get our own creatures,' Syn pointed out. 'Plenty of hybrids on the underground.'

'Interesting you say that,' Brynd continued. 'That is a matter I'm looking into. But there are, for now, some interesting specimens I honestly believe we should use to our advantage – and I say that because preserving our culture here – helping the humans and rumel who make up the Boreal Archipelago as it is – they're also a priority right now. Of course, whatever is in the encampment to the south, once they're here for good, then their integration becomes a shared responsibility.'

'Have you seen anything of particular value in their encampment?' Brug asked.

'I have,' Brynd said. 'It wasn't so much a creature based there – it was someone who managed to break through into our world of their own accord. I have mentioned this Frater Mercury figure before. He could be key to bringing down that sky-city but, as far as I'm concerned, we'll have to go through Artemisia's people first.'

'Is he their god?' Tiendi asked.

He's a god to all of us, apparently, Brynd wanted to say, but thought better of it. 'Of a sort, yes. We've already seen that he has staggering powers – he created those land-vehicles, after all, so it's safe to say that without him most of our people would already be dead. I need to . . . negotiate, with Artemisia, with their elders, with Frater Mercury himself, if I can somehow schedule a proper meeting with him. That will be my biggest concern for the immediate campaign – if he is to be a weapon of sorts, just how we can use him.'

'Who will you send first to meet with their people?' Tiendi asked.

Brynd contemplated her question for a moment, and looked at the men – and woman – gathered around the table. 'You're all the best soldiers I will ever know. You're all suited for combat. You're all intelligent people. Any of you will, I'm sure, do a good job in promoting our concerns and gathering information. I will make sure you all get to investigate what's there within five or six days – each of you will help me form a strategy.'

Nineteen

Malum waited in the afternoon shadows, mulling over his plans.

The garuda had informed his men that there was in fact no immediate threat to Villiren. The Okun were nowhere to be seen on this island. There was no more threat from the north. In fact, the only issues were in the west, on another island entirely, too far to be of concern to him. So in fact the posters found around the city, telling of this so-called immediate threat, were lying.

So what was the commander really up to?

There, the man Malum was waiting for. Derrouge was skinny, well dressed, and walked with a gentle stoop, so he constantly had to peer slightly upwards to see where he was going.

There's a man who's spent far too long sitting at a desk, Malum thought. *Should have no trouble overpowering this fool.*

Derrouge left the bank, a compact, whitewashed building. Two men were standing by its front door; they wore no uniform, and were only noticeable to those who knew the drill. They were private militiamen, skilled fighters and paid highly enough so that they wouldn't trade secrets with the gangs. Aside from those men, the building bore no signs that told you money could be stored there. Then again, the banks didn't like to attract attention to themselves. It was said they were small, impenetrable fortresses. That there were cultist traps deep in the vaults, all sorts of trickery that was more trouble than it was worth to tackle. Malum had never tried his luck with them – besides, he had a lot of coin himself, from his various rackets, which he wanted to protect. The banks guaranteed anonymity so criminals – often the wealthiest in the city – could have their money well looked after.

If it wasn't for the banks, there would be no criminal underworld.

Malum pulled up his hood. The day was winding up, and what people there were began to head indoors. He moved along the walls, swift and cautious, all the time looking around to see if anyone would interrupt the mission. He had to be careful and felt he couldn't rely on the same networks to do his bidding, or on the fear of the public keeping them from intervening. Derrouge, wearing elegant, long crimson robes and a black waxed raincape, took the predictable route towards his home, situated at the north-eastern end of the Ancient Quarter. On edge, Malum trotted down through the same high-walled alley, noting all the details, the rubbish and the homeless man slumped on the corner. Three old women were standing in a doorway talking about the weather. A young man was pulling in a washing line between buildings and somewhere indoors was the sound of a baby crying.

It began to rain, thick and heavy drops. Up ahead, Derrouge pulled up his own hood and continued on his way. Malum shook free his messer blade from his sleeve and pursued the banker down an even narrower alley. He closed the distance in stealth, thirty feet, twenty, ten and he was upon him: he stamped down on the back of Derrouge's left knee, bringing him to the ground, sprawling on his back. Malum stood on the man's chest, grabbed his collar and pressed the messer blade up against his throat.

'You do exactly as I say. You're coming with me. You're going to stand up and calmly walk back the way you came.

You're going to walk in the direction I tell you and when we get to an agreed point you're going to wear a sack over your head. Do we understand each other?'

'And . . . if I don't?' Derrouge squirmed.

'I'll cut a diagonal line across your torso, grab your innards while you're still alive to feel the pain, and tie them to the door of your family home.' Malum held up his blade to show the man the tool he would use to do that.

'OK.' Derrouge nodded as much as he could manage.

'Good.' Malum stepped back and hauled him up by the scruff of his neck. He spun the banker around and pulled back on his raincape; he cut a slash through the clothing, slipped his hand and blade inside, resting the steel on the man's back. 'You try to move out of line, I cut and you don't walk again.'

Malum steered the visibly nervous Derrouge back through the streets, almost the way they came, but then taking a radically different direction. The two of them must have looked like close friends, being so close to each other like this.

They walked for about ten minutes and, in an alleyway on the edge of the Ancient Quarter, safely away from those who might draw the attention of a military patrol, Malum produced a hessian bag to go over Derrouge's head. 'This is so you don't go blabbing our whereabouts.'

The banker begrudgingly obliged, and stood limp while Malum pulled the bag over him. Malum guided him to a house a few streets further into Deeping, a modern bland structure with a straight roof and little in the way of ornamentation. It was enough for their purposes today. Malum banged on the door and a hatch opened for someone to identify him.

'It's me,' he grunted.

The door opened and Malum was ushered inside.

*

They tied Derrouge to a sturdy chair in an upstairs room, which was composed of bare floorboards, rough walls with a small window that overlooked a backstreet. Malum lit a fire and, after deciding the banker had suffered for just about the right length of time, he took the bag off his head.

'There, that wasn't so bad, was it?' Malum asked.

'If you want money, I can arrange for that,' Derrouge slurred. 'We . . . we can have it to your doorstep in less than an hour, no questions asked.'

'I've got enough money already,' Malum replied. 'But thanks for the offer. It's nice to know you can piss people's savings away like that.'

'Hey, Malum,' one of the youths said, poking his head through the door, 'you want a drink or somethin' to eat?'

'Nah, I'm good,' Malum replied. 'You can leave me alone with this guy for now.'

The kid sauntered downstairs and left them to it.

'Malum,' Derrouge said, squinting to make out his face better. 'I've heard that name before.'

'Good, then you should be scared,' Malum replied.

'What do you want if it's not money? I can't think of anything else we'd have in common to discuss. We operate in quite different circles, you and I.'

Malum struck him across the face just to let him know who was in charge and the banker lurched to one side, before looking back at Malum with the appropriate level of fear. 'I've killed more people than you've closed deals,' he said. 'Don't think I won't hesitate to cut your throat when the time comes.'

'Why did you bring me here then?' Derrouge spat. 'You could've killed me in that alleyway if my death was all that you wanted.'

'You're a smart guy,' Malum admitted. 'You're alive because I want information out of you, and it usually requires the informant to be alive.'

'What information?'

'Now we're talking. You're one of the bankers involved with the military's schemes.'

'We all are,' Derrouge confessed.

'I want to know all about your dealings with the albino commander.'

'That's all?' Derrouge replied, surprised. 'Well, the fellow is looking to rebuild the city and he needs our finance. One can't build an Empire without capital.' He gave a look of disdain to Malum, as if he was too stupid to understand.

For that, he got a punch to the stomach.

Malum gave him a couple of minutes and paced around the room, behind Derrouge, then back around in front of him. 'Is that what he claims he's after then, to *rebuild* the Empire?'

'More or less, yes. I believe he has the city's interests at heart.'

'Does he fuck – he wants to stomp the Imperial seal on Villiren, a free city, bringing with it his military law.'

'Well, that's no issue to me. I'm simply looking to grow the bank's finances, and the military is a very safe bet.'

'Why?'

'If the worst happens, they just invade somewhere else and take the resources to pay us back,' Derrouge chuckled.

'Didn't you make enough money from the war?' Malum said. He walked over to the window and folded his arms. 'I know of your dealings with arms manufacturers.'

'It is true we made money from them. They needed loans for ore, we provided them, and the military gave them more orders than they could cope with. There's nothing illegal about it.'

'You're profiting from death,' Malum pointed out with a smile.

'Business is business.'

'Well now, there ain't much difference between you and me, after all, is there?' Malum grunted.

233

Malum walked around the room contemplating his next question. Derrouge simply sat miserably, staring at the floor. The fire crackled in the stove.

'I want details,' Malum said. 'I want to know not just the plans for any rebuilding projects, but I want to know what the *military* schemes are likely to be. You must know that. Most importantly, I want to find out what you know about the aliens south of the city – what their role is likely to be? Are they likely to be given their own island or shipped in with us lot?'

'The aliens are to be integrated,' Derrouge said. 'That much I know.'

'Are they likely to come to the cities? To Villiren – will they come into Villiren?'

'It is possible,' Derrouge said, his head low. 'That's what the commander suggests.'

'They're going to be treated like ordinary citizens?'

'They are going to earn that honour by fighting alongside the Imperial soldiers,' Derrouge replied. 'I think that's what the commander is after. He claims there's little choice – it's either that or fight against them, which he says is a battle that cannot be won.'

Nothing but Imperial lies to control the city ... This contradicts what the garuda told us. I've got plans for this damn city and the military does not feature in them. Malum tried not to let his anger show.

'Where exactly does Villiren fit into all of this?'

'How should I know?'

Malum lifted a blade and rested it on the banker's collarbone. 'Perhaps this'll clarify your mind a little.'

'Honestly, I don't know the full plans,' the man spluttered, 'but I know that the commander wants to protect the city, and funding for that is about as honourable as our profession gets.'

'I want numbers, banker,' Malum ordered. 'I want numbers, I want plans. How many aliens are south of the city?'

'I don't know, honestly. Perhaps several thousand at the moment, but there are likely to be far more than that. To my understanding they are escaping problems in their own world – that could mean tens, possibly hundreds of thousands, possibly millions – and they all need communities to be built, which is why the commander is seeking finance – that, and to defend our islands in case of another war.'

'So he's using *our* money – money put in by the hard-working folk of this city – to spend on the welfare of creatures from another world?'

'Who will then create prosperity with that money, making us all richer in the long run.'

'That's a fairy tale.'

'You can look at it like that if you choose, but this is all I know. Please, I will help you if I can, I have knowledge of how the finance will flow, and in which direction.'

Malum walked behind Derrouge and cut one hand free. He went to fetch a piece of paper and a pencil and thrust them at Derrouge. 'You write down these names for me. Write down everyone who's involved in financial dealings with the aliens, and you write them now.'

This is a futile lead to pursue, Malum thought, as Derrouge hastily scribbled down the details.

Malum also realized that he didn't know precisely what he wanted from Derrouge any more, which was a desperate state to be in. He wasn't used to such amateurism from himself.

Still, he had now confirmed his great fear: aliens were indeed coming to invade their culture to make a ghetto of Villiren, and he vowed never to be a part of that. He would take this city for himself and make sure that both the military and the aliens had nothing to do with the city's future.

*

Later, once Malum had dumped the banker on a street deep in the Ancient Quarter, he headed over to his underground hideout to meet up with some of the others in his gang. The only light came from the glow of a few cressets lined up to mark the way. There, in the subterranean darkness, he found them drinking home-brewed alcohol on upturned crates.

Since the war, the Bloods – along with affiliate gang members – had secured various pockets of the city and, surprisingly, the military had done nothing to take back control. Businesses carried on, with the Bloods overseeing protection for their areas: a few streets in Deeping, Althing, Scarhouse and two in the Ancient Quarter, with larger communities of the Wastelands likely to be at their disposal, if they were actually worth maintaining.

What had begun as the result of his wartime rage had become something he managed, and ultimately it wasn't the fact that the commander was working with bankers that disgusted Malum – after all, he dealt with the rich himself.

There were a few businessmen who had teamed up with Malum, worried that the military rule would stifle their markets. It was they who were most concerned about alien communities, worried about how their land might be taken from them. While the likes of tavern owners, landlords and butchers didn't have the chutzpah to take up this cause against whatever Imperial plans were brewing, they knew that Malum did. They also knew that he had a proven record of dealing with Commander Lathraea and standing up to him. There was one other thing that businesses could not control, which was the wider population. They needed to manipulate the citizens, to cause problems so that control might be levered away from the military. That was where Malum came in, and he was happy to use the businessmen as a platform for his own plans to free Villiren from Imperial rule once and for all – and to make plenty of coin in the process.

He had dreams of creating a pirate city, a free city.

Something independent of the Empire, and which he could control in alliance with business owners. A few rogue cultists, fearful that they were going to be purged by military occupation and martial laws, had also pledged their allegiance. A force was building up and his tendrils were stretching out further. Malum was now dreaming of taking up the position of portreeve of a free Villiren: he would be the king of this city, officially, and not just the head of a gang.

'How did it go?' someone said, distracting his thoughts.

There were about ten of his men here, some playing cards, some drinking, and one reading a book. These were his most trusted, those who felt uneasy about leaving an underground they were used to. Most were below the age of twenty, young men from various backgrounds, none of them particularly blessed. As the years rolled on Malum began to feel like a father to them.

'Yeah, did he spill anything good?' another asked eagerly. Soon their respectful attention all turned to him.

'I got a little information out of him,' Malum announced. 'It wasn't quite what we wanted, but I think I can act upon some of it. The fucker confirmed a lot of our worst fears though – the soldiers want the aliens to live with us.'

The lads were silent.

'Look, I need a hand,' Malum said. 'We're running out of time and we need to start taking control of things. There's a package I want to collect and the time is right. I need a couple of you to help transport something around the city.'

'What've you got in mind, boss?'

*

Jeza didn't like Malum all that much, though she didn't know why specifically. However, she decided that she did like his money – if he was a paying client, she couldn't exactly say no just because he was a bit of a weirdo. The city was full of weirdos.

There was something about him that unnerved her – it

wasn't his lack of manners, since he had those in spades; he had all the charm in the world. It wasn't the air of mystery around him, either – there were plenty of people in Villiren who had secrets. No, it was something about his nature – as if he was always trying to suppress something about himself. That he was holding something *within* that could burst out at any minute. His unspoken potential frightened her.

When Jeza got Malum's message she was agog at the amount of money he was offering. All she had to do was provide the *remains* of one of their botched operations – of which there were plenty. If anything, he was doing her a favour by helping remove one – it wasn't as if she could dispose of them easily. What would people think? He had asked for the most bizarre-looking creature she could find, and she was fine with that, though she couldn't help but feel a little dirty standing outside, waiting for him to come. There was an illicit feeling about this whole operation, prostituting everyone's talents like this.

This is what business is, Jeza told herself. *Get used to it if you want to build up a big enterprise.*

As she continued waiting, something else niggled her. Why, for example, had she not told the others she was getting rid of the waste grotesques? Was that a sign of her guilt?

She now lingered by the corner of Factory 54, while the rest of the gang headed out into the city to get food. Just outside one of the rear doors to the factory, no more than a dozen feet away, sat a crate containing a grotesque, which had not been able to cling on to life.

The first time one had died, everyone felt sad. Of course they did. The second time, less so. They were, the gang warranted, creating life in the first place. There was no death first without life. The third and fourth time they were almost indifferent to the whole operation: their aim was simply to keep them alive for as long as possible, but no matter what dimensions the creatures took, most of them seemed to die quickly.

But not this one.

Eventually she saw movement at the end of the street. A horse was approaching, pulling a cart, and on top sat a man with a tricorne hat pulled low over his face, with the collars of a wax rain jacket covering his mouth.

The horse approached and pulled in alongside her. The rider nodded and jumped down; suddenly four other men, whom she hadn't seen previously, and who were dressed like the rider, leapt off the back of the cart and their boots thudded on the cobbles.

They approached in a line. Nerves almost got her voice, but she managed to ask, 'Is that you, Malum?'

'That's right, lass,' Malum replied. 'So, have you got what we're after?'

'Sure.' She gestured behind to the crate. Whether or not it was the cold, she didn't know, but she shivered as he moved past her with a crowbar in his hands.

Malum approached the crate, levered open the top to look in and nodded to himself. He looked up at her and she realized suddenly that she could read him better. He now seemed very dangerous and she was scared. He looked across to his accomplices behind her, and said to them, 'It's all fine. Hand over the money to the lass, and we'll be done.'

Then he approached Jeza and gave a smile that seemed utterly unnatural. 'You, uh, you might hear one or two things relating to this creature. I'd like it if you were to remain quiet about it, if you do hear anything. If anyone comes asking questions, please – your silence is expected, part of the contract.'

'Hey, what you do with this from now on isn't my concern,' she said and laughed awkwardly. It took all her willpower not to enquire what he'd do with the corpse of the creature.

'Good,' he replied. 'Then we have an *arrangement*.'

Why was it that every word seemed like a threat? She hoped all future clients wouldn't be like him.

The four men lifted the crate under Malum's direction and loaded it onto the back of the cart, then they jumped back on board. Malum climbed back up onto the seat and addressed Jeza one last time. 'You might want to put the money somewhere safe now,' he said, smirking. With a flip of the reins the horse plodded in a wide circle back the way it had come.

Only when she saw the small sack by her feet did she realize what Malum meant. Glancing up, she watched the cart move away into the distance and on through the streets.

She lifted the sack, noted the weight of the coin and, peering around sheepishly, headed back into the warmth of the factory.

*

Malum knew that if he was going to do this properly, to create the right amount of public fear, it would have to be in one of the most public places possible, an iren. The large one recently set up behind Port Nostalgia, where all the traders would be going about their business, would be ideal, and the irens were always busiest first thing in the morning.

He worked through the pre-dawn darkness, getting every-thing ready. A stall had already been rented right in the centre – something in a prime location. He had his men set up a few trinkets on display, cheap cookware and the likes, in order to make the stall look *genuine*, but beneath a sheet weighed down with stones was the grotesque. They had bought a bucket of pig's blood the night before from a butcher's shop in Althing, and spread it liberally on the cobbles around the creature. Previously Malum had ordered one of his gang to locate the body of a child. He didn't ask how or where they got it, but they managed to find one and the young boy's body was intact. The corpse was placed by one of the creature's outstretched paws, which poked up from under the sheet.

'It has to look as if the creature killed the kid,' Malum ordered, and his men began making the necessary adjustments.

The city architecture began to define itself against the light of the pale dawn sky.

'C'mon, you guys,' he ordered. 'We need to get this done before the sun's up, and be clear of here as soon as possible.'

Finally, they peeled back the sheet, rolled it up and stuffed it in the far corner of the iren, just as the first traders rolled their carts to unload their wares. The monster was unveiled in all its hideous glory.

*

Malum ordered his most presentable men to knock on the doors of local administrators and politicians, anyone who was *someone* in the Ancient Quarter. They were woken up from their slumber or dragged from their breakfast table to listen to the hottest rumour of the day, and the lines the gang used were simple:

'Hey, have you seen what's kicking off in the iren in Port Nostalgia? They say a monster's come to the city from the south. It's just died right in the middle of everything. They say it tried to eat a kid. There's blood everywhere. Come quick!'

It wasn't a truly calculated plan, and certainly wasn't his finest hour, but Malum was happy enough watching, from a distance, as influential people moved towards the harbour, alarmed at the alien *threat*. After a short while, he decided to go back to see what was happening at the iren.

Upon entering the area, Malum smiled widely.

Everyone else's stalls were not fully set up, trade had not commenced, and there were a good few hundred people – traders and customers looking to fill their baskets with sup-plies – clustering around where Malum had left the beast. He recognized the faces of influential people, cowering behind or their faces half-hidden beneath hoods. He pushed his way forward, in the game now – he knew people would recognize him and he had to be careful.

The nearer he got the more hysterical people's conversations were.

Two or three traders built like barbarians were investigating the corpse, which in the morning light was clear to see in all its glory. The thing's skin was almost reptilian, with scales along its underbelly; four crude, fur-covered arms jutted out from this, and two legs that seemed more at home on oxen. The head was a mash-up of all sorts of creatures, with a cluster of eyes and two long fangs. From head to foot, stretched out like this, it must have measured a good ten feet long. Blood had soaked into the fur nicely, and the overall effect was that it appeared to have killed the child and somehow had died in the process.

It was a marvellous design, truly horrific, and it was having the desired effect on the gathered throng. It would also make the commander's dream of alien integration a lot more difficult.

Malum could overhear one or two of his men, deep within the crowds, shouting the message he had ordered them to spread:

'This is one of those monsters from south of the city, I know it.'

'I can't believe we're not being protected from these alien immigrants.'

'The army needs to kill these brutes and quick.'

'Do they really expect us to live alongside such foul things?'

It didn't take long, either, for people in the crowd to mutter their agreement. Opinions were *that* easy to change, when confronted with the right image.

A unit of Dragoons came a little later, parting the crowds and invading the iren. People were steered to one side of the iren while the army sealed off the area. A lot of people clambered around the walls and rooftops to see what they were up to, and it seemed they had no clue what to do or what to make of this turn of events.

They were as dumbstruck as the citizens.

TWENTY

Investigator Fulcrom was hoping to have a day or two's rest, but apparently that was not going to happen.

His and Lan's quarters were luxurious compared with life on the road. There was warmth and comfort, and most of all peace from the constant demands of leadership. A slender, arched window offered a view towards the far east of the city, which seemed relatively untouched by the brutal war.

While Lan was changing into her freshly laundered Knights outfit, Fulcrom stood browsing the selection of texts on a high shelf, most of them on fishing or local history. His musing was interrupted by a loud thump on the door.

'Fulcrom, it's Brynd.'

'One moment, Lan's just getting changed,' Fulcrom called through to him.

Lan glowered at him. 'Can't you learn to lie from time to time?' she whispered, hurriedly yanking on her breeches.

When she had finished, Fulcrom opened the door and the commander strode in sheepishly. Only now, in this calm situation, did Fulcrom realize how striking the commander's white face and red-tinted eyes were.

'Is everything well, commander?' Fulcrom enquired.

'As well as can be expected here, yes, but I came to start you up with a few tasks, if you're willing.'

'Of course, yes. Is this for the Villiren Inquisition?'

'If you want to call it that, yes. At the moment the city is under military law, and I would like to work on a transition to something more stable, local and meaningful. That is, if you are both happy to get started immediately?'

Fulcrom looked to Lan, who nodded back.

'The Inquisition is just the two of you at the moment.' Brynd reached into his pocket and pulled out two small leather cases. He handed one to Fulcrom and one to Lan.

Fulcrom opened his and found an Inquisition medallion inside, much like the one he wore in Villjamur, with the same triangular crucible stamped upon it. The ribbon was black. Fulcrom put it on over his head; it felt good to have one there again, after having discarded his old one in disgust at his superiors in Villjamur. Lan followed suit, smiling then staring down at the medallion. 'Our deepest thanks, commander,' Fulcrom said.

'As for what I'd like you to do,' Brynd continued, 'well ... we've heard reports this morning of a creature being found in the middle of a large new iren. A creature that has *apparently* killed a child. It's causing a bit of a stir and the iren has been closed for a while. It seems the whole city is talking about it, and we're the last to know.'

'Killed a child?' Fulcrom frowned. 'What sort of creature are we talking about?'

'We'll find out soon enough,' Brynd replied. 'Come.'

*

Fulcrom and Lan, wearing thick robes to cope with the colder conditions, followed the commander on horseback across the city to the iren. The sky had quickly become grey, filled with the promise of snow, though none came. When they arrived, they tied their horses and dismounted in silence, Fulcrom too fascinated by his new surroundings to talk.

The city was busy, much more so than Villjamur, which surprised Fulcrom. The buildings were old and frail, in much need of repair. Slates were missing from rooftops, some lay on the ground in shattered pieces. On closer inspection there was poverty here, even more than he had seen in Villjamur's caves, but it was kept to side streets, alleys in which people clustered around pit fires – he could see people's blankets stacked to one side, food rations piled alongside weaponry. Exotic smells drifted from houses, spices he wasn't familiar with, colours and sounds that seemed a world away from Villjamur. It could take a lot of getting used to.

'It's this way.' The commander led them into a busy thoroughfare and then into an enormous open iren, now up and running again. For a post-war city the amount of trade was incredible: everything from grain and vegetables to metal-work from other islands, from spices to scribe services. The economy was certainly starting to recover again.

'We cancelled pitch rents for the poorest,' Brynd said proudly. 'The previous portreeve had privatized the irens – which was public property would you believe – in many districts, so that landowners were taking profits from the traders and the market barely made any money. The prices were ridiculous. We took the irens back, slashed rents, prices fell and now look at the place – it's busier than it was before the war. I think that speaks for itself.'

They moved forward through the crowd until they reached a sealed-off military area. Thirty or forty Dragoons were standing casually in a line, but stood to attention when they spotted the commander advancing towards them.

'At ease,' Brynd called, but they weren't half as slack as they were a moment ago.

A gap parted, and the newcomers moved in to examine the scene.

Fulcrom was admittedly shocked. On the floor was a truly strange creature, in all its gruesome multi-limbed glory. It lay there giving off a strong aroma of decay. He had never seen anything quite like it. Not even the new races who had helped out the refugees on Jokull were so alien.

Lan cringed in disgust, but Fulcrom coolly crouched down

to get a better look. 'I'm going to ask the obvious – this isn't part of the local habitat, is it? Something that lives further out of the city?'

'There's nothing natural about this,' Brynd said.

'Is it a hybrid creature often talked about but rarely seen?'

'No – hybrids are more coherent, more logical than this. Besides, we've done research into what creatures there are and there is nothing like this.'

'Look over here.' Lan was crouched down pointing to foam surrounding the body.

'Well spotted,' Fulcrom said. Then, aloud, 'Who washed away the blood? There are soap bubbles here and here.'

Brynd looked over to a Dragoon soldier, who answered, 'A couple of traders cleaned it away, sir, so they could get on with business.'

Fulcrom sighed. 'We could have done with knowing just a little more about where that blood came from.'

'You don't think it was from this thing itself?' Brynd enquired.

'The cobbles have bloodstains over too wide an area to have come from the creature.' Fulcrom gestured in a wide circle to denote the extent. 'And the creature itself does not look as if it has lost that much blood. Not that I know much about the creature's anatomy, of course.' Fulcrom stepped around the giant corpse, examining it in detail. *Could've done with my notebook* . . . 'Can someone help turn it over?'

No one moved for a moment; the soldiers just looked at each other sheepishly.

'For Bohr's sake, you heard the man,' the commander called out. 'Four men, you three and you, one of you get an arm and the rest of you shove from the other side.'

The four Dragoons moved into place and reluctantly began to try to lift the monster. They struggled a little before giving up.

'Sir, it's rather heavy,' one of them said.

'Oh, really – I'll give you a hand.' Lan marched to the side with the three soldiers, who looked askance at her. Fulcrom smiled as Lan took hold of the corpse, closed her eyes and gently tuned in to her powers. The creature's body began to lift up from the cobbles and soon the rest of the soldiers joined in, not to be outdone by her. With them all helping shove it, the thing eventually collapsed onto its front.

'Thanks for your help, lads.' Lan winked at the soldiers as she rejoined Fulcrom. The men shyly stepped back into line, muttering to themselves.

The creature's hairs were soaked with blood, and yet Fulcrom couldn't help think something wasn't quite right with the scene.

'Strange,' he said to Brynd. 'There are no wounds anywhere on its body, and yet there must have been quite a bit of blood on the floor – until it was cleaned away, of course. So unless the creature has somehow vomited up such blood, which, I have to say, usually has a particular scent not present today, this was made to *appear* as if it had died here – but I don't think it actually did. And look.' Fulcrom crouched down by the creature's immense hand, which was leathery and clawed, and which had lain by the child's corpse. 'If this thing had actually killed the child, why are there no wounds or tissue damage? There are no signs of a struggle. There is no ripped flesh to denote any hunt, not to mention it seems that rigor mortis has begun to set in . . . No, none of this sits right with me, commander.'

Fulcrom tilted his head to suggest they step aside, and Brynd obliged.

'Everything here says to me that someone has placed the corpse here deliberately and, given that we're in an iren, this seems as if it was staged to catch the eyes of as many of the citizens as possible. Someone, somewhere in this city, wanted people to think a monster had come here to kill. Now that presents us with a few questions, admittedly. The first one, where did they get the creature's corpse?'

'I have a suspicion,' muttered Brynd, but seemed reluctant to expand on the issue.

'Really?' Fulcrom asked.

'It's only a thought, mind you – there's a factory in the city that specializes in things like this. You could start there, but I can't see why they would be involved in *staging* something like this.'

'What makes you say this?'

'They're business people. And they go to great lengths, generally, to keep such things away from public eyes. No, they wouldn't want this out here in this state.'

Fulcrom nodded. 'If I could take the details of this factory, back in the Citadel, along with any other information, I'd be very grateful, sir. Now, point number two then: if this corpse was acquired, somehow, that leaves the question of *why* it was left in public view like this. Why would someone create a scene? What is there to gain from the act? And there's little to follow it up, either – so what was the purpose of something so isolated?'

Brynd looked around at the iren, which by now had returned to normal.

'Given we're in a public place, the purpose could have been to get people talking and, possibly, for people to be frightened of the creature.'

'Why do you think someone might want that?' Fulcrom asked. 'You know this city better than I do, of course.'

'There are plenty of tensions here,' Brynd admitted. 'I had considered, since the war, that most of those concerns were no longer valid – that it was a fear that came from the war itself.'

'This invasion came from the north, am I correct?' Fulcrom asked.

'Indeed.'

'And the alien threat, that's nothing for people to be worried about?'

'There may well be concerns about those from the other-world who are camped south of the city.'

'I can understand that.' Fulcrom nodded. 'Do you think someone wants to make a point of their dislike of this arrangement?'

'People are going to have to learn how to cope sooner or later.'

'If there's anything I've learned, it is to never underestimate the will of the people,' Fulcrom replied. 'They can be over-whelming if a notion spreads wide enough.'

Brynd sighed and glanced at the corpse one more time. 'Do you think you can find out who did this? After Jokull, you've earned my trust.'

'I will give it my best shot,' Fulcrom replied. 'At the same time, I'd like to seek permission to build a team – volunteers at first, most likely – but if an Inquisition needs forming, we'll need people – perhaps even some surviving members of the Villiren Inquisition.'

'I probably wouldn't bother with them,' Brynd urged. 'Start fresh. Get smart, honest people.' He marched over to the gathered Dragoons and said, 'Right you lot, Investigator Fulcrom is hereby in charge of this situation and you're to follow his orders, do I make myself clear?'

A chorus of 'Sir' came.

'Good.' Brynd returned to Fulcrom. 'If they give you any trouble, let me know. This is all yours now.'

*

Back at the Citadel, Fulcrom had requested a cool basement room to use as a temporary office. As it happened, Brynd had already located a little network of chambers and antechambers situated a couple of levels underground, beneath the kitchens, and offered them to Fulcrom's operation. Some of the rooms still contained crates of foodstuffs and bottles of wine hoarded during the war, but a few insouciant Dragoons carried them elsewhere while Fulcrom and Lan settled in.

In the furthest room from Fulcrom's intended office, the corpse of the iren creature was brought in. Soldiers stacked packs of ice around the body so it didn't decay further and reek the place out.

Fulcrom and Lan studied it in detail and made notes, before abandoning this in favour of a better idea: Fulcrom decided to send messengers to bring in whatever medical staff there were at hand. At first these people protested, said they didn't want to see any monsters, but Fulcrom went out of his way to charm them into helping him.

One woman obliged, a plump former nurse with a penchant for art, and who seemed to want something more interesting to do with her days; she set about scrutinizing the beast, humming a little tune as if she was baking. She prodded it and sketched it, and Fulcrom left her to her own devices for an hour or so. When he returned, he asked her if she had found any visible wounds; she'd located none, just a few casual grazes where its body had been seemingly dragged along a harsh surface – such as a cobbled street – and her report confirmed much of what Fulcrom had suspected.

*

Lan, meanwhile, set about creating an office out of their intended chamber. She hauled huge pieces of furniture about the place with apparent ease. This had been, in the past, some kind of accounts room, and there were ledgers running way back – books that covered the movement of grain, ore, gemstones and money. She opened them up and was startled to see how intermittent they were; in some of them, whole years of accounts seemed to be missing. Lan acquired a rag, dusted down a desk. She arranged the chairs. She managed to find some scented oil and lanterns to scatter about the place. Within a couple of hours, she had transformed the room from a reasonably large but forgotten dusty corner of the Citadel into a welcoming office.

'There,' she said to herself, 'we're going to do things properly or not at all.'

Fulcrom came in and his expression pleased her greatly. 'This looks fantastic, Lan!' He walked over to the desk, where he immediately began arranging some of the books and pencils into something more orderly.

'You just can't leave things be, can you?' Lan suggested.

Fulcrom smiled. 'You've found a notebook too – excellent.' He pocketed it and looked around. 'We can put up some legal texts here.' He pointed to a shelving unit.

'Yes, and I've even found a blackboard you might find useful,' she said, and lifted up a large, four-foot-wide board. She stood it on the desk, leaning it carefully against the wall. She picked up a piece of chalk, wrote the word 'monster', and circled it.

'Your handwriting is messy,' Fulcrom said.

'Stop being so damn *neat*,' she replied.

Fulcrom moved closer to her and said, 'And that's why you love me.'

'Yeah,' she said, pausing. 'I do love you.'

They said it so little recently, but now things had calmed it seemed more powerful than before.

'We should do something tonight,' Fulcrom said. 'Just have dinner in our chambers. No one else. Get some candles, make a night of it.'

'That'd be nice.'

'Just *nice*?' he asked.

'OK, that would be *great*,' Lan replied.

'That's better.'

'So have you had any more thoughts about the creature?' she asked.

'Many,' he replied. 'Once I make a detailed sketch of it, I'll be satisfied that we can probably burn the corpse and be done

252

with it, the poor thing. If it has a soul, we can at least free it. In the morning, I'm going to head to the factory the commander spoke about. I'd like to speak to some people in the irens, too, to see if they witnessed anything out of the ordinary beforehand.'

*

That evening they acquired some roasted meats, cheese, bread and even commandeered a bottle of red wine Fulcrom had spotted being carried out of his new headquarters. They had both washed in hot water, and dried off, by the firelight, eating the food in its warm glow, sitting semi-naked together on a bearskin rug.

They took their time. They ate slowly. Fulcrom relished the fact that he could finally enjoy the lines of Lan's body – the cold conditions had always denied him this luxury. She was wearing a long, dark silk skirt and a wrap-around top that only really covered her breasts. He could see her firm stomach as she lay on her side. Her long dark hair, drying in the firelight, seemed healthier than ever. She had trimmed her fringe so that it was as short as he remembered in Villjamur.

Her skin glowed in the light and she seemed too hot to touch – but touch her he did. He placed a palm on her hips and ran it onto the small of her back. He pulled her towards him so that he lay on his back and she on top of him, her hands on his chest. She seemed more relaxed than ever before, which was the most important thing. He pulled the knot holding her top together and gently slipped it to one side; everything in her eyes told him that she wanted him. He kissed her collarbone, kissed her neck, kissed—

A banging at the door.

'Are you in?' came a voice. 'It's Brynd.'

'Just a moment,' Fulcrom spluttered.

Lan glanced at Fulcrom wide-eyed, then climbed off him, pulled on a robe and sat on the bed with her legs crossed.

Fulcrom stood up hastily, and shambled over to the door.

He looked back to Lan to check she was all right before he finally opened the door. 'Commander,' he said. 'Is everything OK?'

'Not disturbing anything, am I?' Brynd asked tentatively.

Yes. Yes, you are abso-fucking-lutely disturbing something. 'Not at all, commander,' Fulcrom replied. 'How can I help?'

'It's Lan I'm after actually,' Brynd told him.

'Oh, really?' Lan said, coming to the door in a rush.

'Yes, we've a bit of situation I'm afraid.'

'Anything serious?'

'That depends on what you mean by the word *serious* ... Now, I believe you have quite a few powers, by all accounts.'

'That's true, yes.'

'How are you at scaling buildings?' he asked.

'Could scale a couple before breakfast,' she muttered. 'Why d'you ask?'

'It would appear that Lady Rika, formerly the head of the Jamur Empire and now head of whatever future civilization we're building, is currently three-quarters of the way up the south wall of the Citadel. We'd like to get her back, somehow, without her presence being known to the entire building.'

'Give me a second to get changed into something more appropriate and I'll join you.'

The commander nodded. 'I'll leave an escort outside the door to guide you to our location.' Then he left the room.

Fulcrom closed the door and began to laugh to himself. Lan placed a hand on his back and breathed, 'We've waited long enough. Another day won't hurt us.'

*

Lan wore her Knights outfit proudly, and had acquired a few loops of rope, which she slung across her chest. Their escort led them to the balcony, where a small number of the Night Guard had gathered. They weren't enjoying the view of the harbour – they were looking directly towards the sky.

No one said anything on her arrival until the commander introduced her as a hero of Villjamur, and then they gave her a salute that made her blush.

'I'll explain to them fully who you are once you're up there,' he said. 'We need to be quick about this.'

'How did she get up there?' Lan asked.

'Your guess is as good as mine.'

'Have you got any idea where she is precisely?' Lan craned her neck to get a better view. The sheer height of the Citadel was intimidating. It was a fairly featureless structure, apart from the crenellations situated at the very top. *That would make it difficult to get up there*, she thought. Few nooks and crannies to use as assistance. Few gargoyles to hook her fingers on.

'Be careful when you're up there,' Brynd warned. 'We don't know how volatile she will be.'

'Volatile?' Lan said. 'I thought she was just a bit mad.'

'Well, that may be the case – however, she has been spotted by one person engaged in potentially violent conduct. This could be something similar or nothing to worry about at all – either way, we'd like the ruler of what's left of the Empire safely ensconced in a secure cell as soon as possible.'

'Right,' Lan replied. 'Anything else that I should know about?'

Brynd shook his head. 'This remains as much a mystery to us as it does to you.'

'You'll be OK?' Fulcrom whispered.

'Don't worry,' she replied, squeezing his hands. Then she moved into a clear space on the balcony, closed her eyes to tune in to her powers, and glanced directly up. The wind buffeted her, sending her hair spiralling in front of her face. She tied it back, and then stepped up into the air and glided onto the stone rail of the balcony; a window ledge up above caught her eye and she levered herself up even further; she misjudged the angle, slipped and clattered into the glass, though it didn't shatter. Luckily, no one down below saw her error.

Peering up, left and right, she couldn't see anyone. The wind was even stronger, a bitterly cold breeze from the east. The lantern lights of the harbour and the windows of the city were mesmerizing, but she didn't let them distract her. Instead, she scanned the walls for another window ledge; the jump up would be difficult, she thought, because she had to go in an arc. She gave it a go, knowing curve jumps were more dangerous, and luckily the wind blew her back against the building anyway.

Another look around, and this time she thought she saw something horizontally to the east. She flattened herself against the structure, hoping not to be seen; she wanted a better look.

It looked like the pale skin of someone's arm.

Lan looked up again, and noticed that she was only twenty feet away from the crenellations at the top of this section. Another push and she scrambled up the wall with all her might – she reached the top, banging her shin against the stone, but she was careful not to let out a cry of pain.

Once at the top, she found she could dash easily along the rim of the wall. She lifted one loop of rope off over her head and tied a quick, firm knot as she ran. Then she paused to check over the side along this section of the wall.

There. Down below was, very definitely, a female figure, bizarrely twitching and clawing her way *on* the wall – not ledges, not on the crenellations, but clawing the actual stone-work itself. It didn't seem possible. Lan tied one of the ends of the first piece of rope to a crenellation and made a loop at the other end, which she attached to her waist. She made it long enough for the fall; then she took the second length of rope and jumped effortlessly through the gap in the crenellations.

Her passage through the air was as gentle as she could manage with her powers; she focused on Rika, with the rope ready in her hands. It happened as planned: as she fell inches behind Rika, Lan dragged the rope over her body, snapping it tightly around the woman's torso. Her own rope snagged, stopping her descent. Rika was bound and snarling, like a trapped wolf, pressed up against the stone. The Empress lurched back, her face twisted and cortorting, her teeth a little too long to be human.

From her pocket, Lan withdrew a small hessian sack. With one hand firmly on Rika's throat, Lan climbed up her bound body, and eased the sack over the viciously struggling woman. She pulled the ends tight, being careful not to strangle her. Satisfied she had the woman bagged, Lan tied her own rope around Rika's waist, tied her hands, layered the rope around her again and again, and moved down to bind her ankles. Lan breathed out, relieved.

It had been simpler than Lan thought. Tuning in to her powers, she hauled Rika up with a jump and dropped her gently onto the walkway at the top of the crenellations. Lan landed gracefully alongside her.

The night sky was gathering clouds; a few flecks of snow began to fall, but Lan had her woman. Rika was now trying to tear her way out of her restraints, and Lan wanted to deliver her to the commander as soon as possible. The only way to get her down was back through the Citadel, so Lan dragged the Empress along the stone floor like a pugnacious dog.

*

'Nice work, Lan,' Brynd said. 'I'm impressed. That was a skilful display.'

Despite his positive words, he seemed deeply uneasy, as if uncertain what he would now do.

They had placed the bound Empress in a gaol cell within the Citadel. Only Brynd, Fulcrom, and two Night Guard soldiers were there.

Lan leant back against the bars with her arms folded, happy that she had proved herself to the most important person on the island.

'We used to keep these cells,' Brynd said, 'to imprison any Okun we captured from the war. We wanted to observe them, study them to see if we could get any information from them to use in the war. We got very little, it turned out. But I never thought we'd be using this room to imprison our own Empress. Would you mind stepping out of the cell for a moment? This could get a little tricky.'

'Of course,' Fulcrom replied.

Lan followed Fulcrom then turned to watch.

Brynd gestured to his soldiers and they both nodded their acknowledgement of the order, stretching out Rika's body horizontally, grabbing her legs and arms, pressing her down on the floor at one end of the cell until she stopped resisting. When she quietened, Brynd moved towards her feet and cut those restraints. Then Tiendi, who held her arms, looped a piece of rope around Rika's waist before handing it to Brynd, who then tied it around the cell window bars. The soldiers by her feet stepped away and both of them came out of the cell. Now only Brynd remained. He signalled something again with his hands before quickly cutting the restraints on her wrists, leaving just the bag over her head.

He walked out of the cell, slammed the barred door shut and locked it.

Everyone waited. The bars were as thick as Lan's thumb, spaced an inch apart, and crafted from iron, so Lan had no fears that their lives were threatened. It all suddenly seemed as if she were back in her circus days, watching one of the beasts in its cage. Rika pushed herself to her hands and knees, before staggering to her feet. Then she began pulling at the bag restraints, and managed to untie them quickly.

Rika pulled away the bag and dropped it on the floor. She turned, slowly, to face her captors.

'Dear Bohr . . .' Brynd breathed.

Her face was clearly once beautiful, yet it had distorted into something hideous: her eyes were enlarged slightly, her teeth so big that her mouth had become misshapen, and her nostrils flared like some furious beast. With alarming speed she flung herself against the bars and everyone either flinched or took a step back; as if Rika could have actually snapped the metal and leapt for their throats.

Brynd stepped forward until he was an arm's length away from the cell. 'Rika,' he called. 'Lady Rika.'

Lan watched the woman for a reaction, but there seemed no acknowledgement of her name.

'I am Brynd Lathraea, Commander of the Night Guard,' he said louder. 'Do you recognize me?'

Again, nothing. Rika merely glanced aggressively at everyone who had gathered to watch her. Cursing, Brynd turned to address them. 'It seems as though she may be beyond help. For now, no one is to enter this area. Tiendi, Mikill – I'm putting you two on the door. No one comes in, no one comes out without my say-so.'

'Yes, commander,' they replied.

Mikill said, 'Should her sister know?'

Brynd considered the question, but replied in hushed tones: 'Soon.' He looked at Lan and Fulcrom: 'Obviously you're both now witnesses to this – and Lan, while I do indeed appreciate your remarkable efforts, I would be grateful if no one was to find out about this. The ramifications could be huge.'

'You have our word,' Fulcrom announced. 'And if you need any assistance in the matter, you only have to ask.'

Brynd nodded his thanks before escorting them out. Two doors closed behind them. Two sets of lock mechanisms clicked into place.

TWENTY-ONE

The morning was wet and miserable, but Fulcrom and Lan headed across the city to the address given to them by Commander Lathraea. They were surprised at the lack of life in the area, as if everyone had simply been evacuated.

'Maybe the people here were lost during the war?' Lan suggested.

'Could be. Or perhaps they left as a result of industry lost after the war, who knows. There's a lot we don't know about this city.'

'Why have you asked me here today?' Lan asked. 'Wouldn't you rather have me back at headquarters than getting in the way?'

Fulcrom laughed. 'No, you're part of the Inquisition now.'

'I'm not particularly good at questioning though. You're the brains of the operation.'

'If that's so, then you're the brawn,' he replied. 'I'm still aching from the way I was treated in the cells of Balmacara.'

'You should've said something,' Lan replied.

'I've not let on because rumel skin doesn't bruise and I didn't want to make a fuss. You know what I'm like. It's strange that, during the escape and fighting, I couldn't feel much in the way of pain – I guess adrenalin kicks in and I just continued as if nothing had happened. But now we've relaxed, now we're settled somewhere else, the echoes of it are coming back.'

'There's only one thing you can do then,' Lan said, 'and that's to throw yourself back into the thick of it.'

'Which is why we're here.'

They located the vast structure called Factory 54, an unusually bland name. They tied their horses around the end of the massive structure and, locating the door, Fulcrom gave a loud knock.

There were a few curious sounds from inside, and eventually a young man opened the door. 'Hell do you want?' he said grumpily. 'We're busy.'

'We're here on behalf of the Villiren Inquisition.'

'Ain't no Inquisition any more. Barely was in the first place, bunch of corrupt buggers. We're not paying any protection money, if that's what you want.'

'No no,' Fulcrom interrupted. 'I'm not sure you understand. We're here on behalf of Commander Lathraea.'

'The albino?'

'That's correct,' Fulcrom said. 'Now, I'm not sure what went on before, but the Inquisition is being reconstructed and I'm not here to ask for money.'

'So what d'you want then?' The young man slouched in the doorway, then suddenly turned back and bellowed, 'It's the Inquisition!' Then, back to Fulcrom, 'Sorry – go on.'

'I want to know if you can help me. The commander suggested you people create monsters, is that right?'

'Yeah, what's—' He was cut off by the arrival of a young woman, no older than twenty, Fulcrom guessed.

'Sorry, sorry,' she said. 'Coren, why don't you head back and let me deal with this.'

The man shrugged and skulked off into the darkness. The girl smiled and introduced herself as Jeza.

After repeating who they were, Fulcrom reached into his pocket and pulled out a piece of paper. He unfolded it and held it up to Jeza. 'Do you recognize this?'

'Sketches of a grotesque, by the look of it.' She handed the

261

paper back to him and, despite her attempts at nonchalance, looked incredibly sheepish. She was someone who could not tell an effective lie.

'This was found yesterday in a major iren near Port Nostalgia, and it was made to look as if it had strolled in there before dying. There was blood. It had been staged so that it held a dead child in its claws.'

'It shouldn't have been, um, able to do that . . .' Jeza started.

'Because it was dead in the first place, right?' Fulcrom said. Jeza nodded.

'Did the grotesque come from here?'

Again, she nodded.

'I'm guessing you sold it to someone,' Fulcrom suggested. This didn't look as if it was going to be his most demanding case to date.

'I did, yes, but I really can't tell you, because . . . because I want to keep all my clients a secret – cultists can't do good business without confidentiality. We just don't tell.'

'But you realize the consequences of us not finding out?' Fulcrom asked, thinking she was showing signs of having been intimidated. 'This might not be a one-off incident. This might be at the heart of something more sinister, and the commander has asked me to find out who did it.'

'I can't help you!' Jeza said, raising her voice with nervousness.

'Look. Hundreds of people are panicking. There could be great social unrest. The commander has had dozens of worried parents protesting about their children's safety.'

'They're not under threat though – it's all staged,' Jeza suggested meekly.

'It doesn't matter, it's the fact that they're being used as a tool. We just want one name, that's all. No one will know and you'll be doing a service to the whole city.'

'You promise you won't let the trail get back to me?' she asked, tears welling up in her eyes.

'You have the word of the Inquisition,' Fulcrom replied confidently. 'As well as the commander.'

'And you'll go – if I give you his name, you'll go. No more questions?'

Fulcrom nodded.

'OK.' Jeza leaned in close to whisper. 'His name is Malum. That's all I know.'

With that, she said a hasty goodbye before closing the door on them.

Fulcrom turned back with Lan to find their horses.

'Well, that was simple enough,' Lan said.

'She was scared of him, this Malum,' Fulcrom replied thoughtfully. 'That was one defiant young woman, and if she created that monster, she doesn't frighten easily. Now to find out who this Malum fellow is, and what he is up to.'

*

Jeza dashed inside, breathing heavily, and sat down at the kitchen table while the familiar noises within the factory echoed around her. There was the whirr of machines working somewhere, relics churning out cultist energy; then came the guttural call of one of their creatures. She closed it all out and put her head in her hands and took deep breaths.

Coren came down the stairs with a few flecks of blood on his face. 'Hey, what was that all about then?'

'I did something I think I shouldn't have.'

'Bad enough to bring the Inquisition to our door? What did you do?'

'I sold one of the dead grotesques.'

'A dead one?'

'To that guy – who wants monsters made like we're doing for the commander.'

'That's not so bad. Hell, it means we don't have to deal with cleaning up after it.'

'I know, but he used it to scare people in an iren – put a body and blood all over the place apparently. I think he was trying to use it to cause trouble. Will you promise not to tell anyone?' She could feel the tears in her eyes now.

Coren moved around to put his arm over her shoulders. 'Don't worry. Your secret's safe.'

'I didn't think it'd do any harm, and I thought we could just make a little extra money on the side. I'm not sure we should deal with him any longer.'

*

Fulcrom and Lan headed into a questionable tavern on the edge of the Ancient Quarter. It was run-down, with paint peeling off the sign, a shutter missing from one of the windows, and graffiti plastered up along one of the walls – but it seemed busy enough that Fulcrom thought it'd be a good place to begin inquiries. Lan and Fulcrom headed to the bar. 'Keep an eye out for any trouble,' he whispered, and she nodded her understanding.

'Got a blade in my boot,' she replied, before glancing around.

At the counter, Fulcrom eventually caught the attention of the barman, a tall, skinny man, with greying hair and a large moustache.

'A moment of your time,' Fulcrom said. 'We're new to the city and just want a quick word.'

'Time's money to me,' the barman said, wiping his hands on his apron.

Fulcrom reached into his pocket and drew out a couple of coins, which he slapped on the bar. 'This'll do?'

'Now that's how we work around here – welcome to Villiren,' the barman said, pocketing the money.

'We're actually looking for someone, an old acquaintance of ours.'

'Whassis name?'

'Malum,' Fulcrom declared.

The barman's expression darkened in a heartbeat. He took

thing was coming into the city – this sort of meeting looks like the same kind of strategy, trying to whip the people into excitement over the issue.'

'You're right,' Fulcrom said. 'I guess Malum's been a busy man.'

TWENTY-TWO

Brynd rode out through the morning mist with two other members of the Night Guard, out of the city's southern limits and towards the alien encampment. The journey was becoming a routine, a well-trodden path, but that didn't make his nervousness vanish. Each time he arrived there were more exotic creatures, more unfathomable languages, and the realization that somehow they all had to fit in to the fabric of the Archipelago.

His two companions, Brug and Mikill, were consulting him on the size of their own military. The latest figures showed that they had, somehow, built up a force of over a hundred thousand warriors in military stations and training camps assembling on Folke now, where they were undergoing an intense training regime as per the Imperial rulebooks.

'This is good,' Brynd called out. 'This is very good. What about grain?'

'Fine for the moment,' Mikill said. 'We've got the cultists working on speeding up the crops even further, which should guarantee future yields if this next campaign turns out to be a long one.'

'Good. What about increasing the military force even further – alliances with the tribes, conscription, and so on.'

'We've not had to resort to conscription yet,' Brug replied. 'My gut instinct tells me it's a bad thing.'

'Then I believe it is a bad thing,' Brynd agreed. 'I suppose a forced warrior is never a good one anyway, and will desert us at the earliest opportunity.'

'As for the tribes,' Brug continued, 'several communities have offered to help – in exchange for gold.'

'What the hell do they want with gold?' Brynd asked. 'They're usually after nothing but bone, meat and fabric when they're not fighting.'

'They're becoming savvy,' Brug replied, smiling. 'They say they want to stockpile gold, to buy food and clothing in the new culture. And – get this – property. Some are willing to surrender their nomadic ways.'

'How can they know of the new plans?' Brynd asked.

'They're not stupid,' Brug replied. 'They've got trackers all over the island reporting back.'

'How many does that add to the force then?' Brynd asked.

'Between twenty to fifty thousand, if the negotiations go well. We've promised them the gold, but it's up to you whether or not we actually do that, or if it goes . . . missing.'

'We'll keep to our word,' Brynd replied.

'Sir?'

'We will keep to our word,' he repeated. 'Just let me know in future before you give away what's sitting back in those vaults.'

*

The soldiers arrived at their destination with the sun high above the encampment, casting a red-orange glow across the scene. Rows of tents now stretched to three times as far as when Brynd had seen them first, and it was more than just an awe-inspiring sight: it was a hugely intimidating one. This was a civilization that had just inserted itself alongside his own. Though they had – and would still – fight side by side, the thought struck Brynd that they might one day disagree. And then what?

They were met by a unit of human guards, which – as it was explained to them in crude and broken Jamur – was a gesture of welcome. The men wore red tunics and bright armour, with the sun emblem etched into the surface. Other than that, they wore stout boots, but little to ward off the cold. It didn't seem to bother them.

'How many humans live in your world?' Brynd asked optimistically.

'Some millions,' came the reply. 'Fewer after the fighting.'

The men marched them through to meet with Artemisia. It surprised him, then, just how similar military camps smelled. There were now sturdier, more permanent-looking structures than tents: wooden temples crafted in elaborate designs, with all sorts of banners and insignias across the framework. People drifted in and out of wide lanes; patrols of foot soldiers – humans and rumel and the more exotic shambling creatures – which seemed to enforce a reassuring sense of discipline. There were metalworkers and weapons manufacturers, cooks and priests, in fact there were so many shared similarities between the cultures it was strange to think that they had been separated for so many millennia.

Eventually they met with Artemisia in one of the wooden temples and, as they were sitting on cushions around an ornate brazier, the group partook of sweet-flavoured drinks. Guards surrounded them in a circle, but it didn't seem at all threatening. Time stretched out. There was patience and consideration to the ceremonies. Artemisia stared into the flames of the brazier before issuing her greetings in full.

'So the white-skinned commander visits today,' she said. 'Welcome. How shall we begin today's discussion?'

'What did you do to Rika?' Brynd demanded.

'I am not sure that I follow you fully, commander.'

'Recently we have caught Jamur Rika engaged in very strange behaviour. Not only were there reports of her eating flesh, but we found her scaling the external walls of the Citadel in Villiren. We are now forced to keep her imprisoned – for everyone's benefit – in a cell, like a common thief.'

Artemisia nodded slowly.

'She's insane, now, and we've very good reason to believe the origin of the problem was on your ship.'

Artemisia remained silent, her blue face impassive. She lifted her cup in huge hands to drink from it. 'It is that Randur Estevu who speaks too much.'

'He told us what we needed to know. Now, could you please share with us what is going on with the woman we supposedly both want to lead our cultures?'

'It is partially, I believe, my fault. And partially, I believe, her own.'

'Go on.'

'When I collected the group, I intended to secure her trust, which I did. But I was also under instruction to make what . . . there is no translation, I believe for this, but a comparison would be something like "mind-bond". It would have made sense for all concerned to be bonded – in our minds. One of instantaneous connection.'

'You and Rika, this is? Why her?'

'She was, according to our intelligence, the most important person in your world, someone with whom we could openly negotiate. We had previously tried making connections with her father, though he was . . . unreceptive. Rika needed to be mind-bonded to me so that we could secure a peaceful path forward. However, what I did not understand is that she believed me to be a goddess, or something equivalent or related to one of the ones she worshipped. She possessed an improbable amount of faith, a strong – or weak depending on your understanding – mental capacity. I did not realize quite how dangerous it might be to mind-bond with someone of such religious fervour. Whenever someone who is mind-bonded is kept apart from the person to whom he or she is bonded, it creates difficulties in normal circumstances, though nothing more than uncomfortable . . . yearning.'

'How does one mind-bond exactly?' Brynd asked.

'It is similar to a sexual ritual, but one only of the mind. There is penetration from one mind into the other, a release, a union. It is common in many of our cultures to do this. There is no physical connection.'

'So what's gone wrong in Rika's case? Why has she transformed suddenly?'

'Two things, I believe. One as discussed – the issue of her faith. Her mental state was not right to begin with; there was something inherently unstable in her mind. Perhaps it is hereditary. When she is away from me, she has obviously crossed a mental threshold and gone too far in her ways. Her mind has now *changed* her. The second issue might be merely that I conducted the ritual incorrectly.'

'Is there any way of reversing the bond?'

'No – unlike sexual bonds, mind-bonds may not be withdrawn quite so easily. You say she has transformed?'

'Her face is distorted, she's grown more feral, she's feeding on flesh.'

'An animalistic path,' Artemisia concluded.

'And that's it then?' Brynd said. 'You simply ruin the leader of our people and that's that?'

'Please, you must forgive me. I did not know this would be the way of things. It very rarely is. I was acting under instructions to bond, to connect, but this is most unfortunate. You have my sincere apologies.' She seemed quite matter-of-fact about the whole business. 'But, you mention she is your ruler, yet you, commander, are the one who does most of the organizing. It is you who is more like the Emperor.'

'Nonsense,' Brynd scoffed.

'I do not believe you felt Rika suitable for the task in hand. I could sense such things.'

'Only because you changed her in the first place.'

'For that I have apologized. It was an act not from malice but from one of seeking union – that, you must understand. I assure you it was accidental, and please remember that myself and my people are at your service.'

Brynd tried to calm himself. It would do no good to continue the conversation in a fury. He wondered if cultists could help Rika regain her former self? It was probably worth a shot at some point, though for now it seemed he had to find a new ruler – and it would not be himself, he would not become a military dictator.

Brynd mercilessly processed his options. Did Artemisia's confession change the relationship between their cultures? No. Could he trust Artemisia on the matter? It seemed she was at least telling the truth, for whatever that was worth any more. How important was Rika? He cared for her, of course, from a sense of duty and nostalgia, but the people of Villiren had not exactly taken a shine to her – and they did not so far have the opportunity to do so. There was nothing lost there, at least.

'Jamur Eir,' he announced. 'She will make the transition to being leader of our nations. The blood lineage is there, enough to keep the establishment satisfied.'

Brynd glanced to Mikill and Brug, whose expressions seemed positive. Brug leaned over and whispered, 'She'll be compassionate. That'll come in useful when we need to be hard with regards to rations or taxes.'

'Besides, I do understand your current pain,' Artemisia continued.

'What do you mean?'

'It may well be that we are experiencing a similar crisis with our creator.'

*

'No, it is really best if I show you,' Artemisia said. 'It is not the sort of thing that can be explained.'

The level of security around them increased; whereas before there were no more than ten soldiers, now there seemed to be an entire regiment surrounding them. They were escorted down a long, straight avenue between the tents, and one thing that struck Brynd was just how clean and organized everything was. This was military discipline at its finest.

Artemisia walked alongside them, which was to Brynd an important gesture. Orders were given and the military escort separated, allowing a path to open up to the right. It led to yet another wooden structure, this one significantly more sturdy-looking than any of the others. There were yet more guards stationed here, different insignias, a more intimidating air.

'What's this place?' Brynd asked.

'Our destination,' Artemisia replied. 'When you enter, you must not say anything until spoken to; you will not comment on what you see.'

The three Night Guard soldiers nodded and continued behind Artemisia down a small set of stairs to a vast room. Although the building was constructed from wood, the walls appeared blackened and contained specks of light, like some kind of projection of constellations. At the top, to the right, a row of this culture's elders were seated within a ghostly white light. In the centre of the room, however, Brynd could make out an enormous enclosure – except there were bars of translucent purple light that seemed to shimmer where bars of metal ought to have stood. Every now and then something would crackle and spark off onto the floor a few feet away.

Inside this prison of light sat Frater Mercury. He was perched on a stone slab and the light from the bars reflected on the metallic half of his face.

Brynd tried to remember what Fulcrom said, and communicate via his thoughts, to enquire if the man was OK being treated in this way.

'Are you here of your own will?' Brynd muttered, but Frater Mercury did not look up.

'He cannot communicate with you from within this cage,' Artemisia declared.

'He's your god, right?' Brynd asked.

'He is our *creator* and we respect him as thus,' Artemisia replied.

'Why are you keeping him prisoner?' It seemed absurd for the being who had crafted her civilization to be held behind bars.

'Our elders would dispute the term "prisoner",' she replied.

'It doesn't seem an appropriate way to treat your creator – surely he's too important.'

'We keep him here, in this way, for precisely that reason. He is too important to our culture for him to wander off like some idle youth. We do not want harm to come to him – and he would be in great danger if our rivals captured him. You have witnessed what he is capable of – so you understand why we wish to keep him safe.'

'Safe,' Brynd whispered, glancing at Frater Mercury once again. He tried to understand and respect their culture's decision, but failed.

'Besides, he is reluctant to go anywhere. We know he is disappointed with our people – with all his people – for having taken our respective paths, despite his efforts many thousands of years ago to broker peace. He has tried it all, long before you and I were born. He is a tired man.'

'He could be useful. He could have his chance to help.'

'You view him as a weapon,' Artemisia said. 'I know this. I can see this in the way you regard him.'

'I think he can help save many lives,' Brynd confessed. 'He's already done so, and yet you keep him here, like a caged bird.'

'Poetic,' Artemisia said. 'But you want to use him to create ways to destroy our enemy, as we did, and this is understandable.'

'Have you ever asked Frater Mercury what his wishes are?'

'We know what it is that he wants.'

'And that is?' Brynd asked.

'A release from it all,' she replied. 'He is tired of life. He has lived for an unfathomable number of years. His ascension from a life technician to god was merely the beginning of things. He was forced to leave this world and create a new realm, what I call home. He has seen his creations rise up and create mass violence on a scale he did not think possible. And he has done this as someone who had conquered Time itself, having lived on and on without end.' Artemisia walked along one side of the light cage. 'Convinced he had no future, he only ever had one dream, and that was to break free of our world to this one, his home, his past, so he might look upon it one last time. Now he has done that, of course, by methods that we were not aware of. Now there is nothing left for him.'

'This is why you keep him in the cage then,' Brynd observed. 'We have a term for something similar in our world – it's called a suicide watch.'

Artemisia looked to her elders sat within their raised, glowing antechamber, and then back to Brynd. 'You are most perceptive, commander. We are watching, as you put it, to see if he attempts to end his existence – for we do not entirely know what will happen.'

'How d'you mean?' Brynd demanded.

'Simply that,' Artemisia replied. 'He's an entity of immense power. For him to end his life, our own technicians think that it would mean . . . that power would have to be redistributed.'

'How do you mean? As in, he may explode?'

'That may well happen,' Artemisia said. 'And it could be severe enough to cause great instability to his surroundings.'

Brynd eyed the man behind the light cage for a moment or two longer. It was true Brynd had hoped the man could help them, and now he felt only a deep sense of frustration. A key piece of his military operation had suddenly collapsed.

Brug suddenly approached Brynd's side. 'A word, sir.'

'Go ahead.' Brynd turned to him as Artemisia continued her slow pace around the cage.

'You may recall some of the warriors of the Aes tribe when they undergo their birthing ceremony,' Brug began.

'What of it?'

'Well, the birthing is *rebirthing* in that instance, of course, but the principle may remain the same: that of a possibility of a glorious birth in a new realm through the notion of *sacrifice in battle.*'

'I still don't follow,' Brynd muttered. 'Get to the point.'

'If Frater Mercury wants to die and is going to explode, why doesn't he do it in battle in order to help us?' Brug grunted. 'Better still if he's in the middle of a thousand Okun.'

'Better *still*,' Mikill said, 'if he can kill himself up in that sky-city thing, he may well bring it to the ground.'

Brynd let the thoughts move around his mind. It seemed perfect. Frater Mercury would get his wish to end his life, leaving the greatest possible chance for lasting peace behind, and the united forces would stand a better chance of wiping out the invaders on Jokull.

'Excellent suggestions,' Brynd whispered, and turned to Artemisia.

'How does Frater Mercury view your enemy? Does he care for them in the same way?'

'No. Do not forget they rose up against a vastly peaceful culture, bent on destruction – they would see all his creations destroyed. It is our understanding that he views them as he would a violent, murderous son or daughter. With sympathy, disappointment, wishing he had never created them in the first place. It is why he remained with our culture.'

'In that case, could we liaise with you and your elders?'

*

They negotiated for the better part of two hours before the elders would even grant permission for Brynd to consult Frater Mercury.

Brynd stood before them – *below* them – staring up into their illuminated faces, sagging with age, as they painfully contemplated his requests. Artemisia and some of her colleagues mediated, and Brynd could never be certain just how much of her own feelings she was inserting into the conversation.

As expected, the elders were reluctant at first. A culture did not simply abandon its god so easily; however, the way Brynd presented the case, it was logical, almost irresistible for them to use Frater Mercury as a weapon in such a way, providing he agreed.

Problems were mooted from the off: 'One simply does not drop him into the heart of the Policharos,' they claimed, via Artemisia. 'He might not want to die in such a way,' they asserted.

Immediately it became clear that these people were unsure how to proceed after having treated Frater Mercury a certain way for so long.

They had kept him prisoner in the tallest structure in their home city, a cage he had built himself so that he might never escape. He had been given moments of freedom, of course, but these were strictly rationed. People came from far and wide to worship him. They offered prayers and asked if he could help them, be it for some pathetically trivial matter in their own lives, to more elaborate tasks like moving islands through the sky.

Brynd couldn't be certain, but it seemed as if these elders – or whoever had imprisoned him – saw this not as a form of torture, but as an attempt to show how vital he was to people's lives.

Brynd tried to understand why, if Frater Mercury was so powerful, he had not found some method of escape.

By this point, time had ground him down, they explained. Millennia came and went, and Frater Mercury was witness to all of it, to the repetitions of his creations: races would continue to wage war, to take what was not theirs, to fail to notice any obvious signs that their cultures were under threat. He watched them, passively, as if it were some enormous experiment unfolding before his eyes – and perhaps it was. Ultimately, he was a scientist, after all, and he had created these cultures.

'What changed?' Brynd asked.

Time began to run out and Frater Mercury was the first to see it, to read it in the elements. The sun was fading from the sky and soon the wars had reached their peak and the city in which Frater Mercury was held was being eroded by the advancing armies. The elders requested Frater Mercury's aid to help prevent a staggering loss of life and, despite the apparent futility, he obliged and found himself trapped even further as the elders showed him just how dependent on him their civilization was.

Perhaps, the elders admitted, they had not treated him fairly, but they did it to preserve their culture.

'So we both want to use him as a weapon,' Brynd observed. He turned to the so-called god with an overwhelming sense of sadness. Beneath the veneer of magic and science, beneath the experiences of millennia, here was someone trapped by the very creations he'd given life to.

No, the elders continued, they wanted him to help save lives, not cause harm like a weapon.

Frater Mercury decided that with no future, he'd look to the past. He began to yearn for home, to return to this world – the one he was banished from so long ago due to their fear of his ways with science. He had created many races here, too, and pushed the boundaries of what was acceptable. Cultures could not appreciate him. Religions wished to banish him. People no longer accepted him and he was forced to flee, to our world, and brought his creations with him.

Later, after many wars, pathways of science opened up.

When, thanks to spies, the elders went on, their enemies learned of his scientific methods for breaking through dimensions with Realm Gates, they stole his secrets and mastered the arts. Armies came into this world, bringing slaughter to new shores, to Villiren.

All the while, someone began communicating with Frater Mercury. Somehow, during his few moments of freedom, he managed to communicate back and make it possible to walk away from it all.

And that was exactly what Frater Mercury did.

Now here they all were, facing a stand-off against the races that wanted to cleanse the Boreal Archipelago so it could be resettled by their own kin rather than working together for a peaceful solution.

As the elders stressed again, Frater Mercury should not be allowed to die – he could still offer some kind of help.

'Your way is delaying the inevitable,' Brynd concluded, 'negotiating, settlement, asking small favours to keep people alive long enough to be killed by your enemy. With the proposed solution, it could end these skirmishes once and for all. Besides, if Frater Mercury wishes to die, he should have some say in the matter.'

On that, they eventually came to an agreement.

*

The cage was deactivated, the light fell away, and there was a sudden stillness in the building, but Frater Mercury showed few signs of acknowledging the change in his situation. The Night Guard soldiers stood to one side next to Artemisia, their arms folded, in respectful silence.

The elders, still illuminated, presented their question in their own language. Artemisia translated for Brynd: 'Reverend Frater,' she said, 'we have entered discussions with the aged races, represented here by the white man. That's you.'

'Thanks for pointing that out,' Brynd muttered.

Artemisia held out her hand, despite the silence that followed. Brynd wondered if Frater Mercury was talking only to the elders.

'He just asked them if they have let him free. In a manner of speaking, they replied. They continue: "It is clear that you have made your wishes to terminate your existence fully over the recent ... uhm, a unit of time equivalent to three of your years ... If your wish still remains, then so may it be."'

Brynd watched Frater Mercury for any signs of a reaction. Suddenly a voice rushed into his head: *Did you come here to free me?*

He thought his reply back, not wanting to speak it aloud. *Yes. But I ask one final act of sacrifice.*

Can I die then? Will I be finally left alone?

Your sacrifice will be your death, Brynd replied, *if I have my way.*

Poetic enough, warrior.

'He must be contemplating his option,' Artemisia said. 'The elders have asked if he requires more time to think on the issue, but he has replied already. They have mentioned you and they have mentioned the way in which his life will be terminated – with sufficient power to cause destruction. They are trying not to use the word suicide ... He will comply.'

Brynd's relief was genuine. He had his weapon, and the poor man could end his existence now that he had seen his home world.

'That's the easy part over,' Brug whispered. 'Now how the hell do we plan to get him up in that sky-city?'

TWENTY-THREE

As the sun reddened behind the clouds, the Night Guard rode back to Villiren. He noticed the distinct lack of snow in comparison with the first time he approached the camp. The landscape seemed far more desolate because of it, the melting snow revealing broken carts abandoned along the side of the road, or the occasional corpse with an outstretched arm. The soldiers rode in thoughtful silence. They had left discussions with Artemisia's people in a profoundly positive manner – Brynd had negotiated what he wanted, to use Frater Mercury as a weapon, but the task ahead was now one of planning, strategy, logistics.

During the siege of Villiren he felt he had done enough of that to last a lifetime, but he had already begun ordering more soldiers to move across the island and then by sea to congregate on Folke with the others. That was where the threat was gathering, his garudas were informing him; it was on those shores that an invasion would come, it was where he had to send troops first.

Tundra soon became villages, melding into the southern fringes of Villiren, the Wastelands, where there seemed to be more hastily constructed shelters and crude housing being erected daily. Brynd also noticed there were small groups of people marching around the streets as though on a military drill. They wore no uniforms, but carried crude weapons, machetes or messer blades; and some even seemed to be taking look-out positions.

'Is this some kind of civilian militia we're unaware of?' Brug muttered.

'They're probably still afraid the Okun will come back and want to defend themselves,' Mikill said. 'It's quite natural.'

Brynd wasn't so sure. He couldn't ever hope to know all of what was going on in Villiren, but this didn't feel right for some reason. 'Wait here,' he called to the others.

He pulled his horse to a slower pace, and nudged her nearer to the patrols. Tugging his woollen cloak around his uniform, he concealed anything that might suggest he was a military man. He even pulled up his hood to put his pale face into shadow.

One of the men looked up at him, a bearded fellow with a scarred face, dressed in little more than a bundle of rags. In his right hand he gripped a blade.

'What's all this?' Brynd gestured to the unit of six other people. 'Some kind of citizen militia?'

'Sommat like that, yeah,' the man muttered. 'What's it to you anyway?'

'I wondered about joining up, that's all.'

'We ain't no military and we don't trust outsiders. Military don't care about the likes of us. They make things worse.'

'Really?' Brynd said. 'How so?'

'Monsters,' the man muttered. 'They're too busy inviting monsters into the city. It's why we're here.'

'Ah, I see,' Brynd said. 'You mean the camp to the south.'

'Aye, that's right. You seen anything strange, traveller?'

'Nothing at all out of the ordinary,' Brynd replied. 'There's no reason to be afraid. But I thought they were our allies?'

'That's what the military wants you to think, get it? Don't believe a word of what they're saying.'

'Why would the military lie?' Brynd asked.

'You ask too many questions . . .' the man replied.

283

'Well, I'm not from around here.'

'The military wants us to believe anything so that we'll be forced to live with freaks. Make us live in fear so we think it is the best choice. We don't wanna be sharing our city with the likes of them, is all.'

'But you're not actually sharing anything yet,' Brynd pointed out. 'Nothing at all has come around here.'

'You know an awful lot for a traveller,' the man replied, eyeing Brynd with suspicion. 'Nothing's come in yet because there are people like us to stop them coming in.'

'I'm sure the city's grateful for your ... protection,' Brynd replied. 'How many monsters have you stopped so far?'

The man didn't seem to like that question, judging by his sour expression. 'Ain't the point – it's about having a presence, like. Having men on the street so things can know not to enter these parts. Makes some of the families feel safer, too.'

Brynd nodded and decided not to press the issue any further. The man had decided to believe there was a threat and act in this way; nothing Brynd could say would change matters. 'Good luck, then,' he replied, and turned his horse back.

On getting back to the Night Guard, Brug asked him: 'Anything the matter?'

'Yes,' Brynd replied, 'we need better propaganda. They're convinced monsters are going to come into the city and take what's theirs. It bothers me.'

'We know better than to believe nonsense like that, though,' Mikill replied.

'Sure,' Brynd replied, 'but they do believe, and what concerns me is why they believe these things so *strongly*.'

*

They headed into the Citadel where Brynd immediately called a meeting, in private, with Jamur Eir. He could put it off no longer. Within half an hour she was sitting next to him in the obsidian room. She had just returned from the hospital, and there were still a few bloodstains on her clothing.

'I'm sorry,' she said, 'but I didn't have time to change.'

Brynd waved her apology away. 'Quite all right. I've seen more than enough blood on uniforms in my time. At least yours is present for a more constructive reason.'

'Have you seen my sister at all?' she asked. 'I've spent a lot of time working, but I've not noticed her around the Citadel. And when I do ask someone, they put me off with one of your instructed answers.'

Brynd smiled awkwardly before explaining, with as much sympathy as he could manage, what had happened to her sister, the events outside the Citadel, and her new-found cannibalistic nature. He even explained the context that Artemisia had given him, of some failed union of their minds. She listened silently, though showed little in the way of shock.

'So,' Eir said calmly, 'there is no way we can get her back to her previous state?'

'It doesn't seem so, I'm afraid. She is what she is now. Pardon my saying, but you don't seem overly ... concerned, Eir.'

She gave a huge sigh before standing up and moving to the window. It was night, so she couldn't see much outside. 'I've seen plenty of horrific things in the last few weeks, so perhaps I am numbed by such experiences. Although she's not dead, it seems like I lost my sister long ago. What do you suggest we do about her situation?'

'I'm not sure,' Brynd replied. 'One idea I had was to allow cultists to take a look at her. But one thing is obvious: she can no longer be head of the new empire.'

Eir looked at Brynd, as if she knew what he was about to ask her.

'Which means we'd need someone else of the Jamur lineage ...'

'Must it be someone from my family?' she asked.

'It would be easier to have a figurehead.' Brynd stepped over to her side and followed her gaze outside. 'It could even be symbolic if you like.'

'I'm not a ruler, Brynd,' Eir whispered. 'It isn't a matter of helping people. I do that at the hospital – that's helping. Being Stewardess, even for that short while in Villjamur, all I really ended up doing was administering the affairs of the well-off. I'm not interested in doing that again.'

'I understand that,' Brynd replied.

'Besides,' Eir continued, 'you've done a good enough job running things as they are. Why don't you become overall ruler?'

Brynd gave a hollow laugh. 'Me? I'm ... no. We'll need a Jamur leader to unite the people and, I suspect, for stability.'

'You don't need anyone but yourself and your army. The people love to see strong leaders, and you're rather well thought of since the defence of Villiren.'

It was true and Brynd knew it. The temptation was great. He was well aware that he could run this operation on his own, and he was even starting to become attached to the idea of leadership. 'What if I get killed on the next mission? How can I make such promises when I'm about to drop into the dark heart of our enemy? What good would I be as a leader, then, if I've been sliced into a thousand pieces—'

'Don't talk like that,' Eir cut in.

'It could happen. I have to plan for every eventuality. Anyway, I know that people don't fully respect me because of what I am.'

'How do you mean?'

'My skin, Eir. I've seen the way people give me a mistrustful gaze across the bargaining table. They wouldn't stand for someone so unnatural being their leader. They only do as I say because I've got some of the best warriors that have ever walked the land by my side. No, these people – bankers and landowners – they respect and trust only good blood. With Jamur blood at the helm, it means the status quo can continue. It means they can relax. You never knew the lengths your father went to protecting their wealth, did you? You never saw the way he'd manipulate things to keep people in their place, to keep them happy – making sure their money went to Villjamur. These people own all the resources you can imagine, and with me – a military man – in charge, they'd panic, and assume it was a dictatorship. They'd keep things away from me, scared I'd send in my soldiers and take it all away.'

'And would you take it all?'

'I confess I'd like to, in order to get things done quicker and give more people a job, but no. Even if I did want to do such a thing, now is not the right time. We need to rebuild things first. People in all walks of life need stability. Only you can offer them that, Eir. I need you to do this. Perhaps you would not need to be a nurse . . .'

She took a deep breath and glanced at him with more determination than he had ever seen in her. 'You won't stop me doing that in order to hold a banker's hand.'

That's the spirit, Brynd thought. He tried not to smile. That she cared about the lives of others would be a good thing. That she held the moneylenders in contempt was a boon. 'Can I take it that you'll consider it? You won't be alone. We'll stand side by side all the way through it.'

'I'll do it,' Eir said. 'I know all about duty.'

'You'll be popular,' Brynd continued, his voice with more gravitas now he knew she would do what he asked of her. 'People are already talking about the royal who isn't afraid to get her hands dirty.'

'Brynd, you don't need to butter me up. I know people will like that. Any leader who isn't mad or cruel will be well received. Listen, before we go on, may I please see my sister?'

'Only if you're certain you wish to. I've told you what state she is in.'

'I'm positive, Brynd. Please, I would like to see her.'

*

Two soldiers on the door stepped aside as Brynd and Eir approached. He paused as the men opened it, and two of the Night Guard soldiers on duty filtered out.

'Commander, would you mind waiting outside momentarily? I would like to spend just a moment with her on my own.'

'As you wish. I'll join you in a moment.'

She slowly stepped inside, leaving Brynd in the companionable silence of the soldiers. He turned his back to the door for at least half a minute, then turned to look inside. Eir was standing there, her face impassive, watching through the bars. Rika had approached the bars to almost mirror her pose. By blood rather than magic, these were the two most powerful women in the Boreal Archipelago. He felt a sudden nostalgia, and could remember only too well what they were like as younger girls; they had brought a much-needed light into Balmacara, ridding the place of the darkness of Johynn's paranoia.

And now look at them, Brynd thought. *One altered into some cannibalistic beast; the other preparing to take her sister's place at the start of an uncertain future.*

What would Johynn think of the situation now, if he were still alive and of sound judgement? It was Johynn, after all, who put Brynd in charge of the military; who trusted Brynd with the safety of his family, with the protection of his ancient domain.

Brynd decided, then, that he could not dispose of Rika in some cruel manner; it would be up to Eir to decide her sister's fate.

'Commander . . .' Eir called.

Brynd marched over to Eir's side. Rika was slumped

against the far wall now, her knees drawn up to her chin, her gaze set firmly on Eir as if she was looking right through her. Brynd tried to read Eir's expression, but if the young woman was emotionally affected by this scene, she wasn't showing it.

They turned and went back through the door into the corridor.

'How is she?' Eir's question came matter-of-factly, as if this was merely another patient in the hospital.

'According to the notes left in my room, she has not made any signs of a recovery, if that's what you mean. She's lashed out at whoever's passed and eaten her food in what has been described as an "animalistic" manner.'

Eir nodded and moved to the doorway to look at her sister.

'Are you all right?' Brynd asked.

'She is ill,' Eir replied. 'Nothing more. It may be that she cannot be cured, but she remains simply ill – and, importantly, she is not dead.'

'What do you want done with her?' Brynd asked.

'We will keep her here, under observation, for now,' Eir replied, and fell silent for a moment. 'I won't have her killed, if that's what you're implying?'

'I wouldn't have suggested such a thing,' Brynd replied. 'Hardly seems fitting, does it?' Only then did he notice the irony of the statement – this gaol cell wasn't exactly fitting either, with its damp stone walls, lack of light, and musty stench. 'No, it is appropriate that, as her sole family member and guardian, you should have the final word in how she's treated. She's dangerous, I'll say that much. She has *killed* people.'

'I know you say it, but it just seems so hard to believe.'

'Believe it,' came another voice. It was Randur Estevu, approaching quietly. *Guards doing their jobs well*, Brynd thought. 'Evening, commander.'

'It was Randur who first saw her acting strangely,' Brynd announced.

Eir glanced at him, wide-eyed. 'Why didn't you say anything to me?'

'Well, I didn't think you'd really want to know your sister had starting munching people,' Randur replied. 'Besides, I was scared shitless she'd do something.'

Randur related the incident outside his window.

'So I told the commander, which was shortly before she climbed the Citadel. What else could I do?'

He moved close to Eir and tried to put his arms around her softly, but she shrugged him off and peered back through the doorway to her imprisoned sister. Randur looked as if he wanted to say something to her, but then thought better of it.

'I'll leave you two to it,' Brynd announced. 'You know where I am, Eir, if you need to find me. You two probably have a bit of catching up to do about your new role.'

'What does he mean by that?' Randur asked, but Brynd was already walking out of the room.

*

The next thing on Brynd's list that night was to head to Factory 54 to check on developments there. He rode across town without a guard; this time he noticed more civilian patrols on the streets.

If they're that keen on playing soldiers, perhaps they should have enlisted in the army with everyone else...

He knocked on the door, banging four times as he always did, the sound echoing through the cavernous rooms of the factory. It was with a sense of excitement that Jeza opened the door for him.

'I got your message,' he grunted. 'Is tonight really going to be of use?'

'As I said in the note, it really is,' she replied. 'You look anxious.' She was going to say white as a ghost, but he always was; this time there was a hint in his expression that suggested he was deeply uneasy about something.

'War will be coming sooner than I thought. If you've not noticed already, the last of the soldiers have been leaving the city and the island.'

'Is that safe?'

'Yes. Surveillance has confirmed no threats remain to the north, only in the west. You'll hear news soon enough.'

'Are you happy with the orders of armour?' Jeza enquired, leading him down the dreary passageway, deep in the factory.

'It's not enough, admittedly, but it would take the better part of a year to supply every soldier. Time is against us, unfortunately.'

'Don't be so downbeat!' she enthused.

'If only I had your optimism,' Brynd replied.

'If I'm your symbol of optimism, you really are in trouble.'

He chuckled, which seemed to diffuse his mood somewhat. 'Come, show me what you have this time.'

'We've been secretive about this, because we wanted to make sure it would work, and that it was stable,' she declared, leading him to a door. The droning noise could be heard from outside the room.

'What have you got in there?' he asked.

'You'll see.' Grinning, Jeza pushed back the door.

Brynd's jaw fell in disbelief.

The Mourning Wasp was hovering a few feet above the floor, its wings beating so fast that he could hardly see them – there was a huge downdraught of wind. Standing against the far wall were Coren and Diggsy. They waved to the commander, but he wasn't paying attention to them.

'What . . . ?' Brynd began. 'What is it? It has a skull?'

Jeza explained, loudly, above the droning. She told him a shortened version of the events that led to this point. She said it was quite safe and explained why.

'There's more,' she said, walking along the side of the huge room. She took him by his arm and dragged him to follow her. The look on his face was priceless.

'Here's a helm we manufactured. If you notice, we've included a transparent visor.'

Brynd acknowledged the items and looked back to the wasp still hovering above the floor.

'I want you to wear it,' she said, pressing the helm into his stomach.

'Why?'

'To keep the wind from your eyes.'

The commander frowned. 'Why would I want to do that? Do you want me to stand behind it?'

'Oh no,' she laughed. 'It's much better than that.'

*

They reconvened outside the rear doors of the factory. It was way past midnight now, there had been a sudden shower, and the streets were glistening in the moonlight. It was cool and clear. Perched on stone slabs was the Mourning Wasp, its legs poised, always on edge, ready to take flight.

There was little or no gang activity in the surrounding districts – you could usually hear their calls or bottles smashing, but there was only the groaning of the wind, or the distant sound of the surf. Tonight the quiet, desolate district was to their advantage.

Jeza slipped on her own helm with the visor sitting perfectly in front of her eyes and she encouraged Brynd to do the same, which he did. They approached the Mourning Wasp, which was inert, like a statue. It was only now that Brynd seemed to notice the modified saddle.

'Where did you get that from?' he enquired.

'Clever, isn't it? We had to modify the design of a horse saddle, but it does the job remarkably well.'

'Let me be perfectly clear,' Brynd said. 'You expect me to ride this?'

'I do, yes, and once you do, you'll realize why. Come on – you're a big brave soldier, and I'll be sitting right behind you.' She half expected him to cuff her around the ear.

She prodded him forward, and he put his foot in the stirrups and levered himself up and onto the creature. She hopped up behind him, peering over his shoulder towards the vacant stretch of road that lay ahead of them. It was perfectly straight, as a lot of the newer parts of the city tended to be, and lined by tall warehouses or factories.

'The road south of here heads straight towards the Wastelands,' Jeza said. 'She knows the way already – we've taken her out a few times now.'

'*She?*'

'That's right, she's a female,' Jeza replied. 'Right, now, you see those two leather-looking reins in front? They're not leather, they're made of a specific bit of tissue, which connects to nerves within her skull. Now, think of them as like normal reins. You pull to the right, she goes right. You pull to the left, she goes to the left. Both at once, she slows down – release and she'll go as fast as she can. There's a middle rein that controls her height, but she tends to make her own judgements for the most part. I haven't quite worked out how to get a steady pace out of her, so you'll just have to see how you get on.'

'OK,' Brynd replied grimly. He set his gaze forward and they waited, on the back of the wasp, for a minute more. 'How does it get going?' They had to speak louder now, their voices muffled by the helms.

'Tug the reins back firmly.' Jeza chuckled, reached behind and patted the muscle where the wings met. The wings began to move, the drone commenced and, very slowly, the Mourning Wasp began to lift.

Its legs lightened and drifted behind, the whole beast inched forward, the noise increased. Vibrations rattled through them. Dust and debris skittered away in the wind caused by the rapid wing beats.

Jeza could feel Brynd tensing up. 'It's OK, just relax!' she shouted. 'You won't fall off.'

'How can you be certain?'

'Well, even if you do, we'll keep to street level, so you'll only fall a few feet at the most.'

'That statement doesn't fill me with confidence.'

'We can look at building some kind of attachment to keep people firmly in the saddle at higher altitude, that's easy – but you should really just enjoy the ride first.'

'OK. Now what?' Brynd called back hesitantly. It amused Jeza greatly to see a war hero act so tentatively.

'Gently ease off the reins, but remember, pull left for left, right for right – you must do that.'

'I can manage that—'

The Mourning Wasp lurched forward at speed, the buildings began to whip by, and Jeza made the unlikely move of placing her hands on Brynd's hips. Cobbles and stone walls became a blur at the periphery of her vision, and she could feel the chill wind on her hands. She leaned over to get a better view of what was going on: up ahead a wall seemed to race towards them, her heart beat incredibly fast, then she felt Brynd's right arm move: the Mourning Wasp tilted and made a right turn, maintaining its height a few feet off the ground, almost skimming the stonework as it completed the manoeuvre, where it levelled off, stabilized, and continued at high speed.

'You've got the hang of it now,' Jeza called, but Brynd showed no sign of hearing her words.

*

Street by street, building by blurred building, they raced through the southern neighbourhoods of Villiren, skimming the decrepit roads at phenomenal speed. What few citizens were out at this hour stood and gaped, slack-jawed, at the sight of two figures riding the Mourning Wasp past them. Not that it mattered – not at this speed.

Brynd had soon mastered the basics of controlling the

steering: one of the benefits of the wasp was that being a sentient creature, she knew to avoid danger, she would instinctively avoid hitting a wall; the nerve controls simply nudged her where the rider wanted to go. Two minds were involved in the process, working symbiotically. There was one moment as a horse lurched into view at a crossroads, but the wasp's reactions were quicker than the commander's own, and the creature simply drifted up and over, steadying herself once again after they had passed.

*

'Do you want me to take over yet?' Jeza asked eventually, as the streets became sparser, more barren, devoid of notable buildings until they were at the limits of the city. 'Do you want to head back?'

'Not a chance,' came the reply.

Brynd was clearly enjoying himself. They drifted into open country, past smallholdings and larger farmhouses. Out here there were few walls to avoid, and as a result he simply let go of the reins altogether.

'Are you crazy?' Jeza snapped. 'Pick them up again.'

'I want to see where she wants to go herself. I want to know what she *thinks*.'

'That's a bad idea!' Jeza snapped.

'Now who's scared?' came Brynd's smug response.

The Mourning Wasp began to bank a little higher, at tree level now, gliding above the snow-covered hills. Her speed increased and, at one point, they spotted two pterodettes flying alongside before they fell back, unable to keep up. The wind was stronger here. Jeza's heart skipped a few beats – she had not been prepared for Brynd letting go. Yet the wasp seemed to enjoy the freedom: she slowed down along the sides of an iced-up river, and drifted lazily along one of the tributaries, until she met the open sea. There, he took the reins again: and steered her back towards the ground, towards the city, whereupon they picked up speed to race the final few streets home.

*

Outside the factory, Brynd pulled on the reins with confidence. The wasp lowered her legs straight away, barely waiting for them to stop, and shuddered to a standstill. As they dismounted Brynd stumbled slightly, probably dizzy from the speed, as Jeza was herself, despite being more used to it.

Brynd took off his helm and ruffled his hair. He was laughing. He looked back at the wasp in disbelief, then walked a slow circle around it.

'I can't believe how you just trusted her like that,' Jeza said. 'We could have fallen off at high speed.'

'It wouldn't have been a bad way to go,' he smiled. 'You never once took the reins off me. You could have reached over to slow her at any point. You didn't, because you knew she'd be OK.'

'That's not the point,' Jeza replied. 'I didn't think we were ready for that.'

'I'm not the sort of person who hangs back worrying about those sorts of things. It seemed right to let the lady have a go herself. So this . . . Mourning Wasp, is her name? She really is breathtaking.'

Jeza managed to remember to smile. 'You like her then?'

'I didn't understand half of what you said when you talked about resurrecting her, nor do I really want to know. I think she's the most important creature I've seen in a long time.'

'Do you reckon you'd be interested in buying more of her?'

'Yes. Without a doubt. How many more do you have?'

'Four, but you can have as many as you need,' Jeza told him. 'Now we've established the design, the technology is based on the same replicating principle as the armour, more or less. We've two more Mourning Wasps in the basement. I could make a few in a day.'

'The military will require many of these,' he said, more sternly now. 'I want the Night Guard to familiarize themselves with this urgently. And tomorrow I'd like to commence their training.'

'We've not talked about money,' Jeza reminded him.

The look in Brynd's eyes suggested that money was an irrelevance. 'You can have what you need. I hope you know our payments are valid.'

'The best in the city.'

'Good,' he replied. Then he stood in front of her and gave his most serious look of the evening. 'Jeza, when the war is over, consider all of you at the factory to be friends of the Night Guard. If you ever seek employment, you have my word, you'll have a place at my side.'

*

'He said what?' Coren muttered.

'A place at his side. Employment. Jobs for life, or something like that.' Jeza looked across the breakfast table.

'Who wants to work for the fucking Empire?' Coren asked. 'We make our own rules.'

'I know,' Jeza replied. 'I'm just telling you what he told me, all right?'

'Cool it, Coren,' Diggsy said, palming the air. 'Jeza's right to build relationships like that. That albino's the most important man in the city, and we've got him in the palms of our hands. That's pretty incredible, right?'

'Maybe,' Coren grunted.

'Good,' Diggsy said.

'Did you bring the wasp down to the basement?' Jeza asked.

'Yeah, through the rear doors. She seemed fine.'

'They want to bring the whole Night Guard here tomorrow to learn how to ride the Mourning Wasp,' Jeza said.

Coren shook his head.

'What?' Jeza demanded. 'You wanted me to negotiate deals, we negotiate deals – quite a big deal this time, if you must know. They want more wasps made, hence the training.'

Everyone else seemed jubilant, except Coren.

'Just feels too close to the military,' he grunted. 'We wanted to be free to do our own things, not be slaves to soldiers.'

'Yeah, well, we need money to be free in this city, and the military pays the best rates going. We just have to deal with it. Besides, I'm sure I'm not the only one who feels guilty we didn't play our part in the last war. This is our chance to help them defend the city.'

'She's right,' Diggsy muttered. 'Leave things be, Coren.'

Coren exchanged a strange glance with Diggsy then. Jeza made a mental note to follow that up later.

'I'm going to bed,' she said, 'it's been a long night and I want to be ready for the Night Guard tomorrow.'

'I'll be up soon,' Diggsy said, still locked in that weird exchange with Coren.

*

It was late when she shambled about the top floor in her nightwear, wondering what book to read before she went to sleep. She walked barefoot, hardly making a noise. Moonlight came through the shutters in slices, and she saw two figures move in the shadows on the floor below. Crouching, concealing herself behind a metal post, she peered down.

Pilli and Diggsy were embracing, their lips touching.

Her heart stopped. She swallowed. Welled up. She forced herself to take a second glance to confirm the betrayal, then shuffled away into the darkness.

After she entered the bedroom she reached for a bottle of vodka, sat on the edge of the bed, took three huge, eye-stinging slurps from the bottle, and that was OK because she knew she was crying then anyway, could feel the tears streaming down her face. She struggled to take in breaths.

'That's not how to deal with it.' Coren lingered in the

doorway, his body in darkness. He walked towards her, then sat on the floor at a distance.

When she could manage it, she asked, 'How long have you known?'

''Bout ten or so days.'

'Why didn't you tell me?'

'Thought Diggsy would sort himself out. Also, was a little scared of what might happen should Pilli suddenly decide to up sticks and leave.'

'What . . . ? What do you mean?'

'Her dad owns this place. If she fucks off, who knows what would happen to us?'

'I didn't think.' Jeza cradled the bottle. 'What should we do?'

'Drinking now will make it worse. That's not how you get control over the situation.'

'Don't tell me what to do.'

'You just asked me!' Coren continued in an even gentler tone, a level of softness she didn't know he possessed. 'Sleep in my bed tonight.'

'Nice try.'

'Not even I'm that obvious,' he replied. 'I'm off out to see one of those late-night poets in Saltwater. Friend of mine – last on. Take my room, I'll bring in a load of cheap food and pass out in the kitchen. No one will spot the difference.'

'Thanks,' Jeza said, wiping away the last of her tears.

'You know what I think?' Coren asked, standing and moving to the door.

Jeza looked up at him, silently.

'You never liked Diggsy because you were in love with a dead man. Diggsy was your stand-in, a surrogate lover.'

Jeza stared at him, opened her mouth to say something but nothing came out.

'That's right, I have *emotional awareness* when I want. I'm not stupid. You wanted my opinion? Sleep it off, don't

299

mention it. Break it off with him at a more appropriate time, but don't let on you caught them. We can't risk losing the factory.'

He left her in stunned silence.

*

The Night Guard came before daybreak, and Jeza felt like hell despite having stayed away from the vodka. She had cried herself to sleep and descended into deep dreams that left her feeling restless. When she passed through to the kitchen, Coren was slumped at the table with weird tribal food stuck to his cheek. She woke him gently and sent him back to his room.

She answered the door to the Night Guard and nearly had a heart attack at the sight of a dozen of the Empire's best warriors looming over her in the morning mist. They were garbed in black and arranged in a curved row, while to one side Commander Lathraea introduced them.

He wanted each of the soldiers to have their turn with a wasp. First they began to familiarize themselves with the creatures in the basement, overcoming any fears they might have, getting used to the concept of riding on top of them. Later, they each took turns to ride around the nearby streets before they became too busy with activity – it was, Brynd said, of great importance that no one see what was going on because people were sensitive to the new races south of the city. He didn't want to stir up any further tensions.

*

After several successful efforts, the Night Guard went away to work on their personal fitness, only to return later that evening, when darkness came again to the city's streets.

Jeza watched as they became more relaxed and confident. Their reactions became far quicker – their desire to master the skills was unsurpassed. She was both in awe and jealous at their skills.

Brynd soon pushed them to try riding with one hand then

asked them to hold out their swords to see if they could master both swordplay and flying. She began to realize exactly how the Mourning Wasps were to be used.

By the time both moons were unseasonably high, Brynd was encouraging his men and the Mourning Wasps through ever-more complex manoeuvres.

What struck Jeza was how the Mourning Wasps thrived under their military masters. They seemed to enjoy the challenges, which had unearthed a new sense of vitality. If the creatures had once mourned, as according to the legend, it appeared that they no longer felt any sadness. The only sadness was Jeza's: she felt like a mother handing over her child in exchange for a fat contract, but she forced herself to be strong.

And in just a day and a night, the soldiers of the Night Guard had mastered the complex arts of riding the Mourning Wasp.

TWENTY-FOUR

The streets were slick with rain. Street traffic picked up after the rainstorm: people heading quickly on their way home before the skies opened up again. Fulcrom and Lan had waited for the rain to stop before leaving the Citadel.

Dressed in crude civilian clothing, brown breeches, woollen tops, raincapes and heavy boots, they blended into the Villiren dusk.

'These jumpers make my skin itch,' Lan said.

'Never mind,' Fulcrom replied, smiling.

'It's all right for you, with your rumel skin. What about poor little humans like me?'

'You're tough as old boots,' Fulcrom replied. 'You'll live. Besides, it's either that or give ourselves away.'

'I get it, but that doesn't mean I have to like it,' Lan said, rearranging her raincape.

They continued through the cold streets to their destination in the Ancient Quarter, the Partisans' Club.

Fulcrom had done his best to speak to locals that morning to glean the mood on the streets; he also studied maps, memorized street names and corporation names registered with the Citadel, so that he might pose as a civilian more effectively.

The road around the Partisans' Club was noticeably different. There were people here coming for the meeting, that was clear. But amidst the moving tide of people, Fulcrom noticed individuals who were standing still like islands. Big men with their arms folded lined the wall nearest the entrance. Behind the flick of a cloak, Fulcrom spotted a blade or two. 'Keep an eye on those,' Fulcrom whispered to Lan. Her gaze immediately scanned around and she nodded her agreement.

Men stood by the door of the club, occasionally pulling certain individuals out to inspect them, before pushing them back into the flow. As the last remaining light vanished from the day, Fulcrom and Lan headed inside.

Down a stairwell and they were inside the plush club. At one end was a stage with spotlights and dreary lanterns, which gave the room a vaguely sinister air. There was a heady smell of damp, sweat and cheap incense, and the place was rammed with people of all ages. Fulcrom had expected a few tough-looking disillusioned types, but was surprised at the variety of ages and classes: there were old and young, well-to-do and both men and women, humans and rumels present.

It was mostly standing-room only. There was cheap art-work on the wall and, judging by all the tankards of beer, and glasses of wine or vodka, there was a bar somewhere out of sight. At least it was warm. Fulcrom and Lan managed to find a spot against the far wall, so that the stage stood on their right and the rest of the room opened up to the left, allowing them a full view of everything.

The noise of the crowd grew and people became restless. They were whistling and jeering, and when three men walked on stage the people cheered sarcastically.

The centre figure walked to the front of the stage with his legs apart like some dodgy actor soaking in the admiration of his crowd; this was sheer arrogance on display. Even though he was thirty feet away, Fulcrom guessed he was a handsome man, a swarthy-looking fellow with a day or two of stubble. Everything about his outfit said he was a man used to the company of thugs – the handle of a dagger was sticking up out of his boot – but he had a vaguely refined air about him.

'Who's the show-off?' Lan whispered.

'I suspect this is the man who runs the show, and the very man we're looking for. Malum.'

The two men that had accompanied him on stage suddenly drew out enormous swords and rammed them in the stage – and the crowd fell silent.

Malum placed his hands in his pockets and waited just a little longer before beginning. 'Thanks for coming,' he started. 'It's much appreciated. Feels good, doesn't it? All of us together like this. You know, humans and rumel, folk from all across Villiren. That's us. That's community. That's what this city's built on, right?'

A few cheers scattered about the club.

'Good,' Malum continued. He walked slowly across the stage as he spoke. 'My lads have good evidence, you see, that all of this is under threat. You heard about the monster in the iren, yeah? The child killer?'

A murmur of agreement from the audience.

'You ain't seen anything yet. There are worse creatures to the south. We've seen them.' He gestured to his accomplices on stage. 'Me and the lads, we've seen just what lies on the edge of the city. You want to know what we saw?'

Malum marched across to the other side of the stage. 'Oh, we saw some of the sickest shit. Creatures with more arms than you've had hot dinners.' He pointed to a heavyset man in the audience, and got a few laughs.

That seemed important, to show his charisma, Fulcrom thought. *He's looking to win them over all right, but for what? Why does he need their support?*

'Creatures with rows of vicious teeth, creatures with the blood of our children on their hands. That's right, we've seen them taking people off the streets. Kids, animals, you name it.'

'That's not actually true, is it?' Lan whispered to Fulcrom.

'No. But he's very convincing, isn't he?'

'So, the commander who fancies himself as a bit of a ruler over you and me – someone who doesn't know how tough things are for honest people in this city – seems to think it would be a good idea if we lived side by side with these things. He's spending all his time meeting with them, preparing the way for millions of those aliens to come to our islands. He wants them to work with us – can you imagine that? There's hardly enough fucking jobs as it is – he wants to hand over what's left to a bunch of evil monsters?'

'He's stirring up a little racial hatred,' Fulcrom whispered. 'You see it all the time from various businessmen trying to keep the masses angry and accept low wages, but what's this guy trying to achieve?'

'Maybe he wants to lead them?'

Fulcrom's attention skipped back to Malum, who was continuing his monologue of hatred.

'I'd like to invite anyone who supports them aliens south of the city to stand up here on this stage and tell me why,' Malum demanded. He now stood centre stage once again. There was nothing but silence to his question.

A voice eventually hollered from the audience: 'OK, you got us on your side, pal. What can we do about it?'

'I'm glad you asked that,' Malum replied. 'In terms of your safety, I'm already on it – not the military, you should note, but a lot of genuine people who I know well. We've got civilian patrols organized keeping watch on the fringes of the Wasteland . . .'

As Malum spoke, Fulcrom caught some movement to one side. It looked like a scuffle, and two men were pulling a third out towards the exit. 'Wait here,' he whispered to Lan, before pushing his way through the attentive crowd towards the doorway. He poked his head around the corner and glanced through to the dimly lit corridor beyond. There, two thugs were laying into another man, striking firm blows to his stomach and face. They pushed him up against the wall and spat in his face.

Fulcrom could overhear a few words. '. . . You breathe a word to anyone and we'll kill you.'

The victim, a male in his late thirties, with a torn shirt, brown breeches and heavy boots, spluttered his response. 'Didn't . . . didn't mean to disagree with the man. Just seemed a bit over the . . . over the top.'

'You said you were heading to the Citadel,' one of the attackers snarled.

'Was jokin'. Empty threat. Nothing more.'

A third man came to enquire what was going on and the thugs dumped their victim on the floorboards before speaking to the newcomer, a broad-faced, red-headed man who looked as though he'd been in a few fights in his life.

'Citadel you say.' The red-headed man scratched his chin. 'Malum wouldn't like that. Better get rid of him. Keep it clean.' And with that he began to walk away.

The thugs nodded, pulled out a blade, hauled the victim up off the floor and, with his eyes wide and his hands up in protest, they slit his throat. It happened so quickly. Blood pooled across the wooden floor.

'Aw, for fucksake,' the red-headed man called back. 'I said keep it clean.'

'Sorry, JC. You want us to sort it?'

'Yeah, we've got a reputation. People respect us. Get a mop and a bucket and sort it out, and get rid of that fucking body.'

Fulcrom quickly pulled back into the room and, his heart beating rapidly, he pushed his way through to Lan's side. Malum was still talking, and there was now the acrid stench of arum weed to add to the sweaty musk.

'What was it?' she asked, and he told her.

'If I'd have intervened they would have taken me too.'

'Shit.'

'Exactly. I'd like to see what the commander has to say about this.'

'They're not messing around, are they?' Lan whispered.

'No, this is serious,' Fulcrom replied. He eyed Malum, who was at the far side of the stage, continuing his diatribe.

'Tell you what I'm going to do,' Malum called out across the crowd. 'I'm gonna repeat this little speech of mine on another night or two. Or three. Fetch your friends and family – and if they can't make it, tell them all will be fine. I'm here. I'll not let this city become some kind of military dictatorship or alien ghetto.'

The raucous cheer was louder than ever. People banged tankards on tables and stamped their feet on the floorboards.

After this settled, a few people began to ask what he'd do next?

'All in good time, my friends. All in good time. I'm getting some of the old underground networks to unite. We're starting to form a new network with some of the tavern owners and shopkeepers around the city – all nothing to do with the alien-lovin' soldiers. We've got plenty of money on our side. We've got all we need to take our city back and protect it from aliens. Expect more news very soon.'

With that, he turned and walked off stage, leaving the crowd demanding more.

'That guy knows how to play to an audience,' Lan commented.

'It all explains why he created that scene in the iren, anyway,' Fulcrom replied. 'We need to report back to the commander right away.'

TWENTY-FIVE

The military were packing up for the final time. People were bustling through the corridors on each level, carrying supplies, blankets, armour, swords, food – everything that said something big was about to happen. Fulcrom found Brynd surrounded by clerks and piles of paper.

'You look busy,' Fulcrom commented.

Brynd didn't reply for a moment, simply staring at the papers before him on the table. 'It's war this time, investigator. This is it. This is the big campaign.'

'Will you be gone from the city for long?'

'I've no idea. It could be over pretty quickly. It could be a more sustained campaign but I bloody well hope it isn't.'

'Where's the conflict?' Fulcrom enquired.

'It's looking like the coast of Folke, if the surveillance is correct. There's another coastal invasion being planned. If Folke falls, so does the rest of the Archipelago.'

'I hope it goes as well as these things can do,' Fulcrom replied.

'Thanks, but I take it you didn't come here to discuss that.'

'No, I've found out who acquired the corpse of the monster in the iren, and why.'

'That was quick.' Brynd gestured to the chair opposite.

Fulcrom sat down to reveal his findings, from his dealings with the youths at Factory 54 to the meeting in the Partisans' Club. 'Those kids were probably quite innocent in all of this

I believe. The girl – Jeza – felt pressured by Malum. She probably regrets ever having met him.'

Brynd had kept calm while Fulcrom related the information, but as soon as he recalled the threats that Malum had made to him months ago, his temper began to show.

'You know who Malum is, I'm guessing,' Fulcrom ventured.

'I certainly do.' Brynd sat back in his chair, made a steeple of his hands and contemplated his fury. 'He was a vicious gang leader and used to be a powerful man – for his position. He tried a few tricks on us. If I'm honest, I hoped he'd died in the war, but I knew there were still a few issues with the gangs in some districts. It's the gangs who rule the streets in this city, investigator – or so they'd like to think.'

'What do you think of the meeting at the club?'

'I've not got time to deal with it so I'm going to entrust this to you – but be careful. The man was once capable of great evil. Because of that, I'll release what few guards we have left at the Citadel to be at your disposal, but tread carefully. I'll see if we can spare fifty newly enlisted soldiers and have them patrol the streets, but that really is a maximum.'

'Of course,' Fulcrom said. 'How many soldiers from the city are going with you?'

'Nearly all of them – it has to be that way. We really do need *every* fighting man and woman for the battle.'

Fulcrom nodded and rose. 'I'll do my best, commander.'

'I want to repeat: be cautious,' Brynd replied. 'Malum isn't your typical criminal.'

The rumel smiled. 'I've dealt with more than a few unusual criminals in my time, commander.'

*

'Hey, Malum,' the kid said, stirring Malum from his slumber.

Malum recalled his surroundings: he was sitting in a plush chair in an empty underground tavern. Everyone had gone home. The party had ended. It was just him and the embers of the fire, and the empty lager bottle that lay by his feet. He breathed deeply, trying to clear his head.

'What is it?' Malum tried to locate the kid's voice, and his blurry vision eventually located the doorway, in which a blond kid was standing.

'JC told me to tell you that the army's leaving.'

'What? Say that again,' Malum demanded. His head didn't pound these days, but the kid's voice was dulled slightly.

'The army is vacating the city.'

'Why?'

'They're going to war, JC says.'

It took Malum a while to process this.

'Tell JC to get the Bloods together, in here, tonight. What time is it anyway?'

'Mid-afternoon,' the kid said.

'Fucksake,' Malum muttered. 'All right, let JC know that. Get them all here real quick. Tell them to sober up, too.'

*

Later, the tavern was rammed with his core gang members, a good few hundred of them. These were the remnants of the war – not that many, but enough to get the word about. They were his brethren, the people he could trust. They would do anything, kill anyone, if he asked it of them.

Malum stood on the bar and regarded them all. Like he had done on stage, he waved for silence and it duly came. 'It's come to my attention that the military is leaving the city. I thought there'd be a thousand or so soldiers in the city – turns out there are less than a hundred left. I'm sending out scouts to confirm this, but this new situation changes my plan somewhat.'

'We sending out raids on the aliens now then?'

'No,' Malum said, 'not immediately. We've always sought for this to be a free city from the Empire. Only when it's free of military and Imperial rule will we get to do what *we* want.

We get control then, and we can only do that if the people want the same thing. We'd hoped to start doing this across the city after the war, but it didn't really happen like that, did it? No, because the military got there before we did. Effectively, there's one place we need to occupy to make Villiren what we want.'

There was a stony silence in the tavern. No one knew what to say.

'The Citadel,' he concluded. 'With all the soldiers heading to war, this leaves the Citadel *unguarded*.'

'It won't be completely unguarded though, will it?' someone called.

'Probably not, no. There are most likely going to be a few units on the streets too. But we're never going to get a better chance to take the place, are we?'

'What, we just *take* it?'

'We just take it. Like a repossession, break things down from within. Without the same level of defence, it'll be like walking in. Any soldiers on the streets, we'll slaughter – we'll overwhelm them. It won't be that easy, obviously, but if we're ever going to do it, now's the time. Once we're in the Citadel we can loot the place and burn what we can't take.'

'But that Jamur lass is still going to be there, isn't she?'

'Probably, unless she's going with the military,' Malum said. 'If she is, we could keep them hostage, or hang their body parts on the outer limits of the city – like the old days. Either way, they're not going to provide much of a challenge against a few thousand of us.'

'Where are we going to get a few thousand from?' came another voice. 'There's barely a thousand of the Bloods left.'

'We put the word out. We make offers of sharing the spoils of the Citadel with the people – whoever would like to help us. They'll accept that. Tell everyone that the aliens will soon be coming. We unite what's left of the gangs under one common aim: to reclaim Villiren while the commander's at war, to take the city for our own, to stop aliens coming in. Who knows, the commander might die while he's at it, meaning there'll be nothing to trouble us afterwards. And when the military does decide to come back – depleted after the fighting – there'll be nothing here for them. The people are already on our side.'

'We doing this for the people or for us?'

'For *us*, of course. We need the people to be on our side so we can take what we want. But everyone wins, think about it. This is the chance to make the city ours. To free it from the Empire, let people do what they want, make their own rules. Meanwhile we can live like kings and make sure there's no aliens at the same time.'

The lads seemed to like that. They hollered and cheered. They banged tables and shook their blades in the air.

That's more like it, Malum thought.

TWENTY-SIX

They were getting used to the flying. That morning, as the Night Guard ascended high above the Y'iren countryside on board the dragons, none of them vomited. They were travelling in smaller numbers than before, to make room for the Mourning Wasps. Four travelled per cage, subdued by a small chemical treatment that Jeza had provided. There was a stimulant to wake them fully before they were required to be used.

Brynd stood over them watching curiously. He was concerned with whether or not they could be used in battle and that his men had complete control. In his brief conversation with Artemisia that morning, he had confirmed the tactics required for the forthcoming operation.

At this time enemy forces were preparing another sea invasion with the sky-city, aiming to slam into the coast of Folke with their trademark ferocity. Brynd's and Artemisia's combined forces were making their way to that western coast at great speed in order to meet the threat. As for the enemy, they would comprise dozens of races, many of which Brynd hadn't encountered and, therefore, he couldn't assess their strengths or weaknesses. This made tactical decision-making awkward: he could advise his own people on their tried and tested formations. They had an advantage from knowing the best ways to navigate these islands, the most effective terrains on which to fight. He also communicated with Artemisia about the effectiveness of her people, which made planning a little easier, but what they would actually face was still unknown.

Artemisia had conceded that command would be his – up until the point where he and his Night Guard soldiers would escort Frater Mercury into the sky-city.

Given Artemisia's numbers and estimated figures for the enemy, there could be up to two million lives on the field of battle. By now, he liked to think his numbness to death, and the fact that not all of them were humans or rumels, were the reasons that he was not intimidated by these numbers. Yet no matter how he looked at it, his decisions would probably contribute to the biggest loss of life ever to have been witnessed on these islands.

Artemisia had given instructions to fly to a specific destination. Having studied maps of the island of Folke, she said that there would be a vessel in the sky above a particular coastal lagoon, which was not to be attacked since it carried her own elders. There would be a docking platform on which the dragons would land. She stressed that the vessel was a place of great importance for her culture, and that he was to think of it like a floating cathedral.

That place was where they were now headed and, despite the occasional gust of wind that rattled the cages, all was as calm as it could be. The Night Guard were looking resplendent in their new, black armour – as intimidating a sight as any Okun.

*

The landing came suddenly. Brynd marched to the back of the container, as one of the others unlocked the hatch, unhooking the landing ramp, and opening it.

'Bohr . . .' someone in front of him muttered. 'What the hell is this place?'

'Artemisia's so-called cathedral in the sky, I assume,' Brynd replied cheerily. He marched down the ramp, into daylight, no longer surprised at the fact that nearly every new experience these days left him in awe.

Some hundred feet long and just as wide, the platform was bordered by an ornate, green balustrade. It was large enough to fit at least five dragons and their dismounting troops and was crafted from the same greenish stone, very much like marble. Brynd crouched down to assess the material and saw that gemstones had been pressed flat in its fabric. Beyond the balustrade, everything was lost to cloud, so it looked as if they were on another world entirely. He turned around and gazed up a cliff face of architectural elements. He could understand why Artemisia had compared it to a vast cathedral. Huge pillars disappeared into the cloud. Massively ornate gargoyles stood either side of long balconies, on which there were people in blue and red robes standing, observing them. There were at least three arched doorways nearby, each one high enough to accommodate a dragon stretched tall. It was cold up here – and there was the groaning sound of a strong wind, yet little of it seemed to reach the platform; it was as if they were protected from the elements, but there was no shelter.

Brynd turned to see Artemisia heading towards them, strapped up in full battle gear, her sword handles poking above her shoulders.

'Welcome, commander!' she bellowed. 'Your arrival is an honour. This is *Ekkpolis*, our most important vessel.'

'It's enormous,' Brynd replied.

'This is true, yes,' Artemisia said. 'You are on the first of ten such landing . . . harbours? Bays?'

'Landing bay would make more sense in Jamur.'

She nodded firmly. 'Yes, landing bay. There are nine more, and this is the smallest.'

'What is this structure precisely?'

'It is where we accommodate the most important members of our civilization. Come, let us not talk out here. Bring your soldiers.'

'I wanted to show you something first.' Brynd took Artemisia back to one of the dragons and up the ramp to reveal his new weapons – the Mourning Wasps.

Artemisia looked impressed, which was saying something for her. Brynd explained that the Night Guard intended to ride the creatures instead of horses, and discussed the advantages this would bring.

'Narrow spaces, different altitudes, and all at high speed. I don't think they cope well with long distances, but they're certainly an improvement in all other aspects on our usual military horses.'

She nodded, thoughtfully. 'This will be useful, very useful,' she said. 'It may change our plans perhaps. We will talk more of this inside. We must now refine the final tactics. These . . . Mourning Wasps' – she stressed the name slowly, as if to commit it to memory – 'will help us when we need to enter our enemies' inner sanctum.'

They headed back down the ramp and on to the platform. There, they progressed as one unit inside the *Ekkpolis*.

*

Once inside, it no longer felt as if they were in the air. What struck Brynd most about the *Ekkpolis* was not how alien it was, but how *normal* it appeared. Admittedly, there were sophisticated alien technologies obviously running in the background, but the layout, structure and function was much like a grand building found in the Archipelago.

As Artemisia escorted the Night Guard soldiers through the main doors, they headed on to a large street, which led through apartment-style blocks. Here it was generally dim – lighting coming from a few large torches and a thin skylight.

The buildings were made of varied materials, a stone like granite, but possessing more interesting textures; there were shimmering sheets of white stone, fat bricks with precious stones pressed into the surfaces. There were ornate signs in a language Brynd could not understand, though he vaguely recognized some of the symbols from the military camps, so he guessed they represented clans or families.

Clusters of humans, of all ages, peered over their balconies to watch the Night Guard as they were escorted past their homes. Further along there were stalls lining the streets, though there were no basic goods to be found here – these were craft items, jewellery, decorations and the like. A few people meandered underneath beautifully textured awnings, but there wasn't any of the energy of their own irens; people wore morose expressions, there was no haggling, and barely any coin being exchanged.

'Everyone looks so tired here,' Sergeant Tiendi observed.

Brynd didn't say anything in response. *Perhaps eternal warfare tends to grate after a while . . .*

There were further city blocks, people crammed above each other in tight spaces; there was the drone of distant, indecipherable conversation. There were plenty of new aromas, too, sweet and bitter, and he did not recognize them.

Brynd admitted to himself that he was disappointed with this place. He had expected the most exotic structures, the most baroque cityscape, confusing and baffling buildings – but there was little of that. More unusual goings-on could be seen on the streets of Villiren.

No, this seemed a sanitized culture, as if the most conservative elements had been ring-fenced and shot up into the sky.

He told Artemisia his thoughts.

'You are not entirely incorrect in your assumptions.' Artemisia walked by his side, stooped slightly, muttering her words with discretion. 'You must understand that the people gathered here are our elites. These are the royal bloodlines, the assemblage of noble kin.'

'I thought your culture more . . . democratic than this?'

'It is indeed democratic for the most part. But the *Ekkpolis* is a relatively new vessel, the result of great expenditure, which has been partially commandeered by our military rulers. The people here feel safer with protection and the military have a first-class vessel on which to base their operations.'

'Why are all of the people here *human*?' Brynd asked.

'It is humans who have hoarded the wealth. Other races do not seem so bothered by coin and manage by other means. So it goes in your world, too, does it not?'

Brynd confessed that it did, more or less.

*

They headed along increasingly empty roads. Admittedly, the further away from habitation they marched, the more interesting the architecture became, but it still felt perfunctory to Brynd, as if the buildings were mere shelters. There were a few other races – some small, interesting creatures with complex body shapes and bizarre faces, engaged in menial work, polishing some of the surfaces, carrying items that looked like building materials. The streets were curved as gracefully as a river's meander, passing through minimalist decor. Soon it became nothing more than a path between pale, glossy walls, with thin slits for windows, which overlooked nothing but patches of cloud. The walls met at the top in a vast arched ceiling. There were no other markings, nothing else to suggest they were going somewhere important.

They arrived in a small antechamber, which again was minimalist in style. Artemisia ushered them through a white door, then another. The soldiers found themselves in a room around fifty paces wide, with a large, black table upon a raised platform, around which Artemisia's elders were seated, along with other people garbed in military-style clothing, one human wearing bright-silver chest armour and a sour expression. The elders regarded the Night Guard pensively.

At the other end of the chamber, Frater Mercury was seated in an immense glass-like throne. Around the room were large, golden cauldrons, each with levers and dials, and when he passed one Brynd peered in to see a clear liquid inside with steam rising. The floor tiles they walked upon were almost porcelain-like in their appearance, but they remained strangely soft underfoot, like a luxurious carpet. The white walls contained designed panels here and there; whether they had function or not, he didn't know.

The man in silver armour, grey-haired yet still young-looking, marched down to Artemisia, and began to speak in hushed tones. His uniform was interesting, not dissimilar to some of the more ancient costumes from the Boreal Archipelago: a white tunic over which he wore stylized armour that had been moulded to look like a muscular chest and boots of dark brown leather.

Artemisia turned to Brynd. 'My people wish to confirm our plans.'

'Of course,' Brynd said. 'How shall we continue?'

'Stand by any one of the cauldrons,' she instructed.

Brynd turned to his comrades and shrugged. They peeled off in small groups to stand around the vessels.

They were tall objects, reaching to just under Brynd's ribs, and they were at least several feet wide. On closer inspection, the fluid within was not transparent, it was mirroring what was above. Brynd saw his own pale features reflected, though his face was distorted slightly by slow ripples passing across the liquid. 'What should we be looking for?'

Artemisia was looking at the elders, who were conferring and gesturing to their table. Were there maps on there?

Suddenly the liquid began to bubble slightly, then simmered, though Brynd could feel no heat from the container. He looked at the expressions on his comrades' faces, and they were as cool as his own.

'Look down into the cauldrons,' Artemisia called.

The liquid began to change tone – its mirror-like qualities dissipated, and in their place appeared images of small black dots.

'What are we looking at?' Brynd enquired.

'These are the . . . Boats?' she looked to Brynd for confirmation of the word and he nodded. 'These are being sent out, as we converse, across the waters towards the coast of Folke.'

Brynd looked down again into the liquid. He could now see that while there was a cloud around the perimeter of the cauldron, the liquid was in fact the surface of the sea, and there were hundreds of small dots. 'Just like Villiren,' he breathed. 'Where did the boats come from, another Realm Gate?'

'Not this time. These were contained within a limb of their vessel.'

'So the enemy has launched their offensive already?'

'They have indeed.'

Brynd's heart skipped a beat, but he wanted to be sure. 'How are you acquiring such . . . such pictures? Moving ones, of that.'

'We have our . . . surveillance beings, not dissimilar to your garudas. They are equipped in a fashion that means what they see is transmitted to these cauldrons.'

'What size is this force?'

'There are approximately ten thousand ships heading to the shore in the first wave, and one of your hours behind them lies a second, larger wave. Our estimates suggest the first will arrive in two hours.'

'Most of our forces will take another day to meet us. They're currently protecting towns situated further from the coast, where the populations are dense.'

'They will be of more use there, for we have tens of thousands of our own people ready to meet this. We will, however, require your guidance. The elders,' Artemisia gestured respectfully towards them, 'will need to know what this terrain of sand is like.'

'It's nothing you want to fight on ideally,' Brynd replied. 'Depending on where they make landfall, however, your best bet is to assault them hardest as they land on the beaches. The waters are shallow, which means that the boats won't be able to penetrate deep enough. If the ships are of the same type as those that hit Villiren, they'll probably run aground thirty or forty feet before the low-tide mark: this means wading through water.'

'We will need to know the quality of your water. Is it saline?'

'It is.'

'We have oils that will be useful here. Liquid fire, commander.'

Brynd raised an eyebrow. 'That will be more than useful, if it does what I think it might. After this, I suggest holding them up as best you can with airborne assaults, archers, catapults, anything to keep them from establishing a position on the beaches. It will be messy. We'll have the advantage as there will be nothing for them to shelter behind at first. They will suffer a lot of casualties if you've the numbers to keep the attack up.'

'Be assured we do.'

'Good. I'm guessing your enemy knows this already since they've split their assault into two sections.'

'At least two.'

'So why do they not send their sky-city to deploy ground troops?'

'It doesn't move well across water.'

'You could have mentioned this earlier!' Brynd snapped.

'The . . . forces it uses require it to be above land, otherwise they have to adopt different fuel sources and it can very much inhibit their mobility. This works to our favour, for it may be that our attempt to land on board will be far simpler.'

'And are we to attempt this boarding while the war rages?' Brynd asked.

'Yes.'

'It feels wrong. We should be on our islands, protecting our people and our land and our children.'

'This is not the time for seeking glories.'

'This is not,' Brynd growled, 'about glory. This is about doing our *jobs*. We *will* stand alongside our people.'

'You will have time for such matters, if you wish,' Artemisia replied coolly, 'but we should concentrate our primary efforts on where their communications are most focused.'

'The sky-city,' Brynd said. 'I'm guessing that their military will mostly be concentrated on the invasion, leaving the sky-city less defended?'

'Indeed that is so, much like our own. We strike when the battle is at its most intense, but it will not be simple,' Artemisia replied firmly, and with outstretched arms she gestured to the cauldrons once again, which bubbled furiously.

A new scene then presented itself: there were clouds or white smoke at first, a hazy bird's-eye view of landscape, rolling hills, snow-covered tundra perhaps, it wasn't easy to discern. Then, dark patches of land.

'What are we looking at now?' Brynd enquired.

'This is our army,' Artemisia said, with pride. 'One and a half million individuals, made up of several different races, all of whom are trained ... soldiers, I believe your word is, though we would call them mercenaries and conscripts, too. It is all we could muster at such short notice. More are coming, but we are currently engaged in the business of evacuating our largest city. It is not, as you may appreciate, a simple and clean effort.'

'Indeed . . .' Brynd peered once again into the liquid, only to see a clearer context now: there was the coastline, along which Artemisia's forces were gathered.

'We are adjusting our tactics according to your advice,' she announced.

How the hell are they doing that so quickly?

'I can sense you are wondering how this may be so,' she continued. If she was capable of pride, she was certainly capable of smugness at how her culture was more advanced than Brynd's.

'Not really,' Brynd grunted. There was a chuckle from one of his soldiers. 'But since you mention it, what facilities are you using?'

Artemisia described a complex system that seemed to cross shamanism with high technological genius. The elders were connected telepathically to the generals on the ground, where they in turn had cauldrons and methods of viewing the entire operation. There was a vast system of communication that her army depended upon, and Brynd remembered how the Okun, too, relied on an elegant form of contact with each other. It maintained their uniformity, their progress. Their devastating force.

Artemisia concluded, 'We shall settle final tactics on the ground, then for our own operation – for which we have gained new intelligence and our cartographers have supplied us with internal maps of the Policharos. After this discussion, we may watch the first wave of conflict.'

'What, we just sit up here and watch the war like spectators? Shouldn't we be down on the ground, rallying the troops, boosting their confidence, giving direction?'

Artemisia translated this statement to the elders, who seemed greatly amused.

'Our people do war on an enormous scale, Commander Lathraea. More often than not, if we are on the ground, any information we give would be too slow and ineffective. No, it is better we stay up here, and view progress through our usual means.'

Brynd did not like this at all. It was his way to be on the ground, with his own people, protecting his towns and cities from whatever forces assaulted them. It seemed an artificial warfare, conducted from a distance, as if he were one of the ancient gods.

I am no god, he thought to himself. *We* will *fight alongside our people.*

TWENTY-SEVEN

Fulcrom and Lan headed back to the Partisans' Club in the morning. When they arrived, Fulcrom made up some excuse about having lost Lan's necklace the night before and asked to take a look around to see if he could find it.

'You look like decent sorts,' the doorman said, and let them both in.

While he was there, Fulcrom planned to engage the owner in a conversation about the event with Malum. It pained Fulcrom to praise the scenes he had seen that night, to wax lyrical about what was at best small-mindedness, racism and violence. But he knew he needed more information about what Malum had devised next and this was his best – his only – lead for now.

The owner turned out to be a woman in her fifties. She looked as if she could have once been a starlet in her day, and there was still something about the way she moved, and the make-up she wore, that said she hadn't fully left the stage alone. She had greying blonde hair, a huge smile and wide, pretty eyes. Judging by the look of her she liked her food now, and almost anticipating such thoughts she said, as they took a table by the empty stage, 'I'm not what I used to be, you know. When you have your own cook, sometimes the temptation is too great!'

'There's no harm in liking a good meal,' Fulcrom said.

'You rumel might be able to cope, but it's not that easy for me. Now, can I get you a drink? I've more than one handsome waiter around here somewhere . . .'

'No, that's OK,' Fulcrom laughed, 'we shouldn't be that long – hopefully Lan will find the necklace soon enough.'

'She's a pretty girl,' the woman observed.

'She is,' Fulcrom replied. 'If you want to get yourself something to eat or drink, don't let me stop you.'

'I don't get enough exercise to eat and drink all the time! I used to be on that stage every night in my youth.' She gestured with a wave to the dimly lit platform just behind.

'You've some interesting shows these days,' Fulcrom told her. 'That one with Malum last night was different. Not your typical piece of theatre.'

'You could put it like that. Must confess, I don't normally like to entertain the likes of him.'

'You disapprove of what he said? I thought it was . . . interesting.'

'Not his message, no,' the woman replied, leaning back in her chair and drawing a leg over her other knee. 'No, he speaks wisely on that front, does the young man. I make no issue about being scared of the aliens – most of us are.'

'It's understandable, given the times we live in,' Fulcrom said. 'So how did you end up hosting his . . . well, his little show?'

'Oh, he's a regular here – well, he used to be before the war. That was his chair over there, by the wall.'

'He had his own chair?'

'He was in the *gangs*.'

Fulcrom nodded, pretending to understand the significance of her statement.

'Those gang types,' she went on, 'tend to have their own way around these parts. You don't mess with them.'

'It shouldn't be like that,' Fulcrom observed.

'That's the way this city is,' she said. 'There's no point in complaining about things.'

'How does a gang type end up here? And how does he go from having a table to going on stage?'

'Well, he asked for a favour, and I was too scared to say no.'

'I don't really get the chance to mix with people like that.'

'Count yourself lucky.'

'I was interested in what he had to say, even if he doesn't impress everyone. I had this silly idea in mind of offering my help.'

The woman eyed him suspiciously. 'There are better people to help.'

'But I agree with his sentiments.'

'You know, I'm feeling generous.' She then went on to describe the address at which Malum could be found. 'That's if you're serious in your offer.'

'I'm very serious,' Fulcrom replied. As if on cue, Lan came over with a necklace in her hand and a wide smile on her face.

'Well,' the owner declared, 'would you look at that. What were the chances?'

'I know,' Lan replied, with fake elation.

Fulcrom rose and stood alongside Lan. 'That's wonderful news. Now I won't have to buy you another.'

'We should probably be going.'

'Let me show you out,' the woman said. She walked them back through the musty corridors, which smelled of spilled alcohol and arum weed.

'One last thing.' The woman paused at the bottom of the stairwell to the exit. 'You are both awful liars and performers.'

'I'm sorry?'

'I know lousy acting when I see it. You should have just been honest and asked for his details outright. I'd be glad to see him stopped – that's if you think you have it in you.'

Fulcrom considered continuing the charade, but decided it

wasn't worth it. 'We have to be careful. We know who we're dealing with.'

'I know. Make sure you watch your back.'

*

Outside, Fulcrom consulted Lan on their next move. They weighed up their options, but with nothing else in their way they decided to press on to the address.

'With the military out of the city, we need to see if we can stop this sooner rather than later,' Fulcrom concluded. 'At the moment, though, I'm short on ideas . . .'

The two of them headed through the wet streets. The cobbles were shiny in the afternoon sun. A giant trilobite, which Fulcrom had heard of but never seen until now, skittered across their path dragging a crate of tools. The devastation from the war was clearer here, but Fulcrom guessed that things had been far worse before they turned up. There wasn't so much rubble, but it was the lack of activity in what should have been a thriving district that was disconcerting.

It took them the better part of an hour to reach the area they wanted, a well-to-do zone with a few taverns, faded shopfronts, and that kind of architectural spirit far too lacking in the rest of the city.

The building was a whitewashed affair with timber frames and a flat roof. A few people milled around nearby and Fulcrom tried to assess whether or not they were related to the operation Malum was running. A cluster of youths came out of a side door and marched with deliberate purpose and an air of nonchalance. He spotted a few knives being carried, so they decided to hang back a little while longer.

'So what exactly is the plan?' Lan asked. 'We just storm in, the two of us?'

'No,' Fulcrom replied. 'I think we need a little more confirmation of what's going on. I suspect our next move should be a stealthy one. I want to get up on the roof.'

'Easy enough.'

'For you, maybe, not for the likes of me.'

'Should get yourself some powers someday,' Lan chuckled.

The roofs were all flat and the buildings close together so Fulcrom decided they should head to one of the nearby taverns, get up on its roof, and jump across until they were on the roof of Malum's building. Lan happily enough skipped up onto the roof when no one was looking, but Fulcrom had to find his way around the back to scramble up. Lan gave him a hand up at the top, and with an effort he found himself on top of the tavern.

'Thanks,' he spluttered.

'No problem,' Lan replied.

The place offered a good view of the area. The sun was higher in the sky now and a cold wind blew half-heartedly. The youths had moved on a few streets, and Lan spotted them heading towards the east.

'Let's go over.' Fulcrom steadied himself, took a run and leapt across the three-foot gap between the rooftops. Lan effortlessly took a large step, her foot hardly touching the adjacent roof before she'd moved on to the rooftop of Malum's building.

'All right,' Fulcrom muttered as he landed alongside her and wiped the gritty rainwater from his palms.

There was a hatch on the top, a mouldy bucket to one side, but otherwise nothing else of use. Fulcrom headed towards the hatch, saw that it had not been opened for a while.

'Lan, can you give a hand here?'

'Sure, is it locked?'

'I'm not sure. It just needs a yank to pull it open, but I don't want to make a noise.'

'I'll see what I can do.' Lan hunched over the hatch and tuned in to her powers; then, with a quick heave, she snapped up the hatch. It came loose, and the noise was discreet enough not to raise an alarm.

After a few minutes, confident that they were unheard, Fulcrom poked his head into the opening: there was only blackness down below, but with enough daylight leaking in he could make out floorboards.

'OK, let's head in and leave the hatch open.'

They both descended into Malum's building, Lan more fluidly than Fulcrom, and they left the hatch half open so that they could see what they were doing. They found themselves in an attic space, with old fishing crates, nets, buoys and paintings all gathering dust. Some of the floorboards seemed rotten, and Fulcrom cautiously tested them with his foot before applying his weight.

'So where next?' Lan whispered.

'We listen and we wait.'

They nestled themselves in one corner and, from their position sitting on the floor, Fulcrom spotted a door. He gestured to it and, in hushed tones, said, 'We can head through that if we want to hear more, but for now I suggest we just hang about for a while to see who's around and find out what their plans are. Without the backing of a great force all we can do is spy on them and work out what they're up to.'

'Fun,' Lan whispered sarcastically.

'Hey, this is the dull side of working in the Inquisition – a lot of waiting around to see if something happens. It isn't that glamorous.'

'I'd better get used to it then,' Lan replied, reclining with a sigh.

*

A door slammed somewhere down below.

Lan and Fulcrom snapped to attention, Fulcrom's heart beating quickly now. Voices drifted up from below, commanding tones, precise instructions.

'It's him,' Fulcrom whispered. 'It must be.'

'How long have we been here now?'

'No idea.' Fulcrom stood up, brushed himself down and looked up at the hatch. The sun had moved significantly since they had entered the building. 'I reckon at least three hours.'

'You were right, this is dull work.' Lan joined him as they moved towards the door.

Fulcrom pressed his ear against the wood.

Malum ... we've got most ... east city.

Killed ten soldiers already, bodies dumped in the harbour.

When shall we start?

More time. More numbers? We've thousands right?

Military ... unguarded.

Empress? Haven't seen her for weeks.

Fulcrom peeled back a minute later, when the people who had entered the building began laughing about something else.

'Well?' Lan asked. 'I say we head down there and get them now.'

'We don't know how many are down there and how well armed they are. We're not an army.'

'So what? We can take them, surely. I've got my powers.'

Someone shouted from underneath.

Fulcrom watched in horror as Lan, almost bouncing on the spot to ready herself, suddenly put her foot through a floor-board: as she tried to rebalance herself, she engaged her powers, which worked against her. She flipped her head back and smacked it on a timber support with the full force of her enhancements.

It happened so quickly.

'Fuck.' Fulcrom dashed to her side and was relieved to see that she was still breathing, although she had cut open her head on the sharp edge of the pillar.

Footsteps on the stairway.

Fulcrom glanced to the door and back to Lan. He tried to lift her up, to see if she was still alert, to see if she could tune in to her powers.

331

Footsteps were now outside the door. There was a silent pause then the door was kicked open. Four men each carrying a blade ran forward into the room – and there were another two coming up, all of them tough-looking types that looked as if they knew their way around a fight.

Fulcrom held up his hands as if to say something but a punch came to his face and the next thing he knew he was pressed against the floorboards.

'What the fuck should we do with 'em?' someone said.

'Tie them up. Take the buggers down to Malum. He can decide.'

Still dazed, Fulcrom felt the ropes binding around his wrists and twisted his head so that he could see Lan. She, too, was being bound. Together they were dragged downstairs by their feet, each step digging into his back. The two of them were shoved into a brighter, cleaner room that was sparsely decorated. There was a window overlooking the street, a few tables, a row of swords and a few bottles on the floor.

Fulcrom breathed mindfully, trying to force away the pain. *Stay alert, stay smart . . .*

'So,' came a strong, bass voice, 'we have guests. Two more for the takeover, do you think?'

There were a few chuckles from the others, as Fulcrom and Lan were levered upright and pushed against a wall. Fulcrom looked over to Lan to make sure she was OK, but she was still dazed.

His vision settled on one man sitting back with his feet up on a large table. It was Malum. There was a blade resting by his boots. He picked up the blade and pointed it at Fulcrom. 'You. What the fuck were you doing up there?'

'We're homeless lovers, sir. Looking for shelter. Times are tough in the city and we've fallen on hard times. Have a heart.'

'Bollocks are you homeless,' the man replied. 'That medallion around your neck is worth a month's rent for a start. Speaking of which, it's one I haven't seen in a while. Inquisition, right?'

'I stole it.'

'Give up, clown, it's obvious who you are. The Inquisition is usually in the pocket of the gangs, or it was before the war, anyway, so I'm guessing you're new stock, that right? Working for the albino?'

Fulcrom nodded.

'Hear that, lads? This is the albino's last line of defence.' They all laughed.

'So what were you doing up in the attic . . .' Malum mused. 'Hoping to listen in to my progress to report back to the albino, right?'

Fulcrom simply gave a sigh in reply.

'Well then. You know the albino isn't around now, right?' Malum stepped back to get a better look at his two captives.

'He's at war, trying to save people's lives,' Fulcrom replied defiantly.

'I was thinking of leaving your heads for him as a welcome-back present.' At that point, Fulcrom realized he would probably die, and he greeted the thought with utter calm and logic. 'I had hoped for a more adventurous, braver end to things.'

'Ain't that always the way,' Malum muttered. 'No triumphant ending for you two.'

'You know, I meant what I said when I said we were lovers,' Fulcrom muttered.

'What, you and the commander? I can believe that – isn't that right, lads? Queer fuckers.'

'No,' Fulcrom cautioned. 'Me and my companion. We're lovers. That much is true. If you're going to kill us, I just ask that you don't burn our bodies.'

'You think I've got the time for that anyway? You'll end up in the harbour like everyone else.'

That was a relief, at least. Right now, Fulcrom had to put as much faith in what he thought would happen next as he could manage. He tried to recall all that he knew of these matters. 'Thank you,' he breathed.

'What the fuck for? Killing you?'

'Please, a stab to the heart would be wonderful for the both of us.'

'You've balls, I'll give you that, inquisitor,' Malum grunted. 'See that?' He announced to the rest of the room. 'The man faces death honourably. No quivering, no pissing himself like some of the shit-bags you see around this city. Look upon this execution as a lesson in how to go if you ever get to this stage.' Malum reached for his sword and ordered someone else to stand over Lan, a much younger man – almost a boy. Both of them pressed the tips of their blades above the respective hearts.

'He needs to move down a couple of inches,' Fulcrom muttered.

'What?'

'Your young colleague's blade is too high to penetrate her heart properly. I'm guessing this is his first time.'

'Oh, right, good spot,' Malum agreed, and gave appropriate instructions to the nervous-looking lad before turning his attention to Fulcrom once again. 'You got guts, rumel. You could have a place in my operation; we could do with a man like you.'

Fulcrom shook his head. 'I serve only the law.'

'Principles, too,' Malum laughed. 'What a waste.'

Don't look at Lan now, Fulcrom told himself. *Whatever you do, don't look at Lan and remember you've tried your best...*

The last thing Fulcrom noticed was Malum's grinning face as he pressed the blade firmly into Fulcrom's heart, instant pain, the daylight fading from sight, then a lightness ... utter freedom.

A release.

TWENTY-EIGHT

Standing around the cauldron, they watched the battle unfold slowly. Brynd conferred with the Night Guard soldiers, who seemed embittered by their sudden distance – and who could blame them? They were the best of the best, and now here they were, simply watching from the sidelines, humbled by a sophisticated technology. They all knew it wasn't right.

'We'll get down there,' he whispered. 'We'll all have our chance.'

When the engagement commenced, the members of the Night Guard soon forgot their bitterness.

They gawked in amazement, watching from afar as the invasion fleet approached the coast of Folke. Channelling a viewpoint directly above the thick of the action, they stared as thousands and thousands of vessels ploughed straight into the shallow waters, running aground as predicted. Massive doors collapsed into the tumultuous surf, and out spilled thousands more Okun, soon pooling thickly, turning the shallows black.

There to meet them were monstrous creatures, ploughing down the beach or rocky shores in vast swarms that backed up deep onto the land and out of sight. The numbers were so astonishing that the entire scene seemed fabricated, as if it was not happening, and for a moment Brynd contemplated asking to see what was going on from the landing platforms. But, as he recognized many of the landmarks along the coast, he realized this was quite real. This horror was most definitely unfolding on the ground.

For the better part of half an hour, the tide of the battle ebbed and flowed, and it was difficult to ascertain what progress if any was being made by either side.

Brynd glanced at the elders, and at Artemisia standing alongside them, and they were all conferring, gesturing to the maps on the table. Now and then she would stand alongside Brynd to ask his thoughts on troop movements, but it was always in relation to the topography or the weather, as if seeking his confirmation rather than making the decisions with him.

'Do you feel aggrieved she doesn't consult you much?' Brug muttered grimly, as if egging him on for a scrap.

'I don't mind that so much. These are her people, after all. Her soldiers.'

'Her *corpses*, at any rate,' Brug replied. 'Fuck knows how many have died in this first wave. At least they're getting a chance at glory.'

They both glanced down again, watching the scene remain almost exactly as it had been minutes ago. Line after line of creatures, each rank stretching for miles it seemed, piled in to prevent the Okun from breaching the shoreline and up onto the grassland beyond, but even there, waiting for them, would be more creatures.

Whether it was because of his remoteness from the scene, or perhaps because these were not his people – they were not of his world – Brynd couldn't help but think of the clean-up operation, removing this many bodies. There were already thousands, and the conflict had not yet lasted for more than an hour.

'Commander, take a look at this,' one of his men urged.

Brynd faced the cauldron again. This time, something was flying over – a dragon perhaps? – dropping what appeared to be a liquid over the Okun. A moment later there was a flash.

Fire exploded out in dozens of tiny plumes at first and then it became more intense, occupying more of the cauldron's image, more of the scene on the shore – an inferno – while the flying creature moved further up the coast continuing to release fire.

'I'd be surprised if anything survives that,' Brynd said.

'It's annoying we can't see the full scene,' Sergeant Tiendi added. 'This is frustrating, commander. When can we get down there to help out?'

'You think we can help much here? Artemisia's right, even though it pains me to say it. We'll engage in our operation soon enough.'

*

Indeed, the time did arrive for them to begin their operation. After what Brynd estimated to be another hour watching the repetitive carnage, Artemisia invited them around the table with the elders so that they might discuss the final moves. On the table lay maps and technical drawings, some on vellum, some on a slate-like material. Artemisia showed how they delineated the internal structure of the enemy's sky-city. It seemed vast, a place of habitation much like the one in which they currently stood, as well as housing many separate units, limbs of civilizations ready to detach and drop to the ground. Its purpose was to transport a population through another world, driven by arcane powers that would – she claimed – take too long to explain.

As a result, there were several central structures of importance. These not only housed the population's noble blood and ruling individuals but also their sophisticated communications, as well as encasing the 'drive' that kept the city floating in the sky.

'That means the most essential targets are clustered together,' Brynd observed.

'The dangers,' Artemisia suggested, 'of centralized power.'

She pointed out the main access routes – inevitably the hardest part was getting inside, but once they were there, it was much like any other city, with roads and pathways, bridges and so on.

'And Frater Mercury?' Brynd enquired. 'If he is to become our very own weapon, before he self-destructs, we presumably need to get him as close as possible to the central districts?'

'It is indeed the case. Your wasps,' Artemisia continued, 'will certainly help. I did suspect we would have to travel on foot, in the shadows, which would have been a painfully slow option. Now if we can gain speed . . . Will there be room for me? No. Perhaps I need to see what fliers we can spare to go with us. Frater Mercury will need transporting.'

'He can ride with me,' Brynd said, 'or failing that, I'm almost certain the wasps can carry small loads underneath them.'

'This is good . . .' Artemisia said. She whispered to the elders in their exotic language, and eventually they nodded their agreement, and seemed sadly satisfied with the notion.

'Which is the best route inside?' Brynd enquired. 'If possible, we should commit it to memory.'

'I had previously anticipated,' Artemisia said, spinning one of the maps towards Brynd with a huge hand, 'that we would take this road here.' It was marked red on the map, a complex, almost spiral circuit that led towards the centre of the structure.

'How many miles is that – in our equivalent terms?'

'It is . . .' Artemisia said, 'about five miles. It is not, admittedly, the most direct route, but it is one that provides the most secrecy and shelter.'

'This is a big structure indeed,' Brynd breathed. 'But surely if we breach their defences, they'll be aware of our presence, and there won't be much shelter at all? We'll be hunted.'

'This may be so. We are calculating they will be distracted sufficiently by events on the ground.'

'That's too much of a risk,' Brynd said. 'We have the

Mourning Wasps. We have speed on our side. Surely there's a more direct route that doesn't involve us dicking around waiting to be killed?'

Artemisia appeared confused by his choice of words before regarding the maps once again. 'You could be correct in your statement, if I understand it. You wish for us to simply strike quickly, deploy Frater Mercury and get out?'

'It makes more sense, don't you think?' Brynd asked despairingly. How could such an advanced culture have such weak military ideas?

*

Brynd's mind was flitting with last-minute logic at such a rate that he didn't recognize time passing by. The Night Guard soldiers remained at the periphery of his vision, of his mind, committing the route to memory. He had to take a step back and breathe quietly to himself to regain composure. *Don't let the pressure get to you,* he warned himself. *Think how far you've come. To lose control now would be catastrophic.*

The plan was simple. Artemisia's people would provide cover in the sky while the Night Guard and a few other creatures would bust their way into the enemy complex.

Dragons and garudas would patrol the skies outside the city, acting as decoys, distractions, eliminating whatever enemies came their way. There would, Artemisia explained, be aerial combat, so the Mourning Wasps would have to travel over great heights to retreat, something he had not yet tried out. Despite the awkward stares of his regiment, he dismissed the point – he had to put his faith in them. There was no other choice in the matter.

*

Out on the landing platform, Brynd stood gripping one of the ornate rails, looking down on the scene below. The structure was drifting lower, through the cloud base, and towards their enemy – now he could see the swarms on the island of Folke.

Everything appeared abstract from this height. Breathtaking numbers drifted across the landscape, dark tides changing the face of the island permanently. Further out to sea, the ships still lined up to pummel the island.

'Normally I couldn't wait to get into a scrap,' Brug muttered, appearing at Brynd's side. 'We feel invincible, with our augmentations, don't we? Almost immortal, dare I say it. Seeing that down there, I've never felt more humbled. It was frustrating in there, too, going over things again and again. Don't they ever just fancy a good fight instead of being so aloof?'

Brynd said: 'I nearly lost it. I didn't say anything, I didn't let on – but sometimes I wish there was just one person making the decisions.'

'You mean like a dictator?'

Brynd laughed. 'Not exactly what I had in mind, but it would certainly get the job done a lot quicker. I gave them good plans down on Y'iren; I thought it was all decided. Yet, every time I have a question or we make a refinement, Artemisia consults with the bloody elders. Meanwhile, down there, people are having their heads split open.'

'At least they're not our own people dying down there,' Brug said, 'not yet anyway.'

'We'll eventually need to stop thinking in those terms.'

'They're not our responsibility though, are they?'

'They soon might be. Besides, they're sacrificing themselves in huge numbers so both our races can survive into the future – I'd much rather chuck some of those scumbags in Villiren into another dimension to make room for people who are willing to shed their blood in such a way.'

Other Night Guard soldiers approached and most of them remained in companionable silence. There seemed to be nothing left to say any more. Everything had been decided. All that was left was to find Frater Mercury. They milled about for a few minutes, agitated, anxious, eager to get into battle.

Brynd headed back into the wooden cages to tend to the Mourning Wasps. They had been fed some liquid prepared by Jeza, though he was not sure what it was exactly. It seemed to satisfy their appetites. He felt a strange affinity to them; and though he might have been convincing himself of the fact, he felt they responded to him positively as time went on. He took the unusual step of placing his hand affectionately on one of their skulls; it was smooth to the touch, and through it he could feel the minute vibrations from their powerful wing muscles.

It seemed inherently obvious to Brynd why he was drawn to creatures that were so different. No, not different – *unique*. He could never escape the company of others, but he felt consistently isolated. Facing battles never bothered him for this very reason, and at the back of his mind was the niggling sensation that if he did die in battle, it would be no bad thing. Even before the arrival of other cultures, his faith in Bohr had been long eroded, so there was solace to be found in the fact that he might die and nothing would happen. Nothing, other than the fact that his corpse would burn, his ashes would be scattered, and the very fabric of his body go back to the earth. There was something comforting about that fact, especially when confronted with such uniqueness as the Mourning Wasps.

The Boreal Archipelago was full of weird wonders. It was about to receive even more.

There was a hubbub outside the cage so Brynd left the wasps, strode down the platform onto the landing bay. Artemisia was approaching, with Frater Mercury, half his face glistening, his expression as always hidden and out of reach. He was wearing a rich blue cloak and tunic with a fine gold stitching of bold shapes; around all of this were strapped thick metal objects.

'Are those relics?' Brynd asked Artemisia.

'I still do not know what you mean by relics,' she replied.

'They are devices that Frater Mercury will use to terminate his life.'

'And the lives of those around him, presumably,' Brynd replied.

'As confirmed earlier, yes.'

'Is he still comfortable with killing himself for the greater good?' Brynd asked.

I am, came the thunderous reply in Brynd's mind. Frater Mercury seemed furious with those two words, a gesture that hinted at far greater powers – and dangerous powers, too.

'My apologies,' Brynd replied, to strange looks from his comrades, who must not have heard the comment. 'Your suicide is a noble one, a gesture that will last for generations to come.'

I want it over now. No more. I have seen all I need to see. I am more than ever disappointed in the results of the experiment.

Brynd felt as though he'd let the man down, though it seemed irrational to think so.

They all prepared for the mission. Brynd guided down the Mourning Wasps one by one, until they lined up in a neat row. For creatures who could manoeuvre so well in the air, they seemed to cope awkwardly walking down the platform, their movements stuttering and clumsy. They were to be deployed into smaller cages, on the backs of smaller, more agile dragons – lithe, green creatures that appeared more like lizards – so that the intention of a smaller force heading into the sky-city would be disguised as best as possible. Their stance was crouched and alert, their wings massive and venous. As the last few Mourning Wasps were taken to their new transport, Frater Mercury moved towards one of them, his hands aloft. Brynd ordered to halt the movement of the wasps. Three of them stood there as Frater Mercury walked around them.

Brynd tried to sense whether or not Frater Mercury wished to communicate with those around him, but whatever went on in the man's head now remained private. He seemed to recognize the Mourning Wasps. He touched their skulls with great respect and for the first time Brynd saw him appear like an ordinary human. His profound presence fell away: instead this could have been a man greeting his own dog at the end of a hard day's graft. Even Artemisia seemed surprised at Frater Mercury's gestures.

He gradually turned his attention away from them.

It will be, Frater Mercury said to Brynd, *a great honour to travel with these creatures. Where were they found?*

'I believe they were excavated and brought to life on an island further up the Archipelago.'

For a moment Brynd felt as if Frater Mercury was not going to continue with his suicide mission; he felt his heart thumping in his chest as he waited for further communication.

I remember these the first time around, many ages ago, Frater Mercury said.

Brynd stared at the two halves of his face, waiting. He had a thousand questions he wanted to ask them. How this figure could have lived so long was beyond Brynd's comprehension – but then there were a lot of things he did not understand.

Artemisia stepped between them. 'We must go now. The weather is in our favour.'

So it must be, Frater Mercury said, much less intense than ever before.

*

There was a dripping sound coming from somewhere. Wherever he was, the place was utterly dark. The ground was moving softly . . . no, not the ground. They were somewhere else entirely. A boat, on water, drifting . . . Fulcrom sat up and felt a stiffness in his chest, but that soon faded. He then felt nothing at all.

Lan was beside him. Sweet Lan, lying there peacefully. Fulcrom tried to remain as logical as possible, and examined

343

her: there was a hole in her uniform where the sword had penetrated, but other than that she looked exactly as he remembered. Well, not *exactly* – her skin was far paler than before, almost giving off a glow in this darkness. He checked his own body, and he, too, had a sword wound in his chest, right above his heart. He checked optimistically for any sign of his tail, which had been cut off by Urtica's men in Villjamur, but it was not there.

Bugger.

All around them was water, but the boat – a small vessel – was drifting in one direction, that much he could be sure of. Lan stirred and a few moments later she rose up to see what Fulcrom was describing. He explained to her what happened with Malum.

'I can just about remember, though it's a bit hazy. I wasn't unconscious, but I was really, really dazed at the time.'

'He kept good to his word.'

'What?'

'Malum. Once I clicked he was going to kill us, I had no choice but to persuade him to kill us in an appropriate manner and not burn our bodies.'

'We're dead then?' Lan asked.

'Or undead. I'm not so sure how to label the dead, now we're one of them.'

'Why did you do that? Didn't you want our souls to go on to other realms?'

'It would've meant we would be apart. I didn't want that. It was – if you could believe it – a selfish gesture of love. I just wanted to be with you. Is that so bad?'

'No, not at all,' Lan replied. 'Eternity together is certainly more meaningful than flowers.' At least her sense of humour had followed her down here . . . 'So Malum hasn't burned us, and our physical bodies are probably somewhere in the harbour in Villiren?'

'Something like that. I can't be sure, though.'

They both moved in close together, and regarded the distance where lights were flickering along a shoreline. There were spires there, glistening, and as they approached they could see people on the shoreline, one or two of them waving. The boat, through no control of Fulcrom, turned in the waters and began drifting in that direction. The water was black, the sky a phenomenally dark grey. There were no stars to be found, and clearly no sun, but it looked very much *unlike* the city of the dead under Villjamur. Just how many of these cities of the dead existed, Fulcrom had no idea. All he felt now was a continuation of that release from when he was killed, and an overwhelming sense of calm.

'So where next, then?' Lan asked.

'Who knows? Wherever this boat takes us, I guess,' Fulcrom replied. 'Somewhere deep under Villiren. It doesn't matter – we can probably handle anything now.'

*

In the cages, Brynd remained tense as the dragons lurched through the air. This transportation was far more erratic than the previous methods, but it seemed a trivial thing to be concerned about.

He held his helmet in his hands and examined the visor, staring at his own pale reflection. For a moment he felt the usual images of his past flicker into his mind, but then he began to empty his emotions once again. Dwelling on such things would mean his concentration would slip and he'd end up getting killed. His own Mourning Wasp – one of two in this cage – seemed to have been befriended by Frater Mercury, who slumped alongside it in the darkness of the cage, apparently communicating with it. Artemisia was attending to her own creature, a much smaller, red dragon barely any bigger than the Mourning Wasps.

Brynd felt remarkably isolated in the cage. He turned to Sergeant Tiendi, and even she seemed to be struggling in the violent flight of these dragons.

'Is this what you hoped for, when you joined us?' Brynd asked. She had only just become a Night Guard before the war in Villiren.

'No, sir. It's far better than that. We get to fly these wasps into an almost certain death situation.'

Brynd grunted a laugh.

'Have you any idea what to expect?' she asked.

Brynd kept staring at his reflection. 'I told some of the others earlier to wipe their minds of expectations, because what we'll probably see could be beyond comprehension or as quotidian as the place we've just left. It's a civilian vessel, so I understand, but we've already seen the kind of evil it houses.'

Tiendi nodded, but remained resolute. 'I'll keep thinking in simple terms: we're just deploying a bomb. Or, at least, a *bomber* who wants to kill himself.' She indicated Frater Mercury. 'What will his explosives do, precisely? They look no bigger than the kind of thing a cultist might use, but at that size it wouldn't produce much, surely?'

Brynd glanced again at the small metallic devices strapped to Frater Mercury's waist and chest. 'I doubt they'll be explosives in the conventional manner. He's a person of incredible ability. No doubt he'll be able to kill himself in the appropriate manner when the time comes.'

There was a small explosion somewhere nearby. The cage shuddered as the dragon plunged slightly, and Brynd gripped the rails while Artemisia pressed her hands against the roof for stability.

'It is to be expected, commander,' she called over, waving him back down to his seat. 'These creatures are quicker. They have greater awareness. We will be quite safe.'

'What's going on?' Brynd demanded.

'We are being fired at, that is all.'

'Are the decoys ahead of us?'

'They are ahead and behind, and all around us. Our main strike force lies in the middle of the formation.'

'How long now?'

'A quarter of one hour at the most.'

*

Brynd put on his helmet and watched Tiendi do the same. They pulled their visors down and mounted the Mourning Wasps. Frater Mercury shuffled humbly underneath Brynd's wasp, and he watched in amazement as two of the wasp's legs suddenly scooped him up and secured him in place. Brynd placed his hands on the back of the wasp in a way he might do with a horse, and though it seemed absurd he felt it was necessary to ensure the creature felt some affinity with him.

Artemisia climbed onto her dragon. The three creatures lined up at the rear of the cage, facing outwards. They could feel the cage tilt as they began what must have been the final arc when they peeled away from the main squadron of dragons. Explosions came and went, noises bursting out of sight.

They were falling now, at high speed, gravity pushing Brynd back so hard he became instantly satisfied that the modified straps that the youths had made would hold him in place.

He positioned himself so he would be prepared to steer his mount. He looked across to Tiendi and she indicated her readiness with a salute. Artemisia remained totally fixed on the door of the wooden cage. Brynd indicated for the wasps to begin to hover; he felt the tiny vibrations of their muscles become something more distinct.

The dragon tilted. The door gave way to a crack of light, then a full-blown whiteness, then extreme winds, before the dragon levelled off to reveal their hideous destination.

Artemisia gave the word. Her dragon lunged out of the cage and the Mourning Wasps quickly followed.

They spiralled out into the sky, the Night Guard on wasps, following Artemisia's silhouette, wind buffeting their descent. Brynd attempted to absorb what was going on around him – amidst the clouds, hundreds of creatures were spaced apart in rows, at varying distances, engaged in combat, and down below what he initially mistook for land was the dark scar of the Policharos – the sky-city. He glanced over his shoulder to see the Night Guard lined up behind him or drifting from the other cages, joining his ranks, alongside people who looked very much like Artemisia, on reptiles identical to her own. The sound of the wind managed to block out much of what was going on; he could not hear the cries of the dying or the clash of weapons – this was a kind of warfare he was totally unfamiliar with.

Directly above, dragons were engaged in skirmishes with similar-looking animals; missiles or bombs were exploding far away, and Brynd couldn't be certain whether or not they were like the mute bombs or something more hideous. Tucked safely underneath his wasp, lay Frater Mercury.

Artemisia guided their large group in a graceful arc to the left, down towards the Policharos. It loomed into view, black and elaborate in detail. Little flickers of light shot across spires at the top; huge spiked structures leered out on multiple levels; there were platforms on which he could see tiny figures, some of them firing into the sky. Massive alien beings – or possibly statues – stood on others, looking out onto the battle.

Their attack force dashed towards the underside of the Policharos, but not quite all the way. They halted on one of the lowest levels, where there was a void amidst the black architecture. Artemisia levelled out and Brynd steered the wasp accordingly. Another glance to check everyone was following and then straight in towards the void, which turned out to be a doorway beyond a landing platform that headed into the Policharos.

As they flew in low over the platform, Brynd relaxed slightly, before steeling himself for what lay inside the sky-city, which had brought so much death to his world.

*

Walls and buildings appeared to be impossibly tall, lurching up into the blackness above. There were slits of green and purple light scattered around that appeared to be windows, but he was moving too fast to really know. Though Artemisia led the group, it was so dark in here that the benefits of having memorized the way were obvious. They hovered a few feet above the ground and sped along a winding route; their formation changed so that Brynd, carrying Frater Mercury, was at the centre of the group. Surrounded by Night Guard soldiers, he didn't have to worry too much about attacks from any direction, so he could concentrate on their surroundings.

They passed through what he took to be civilian areas; there were hominids, but not humans or rumels, alongside taller, fatter, more grotesque and exotic creatures, whose own noises were weirdly animalistic. Everyone here was panicking. Groups of figures in military-style uniform emerged onto the scene but only after the attack group had passed. As his eyes settled into the darkness he could see buildings defined against the black roof; tall structures that must have been over forty storeys high.

A noise behind drew his attention to two-legged creatures lumbering at the rear, and gaining on their group, but Artemisia's people had this under control; in an instant they peeled back from the flight pack, withdrew their swords and hacked at their pursuers' legs. He heard a faint scream blend into the distance before they were too far out of range. Then artillery – arrows and spears – began to whip by above his head at a ferocious velocity. Artemisia reached down to her side, picked up a small glass sphere, held it above her head and crushed it; immediately there seemed to be a field of

349

translucent light around them and the projectiles aimed their way clattered against it before falling uselessly to one side.

The group rounded several corners at high speed and after that there were long straights; the surroundings were a blur; only the looming buildings in the distance remained in focus. If Brynd remembered correctly then they'd only have a short distance to go now, possibly another mile.

The drones of the wasps prevented him from hearing the attack that suddenly occurred: three metallic dragons crashed into their force field; one of them seemed electrified with static and fell away, taking with it their defences. The other two dragons attacked and dispersed their group. At least two of the Night Guard were sent reeling and clattering to the ground. Brynd looked down to note the area in the hope that he might pick them up on the way back.

He could not stay and fight but had to go straight on and hope that as many of his own could keep up with him. A glance over his shoulder and he saw there was no right flank now. It had been totally decimated – three of the Night Guard and one of Artemisia's lookalikes gone.

The group quickly re-formed around Brynd and his precious cargo. There seemed to be some kind of bell being rung. Lights flashed close by. Strange objects lurched in and out of view. He had no idea what was going on at times. It was all happening too fast to register. Artemisia still led the way, true to her word, and all he could do was follow.

TWENTY-NINE

'It's a shame,' Malum muttered to his gang members. They had just returned from disposing of the bodies in the harbour – just like he said he would. For some reason, it seemed the least he could do. 'I almost liked the guy, despite the fact that he'd expose us. How did you find the killing, boy?'

'All right,' the lad replied. He refused to make eye contact, despite Malum's best efforts. He was only eighteen and Malum was conscious that his nervous nature, his great uncertainty, needed training out of him sooner rather than later. The lad had been a runaway, had spent most of his time working in a decrepit bistro on the edge of the Wastelands, and had only recently come into Malum's gang because he was scared about aliens threatening their way of life.

'It gets easier,' Malum replied, and placed a fatherly arm around him. 'You did a good thing. You helped progress our cause. You did that for the city – you just remember that. You're protecting people. It's hard to see, but it's like an elaborate, strategic game. Every little move doesn't seem much at the time, but when you see it in the context of the game, it all becomes clear. You helped with a great move, an important defensive one. I'm proud of you. Hey, aren't we proud, guys?'

The other men in the room suddenly erupted in cheers, and Malum pushed the boy into their masses so that he could soak up some of their energy.

It had been a productive day, Malum concluded. Despite the minor disturbance earlier, he had managed to muster a decent number of fighters, around four thousand in all, which would be more than enough. What made him most proud, though, was that these were largely people who could have sided with the commander, but who chose not to. They were committed to Villiren, not him. They wanted a city free of alien intent, and they would draw blood to have it so.

*

Evening came. Both moons remained low in the sky. A relatively warm breeze drifted across the rooftops of the city. The night seemed full of energy and promise. The gathering masses in the street outside brought a huge sense of pride to Malum.

He had been disappointed that those cultist youths could not provide a living monster in time for his needs. Monsters would have been ideal to cause havoc, or to use in convincing the citizens that their lives were under threat. Perhaps the military had warned off the youths, Malum couldn't be sure – but one thing he knew in life was never to piss off people who dabbled in relics.

A couple of minor explosions detonating in the distance gave Malum reason to smile.

His plan benefited from a simple fact: the military were now out of the way. He hadn't expected them to leave the Citadel completely unguarded, but his rag-tag army of four thousand would be enough to deal with whatever had been left. There were watchtowers and a few guard stations scattered throughout the city, which about now were being overcome. He had sent groups of youths with crossbows, machetes and munitions purchased from cultists to deal with such stations. He had ordered them to show no mercy. As of now, they were engaged in the business of war. Anyone wearing an Imperial uniform was to be killed outright, and no citizens should be harmed unless they were loyal to the Empire.

Though much of this was hasty planning, Malum needed

to make the most of this opportunity. It was important that such positions were taken out one by one before the rest of the surge could move forward. It meant they could storm the Citadel without anyone forewarning them. Once the Citadel was under his control, then he could go on with the rest of his plan.

Malum had already begun contemplating a vague manifesto. He had some vague notions of protecting people from the Imperial skirmishes, which would be easy enough to do once he had the people on his side, but then he knew he'd have to think about other matters such as employment and prosperity, things that people would rightly care about. His gangs would issue true protection – for a fee from those who could afford it. Once he was in command, he could use an old trick of the former portreeve – issue a new property tax: that way he would force those with a little power and wealth to submit to him. He'd also have to employ people who could deal with all the paperwork.

Malum looked up from his musings. *All that can wait*, he told himself.

He could hear his people outside – the gangs and those they had brought to their side. They were making a lot of noise. He stepped outside to greet them. Instantly, those closest in his gang stepped to his side for his protection, but he quickly leapt up on a barrel to address the gathered masses. It was a wide street, and people were rammed in thickly. From one end of the street to the other, they had come together to rebel against their Imperial rulers and make a show, to give the impression that a powerful force would soon be in charge. Many had come carrying torches that flickered strongly in the calm breeze. Others brandished their swords above their heads like some tribal clan.

They cheered as soon as they saw Malum and he basked in their adoration for a while. He finally held up his hands for calm, which took a while to settle down.

He reminded them of the oppression that the military would bring, of the dangers of aliens walking alongside humans and rumels, of what would happen if they failed. He ordered that no one wearing a military uniform be spared, because if the Night Guard did return one day soon, then they would try to free their comrades. There could be no second chances. If they were to free Villiren and maintain a force to protect it against aliens, they would have to do it properly. They'd raid the Citadel's vaults and make sure people who supported them had plenty of food on their tables to feed their families. Cheers went up again and this time he could barely hear himself talk.

He bellowed instructions. He shouted for them to walk – as one – to the periphery of the Citadel. Then they would try all the entrances and accessible doorways. If that failed, they would use industrial ladders to scale the walls. They would use rope, stone, fire, whatever it took to get inside that building.

*

Brynd arrived at the sky-city district where the power mechanisms were located, which turned out to be in the same region as the huge multi-storey buildings. As they slowed, more hominids revealed themselves; there were houses here, shops, various kinds of market, people, children, all the elements of a society. What did he think there'd be? These were people, too, but registering this fact didn't make his job any easier.

Creatures began to call out aggressively; military figures headed into view. He blanked them out and continued along with Artemisia. Had she seriously expected them to come in here in a small team on foot? It would have taken hours, possibly even days and more than likely they would have been massacred.

She hovered her dragon for a moment and Brynd pulled his Mourning Wasp in alongside her, and flipped up his visor.

All kinds of strange scents reached his nose, but it was overpowered by a harsh, vaguely metallic odour. He had no idea where it came from. There were people gathered in small enclaves, gaping at them. Brynd checked again to see if Frater Mercury was still there, and he was, remaining as inert as ever.

Artemisia gestured to a path between tall, red-coloured buildings, before riding off. Brynd pulled down his visor and they picked up speed again. Everything blurred past – lights and sounds and people becoming one incoherent assault on his senses.

Eventually they arrived at a junction with immense yet thin honeycomb domes arranged side by side. There must have been twenty or more, all of them a good hundred feet tall. They were silver, with a black skeletal framework, each one lit up in a slightly different shade of purple or violet. Surrounding these was a glossy black floor, utterly bare.

Artemisia slowed to a halt. Brynd steered in next to her and opened his visor.

'We deploy him here,' she said.

Brynd was amazed, when it came to it, at how little reverence she had for someone her culture treated as a god.

He leaned over and called down, 'Sir, now is the time. Could you release yourself?'

Making no acknowledgement of having heard Brynd's words, Frater Mercury placed a hand on the underside of the wasp's skull for a moment before the creature slowly peeled away its legs, placing them on the floor one by one, and finally stopping its wings. Frater Mercury slid out and stood up; he rearranged the devices on his person before looking at Artemisia. She spoke in her own tongue for a minute or two, Brynd's heart thumping with impatience. With her sword she pointed towards the honeycomb towers and Frater Mercury walked calmly, like a priest to a sermon, towards them.

Brynd called out, 'We will ensure your gesture is not

forgotten – we will see to it that people know of who you are and what you did.'

Forget me, Frater Mercury said, without facing him.

Brynd could hear more explosions in the distance, more bells, more chaos.

'We should make our retreat now.'

'I want to make certain he heads in there.'

'What did you tell him?'

'To give us the same amount of time as it took us to get here to make our retreat, in addition to a few more minutes in case of attack.'

'Then we've no time to waste.' He turned to do a quick head count and confirmed to himself that three more Night Guard soldiers had fallen, though he didn't know who at this stage. And this was only half the mission. They still needed to get out.

'Now I am satisfied,' she said. Frater Mercury was no longer to be seen, lost in the purple glow of the honeycomb towers.

The Mourning Wasps started up again and this time they would take a different formation, riding in threes, as wide as the narrowest street, and in a straight line. They drifted up off the ground, turned in an arc and sped quickly into the alien cityscape.

THIRTY

'Another dull night,' Randur muttered.

'Sorry, sir?' the guard replied.

'I said it's another dull night,' Randur repeated, leaning in the doorway.

The guard remained impassive. He was a broad young lad, possibly little older than Randur was, and he had stood outside of their chamber now for three nights without saying anything.

'Wouldn't you rather be on the battlefield?' Randur enquired. 'You know, strutting your stuff, cracking open a few Okun skulls, that sort of thing?'

'The commander's orders were for me to remain here,' the guard replied, looking forward, stood to attention. 'And that's where I'll stay. Sir.'

'It's all right,' Randur said, 'you can slouch. You can sit on the floor if you must. Want a chair? Don't stand to attention for my sake.'

'Orders were to protect yourself and Lady Eir, sir.'

Folding his arms, Randur sighed and peered down the gloomy corridor. 'See that, down there? Bugger all, that's what's down there. Nothing but shadows. Shadows aren't going to be much of a threat. Why not grab some vodka and join me for a few card games? We'll keep the stakes low – I know wages aren't what they used to be. Fuck it, why not head downstairs and open up the Imperial coffers for kicks?'

'Wouldn't be prudent, sir,' the guard replied.

'Relax, I was joking,' Randur muttered. 'Well, suit yourself, anyway. Let me know if there's any excitement and I'll give you a hand dealing with it.'

Randur closed the door and strolled back into his chamber. Eir had just finished washing herself after another day at the hospital, and looked thoroughly dishevelled and all the more charming for it.

'You've not been hassling that poor soldier again, have you?' Eir asked, drying her hands on a towel.

'He loves it,' Randur declared, and reclined with a grunt into a cushioned chair. 'Besides, he's not lying dead on a battlefield, so putting up with me is a much more preferable situation to that, I'd say.'

'Randur, don't speak of the war like that. We could be doing well – it's just that nearly every garuda was needed – so we simply don't know.'

'Yeah, that's true. Have to give the commander his dues, he knows what he's doing.'

'That he does,' Eir replied.

'Does Brynd still want you doing this hospital stuff now you're supposed to be overseeing things?'

'The commander has no choice in the matter,' Eir replied defiantly.

'Well, I guess if you're the boss, then he doesn't,' Randur replied. 'So, what's my new position in all of this – did you talk about that before he left?'

'How do you mean?'

'As in, I'm your partner, right? So if you were a bloke in charge, and I was your wife, I'd get some kind of duties . . . titles perhaps?'

'Are you angling for a title?'

'I'd not say no to one,' Randur declared with a grin, standing up. He sauntered over to Eir's side and put his arms around her. 'I have the airs and graces of someone who deserves a title, don't you think?'

Eir burst into laughter. 'Even if you do say so yourself. Randur Estevu, I've got a name for you—'

A knock on the door.

'What is it?' Eir asked, stepping away from Randur, as if to appear more professional.

The guard poked his head around the door. 'Um, Lady Eir, one of the other Citadel guards has just come to me with a report of a little trouble outside.'

'What kind of trouble?'

'A mob, my lady.'

'Well, what does this *mob* want?' Eir enquired.

'Not entirely sure right now, I'm afraid. Just an initial report of a massed gathering approaching the Citadel.'

'Nothing inherently wrong with that,' Randur observed. 'It's a strange city. People have their little meetings. Reckon it's something to do with the gangs?'

'There are well over a thousand of them, sir,' the guard grunted.

Randur whistled. 'Reckon we should take a look?' he said to Eir, with enthusiasm. 'Could be a little excitement. Hey, could be a big brawl!'

'Randur!' Eir protested. 'You shouldn't be excited at such things.'

He waved a hand. 'I could do with some entertainment. I'll head up onto the roof to get a better view.' He turned to the soldier. 'You up for a little excitement?'

'It might be advisable . . .' the guard agreed. Randur swore he could see a glint of excitement in the lad's eyes. No one deserved to be this bored in life.

Randur reached for his sword, strapped it firmly to his waist, slung on a long overcoat and buttoned it up to his collar. 'Sure you don't want to join us?'

'I've had a long day,' Eir replied. 'I'll let you boys play combat.'

'Very decent of you,' Randur smiled.

*

'What's your name?' Randur asked as they jogged along the corridor. It felt good to get a little blood pumping through his veins again, to have something to do. He half hoped there would be a serious situation, if merely to relieve himself of his boredom.

'Private Drendan, sir.'

'Drendan,' Randur repeated. 'So what exactly did you see?'

'Well, it could have been the gangs, sir, but it could have been something more serious.'

They trotted along and up the many flights of stairs until they managed to reach the rooftop. The soldier, much fitter than Randur due to his military training – and Randur's own laziness – reached the door well before Randur. He opened it and allowed Randur to step through first.

A strong wind hit him as he ventured out onto the roof of the Citadel. He immediately faced the sea, and Drendan guided him to the side of the building that faced the danger.

'Over there, sir.' Drendan pointed to a few buildings immediately to the south, where a cluster of people were loitering. Randur followed his outstretched arm, struggling to see in the poor light of dusk. At the base of a tall building, by an alleyway, he could see a group of young men, each of them carrying some kind of weapon. On the other side of that building, another few men could be seen brandishing swords. Then over to the next building, and the next, and so on, until Randur concluded that nearly all the streets behind must be filled with people.

'What do you suppose they're playing at?' Randur asked.

'This is serious trouble, sir.'

'Yeah, you might be right. They've not come at the Citadel yet, have they?'

'Not yet. But they might be doing so as we speak.' Those individual clusters began to drift slowly forward, coalescing into a massive crowd, one that promised to be larger than the Night Guard homecoming not that long ago.

'They're heading this way,' the soldier observed.

'What should we do?' Randur asked.

'We fortify the Citadel.'

'How many is *we* exactly?'

'There are several soldiers who have remained here.'

'Several. Several soldiers against fuck knows how many of them.'

'The Citadel is well built, sir.'

'It had better be,' Randur muttered. 'Come on then.'

*

When they were safely within the heart of the Citadel, Drendan saw to it that all potential routes of entry were locked, the main doors barricaded, the portcullis, which rarely saw use, was lowered, and all windows on the lower floors – not that there were many – were sealed and boarded. It took less than ten minutes, and all the while the noise of the crowd outside began to intensify.

They held a quick meeting with most of the military personnel present, as well as Eir, who was annoyingly optimistic about their odds.

'So we have seventeen men – and myself,' Eir said. 'Not to mention we have quite a few of the administrative staff, each of whom could be given a sword and not remain idle. There's also that cultist, Blavat I believe her name is, who spends most of her time experimenting in the basements. I'd say that puts us in a better position than we thought previously.'

'She has a very good point,' Drendan said.

'I could try reasoning with them first, however?' Eir offered.

'Too dangerous, my lady,' Drendan said. 'My limited

experience suggests an angry mob isn't in the mood for negotiation.'

'If this is the case,' Eir said, 'one of us must use one of the underground exits to get a message out via garuda, to locate Brynd wherever he is and to inform him that the city is under threat.'

'Any ideas as to the numbers out there?' Randur asked. 'At least a thousand, right? So how can we *possibly* hold them off? Come to think of it, why the hell are we under siege in the first place?'

'From what I can gather, it is gang-led violence. Some of their anti-Empire chants suggest that they are against our rule.'

'They picked the right bloody time for it,' Randur said, 'what with the Night Guard away.'

'This sounds more of a planned effort,' one of the older guards said, 'if they waited for the main forces to go, leaving us defenceless. It is a cold and calculated attempt to remove a major Imperial structure.'

'That means they won't stop until they're inside here,' Drendan said.

'Not on our watch,' Randur declared.

'Agreed,' the old guard said. 'We are sworn to you, Lady Eir, to protect you and your seat of power.'

'Oh, give me a sword, for Bohr's sake. I can protect myself.'

Randur smiled and handed her his own blade. 'That she can, lads – she had one of the best in the Archipelago teach her.'

'Are you certain, Lady Eir?' The guard had a genuine look of concern. He was clearly of a generation that wasn't used to noble ladies knowing their way around a blade.

Eir pointed the tip of her sword towards him. 'I have never been more certain in my life. If this Citadel falls, I shall go with it. It is important that this building remains – it is the hub of everything that Commander Lathraea has worked for.

It contains Imperial wealth, food stores, documents relating to distribution of monies from the bank, the allocation of grain . . . I could go on, but I hope I get my point across. This building *must not fall*.'

'Yes, Lady Eir,' the soldiers muttered as close to unison as they could manage.

*

The Citadel was built with defence in mind. The walls were high and, unless you possessed special powers, relatively non-scalable. It was built to an old design, redesigned, hacked back, and new sections added with the same stone so, over the years, it was impossible to know what was left of the designer's original vision. Old-style grates were available so that hot oil could be poured down over those assaulting the main door, and this task was left to two soldiers. The crenellations provided adequate cover from which to launch arrows at those attacking. Someone managed to make contact with the cultist, who reluctantly agreed to lend some explosive relics to the cause.

It was a piecemeal and very slow operation.

Randur became immensely frustrated at the fact that success simply meant that the status quo was maintained. There seemed no way of actually winning – all they were doing was holding off one group of bodies, for another wave to come crashing against the doors and walls. There were a few valiant efforts to scale the walls: ropes were launched upward, only to be cut by the handful of soldiers on the roof. Eir and Randur found themselves directing things more than being much use.

As the hours rolled towards midnight, there was an explosion that managed to blow a gap in the front of the portcullis. Moments later came a second blast.

The gathered defenders reconvened to discuss a new plan of action.

Everyone's tone was noticeably more panicky now. There

was a great deal more urgency to proceedings. People spoke over one another until Eir managed to calm everyone down to develop a solution.

They concluded that, should the doors be breached and the gangs make it into the courtyard, it did not necessarily mean that the Citadel could be accessed easily. The courtyard could be sealed off, and Randur suggested they could hold the gangs in there for a little longer, cutting off routes to the rest of the building as best they could. Having ascertained what would happen if the gangs did breach these boundaries, they planned to close down the Citadel section by section, wearing the attackers down, throwing in more relics, drawing more blood.

A third blast came a few minutes later.

An enormous metallic scraping sound suggested the portcullis was being removed. The cheers were more audible, the noise of the mob accumulating within the confines of the walls. Still they couldn't see the numbers of assailants they'd be dealing with.

Blavat, the cultist, had set off a couple of relics in the entrance way to the Citadel – Randur didn't know what exactly; he could only hear the screams – but it managed to buy them some more time. They locked doors, barricaded passageways, drew down further, smaller portcullises, the presence of which surprised everyone but the guards. It seemed the Citadel was not only built well for an external defence but also for an internal one.

They ran back along corridors, sealing themselves in, moving up a level.

The gangs passed the cultist trickery and flooded in. The noise was intense and frightening. Randur could hear the vile chants now, the names, the curses, their promises. Their anger filtered up through the stone.

As they moved up a stairway, between the cold walls,

Randur caught a glimpse of the courtyard below. 'Eir, look. There are hundreds of them.'

'They mustn't get up. We must keep them there, locked in, and wear them down.'

'They're not going to just go. They'll stay until we're dead.'

'If that happens, then so be it, but we must hold until the commander returns.'

'That could be any time. It could be days. It could be weeks.'

'It could be soon, too, we've just no idea.'

The gangs were milling about the place now, as if they were in an iren. With nowhere to go they had been stalled. Somehow one of them had managed to get up on the raised platform, several feet above the ground. It was too dark for Randur to identify him, but he seemed to be giving instructions . . . no, he was *rallying* them.

'Could Blavat throw something in there to kill them all?' Randur asked. He noticed Eir cringe at his intentions.

They looked down the line at the grey-haired cultist, who simply shrugged. 'The military have taken most of my damaging relics for their operations. I have very few of use any more. At best, things that give off smoke, things that may slow down time for them . . .'

'That'll do,' Randur said.

'All it does is make it appear as if they're wading through treacle, and it doesn't last for more than a few hours.'

'I don't care,' Randur said. 'It's our best chance of holding them off.'

Blavat ran up the stairs to her quarters. Randur and Eir waited by the window as the soldiers continued their work of barricading themselves in.

A few moments later, something whistled outside like a firecracker and exploded over the thugs below.

It was difficult to observe fully, but the crowds below were very definitely moving slowly. It was bordering on comical, the way the man on the platform walked in a painfully slow manner back and forth. Was he aware that he had been slowed down? Randur couldn't be sure.

'There,' Blavat said, returning breathlessly. 'It's done.'

'Thank you,' Eir said. 'Has it got them all?'

'No, only those in the courtyard.'

'There will still be a few kicking about then,' Randur muttered. 'It's bought us time – and time is our best weapon so far. I'd say we should continue barricading ourselves in, working up the levels, and setting traps, all the way up to the roof. We've food on the levels above. We can last a longer siege. If they can't get to us, we'll be fine.'

'I agree,' Eir said. 'We just wait it out. Wait for the commander to return. But what about . . .' She moved in to whisper, 'What about Rika?'

'She's higher up. We'll think about her when – or if – we have to.'

THIRTY-ONE

More attacks came on their way out. Alarms had been sounded. A defence had been mounted. Soldiers in armour lined certain streets and they had to pull their wasps high to fly over them. Artemisia pulled out another one of her strange field crystals, crushed it for protection; it lasted long enough to stop minor explosives from detonating, and whatever missiles came their way rebounded back to cause havoc.

They lowered themselves to the ground and continued to race along the network of roads.

Though it was harder to steer the wasp with one hand, Brynd withdrew his sword and gestured for the Night Guard to follow suit. Their formation spread out into rows of five now, for greater presence and to intimidate; warriors came at them but didn't stand a chance: Brynd cleaved this way and that, beheading and then ramming them with the skull of the Mourning Wasp; and as soon as he discovered his steed's resilience in close combat like this, he gave the signal for others to do the same.

Whenever he identified a block of warriors ahead he ploughed into them at chest height, the wasp's skull knocking people to the floor rather than up in the air. Many spat blood on impact.

When Brynd saw the corpse of a metal dragon he recognized that they'd reached the zone where three soldiers had been downed; he slowed and began circling the region, but it was too late.

Artemisia waved them on. Back along the roads, back the way they came, back past people and buildings and blockades, projectiles firing from all sides, but their plan was to keep up their speed, racing too fast for anyone or anything to catch up.

A white glow appeared ahead.

They headed towards it.

Fuck. The walls started to stutter in and out of existence, flickering dark and light. *What the hell was that?*

Brynd lowered his body as close to the wasp as possible and mentally urged it to go quickly, towards the light.

Whiteness engulfed them. The sky opened up. Wind assaulted them. A sign of his concern, he had to remember to breathe, forcing himself to take in air. The platform gave way and his wasp descended down at a severe angle, but eventually smoothed out. Still they flew fast; still he refused to look behind. He heard something ripping behind him and turned to see only half a dozen soldiers alongside. The Policharos was flickering now, almost vibrating in and out of vision.

It happened so quickly. One moment it was there, the next it was drawn into the centre, folding in on itself. The vast, city-wide presence vanished inwardly. Suddenly a blinding line of light shot past towards the horizon, followed by an enormous bass explosion. Brynd closed his eyes and waited for calm.

He opened his eyes again and began to make a slow arc upwards trying to count how many were present: Artemisia, one of her people, fourteen Night Guard soldiers, and that was it.

There was no trace of the Policharos. An absence stood in its place, and various objects or creatures were circling in that

368

vacant space, but now they'd lost all formation and consist-
ency. They began to drift aimlessly.

Artemisia steered the group away, to safety.

*

They barricaded themselves in a room on the top level of the
Citadel that overlooked the courtyard. As the moons glided
above the city, they watched the slow progress of those down
below, wondering how long it would be until they were freed
from the time trap. The noise they generated was audible
still, but was now a low, dull mumble, nothing that generated
fear or intimidation. They broke bread around a table and
served it with cold meats from the kitchen. Two of the
soldiers sat with them, more for reassurance than security.
Blavat also joined them momentarily. Randur observed this
elusive woman who had played such an important role in the
defence of the city against the Okun, an event that already
seemed a distant memory. She seemed a nervous type and
picked at her bread and ate it in tiny morsels. After a while
she got up and left.

Eir said, 'The woman spends so much time on her own
that she must feel uncomfortable up here, without her relics.'

'She's welcome to bring more,' Randur said. 'I won't say
no to some of the more deadly ones on standby. So how long
must we wait now, do you think? What will the gangs do
next?'

'They'll tire at some point,' Eir observed. 'This isn't an
organized military campaign. They haven't thought about the
needs of their own, like the commander does so well. Not
planned for nourishment and bedding. They will be cold and
hungry soon and then they will dissipate.'

'I hope you're right,' Randur replied, and stuffed a chunk
of bread into his mouth.

They managed to get some sleep, curled up in their same
quarters as if nothing was happening. While they rested, the

soldiers managed to take it in turns to hold back those intruders who had not been slowed by the relics, but they were in small numbers and more confused by what was going on with their own kind. The act of cultist magic seemed enough to scare some individuals away. Those who came up the ramp to join in the uprising were probably shocked by the absurd scene that presented itself.

*

Dawn broke, the sun spilling its muted light cast the scene in the colour of blood. Randur woke to the sounds of the gangs being freed from their temporary imprisonment. The noise built up again. The crowds stirred as if they had been stunned. People were trying to make sense of their surroundings again. Though they did not seem to promise the same level of violence as before.

'Maybe by now they hoped they'd be inside,' Randur suggested.

'Their momentum has been considerably slowed,' Eir said. 'I wonder if they're tired now?'

One of the soldiers came to find them to report that all was well and that no further levels had been breached.

'I guess now we just wait,' Randur said.

*

'Where're you going?' Jeza said to Coren, who was standing with his belongings in a case and a sack full of relics over his shoulder.

'I've bought a place, on the edge of the city – a nice place.'

'Haven't you heard what's going on?'

'What? The gangs? Sure, but that's none of our business. Well, none of my business at least.'

'Why're you leaving?' Jeza asked. 'You can't leave me here.'

'We've got money now, haven't we? There's more than enough for each of us to do our own thing. Why hang around? I've always wanted to see more of the world. You can come with me if you want.'

She pondered the point for a long while. Things had certainly been awkward since she'd observed Diggsy and Pilli that night, and she'd not even had the guts to say anything, or to act upon her knowledge. 'Buying a place on the edge of the city is hardly going exploring now, is it?'

'No, but that's not . . .' He sighed. 'I've just had enough of this, all right. We've fulfilled our contracts. It just feels right.'

Jeza moved over to him and for the first time since she had known him she realized he was someone she would miss being around. What was absurd was the fact that she was the one who should have left by now, but where would she go? The culture at Factory 54 was all she had.

'I've been thinking about it for ages,' he continued. 'Sure, the place isn't quite ready to be filled with drugs and dancing girls, but I'm halfway there.'

Jeza gave a sad laugh. 'It feels wrong that you're going right now. I wanted to help do something about the gangs. They're taking over the Citadel. You know that they used our monster to help plan an uprising?'

'I didn't know.'

'The corpse they bought off us – that's what they used. They tried to create fear. They made it look as if aliens were entering the city so that they could get the people of Villiren to support them in an uprising. It's working, too.'

'I don't want to get involved in crazy politics,' Coren muttered. 'Not my scene.'

'This politics stuff affects *everything* though,' Jeza said in despair. 'They could take over the factory, take our possessions, take our money, who knows what. Every little move we make in life will change as a result of *crazy politics*.'

'They wouldn't do that,' Coren replied.

'They're insane,' Jeza said. 'If they take control of the city, you'll need to buy yourself a new house somewhere else. The commander had plans for stability. This Malum guy is crazy. I've seen the look in his eyes.'

'Can't the commander sort it out when he gets back from the battle?'

'There might be nothing left for him by that point. It could be all over – or worse, a second war for Villiren. I don't want that.'

'All right, then what do you suggest we should do about it?'

'Get the wasps out.'

'What, precisely, would a few Mourning Wasps do?'

'We can scare the shit out of the gangs. We can taunt them, maybe move them away from the Citadel, just keep them from causing too much damage. I know we're in the business of palaeomancy and the likes, but there are a few cheap *Brenna*-based relics lying around that we can use.'

'I don't know . . .'

Jeza took his hands and stared pleadingly at him. 'Just this once, will you help me? One last time.'

*

The numbers of invaders thinned out during the day but, when darkness came again, the advancing gangs, used to their nocturnal lifestyle, returned in full force. It seemed to be the opposite of siege warfare in the military, whereby campaigns were conducted in the light of day. Now the gangs brought climbing equipment, ladders, ropes and hooks, determined not to be outdone.

Randur gave instructions to make sure the windows were all blocked on the lower level and, from the floors above, four soldiers fired arrows or crossbow bolts at those trying to scale the heights.

Is it really possible to defend this place against so many people?

Another hour passed in which the gangs tried repeatedly to gain access to higher levels, but they were not skilled in the arts of combat like this. Perhaps on a street corner they could dispatch bodies with ease, lurching out of the darkness in stealth, but here their efforts fell apart. Time and time again those who tried to ascend were shot and fell to the ground.

Randur almost began to feel confident, up until the point where they began to hear more explosions – first they seemed like fireworks, but then they could feel massive detonations ricocheting around the Citadel. Each was spaced a few minutes apart, and followed by a silence in which people tried to assess the damage. Randur consulted Blavat at this point, but the cultist declared that she had hardly any relics left.

They sealed the level and the group moved up to the obsidian room, the war chamber in which the commander had planned the defence of Villiren. Maps, charts and diagrams were strewn across the table and pinned up on the wall. From here they could see the harbour.

'Only another couple of floors left before we're screwed,' Randur observed as they moved out onto one of the viewing balconies.

'There's the roof after that,' Eir said. 'From these plans, it doesn't appear there are many ways to get up there.'

'They'll find a way,' Randur muttered despondently.

'We'll have none of that talk, Randur Estevu,' Eir cautioned. 'We have held these thugs off for a whole day on our own. We can last a little longer yet.'

Randur withdrew his sword and laid it on the table. 'I'll be ready for them, when they come, that much is certain.'

Eir repeated the act with her own blade and laid it alongside his own. 'We'll do this together.'

The young soldier, Drendan, entered the room short of breath. 'Lady Eir, sir, they're about to breach the next floor, which isn't as well protected I'm afraid. It doesn't have the defensive capabilities.'

'What does the situation look like?' Randur asked. 'How many are coming?'

'There are only dozens of them at this level, compared to hundreds down below. I know for certain the gangs are now moving freely on the floors they have got to – and looting.'

'I hope the buggers haven't got into the basement levels – that's where most of the coin is kept,' Randur said.

Eir shook her head. 'The commander ensured that those are kept safe by several relics. It would take a decent cultist an hour to even get access to the room . . .'

Just then they heard a droning sound from outside; gentle at first, then something much harsher. It was soon matched by the noise of the crowds down below.

'What new madness have they found to use on us now?' Randur said despairingly.

They ran to the nearest window that overlooked the courtyard, where, to their astonishment, men were surging to corners of the courtyard, pressing themselves against the walls.

Two enormous insects – no, two enormous insects with *riders* – were roaming the courtyard at considerable speed, darting this way and that, lurching from one side to another. People were now screaming in fear as the helmeted riders attacked them, forcing them up against one wall before attacking others. There were explosions every few moments, bright flashes of purple light.

'Well, that's an interesting turn of events,' Randur laughed.

'What are those things?' Eir said. 'Are they some of the new aliens?'

'I've no idea,' Randur replied. 'They're helping us, I'll say that much. Just look at them go!'

The sight was impressive. To see people who moments earlier were charged with violence now running like frightened children was absurdly amusing. It must have continued for the better part of an hour, the chases within the stone confines, the insects sashaying and skittering about with remarkable manoeuvrability. Though a handful stood to resist, there was nowhere for the gangs to run but back the way they had come and, eventually, that's where many of them went.

Randur and Eir, along with a few of the soldiers, sprinted across to a room that gave them a view of the entrance to the Citadel. There they could see the bulk of the invasion force being scattered across the streets, dispersed back into Villiren.

'I think we've done it,' Randur said, 'or rather – whatever those things are, them and us, we've all done it.'

Any jubilation was short-lived. Two quick explosions sounded.

'There are still more within the building,' Drendan cautioned. 'There could be hundreds already in the Citadel.'

Another explosion, this one louder, this one clearly signalling that another level was about to be broken into.

Randur closed his eyes and wondered just how much longer he'd be alive. Sure he'd had a few scrapes in his short life, and been in more than one tricky situation, but there was a slow inevitability about what was about to happen.

'We retreat again,' Eir ordered.

'What about . . . ?' he begun. *Rika*, he thought, but then thought now was not the time.

Most of the group, including the cultist, took what supplies they could, blankets and extra layers of clothing, equipment to make a fire, and headed out onto the roof of the Citadel, making sure the way up was blocked and heavily guarded. There was shelter up here, of sorts – high stone walls that acted as relief from the wind. From the crenellations they could observe the situation on the ground, which was now calm after those monstrous insects had done their work.

They set up camp, organized themselves, and started a fire. They bedded down, surrounded in blankets, huddled alongside the fire like the homeless. Randur held Eir in his arms, more than ever appreciative that he had experienced a good and interesting life with her. Three soldiers took watch, their crossbows by their sides, ready to shoot anyone who would dare to scale the roof.

There they waited and prayed for morning to come.

Thirty-Two

Brynd headed into one of the large towns of Folke, having left the Mourning Wasps on the outskirts.

First the Night Guard had reported back to Artemisia's elders that all the threats from the Policharos had been eliminated and Frater Mercury had indeed done what he had claimed he would do. Then the remaining Night Guard briefly mourned the loss of their comrades, though there was not time for the appropriate military rituals.

Brynd had peered once again into the cauldrons, and could see that the battle had indeed changed. There was no longer any precise organization to the enemy ranks. There seemed to be little discipline, no communication; the regiments moved back and forth like ocean swells. Yet the allied forces were still sustaining massive losses.

One particularly large mass of warriors was heading along a road towards Lantuk, a major settlement on Folke, a gateway city to the island.

He could watch no longer. 'We're going down there,' he ordered. 'Within a day it looks as though the onslaught will reach Lantuk. It's the first big settlement in a chain of large urban areas.'

'They will drift away within a week,' Artemisia said. 'There is no central hub, no more instructions.'

'Those warriors can still kill, can't they?' Brynd snapped.

'They can.'

'Then thousands of my people will still die needlessly. We're going down to stop them reaching Lantuk.'

Artemisia looked at him impassively. 'As you wish.'

*

The Night Guard took the Mourning Wasps down and left them a short distance from the moderately fortified city. When the people saw the Empire soldiers approaching the gates, they opened up and cheered in their own soldiers, welcoming them into the muddy central plaza.

It was early morning, and Brynd and the rest of the Night Guard were already shattered. He had dispatched garudas to shift dozens of Dragoon regiments into planned formations, but to plan further he demanded maps of the ground around Lantuk from the library.

With a central citadel not unlike Villiren, and thin crenellated walls, it was a relatively weak position; though it possessed nowhere near the level of defence of a city like Villjamur, its real benefit was to be found in the landscape. Lantuk was fortunate in that the only road to it lay in a steep-sided valley, which meant that the coming hordes would be forced through a funnel of land, a fact that pleased Brynd immensely.

It would make the combat more manageable.

He decided to issue more missives via garudas, informing all Imperial regiments based nearby to travel immediately to the western approach to Lantuk. Certain regiments were to station themselves around the two large hills bordering the road, cutting off any difficult, uphill attacks around the sides. Artemisia's people, too, would scour the hilltops to prevent any access from above.

*

The garudas had done their jobs well. All the nearby troops, stationed within a mile of the city, were gathering, passing from the eastern side of Lantuk and heading into the western valley beyond. Within two hours, four thousand soldiers had moved here from the surrounding garrisons and the city; it wasn't much, and how many of them were part-timers and not professional soldiers, Brynd did not know. For a good number of them it would probably be their first taste of battle.

The Night Guard stationed themselves at the very front, in full battle regalia, new shields on their arms and swords at their sides. Behind them stood seven hundred Dragoon veterans. Each side of the road two steep hillsides towered above to a height of a few hundred feet. The landscape was littered with spindly bushes, snow and rocks, but Brynd had ordered four hundred archers to climb up and he could see them now, dotted on the slopes above. He had decided to leave the Mourning Wasps in the city to rest: they would be no good in close combat battles like the one coming.

'Sir!' Brug shouted, and gestured to the west. The remaining Night Guard snapped to attention, catching Brynd's eye, and he followed their gazes to the road in front of them.

Up ahead, he could see the blue figure of Artemisia running back down the road, followed by many others like her, all of similar blue skin and warrior garb. As expected, there were other creatures too, all hominids, some he had seen before, a few he had not.

'At ease,' he ordered his comrades.

A quick count and Brynd estimated the new additions were nearing a hundred in all – not ideal, but better than nothing.

'Any news?' Brynd enquired.

'The Okun have mostly scattered,' she replied. 'There is chaos on the beaches, but more organization inland. Creatures are swarming across the countryside, but they seem to know that there are dense populations this way. They were given one message, we believe – to cleanse these islands of people. That is what they will continue to do.'

'Have you stationed units around the hills?'

'I have,' Artemisia confirmed. 'Two thousand.'

Brynd breathed a sigh of relief. The hills would not be overrun with so many defenders on such difficult terrain. That meant the only way for miles around would be through this wide path along the bottom of the valley; however, if they broke through here they would have free passage through all the cities and towns on the island.

'Let's send a scout up ahead to tell us of their arrival.'

*

They waited until mid-afternoon and there was still no sign of the scout returning. The sun was concealed behind the hillside, leaving the thousands of soldiers in the cold shade. Spears were being brought forward and stockpiled.

'What's keeping him so long?' Sergeant Tiendi asked.

'He'll get here when he's seen something,' Brynd replied.

They regarded the distance a little longer. The road only stretched so far before arcing out of sight. Brynd could perceive noises in the distance, now, but could see nothing . . .

No, wait . . . What are they?

He could see the tops of siege towers.

'They're definitely here,' Brug said. 'We can hear them.'

'Fetch a horse,' Brynd ordered.

One was summoned, and a few minutes later the reins of a brown mare from the Dragoons were handed to him. Brynd jumped up and nudged her forward, racing along the road, through a chill wind.

A few hundred yards later he pulled for her to stop. He could sense the vibrations in the earth now, could hear the low-pitched horns sounding in the distance; the sheer noise of footsteps on the ground was intense, as thousands upon thousands of enemy infantry were being funnelled into the valley. Monstrous creatures loomed up above the ranks, pulling even taller machines of war.

Brynd lifted up his helmet. 'Dear Bohr . . .' There were things in the distance with several heads, like nothing he could imagine, and before them was a sea of warriors on foot.

Suddenly something flew through the air in an arc and landed some distance behind him. He nudged his horse to canter over, where he saw that the launched object was in fact the head of the scout he had sent to investigate.

He immediately rode back to his line, the noise of the advancing enemy behind him seeming to intensify between the two hills. Artemisia's comrades had spread out across the valley bottom, beyond the road, on either side. Their shields were ready.

Brynd rode in front of his own lines now, loud enough for rank upon rank of soldiers to hear what he had to say.

'They're coming!' he bellowed, 'at least thirty thousand of them against us few thousand; they outnumber us at least three to one, but here, within this valley, they cannot overpower us.'

Led by the Night Guard, the gathered soldiers began to strike their shields with their swords.

'If the enemy breaks through, they will begin ending civilization across the Boreal Archipelago. Your children will be wiped out, your homes will be burned. There will be no future. However, if you die today in glorious victory, comrades, it will be better than being defeated and remaining alive to see what follows.'

The clamour continued and he took the unusual step of riding deeper through the ranks to repeat his message further in; then, finally, he returned to the front line.

Brynd dismounted and sent the horse back.

He stood among the Night Guard, with Artemisia and her warriors alongside them.

They waited as the ground shook and horns blared. Brynd raised his sword in the air and silence fell across the thousands behind. He waited.

The enemy continued to pour into the valley, just a few hundred yards away now, a seething mass of anger marching ever closer . . . then began their charge.

Brynd lowered his arm.

A moment later and the skies darkened with hundreds of arrows, which arced into the distance and over the enemy. Brynd repeated the gesture and another wave of arrows was released, this time at a lower trajectory to take out those at the front. Brynd circled his sword in the air and the archers continued firing freely into the advancing ranks.

'Close the line!' he shouted.

The front row of defence locked shields and spears were pushed forward, a barbed frontier of what was left of the civilized world. Artemisia's hundred took several paces and then locked their own.

The enemy tide could be discerned clearly now: the creatures here were hominid, of sorts, like the Okun but with hideous, blistered skin; there were worse things beyond, a few Okun in between.

The Night Guard braced themselves. Veterans from the Dragoons locked shields behind; Brynd peered over the edge of his shield, which he held with his left arm, and gripped his sword more tightly.

He counted down quickly and loudly as the first, huge wave of the enemy advance crashed into the shields and spears.

Multiple dull thuds clattered into the wall. At first, everyone's feet slipped back because of the sheer force, but the Dragoon veterans shoved back behind the Night Guard, who gave a quick, collective heave, pressing forward with their spears.

'Release!' Brynd shouted.

Shields were unlocked for a brief moment as they turned and stabbed their spears, and hacked at any flesh within sight, cleaving limbs and aiming for faces and necks.

'Lock!' Brynd bellowed.

The shield wall re-formed, spears protruded, and again everyone shoved forward in unison.

'Release two!' Brynd commanded, increasingly out of breath now.

They fought for twice as long as last time, now with drawn swords, stabbing where appropriate, severing limbs, coolly ignoring the snarling faces beyond, before locking once again.

And then again.

They repeated the process with finesse, locking and releasing shields, fighting on the break, continuing for the better part of half an hour before the advancing enemy had been thinned out.

The wall had held.

When they had eliminated the bulk of the advance, Brynd gave the order for the front row of defenders to break free and stride forward over the gathered corpses, to remove what remained. He led from the front, hacking into the gawping, vicious-looking creatures, guessing where there was no armour for a quick, clean kill. He dodged crude spears, and knocked away the rough, heavy swords raised at him. Limbs and throats became prime targets, and he hacked at them like a ruthless, calculating machine.

Three, four, eight, nine, the numbers fell before him, everything slowed down, his enhancements came to light; his comrades by his side, he felt unstoppable. The creatures fell by the dozen; blood was splattered thickly across his dark armour. The ground became a sodden mulch of blood, mud and offal.

Then, lightness and a sudden rush of air.

What was left of this first wave retreated back to their own lines and, even there, chaos appeared to have broken out.

Brynd was astonished to see that Artemisia's unit had progressed some hundred yards further up the valley; they were now surveying the wreckage of battle, thrusting their spears into anything that was still moving.

Brynd gave the command to refresh the lines. The Night Guard and front rows of veterans peeled back into their ranks and fresh soldiers were brought forward.

'They're not wearing much armour,' Brug muttered. 'They're undisciplined and untrained. This should be easy.'

'It's not them I'm bothered about,' Brynd said, 'there's worse beyond.'

Artemisia strode over to him, wiping the blood from her blade. 'A good start, commander. They make splendid sport, do they not? They've mostly fled now.'

The Night Guard marched back through the ranks, informing the gathered men that the veterans were still at the front, and inspired them by revealing how easy the defence would be. The mood visibly changed. It seemed that these newer Dragoons wanted a piece of history.

Despite the lighter armour, Brynd felt exhausted. The Night Guard sat on rocks just up to one side, away from the front, and soon Artemisia joined them.

Brynd lifted up his helmet. 'The infantry is no problem. These soldiers will be able to hold their own now, I'm confident of that. We must see that the dragons and garudas can help out. But there's worse back there, I'm sure of it. Thin it out with that liquid fire – whatever it was I saw being dropped on the sea earlier. We can hold our wall for as long as it takes – but as soon as those machines get near to us, Lantuk is done for.'

*

An hour later, his orders were enacted. As another wave of infantry came and failed against the Imperial shield-wall in the valley below, Brynd watched a squadron of dragons sailing overhead, with what garudas could be spared. Beneath the dragons he could see huge cylindrical tubes. The dragons drifted over the advancing infantry to where there were larger and more dangerous foes beyond.

Moments later they released their cargo and fire erupted on the ground, emitting huge flames and black smoke that licked up the sides of the valley. A deep shudder and explosions could be heard shortly after. The skies darkened. Everyone watched in awe. The fighting on the front line seemed to pause momentarily as the advancing warriors on both sides assessed what was going on.

'What next?' Artemisia asked.

'Send your forces down from the hills,' Brynd declared, 'in order to clean up any of those who are trying to flee. I don't want any prisoners of any kind. And bring more fire – there's a lot down there that needs burning. I'll advance the Dragoons through the valley to kill anything that moves.'

*

Back outside Lantuk, Brynd wanted to see the status of the battle and the situation beyond. He took one of the Mourning Wasps up to survey the remnants of the fighting.

He soared over devastation.

Not even in the urban confines of Villiren had the bodies of the dead been piled so high. First, the valley was littered with them, and the road had transformed into a bloodied river, bordered by the blackened sides of the valley. The charred remains of gargantuan creatures lay on their sides, some still barely moving; there was no blood here, just utter blackness.

He took the Mourning Wasp further up out of the valley and towards the surrounding landscape. From forests to the shore, creatures, humans, rumel, Okun, all lay in bloodied pieces. The whole region reeked of death and faeces; how many had died here to create such a mess, he would never know.

He flew towards the shore to see smouldering fires where

the ships had been set alight; out to sea, vessels still burned. Out of the shallows jutted chunks of metal and wood, and the broken, webbed wings of enormous creatures. Mile after mile of this devastation stretched out along the grey surf. Occasionally something stirred within the bloody mess and Brynd wondered if someone had miraculously survived, but it always turned out to be a looter clipping rings from the fingers of the dead.

As he drifted over the corpsescape, he vowed to himself that this was the end of blood being spilled. It was the most humbling sight he had ever seen.

*

It was nightfall when he returned to Lantuk and no sooner had he landed than a garuda swooped down to land beside him. The impressive, black and white feathered creature, with astonishingly bright armour, breathlessly tried to get Brynd's attention.

'You have news for me?' Brynd demanded.

Aye, the bird-sentry signed. *I have flown all night from Villiren, as quick as I could.*

'Villiren?' Brynd asked, frowning. 'What's wrong?'

The gangs, he signed. *They've risen up to take the city.*

THIRTY-THREE

'I've got an idea,' Randur said suddenly. It was pitch-black, and he'd only managed to get four hours' sleep, but it was better than none. He stood up and stretched himself awake. The cold soon brought his senses back.

He took a mouthful of bread and a glug of water before he crouched by Eir. 'I'm going to head over the side of the building. We've got rope, right?'

'What on earth for?'

'I need to visit someone,' Randur smiled, moving over to a specific bag they had brought up. He rummaged inside, clanked about, managed to scoop something out and conceal it in one of the pockets of his breeches. 'Just trust me, OK?'

'Don't go, Randur, stay. Can't you send one of the others to do whatever it is you have in mind?'

'Nope. No one else will know the way.'

'What are you going to do exactly?' She eyed him with suspicion.

'Just trust me.'

Randur gave orders to some of the men to help tie him securely so he could step over the edge and abseil down one side of the building, near one specific area. He walked down the wet stonework as if he had done it all his life, though he was fearful that he'd fall onto the streets below.

Now's not the time to show you're scared, Randur, he told

himself. *You've blagged your way through life – at least you can give everyone a little hope you know what you're doing…*

After a few minutes of faffing about on his way down, he managed to find the window he wanted. Luckily it was on one of the higher floors, where they had not bothered boarding up the windows, only the doors on the inside. He peered through the glass but knew there would be no one on the inside.

No one from the gangs, at least.

He kicked at the glass and in large chunks it shattered. He cleaned the gap of any shards, and laid a piece of cloth on the windowsill for extra protection. Gripping the sides of the frame, he manoeuvred his legs into the gap, before untying the rope from around his waist. He sat there, momentarily, cursing his lack of fitness. *A year ago and this would have been a piece of piss*, he thought.

Once he had regained his breath, he wriggled through the gap and into the corridor connecting the gaol cells. He looked around for any signs that he had been spotted, but guessed he had got away with it.

Rika was in the corner. She appeared gaunt, skinnier than ever, but her expression was one of deep anger and resentment.

'Evening,' he announced, but she showed no signs of having heard him. 'I'm guessing you're probably quite hungry, right?'

Again, nothing.

'Well, I've got a surprise for you.' Randur pulled the key from his pocket. First he walked to the main door that connected with the rest of the Citadel and checked it would open easily; then he returned and put the key in the lock. Hungrily, Rika glanced to his hand and then back at him. He reached down into his boot, drew out a dagger, and placed it outside the cell, then sprinted to the window, jumped back up onto the frame, tied the rope securely around his waist.

He heard the key click in the lock and the gaol door creak open. He slid his head then the rest of his body up and out of the window. He tugged down three times on the rope and shouted that he was coming up. He began to feel the rope tighten then yank him back outside into the darkness.

*

Back on the roof, back safely with Eir, she demanded he tell her what he had been up to.

'I went to see Rika,' Randur muttered.

Eir contemplated his statement and replied, 'You freed her, didn't you?' There were conflicted emotions in her gaze, and he placed his hand over hers. 'She hasn't eaten in days, but she's capable of causing a lot of damage. It took a superhero to catch her, that other night, you know.'

'I can't believe you did that without consulting me.'

'It was the right thing to do, Eir. They would have killed her if they had seen her in the cell like that. They'd have shown no mercy because of who she was. If we'd brought her up here, she would have eaten us all.'

Eir remained silent, but the fact that she did not withdraw her hand indicated that she could well have supported his decision.

*

Screams filtered up through the night. They were occasional, at first – could have been anything. But the next time Randur woke up, the wails of agony from below were terrifying, far more so than anything the gangs had imposed upon the group. Men seemed to be suffering from horrific ordeals. They were sobbing and screeching like bats.

There must have been very few places to run in the winding corridors of the Citadel, very few ways in which to escape. However, if you were familiar with the layout, as Rika was, then there would be infinite places to take refuge.

Perhaps it was a very cruel thing for him to have done, unleash some mad cannibal in such confines. Perhaps . . .

Only when the screams finally diminished could he fall asleep once again.

*

The crowds began to surge again, down below. The first rays of the morning sun began to show themselves, peeling back the darkness of the night. It had been a quiet evening. If indeed there had been breaches of the higher levels of the Citadel, Randur wasn't aware of it. For all he knew, the gangs might have decided that there was no one around any more; that they had vanished down some secret tunnel. There was nothing to reveal that they were on the roof.

They ate meagre rations and waited. Noises filtered up from below: the Citadel was being ransacked. All that the commander had worked for was probably being ripped up or, judging by the burning smells, being set alight.

'Do you think we should perhaps negotiate with them, lay down our weapons?' one of the guards said.

'Oh that's right,' Randur replied, 'hand them our arses on a plate. Do you really think they'll offer any kind of mercy? These are gangs – another word for c—'

'Randur!' Eir interrupted. 'There's no need for that. The man was simply asking a logical question.'

'Logical?' Randur spluttered, and glared at the soldier. 'You can hand yourself in if you want. They might use your head as a vase if you're lucky.'

'I meant no offence, sir,' the soldier replied wearily. 'My apologies. I will, of course, fight as long as you instruct me to.'

'Good.' Randur strode to the edge of the building to look over the cityscape, feeling the chill wind on his face. He half hoped someone would see him and report that there were people on the roof. He wanted people to come at him now. He was sick of waiting – that was all he had done since he'd been in the city. He was a country lad, a scrapper. What's more, he hadn't had a good fight in ages.

He glanced back to the others, whose attention was now drawn to the opposite side of the roof – there, in the face of the onshore wind, someone was trying to climb up. Randur ran to address the situation, but arrived as the soldiers knocked the individual back down to the balcony a couple of floors below. The thug, a thickset man with a beard, fell flat on his back and lay motionless, staring up at them. Below the balcony, the streets were thronging with people.

'Well, now they know we're here,' Randur muttered.

It wasn't long before people were trying to get through the hatch and over the side of the wall. Not many attempted the latter route – it was too dangerous. The hatch repeatedly clattered until the sun was much higher in the sky, which led Randur to believe that people were taking it in turns to batter it.

Everyone looked to Randur and Eir for guidance now, but when an axe pummelled upwards into the wood, the soldiers stepped back and withdrew their weapons. Eir did the same. Randur took a few paces away to get a better perspective on the scene, before drawing his own blade and channelling in to his old sword techniques.

It felt as if he had met with an old friend again – that familiarity with the tension, the adrenalin, channelling his rage.

The hatch split.

One of the soldiers thrust his blade in the gap, stabbing someone down below. A cry came up, followed by a clatter as whoever it was fell backwards. Then a silence lingered. Randur could feel his pulse thicken in his throat.

Three soldiers stood around the hatch, waiting, swords in hand.

An arrow flew up and through the gap, narrowly missing one of the men. A moment later, more debris was tossed up, then someone tried to lunge out – he got a sword to his neck and fell bleeding down below, but by that point another man had squirmed up, waving a mace around his head as he did so, gashing one of the soldiers in the leg before another came to him with his blade. In the mayhem, more gang members piled out of the hatch, three now, each of different stature, and they shambled around the rooftop, weapons extended, but with a tired look in their eyes.

Randur smiled, knowing that they would not have had the benefit of a decent night's sleep, as suggested by their lazy sword-handling and slowness of step. The soldiers quickly dispatched the invaders before yet more thugs came up in their place. Soon most of the soldiers were engaged in the business of sword-fighting, as one darkly handsome individual clambered up and sauntered around away from the main fight.

He was an onlooker, here, waiting for the mess to be over.

Randur noticed that three of the soldiers now lay dead or bleeding to death on the rooftop. People were dropping like flies – this was messy, useless combat.

The man with the handsome face and three-day-old stubble strode around the edge of the fighting and nodded at both Randur and Eir, before drawing his sword.

'What's your name, kid?' the man asked, above the groaning of the wind.

'Randur Estevu,' he replied.

'Bit of a crap name, that.'

'Can you do any better?'

'Malum,' the man declared.

'Not much better at all.'

'Blame my mother,' Malum muttered. 'I take it this is Lady Jamur Rika?'

'Jamur Eir, her sister,' Eir replied. She was now clutching her sword in anticipation.

Randur decided then was a good time to bring out his own blade, and the three of them stood there, to one side. 'Quite a few screams last night,' he announced. 'Must have been pretty messy.'

'Was that your doing?' Malum replied.

Randur shrugged. 'I don't know what you're talking about.'

'I'll tell you, shall I? I lost forty of my best guys, and five others lost a few of their limbs. Mad bitch, whoever it was.'

'Did you stop her?' Eir replied.

'No,' Malum replied. 'She dined her way down a floor or two and jumped out of a second-floor window. She's somewhere lost in the city for all I know. Who was she?'

Randur began. 'That was Lady—'

'We don't know who you're talking about,' Eir interrupted, glaring at Randur.

The fight continued around them. Randur saw Blavat dropping something down the hatch that caused a blinding flash of light below.

'Useful things, cultists,' Malum said.

The man was strangely confident, cockier than even Randur himself, which was a disarming point to note. The way he strode about the rooftop as if this was already his Citadel was something that annoyed Randur. He stood with one foot up on the low gap between crenellations so that he could tighten his boot laces.

Such arrogance, Randur thought. He cautioned for Eir to move further away. 'He looks a good fighter. It'll be easier if I'm not worried about you,' he whispered, and could see the annoyance in her face. Despite this, she moved back.

'Well, enough of pleasantries,' Malum declared, and with a sudden fury launched into a blazing attack on Randur, nearly catching him off guard from the off. While the commotion continued around them, Malum forced Randur further along the rooftop. Randur intercepted the first flurry of blows with difficulty – he was out of decent practice, and the force of Malum's strikes was incredibly intense.

But soon Randur gained control.

His tactic would be to let Malum wear himself out, to go on the defensive, to guide the strikes away harmlessly. He did not fight in any style that Randur knew of, and there was no grace to the man's aggressive technique.

Two blows to either side within a split second nearly disarmed Randur completely. He stumbled back across the rooftop and caught a side-long glimpse of Eir engaged in combat herself, but he didn't have time to register her progress, he was back on his feet firmly, back on the defensive, the repetitive zing of steel sliding across steel filling his ears.

Malum did not tire. Was he some kind of animal? He still retained the same level of aggression as in his first blows. Randur shifted his focus momentarily to see the man's face, which was a picture of rage – and were they fangs in his snarling mouth?

Randur was breathless. He could only parry so much before he realized he would have to commence his own attack. He dashed to his right, wrong-footing Malum, moving around another fight, taking a moment to register the high red sun and the dizzying cityscape below, before lurching right at Malum with a flurry of attacks.

Malum was now on the back foot, weakened, uneasy with defending. Randur tried a whole range of tricks, but was surprised at how quickly Malum could react. There was definitely something animalistic about this man.

The rooftop began to flood with corpses. There was another flash as Blavat moved across the rooftop. There was smoke now, something definitely burning, and Randur saw a blur of movement behind Malum: Eir dragged her sword across his arm as she whipped by, out of sight, and Malum screamed out, gripped his now-bleeding arm then held out his stained fingers momentarily towards Randur. He licked his blood in some perverse manner.

'You're a bit weird really, aren't you?' Randur said. 'Is all this some kind of ego trip for a madman?' He gestured to the mess all around them.

That seemed to ruffle a few more feathers, not that Malum really needed it. He recommenced his attack, but this time Randur noticed that everyone else had stopped fighting – everyone apart from Malum. People were standing back and pointing up, to the sky. Randur forced a break in the fight and dashed out of arm's reach to get a better look at what was going on.

Black shapes were flying in the sunlight, circling as silhouettes. Soon a few smaller shapes detached themselves and drifted towards them. The gang members began to panic as the shapes – very similar to the ones previously in the courtyard – skimmed down to land at the far end of the rooftop. Several individuals, each wearing strange black helmets, dismounted and began to advance.

The pale face of Brynd Lathraea was revealed.

Malum grinned and twisted his chest to face the commander full on. 'So you're still alive, homo,' he snarled at him. 'It's a bit too late to ruin the fun.'

Brynd gave a despairing laugh. 'The fun will be in personally digging your grave, you little shit.'

If Brynd was tired from his battle, he showed no traces of it. While the rest of the Night Guard began to approach the remaining gang members, who threw down their weapons and backed off immediately, Brynd clashed with Malum with a level of violence that seemed unnatural for such a usually calm man.

Malum instantly stumbled and fell, but rolled away from a blow aimed at his throat. He pushed himself up again to resume his defence. Brynd's strikes overpowered Malum: the man was on the back foot at all times. Brynd was drawing this out, knocking him back, walking slowly, waiting for him to get on his feet. Malum snarled like a feral dog, but Brynd wasn't having any of it. Randur spotted at least three occasions where Brynd could have finished the job, but instead he would throw a punch to his stomach or jaw, sending the man sprawling.

He forced Malum towards the edge of the roof, up against the battlements, where there was no more room to run. With a combination of quick moves, Brynd had put a deep cut in Malum's arm and forced him to drop his sword.

The gang leader fell to his knees in pain. He growled, clutching his arms, 'You wouldn't hit an unarmed man, a man of your dignity? Go on, do it. I dare you.'

Brynd walked around to one side, utterly expressionless. Eir came along to stand next to Randur, and they both watched, waiting to see what would happen.

'I could show you mercy,' Brynd called out, then turned to address those on the roof, those few still standing, those gang members now lying face down with their hands over the back of their heads, his own Night Guard soldiers. 'I could show him mercy, couldn't I?' he bellowed.

Only the sounds of the wind and the sea in the distance could be heard.

Malum spat at the commander's boots. 'Get on with it. I never was a patient man.'

Brynd stood over him. He drew one arm back and sideways, holding up his blade, and in a frighteningly quick swipe he cut off Malum's head. One of the bound gang members gasped. Another called out something inaudible. There was a genuine look of emotion in their eyes.

Brynd watched the body slump down as the blood pooled thickly by his boots. He moved over to one side to retrieve the head and grabbed it up by the hair. He held it aloft to a bass cheer from his own soldiers.

Brynd then walked calmly over to Randur and Eir, still clutching Malum's head. Randur could barely take his eyes off it.

'I wore him down for you,' Randur grinned. 'Erm, welcome

back, commander. Sorry the place is a bit of a mess. Person-ally, I blame Eir.' He nudged her in the ribs.

'Randur!' Eir gasped. 'My apologies, commander. We did our best against overwhelming numbers.'

'You did just fine,' Brynd replied. Only now could Randur see just how tired the man was. 'How long was this going on for?'

'A couple of nights and days, I'd say? I've lost track if I'm honest. It all sprawled into one sleepless night.' Randur turned to Eir for confirmation and she nodded.

'Good work,' Brynd replied. 'I mean that.'

Randur found himself incredibly uneasy when speaking to a man carrying a severed head. Blood still dripped from it onto the roof and Randur casually moved out of the way of the trail of blood. 'What are those things?' Randur pointed to the enormous insects now at the far end of the rooftop.

'They're called Mourning Wasps. New form of transport. Very useful in a tricky situation.'

'Was that you who came earlier?' Randur asked. 'We saw some similar things a while ago.'

'No.' Brynd's confusion gave way to a private realization that Randur must mean Jeza and her friends.

Randur looked over to the wasps, which seemed inert, hardly moving at all. He quite fancied having a go on one.

'The battle – it went well, did it?' Eir asked. 'As well as these things can go.'

'You know the cost of war as well as I do, having seen the remnants in the hospital. Artemisia's people lost more than we did, since our lines were far behind her own, protecting our towns and our people. But the loss of life was many times what we saw in Villiren. Half the Night Guard has gone.'

Eir opened her mouth to say something, but then thought better of it.

'What're you going to do with that head?' Randur asked, pointing to it.

'There are still a few dozen gang types in the Citadel. I'm going to round them all up, show them this head, then place it on a spike by the entrance for everyone to see.'

'Good advertisement, that,' Randur admitted.

'Senior members of the gangs will be executed also. Another warning, another lesson to be given to the people. If we're to move our culture on, and live side by side with one another, we damn well need to have some respect for the operations of this Citadel or we'll have riots every day.'

Eir cringed, but nodded. 'I understand.'

Who exactly was ruling here? Randur reflected.

'Besides, the man whose head I hold made his trade before the war by putting fear into the lives of the citizens of this city. Good, honest people will want to see his head on a spike. They'll sleep easily knowing the gangs have been dealt such a blow.'

'Where's Artemisia?' Eir asked.

'She's still with her people,' Brynd replied. 'They have much grieving to do. We'll grieve with them also, when the time is right. They gave so many lives in order to save their future – and ours – here, on this Archipelago.'

'What next?' Randur asked. 'Clean up the Citadel, start getting things back in shape in Villiren, help Artemisia's culture with cleaning up the dead?'

'All of those things,' Brynd replied. As he turned away, still clutching Malum's severed head, he called over his shoulder, 'And then, we plan for peace.'

THIRTY-FOUR

There was a knock on the door and Brynd looked up from his desk. Warm morning sunlight fell across legal papers.

'Come in,' Brynd called out.

Randur poked his head around the door and sauntered to the chair next to Brynd. He slouched into it and put his feet up on the table. 'Guess what?'

'What?'

'One of the servants downstairs suggested that they'd seen some woman hunched over a corpse near the edge of Saltwater and the Wastelands.'

'And?' Brynd asked, raising an eyebrow.

'You think it's Rika?' Randur asked.

'I don't know. No one's spotted her since you unleashed her.'

'It was a sensible option,' Randur replied coolly. 'The gangs would have killed her if they found her – at least she took some of them down on her way out.'

'Anyway, it's too early to tell if it's Rika. There are a lot of strange things in this city. I'll send out a patrol around the southern rim of Saltwater, just in case.'

Randur nodded his approval. 'Up to much then?'

'I'm checking the laws that have been passed recently; copies have been made and I'm seeing there are no errors. Just one rogue scribe and we'll get all sorts of problems.'

'Nice clothes by the way.'

Brynd was wearing an ornate uniform, similar to the Night Guard clothing of old, but a paler shade of grey, with greater details and a new emblem on the chest: two overlapping stars. It had taken a few weeks for him to decide on this, but the Night Guard wasn't the same now it was so depleted. He needed change, for himself as well as the others.

'Shouldn't you be getting ready yourself?' Brynd asked.

'Probably.'

'Cold feet?' Brynd pressed, largely to amuse himself.

'Nah. Well, yes. I'm not the marrying type – or at least I never thought I would be. And it doesn't seem right, does it? To be having some posh party after all that's gone on?'

'We're not doing it for the party,' Brynd said.

'You don't strike me as the partying kind of guy.'

'I know how to enjoy myself.'

'Sure you do. Anyway, so why are we doing this?'

'Apart from your love for Eir, obviously . . .'

'Obviously . . .'

'People want to know who's in charge now, they're looking up to us, and it's better they see a pretty young couple holding a massive celebration, with free food for everyone and land to dispense to deserving families. It's a focal point and people deserve a little good news in their lives. And it looks like you've picked a good day for it.'

'Huh,' Randur said. Then, looking at the papers, 'So what's new?'

'Nearly everything. We're starting all over again. We've had to encourage new equality laws so that the Newlanders—'

'Is that what they're being called?'

'What, you don't like it?'

'A bit bland for such exotics, don't you think?'

'The more familiar their name, the better. Anyway, the rights of the average citizen have changed. No matter if you're rumel or human, or indeed one of the many races that are now to live alongside us, everyone has individual rights unless they surrender those by committing certain crimes. It's the only way to ensure people don't start hurting each other. People may cross borders freely. People will be given free land to farm, in order to restock our grain supplies. What's more, people are free to worship more than one god – Artemisia's people have many, it seems. People are even free to take sexual partners from the new races, if that's their wish.'

'There's a niche for everyone,' Randur declared.

'As long as it is not abusive – rape laws have had to change accordingly. And due to accommodating the new cultures, men may bed with men, women with women. There are permits for those who wish to take more than one husband or wife, but that will be examined carefully.'

'More than one? Why would you want extra grief every day?'

'As you so often say,' Brynd continued, 'everyone has their niche. Now, go on, get ready. The priests are coming soon. Put some decent clothes on – if you've got any.'

'Just because you've got yourself some fancy new kit, don't go getting ideas above your station. If anyone does fashion well, it's Randur Estevu.'

*

A phenomenal number of species gathered at the ceremony, which was held on an enormous stage in front of the Citadel. Brynd had ensured the setting was as resplendent as could be, without being too ostentatious. Most of the money would be spent on the thousands of tables of free food and drink that would be laid on throughout the city. It had taken a while to stockpile, and wasn't as perfect as he would have liked, but it was a bold and important gesture, and the city responded positively. The stage was decorated in red and gold cloth, with elaborate yet humble craft items and ornaments gathered about the stage. Brynd had even taken down Malum's rotting head from the spike so it wouldn't make the place stink or put people off their food.

It would be another hour before the event started properly, but people were relaxing, drinking and singing already. A band struck up under a bright yellow awning.

Artemisia's elders were present, as well as some of her more exotic kin but, pleasingly, there were also a good number of humans and rumels too. There were only a handful of people to bring across from her world now; very little remained there, apart from the last skirmishes of the long-fought war. Any remaining Realm Gates were being sealed off by their agents, and should be little for anyone to worry about, and given the passage of time anything beyond the gates would be uninhabitable. Of course, when the last of the gates closed, there would be a gradual warming to come. Artemisia's elders had given specific instructions that they never be opened again.

Jokull was still an island to be healed: the enemy had established a few minor settlements around the coast and inland, so Brynd had dispatched several regiments of Dragoons along with some alien military units to eliminate the threat. Soon they should begin sifting through the rubble of Villjamur. One day, Brynd thought, they might even start rebuilding it.

*

There was still some time to kill, and everything seemed to be proceeding well enough. Brynd walked through the warm sunlight before he grabbed a lager from a stand in the shadows of the Citadel.

Out of the corner of his eye, he spotted Jeza dancing with one of the kids that she had been staying with at the factory, not the blond one but the one with all the wisecracks. Brynd never could remember their names.

Jeza was now living at the Citadel – it seemed the least he could do in her desperate situation and, besides, he could now keep an eye on all her crazy inventions and ideas. He felt vaguely paternal towards her – a quality he merely dismissed as a sign that he wasn't getting any younger.

After a refreshing sip, he approached Artemisia at a table near the front of the crowds. She was seated alongside some humans from her world, people old and young. They were wearing green, fitted tunics with bold sashes across their chests. Artemisia appeared much more approachable now she wasn't wearing her swords, garbed instead in a garish yellow and brown patterned uniform. In the rows behind them were businessmen and businesswomen that Brynd recognized. There were bankers here, too, never ones to shy away from a free meal. He didn't tell them it was their money paying for all of this.

'A good offering, by the look of it thus far,' Artemisia muttered.

'Thanks,' Brynd replied, standing behind her. 'Who are these people?' He gestured to the two rows nearby, facing each other and divided only by the banquet.

Overhead a garuda swept by, causing a gentle downdraught before coasting up above the nearest row of timber-framed buildings.

'They are not so much soldiers but dignitaries or ambassadors or organizers,' Artemisia said, 'not unlike me, but skilled in dealing rather than the arts of war. I hope you will speak to many of them in the coming days, for they are important people, representing many of our business houses. Though they still aim to keep fighting-ready, as we say. Be cautious, however, for dignitaries in our world are educated in the arts of seduction – of both sexes, they are not picky when the urge strikes them. I tell you this now, to give you an advantage in bargaining with them, should you find yourself in a tricky spot.'

One of the men caught Brynd's eye, a muscular man about his own age, dark-haired and with a fine jaw. They exchanged smiles. 'I think I can handle myself.'

Brynd took a sip of lager, before he decided to head through the throng and introduce himself.

*

The garuda followed the line of the streets before drifting up and over towards the Onyx Wings that guided her like a beacon in the daylight. She soared above the rooftops, looking down on the activities below. Every street was rammed with festivities; even the poorer districts were making the most of their allocations of food and drink.

Low sunlight forced harsh shadows between buildings, and there were clear patches of dark and light across the cityscape. She turned to bank higher, arcing away from the sea and briefly towards the south of the city. Further beyond Villiren's borders, the Newlanders' encampments were growing daily, big but tidy sprawls that stretched beyond the forest. A few dragons circled in the sky high above her, enjoying the benefits of a thermal or two; she reflected that it would take a while to grow used to the presence of others. These skies were once the domain of the garuda, and now they would have to share the freedoms that flight offered.

But that was better than having no freedoms at all.

The garuda spun in a slow arc and headed north, back in a straight line over Villiren, suddenly eager to catch the start of the official ceremonies.

She didn't want to miss out on what might happen next.